In His Ex-Wife's Defense

Andrew Wolfenson

BALDING LEGAL PUBLISHING

IN HIS EX-WIFE'S DEFENSE

In His Ex-Wife's Defense

© 2014

Balding Legal Publishing

2414 Morris Avenue, Suite 104

Union, NJ 07083

WWW.BALDINGLEGAL.COM

ISBN-13:   978-0692339541

ISBN-10:   069233954X

For my wife and children

and

For those who have encouraged me to continue telling my stories

WHAT OTHERS ARE SAYING ABOUT
IN HIS EX-WIFE'S DEFENSE

Eric Goldberg - lawyer, lover, mensch - successfully defended himself the last time out. But now he takes on a much more difficult client: his ex-wife. Andrew Wolfenson spins another just-real-enough tale of the everyman lawyer to make you think, "Did this really happen?" Sex, politics, criminal justice, and more sex. Read on and be entertained.

- Henry E. Klingeman, Esq., Criminal Defense Attorney and former Assistant United States Attorney for the District of New Jersey

"In His Ex-Wife's Defense" is an excellent legal thriller. The author hit the mark here. He combines an expert knowledge of the law and how things "really" work with a plot line that has more dips and turns than an Olympic Bobsled run. As for the ending - guaranteed that you will not see it coming. This page turner is a must read!

- John W. Hartmann, Esq., Criminal Defense Attorney and Author of Jacket: The Trials of a New Jersey Criminal Defense Attorney

WHAT OTHERS ARE SAYING ABOUT

IN HIS EX-WIFE'S DEFENSE

As a lawyer and former Municipal Court Judge, I read crime dramas and lawyer novels with a grain of salt. Invariably, those not trained in the law misstate procedure and the law and that irks me. Even a novel should educate and not misstate, at least that's my opinion. On the other hand, Andrew's books are refreshing because he does give the reader an accurate reflection of the legal system, right down to a realistic portrayal of the interaction between lawyer and client. I am impressed by his presentation and the ease with which he tells a story from start to finish. I look forward to his books as they are simply a good read.

- John Paragano, Esq., Criminal Defense Attorney and former Municipal Court Judge (Union Township 1999-2005)

In his law practice, the fictional Eric Goldberg once again cuts a swath of deviant sexual activity and questionable ethical practices across Union County, New Jersey. The real Eric Goldberg's law practice? Not so much.

- (the real) Eric Goldberg, Esq.

TABLE OF CONTENTS

ACKNOWLEDGMENTS

I want to thank Margie Koehl Milham, Esperanza Fraticelli, and my father, Gil Wolfenson, for their assistance in the editing of this book. Your honesty and input was appreciated and invaluable, and I hope that you enjoyed reading the draft manuscript as much as I did writing it.

To those who urged me to write a sequel to *"In His Own Defense"*- thank you. Originally, it was not my intention to do so, but the fact that you want to read more about the Eric Goldberg character, and that you have strong feelings for him (whether positive or negative) validates my writing in a way that I could not have previously imagined. Maybe the character will even live beyond this tale.

I also want to thank the best assistant anyone could hope for, Karen Da Silva. As always, you did a good job.

To Diana Ani Stokely, who has created yet another fantastic book cover, a big thank you. You have again taken my vision and illustrated it perfectly, and the result is another cover that I will be proud to display on my bookshelf.

To those fellow members of the bar who took the time to write the testimonials which appear in these pages and on the front/back covers – John W. Hartmann, Henry E. Klingeman, John Paragano, and (what a good sport) the real Eric Goldberg, I thank you for your kind words.

It is not my normal practice to cite movie actors, but I want to include the following two quotes:

"One of the things that binds us a family is a shared sense of humor." – Ralph Fiennes

"Insanity runs in my family. It practically gallops."- Cary Grant

Nowhere do these quotes ring more true than with my extended family. Thanks to all of you, especially my parents and siblings, for your support and love. I truly appreciate it and love you all, even though so many of you root for the wrong sports teams.

To my daughters, all of whom have inherited, for better or worse, my sense of humor and elevated level of cynicism, thank you – I couldn't be happier or prouder as a father than I am with the three of you.

To my wife, Jennifer, who will once again be barraged with questions of whether or not anything in this book is true about her husband (spoiler alert – no), thank you for your unwavering support through the late nights (and early mornings) of writing and editing, and of the long hours put in at the office for my other job. 25 years later, I'd marry you again. I'm not so sure if you would do the same.

And last but not least - thank you, DJ. You're the world's best four-legged son.

CHAPTER I – The Accident

"It wasn't so bad, to be honest with you," said the woman as she drove up Elmora Avenue in Elizabeth, her long brown hair fluttering in the wind as she passed houses converted into offices and stores which bore signs lettered alternately in English, Spanish, and Hebrew. "It's definitely not something that I would want to do every day, but if I have to do jury duty once every couple of years it won't kill me."

A voice responded through Wendi's car speakers, its timbre rising above the noise entering the car through its open windows and sun roof. "I assume you didn't get picked for a trial, Wendi. It seems like you are out pretty early," answered Kim, who was on her cell phone at a local nail salon, reclining in a large leather chair, and enjoying her weekly pedicure. "I mean, it's not even 3:00 yet."

The cars in front of her slowed as they approached a red light, and Wendi brought her car to a stop as she looked down at the clock on her dashboard. The numbers read 2:42. She tapped her own freshly painted fingernails lightly along the top of the steering wheel. "No, luckily I was not picked for anything," she said, "Once I said that I was married to a lawyer, nobody wanted me to be a juror. As if I would somehow know anything just because of what my ex-husband did for a living, or somehow be biased against one side." She paused, and then added, with a chuckle, "He always used to say that he wanted people who weren't too bright, so he could trick them easily into believing a client's innocence even if the guy was clearly guilty. So I guess attorneys think I know that and will be onto their game."

"I should try that sometime," said Kim, laughing, in response. "I mean maybe I will make sure that my second husband will be a lawyer so I can avoid serving on a jury. I can tell the attorneys that I have legal knowledge, you know, by injection!"

Wendi laughed as the traffic began to move again. "I don't know what your current husband would say about that, Kim, but trust me, having a nice husband to go home to is much better than getting out of jury duty and driving home alone in Elizabeth on a Wednesday afternoon, even a sunny Wednesday afternoon." She paused. "That's especially true when you're going home to an empty house." As she inched past the Dunkin' Donuts at the corner of Elmora Avenue and West Grand Street, the smell of fried dough filled her nostrils and she saw several teenagers gathered on the far left-side of the next intersection, at the corner of Elmora and Westfield Avenues. She was somewhat surprised because the youths seemed to be Hispanic, instead of the usual Jewish kids who would filter out of the Jewish Education Center located just past the intersection at the end of their school day.

"Don't knock him, Wendi," replied Kim, her voice taking on a serious tone. "I know that it didn't work out between you, but you were married for a long time and he is a good man and good father. Plus, it seems like you made sure to say 'married to a lawyer,' when asked about serving, right, not 'divorced from a lawyer.' So there is still some status attached to it, right?"

Wendi sighed, thinking about her friend's words. "I'm sorry, Kim. You're right. There is a certain status to it. Can't you hear my mother's voice? 'You have to marry a nice Jewish boy, a doctor or a lawyer.' Like doing anything else would be a failure." She again laughed. "And you're also right about him being a good man. Maybe he just worked too hard for our own good." She paused and eased her car into the left-turn lane. She flicked on the turn signal, and sat, waiting for the light to change to green, to turn left onto Westfield Avenue. "Now let me go, I have a text from my mother that I need to check. Enjoy the rest of your pedicure." She picked up the phone, pressed the "hang up" button, and then looked down to read the text as the light changed to green.

She stepped on the gas, still looking downward at her phone, and could see the time on her dashboard clock: 2:47. As she began the turn, she typed a quick "yes" response to her mother's question, laid the phone down on the seat next to her, and then looked up to see, horrified, two of the Hispanic youths moving off the edge of the curb and into the path of her car. One of the boys stopped, and Wendi was almost blinded by a reflection off of what seemed to be something metallic in his hand, an object which then seemed to fly through the air as the light moved away from him. The other boy continued forward, in what appeared to be a deliberate and lurching motion. Wendi frantically tried to turn the car's wheel more to the left in order to avoid making contact with the boy, who was coming at her wide-eyed and without any signs of slowing.

The clock on her dashboard changed to 2:48 as the boy's eyes slammed shut. He fell forward and, as he was almost horizontal to the ground, his torso was struck by the front of Wendi's car. The impact pushed him downward, under the car, and Wendi felt the car rise as its right front tire rolled over the boy. Wendi slammed on the brakes and brought the car to a screeching halt, but not before the vehicle had dragged the boy approximately 20 feet when his shirt caught in the car's undercarriage. Wendi exited the car and went to see if the boy was still breathing. His clearly fractured right leg protruded grotesquely from alongside the rear wheel of the vehicle. Wendi frantically called for someone to help her remove the boy from underneath the car; she could not even hear herself yelling, however. All that she could hear was the rapid, thumping sound of her own accelerated heartbeat and the cries of the other teenage boy that she had killed his friend. Wendi frantically searched for a way to pull the boy out from under the car, and was oblivious to the fact that another woman was bending over her, yelling at her to stop for fear of causing him further injury. A stream of blood ran from underneath the car, directly into the path of Wendi's right shoe. People came rushing from the restaurants on the corner, and some of the children from the Jewish Education Center, who had left school and were approaching the intersection at the time of the impact, ran toward the car while others returned to the school to alert their teachers as to what had happened.

The other woman pulled Wendi away from the car. The two of them stumbled to the ground, and Wendi's head barely missed striking the curb. They sat, bewildered and in silence, until the other woman asked what had happened. Wendi was too shaken to speak, however, and buried her head in her hands as she began to cry. A few seconds later, she glanced up, through moistened eyes, and could see the young boy still beneath her car. He was not moving. She could not see his face, but she surmised that he was a teenager, and was therefore only about six years younger than her own son, Jason. And she cried harder.

Within minutes, a police car and ambulance arrived, and the paramedics rushed to tend to the fallen boy. Wendi stood and stepped back off of the street, as her car remained in the intersection. The paramedics frantically removed the boy from underneath the car, trying not to cause any additional trauma to him, and, seeing no signs of breathing or a pulse, tried to resuscitate the accident victim. They cut his clothes from his body, including a lightweight green jacket bearing the words "Roselle Catholic". Stitched in white script, above the white block lettering denoting the school's name and above the jacket's left breast panel, was the name "Jose."

Wendi could see his face now, at least that part of his face that was not covered with blood. He was tanned, no doubt of Hispanic heritage. She could now hear several of the onlookers talking through sobs, comforting each other in Spanish. This was the Elizabeth that she knew and, irrationally, feared. The city populated by immigrants, who had come from various parts of Latin and South America. They came from places like Puerto Rico, Cuba, Colombia, Venezuela, and Ecuador, and had settled in the city which rested on the shores of the Atlantic, in the shadow of the New York City skyline.

She was the outsider, the *gringo*. While she did not speak Spanish, she heard some words repeated over and over: *muerto, niño,* and *gringa.* She knew what those words meant – they were talking about how the white woman had killed the Latino boy. She wanted to tell them that it wasn't her fault, but could not summon the courage to speak to them. She feared exacerbating the situation. She could barely speak a few dozen Spanish words under the best of circumstances. In her current, frantic state, there was no doubt in her mind that she would be unable to express herself coherently. She thought about going to them; even if she could not speak their language, she thought, she could still convey to them how terribly she felt for what had happened to the boy. She started to stand and walk toward them, but then she stopped, because as more and more Hispanic men arrived at the scene, she also began to feel worried about her own safety. Her fears of being received in a negative manner by the ever-growing crowd of Spanish-speaking men and women paralyzed her.

Gathering her thoughts and trying to suppress her feelings of fear, she slowly placed both hands on the curb and lifted herself to her feet. Choking back sobs, she walked over to one of the police officers, standing next to him for protection.

One of the paramedics and one of the responding police officers placed the motionless boy onto a backboard and carefully loaded him into an ambulance as the other paramedic quickly, yet methodically, administered CPR; that man shook his head slowly from side-to-side as he attempted to compress the boy's chest and compel it to take in air, seemingly resigned to the fact that his efforts would prove to be in vain.

Once its doors were slammed shut, the ambulance sped forward, sirens blaring, made a U-turn on Westfield Avenue, and sped in the other direction toward the hospital in the center of Elizabeth. Wendi could not even hear the sirens' wail above the sound of her own rapid, pounding heartbeat. The police officer standing next to Wendi asked if she could give him her statement or if she was too shaken up to speak. He told her to leave her car in the roadway, and escorted her to the sidewalk so that they could talk away from the car. Wendi composed herself and began to tell the officer about what had happened, about how the two boys were running at the car as she was turning, and that one of the boys stopped and one continued, until he fell into the front of the car at about the same time that she saw the flash of light to her right.

The officer dutifully wrote this account as Wendi spoke, and then said, "Ma'am, I hate to interrupt you, but the boy on the corner says that he saw the entire accident, and that he could see you holding your cell phone and talking on the phone or texting when you hit the other boy."

Wendi looked at the officer and gasped. "He said what?" she asked, adding "absolutely not," as she tried to process what the officer was saying to her.

The officer looked at her, examining her, trying to determine from her demeanor if she was telling the truth or if she was trying to hide reality from him. Thus far, he was unsure. "The boy said," he replied slowly and in an attempt to elicit a tell-tale response, "that you were using your phone at the time of the accident. He's really shaken up, as you might imagine, but he claims that he was standing on the corner and his friend was crossing the street. He said that you were not probably paying attention, since you were on the phone and he saw your head down, and that's how the accident happened."

Wendi looked at the officer as tears welled in her eyes, unable to properly process what the boy had said or of what she was being accused by both the boy and the police officer. "He said that?" she asked, incredulously, as she shook her head slowly. "No, he couldn't possibly have said that. I wasn't on the phone, and I wasn't texting. That's completely untrue."

"Is it, ma'am?" the officer replied, clearly skeptical, or so it seemed to Wendi in her agitated state. "How is it completely untrue?"

Wendi took a deep breath and attempted, unsuccessfully, to stifle the tears which began to flow down her cheeks. "None of what he said is true," she said through sobs, "I was not on the phone at the time of the impact. I have blue tooth in the car so I don't hold the phone up to my ear when I talk anyway. And when I saw the boy coming at the car, there was another boy running with him. The boy fell into the car; I didn't hit him, he fell into the front of the car! He hit me!" She looked over at the corner, still crying, and gestured toward the corner. "Which boy are you talking about? Who did you speak to?"

The officer pointed to a teenager who was standing near the utility pole at the corner, speaking to another officer. "That boy over there is the one," the officer said, "the one in the Elizabeth High School jacket."

"That's the boy who was running after the other one," Wendi cried. "He was running with the other one. He wasn't standing on the corner. He's lying. I don't know why, but he is lying." She leaned forward and placed her hands on her knees, gasping for breath.

"Do you need to go to a hospital, ma'am?" asked the officer, as Wendi, hunched over, continued to cry and he feared that she would begin to hyperventilate. "I can call you another ambulance, or drive you there myself if you want."

Wendi raised her right arm. "No," she said, through sobs. "I just can't believe that someone would lie about what happened here." She stood up and again tried to control her crying, this time with some success. She was suddenly fearful of continuing to speak to the police without having someone else there, like an attorney, to make sure that she did not say anything wrong or incriminating. "I think I need to make a phone call," she said to the officer, "my phone is in the car. Can I please go over there and get it?"

The officer placed his hands in the air as if to stop her from going back to the car. "No ma'am. I would like you to stay here. I will go and get your phone for you."

Wendi nodded her head approvingly, and the officer walked over to the car, opened the passenger side door, and retrieved the phone from the front seat. "Do you mind if I look at your call record?" the officer asked as he walked back to her.

Her initial inclination was to say yes, because she knew that she was not on the phone when the impact occurred, but then Wendi thought like an attorney, or, more correctly, an attorney's ex-wife. "I would mind, actually, officer. Please give me my phone so that I can make a call. But before I do, I have a question – are you going to be arresting me now?"

The officer seemed surprised by both her refusal to allow him to see the phone as well as her question about whether or not he intended to arrest her. He removed his hat and ran the fingers of his right hand through his hair, looking back over his shoulder at his partner as he searched for the correct response. He motioned to his partner, who looked back and shook his head in a side-to-side motion. "No ma'am," he finally said, "I don't think we will be arresting you now. We need to do some more investigation here, but, to be honest with you, there may be charges brought against you in the future." He paused, and handed Wendi her phone. "And, ma'am, you need to leave your car here for now. It is part of the investigation, and we will be towing it to the police lot later. Is there anything else you need from there?"

Wendi looked down, reached out her hand, and took her phone from the officer. She then looked back at her car, and replied, "Yes, just some stuff that I need to take home. Let me make a call and then I will retrieve what I need, if that is OK with you."

"That will be fine, ma'am," the officer said, "I apologize for the inconvenience, and I am sorry if I upset you. I know that this can't be easy for you." He walked over to the other officer, and the men were then joined by a third. The men began having an animated conversation, with the newly-arrived officer, the one whose uniform sleeve boasted the greatest number of yellow chevrons, pointing at Wendi and yelling, loudly enough for Wendi to hear, that he must retrieve her cell phone. The officer, who had been standing with Wendi earlier turned and, shuffling his feet slowly, approached Wendi and said, "Sorry to bother you again, ma'am, but my Captain is insisting that I take your cell phone. You may not be aware, but the law is that we can examine any cell phones at the scene of an accident to determine if you were on the phone or texting at the time of the accident. All that we need is a reasonable suspicion that you were on the phone or texting, and we have that suspicion based on what the kid said."

"No, officer, I don't care what the law is, you cannot have my phone!" Wendi yelled at the officer, who was standing next to her, head cocked downward, and clearly uncomfortable with the conversation. She tried to sound as if she knew he was bluffing, adding, "Plus, without a proper search warrant you have no right to check the phone." Maybe those years of being married to an attorney did pay off, or maybe it was just watching crime shows on television once in a while. Either way, she suddenly felt a wave of confidence in her own defiance. "That boy is lying," she yelled, "and I will not be treated like a common criminal."

She did not know whether a warrant was actually required, but based on the fact that the officer did not immediately disagree with her or shout her down, she surmised that either she was correct or that he simply did not know any more than she did about whether or not she was correct. Either way, the phone remained in her possession.

"But ma'am …"

"No, officer," Wendi said sternly. "I understand that you have to do your job, but I am not going to speak to anyone or give you anything until I call my lawyer. Now that I have my phone, I am going to call him, OK?"

"Yes, ma'am, but after you talk to him I am going to ask you again for the phone, and I must warn you, if the Captain gets involved here, he's not going to ask very nicely."

"Thank you," she replied softly, "I will take my chances with him," as she went down through the names on her phone and eventually pressed the cell phone number of the only attorney whom she could trust, her ex-husband.

CHAPTER II – A Call Is Placed

The two friends sat in the dimly-lit bar/restaurant, watching the television which dangled precariously from the ceiling, hovering over the far end of the bar. Scattered rays of sunlight filtered in through the windows, and the baseball-diamond shaped clock on the wall read 3:20. Eschewing the work that lay piled on each of their respective desks, the two attorneys had left their offices two hours earlier and had walked down Broad Street to their favorite lunch spot. The television set was tuned to a baseball game, and the Yankees were leading the Orioles by a score of 4-2. It was the top of the sixth inning, there were two outs, and the Orioles had a runner on first base. The Yankee relief pitcher threw a lazy curveball, and the Baltimore shortstop swung, connected, and sent a laser to the right of the third baseman. The fielder, playing in only his fourth game at the major league level, stood motionless, seemingly mesmerized by the ball, as it flew past his right shoulder. By the time the left fielder caught up with the ball, the runner had reached third and the batter strode into second, pumping his fist for emphasis as the Yankee Stadium crowd groaned in response.

The reaction in the bar was equally negative. One of the men shrugged his shoulders, draped in a gray Yankees' jersey over his striped dress shirt and tie, and ran his right hand through what remained from what was once a full head of hair. "Do you believe this shit?" Eric Goldberg growled, almost rhetorically, "They're going to blow the damn game again. How many times can we watch the same movie?" He lowered his hand and reached for the glass of soda that rested on the table in front of him. Gripping the glass and raising it to his lips, he added, "I still can't get used to this losing shit. Guys can't hit, guys can't field. We were spoiled for too long, you know." He looked at the soda in his glass, and then over at the bottles of liquor which beckoned to him from

25

behind the bartender. "It's almost enough to drive me to drink at 3:00 in the afternoon, even when I have to go back to the office and meet clients later."

"Give it a rest, Eric," replied Jon Grant, looking down at the half-empty glass resting on the table directly in front of him, a glass which contained what was left of his second round of beer, "enough of the complaining. I have heard this crap way too often from you Yankee fans over the past couple of years. So they don't win every game. Tough shit. Get used to it."

"Don't be ridiculous. I never liked losing, Jon," said Eric, "never." He took another sip from his soda glass. "I don't like losing in court, and I don't like it when my teams lose. You can't condemn me for that."

"True," Jon said, nodding his head in agreement. "But you can't compare wanting to be a good lawyer with whether or not the Yankees win, you idiot. One part you can control, at least to a certain extent. You have no power over a sports team."

Eric looked at Jon and sighed. "Honestly, sometimes I feel like I have more power over the Yankees than I do as an attorney. You know how it is. Some days it is easy. Others, I can't predict what a judge is going to do." He paused and laughed. "And you know that we can't control our clients. If only …" he said, wistfully, as he felt the vibration of his cell phone in his shirt pocket. Reaching underneath the baseball jersey, he pulled the phone from his pocket and looked at its screen. Recognizing the illuminated face, he looked up, puzzled, and said, "Why is Wendi calling me now?"

He brought the phone to his ear and leaned over, cupping his hand over the black rectangle in order to best hear through its mini-speaker. "Wendi, is that you?" Eric shouted into the phone. All that he could hear through his phone was heavy breathing and a great commotion in the background. There was no answer. He turned to Jon Grant. "I think that she pocket dialed me, because she's not answering the damned …"

"Eric!" he suddenly heard her voice shout. "Are you there, Eric? I can't hear you!"

Eric shrugged with frustration. "Shit, let me take this outside," he said to Jon. He walked toward the front door of the bar, yelling for Wendi to hold on for a second. When he opened the door and stepped to the outside, he yelled, "I can hear you, but barely. What's going on? What is all of that noise in the background?" He could hear Wendi crying through the phone, as she gasped for air. "Is something wrong?" he asked, immediately realizing the stupidity of his inquiry.

"I was in an accident," Wendi blurted out through her sobs.

"You were in an accident?" he replied in disbelief, "Are you OK?"

Wendi could not hear Eric's questions. "I am fine," she continued, "but a teenager died. I think they are going to blame me." She paused, and he could hear her start to cry louder. "I'm so sorry for calling you now, Eric, but I need you to come meet me… I am really afraid." Her voice lowered, "I hope that you can hear me now. I was in an accident. I was driving and I hit a boy who was walking in the street. The boy was Hispanic. There are lots of men here now, a lot of people angry and talking in Spanish. I don't want to be a bigot, Eric, but to be honest, I don't feel safe."

"I'll be right there," Eric yelled. "Where are you?"

"I can barely hear you," she replied. "Where am I? I am at the corner of Elmora and Westfield Avenues." She coughed loudly. "Please get here soon."

"On my way," he cried. He poked his head back into the bar, yelled to Jon that there was an emergency and that he had to leave. "I will explain later," he added, as he bolted out the door and ran to his car, two blocks away. He sped down Broad Street until he reached Rahway Avenue, then turned right and passed through two red lights until he reached Elmora Avenue. He turned right at full speed, almost clipping a car traveling Southbound on Elmora, and continued, as fast as he could, up the congested street until he could not take the traffic any more. When he reached the next corner, he pulled the car into the Dunkin' Donuts parking lot to his left, parked on the side of the building, and raced on foot the remaining block to Westfield Avenue. As he approached, he could see Wendi's car off to the left, and crowds milling all along the intersection. The police had blocked traffic from turning left onto Westfield Avenue, and cars were stopped in all directions as a tow truck attempted to cross beyond the police barricades from the other side of Westfield.

"Mr. Goldberg," he heard a familiar voice call, "what are you doing here?"

Eric stopped and looked to his right, and saw Officer Jack Miller of the Elizabeth Police Department standing on the curb. "Jack, tell me," he replied, "where is the woman who was driving the car?"

"Over there," Officer Miller responded as he pointed in a Northerly direction, "on the other side of Westfield. "Is she a client of yours?"

"Sort of," Eric called as he resumed his trot. "She's a client, ex-wife, whatever." As he neared the intersection, he could see Wendi talking with another officer, whom he immediately recognized as Sergeant Adam Woodman. This was a time, he thought to himself, that being in Elizabeth Municipal Court and meeting the local police time and again might be a benefit.

"Eric!" Wendi cried as Eric neared. "Thank God you made it!" She ran toward Eric, meeting him in the intersection, and wrapped her arms tightly around him. "I didn't do anything wrong," she said, again beginning to cry, "But I was afraid to talk to the police without you here. They said I was on the phone when I hit the kid, but I wasn't."

"Don't worry," he said, gently stroking her back, "I'm here." He pulled away from Wendi and looked into her moistened eyes. Immediately shifting his role from comforting ex-husband to criminal defense attorney, and concerned by her comment about possible cell phone usage at the time of the accident, he asked, "You didn't let them look at your phone, did you?" She didn't answer. He again leaned closer to her and whispered, "Please tell me you didn't let them look at your phone." When she shook her head slowly, he smiled. Again pulling away from her, he motioned to his right. "Let me talk to the Sergeant over there," he said. She nodded, and he walked toward Sergeant Woodman, whom he had known for about a decade, from the time that he first started walking the beat. "Sergeant Adam," he said, "it's been a while. I didn't know they let you out of the building anymore since the big promotion."

"Well, Mr. Goldberg," he replied, "once in a while. The high profile stuff, you know. Spanish kid gets mowed down by a white woman, that kind of shit." He paused and looked toward Wendi. "You know this woman, Eric?" he asked, "I just started talking to her and didn't even get her name yet."

"Her name is Wendi Goldberg," Eric offered as Sergeant Woodman's eyes widened at his response. "Yes," he added, nodding his head, "you heard me right. Wendi Goldberg. She's my ex-wife."

Sergeant Woodman looked at Wendi, and then back at Eric. He sighed. "I am so sorry about the comment, Eric. I had no idea." He paused and looked over at Wendi again, lowering his voice so that nobody else could hear him. "I need to tell you something, Eric, and I am going to be honest with you," he said, "because we have known each other for a long time."

"OK, I appreciate that. Tell me," Eric replied.

"The shit's going to hit the fan soon. I'm here because we got word that Jesus Sanchez is on his way here. He was doing some crap on the other side of town but you know the drill, a brown person gets wronged, he picks himself up and gets over to where the cameras are. It's getting to be where he gets somewhere almost before we do. He has his spies all over," he said, looking around to make sure that nobody else was listening to their conversation. "We got the word from the Channel 7 guys. He apparently called them only minutes after the accident, the fucking media hound, to make sure they were here for his grand entrance."

"Fuck," Eric said, shaking his head. "Sanchez? I haven't seen him in a while, other than when he's raising hell in front of news cameras. I used to see him here in Municipal Court, but I can't remember the last time. I guess I should have expected that he'd come here."

29

The Sergeant looked over his shoulder as two more television camera crews pulled up on the North side of Elmora Avenue. "I don't think he even practices law anymore, Eric," he said, quietly. "I think he just puts himself into the spotlight as much as possible, and usually he's making problems for us. He's an asshole, but he's a shrewd asshole. From what I've heard, he has his sights set on the Mayor's job. And he doesn't care who he takes down to get it, as long as he is the hero of Elizabeth's Spanish population. He wants to be their leader, and with the office and title."

"Alright, I get it," Eric replied. "We're staring at a media circus here today." He motioned toward Wendi, who stood, shaking, as she continued to cry while one of the officers attempted to comfort her. "Can I get her out of here, then? I definitely don't want her here when Sanchez gets in front of a camera and microphone. You think she's scared of those guys now? Just wait until their savior comes and blames the white woman for not only the accident, but for every other problem here in the city."

"Yes, that's why I am telling you this," Sergeant Woodman said. "Take her home, or wherever. Just get her the hell out of here. Leave the car here, though." He motioned to one of the officers to retrieve the car keys from Wendi. He then grabbed Eric by the arm, as if to stress the importance of what he was going to say next. "You owe me one, Eric, and you'd better be careful with this one." He lowered his voice again. "Look, Eric, you probably already know what I am going to say, but the kid is dead. If Sanchez is on his way here, he's not going to let it rest. This is just the start."

"I know, Adam, I know. Thanks for all of your help," he said, shaking the Sergeant's hand. "See what you can do about not letting things get out of hand, OK?"

"We will do our best," the Sergeant said as Eric walked away, toward Wendi, and then turned and led her back to his car. She walked as if in a daze, seemingly oblivious to the tumult which would soon come to envelop her existence, currently manifested in the multitude of camera crews setting up their equipment and the New Jersey local correspondents of what seemed like every New York and New Jersey television station applying fresh makeup as they anxiously awaited the arrival of Jesus Sanchez.

Chapter III – La Voz De La Gente

Jesus Sanchez was born 36 years earlier in Cartagena, Colombia, the fifth-largest city in the South American country. The son of a fisherman, he was schooled in his home country and emigrated to the United States at the age of 18, arriving in the New York area in 1996. The charismatic Sanchez attended night school while working during the day at a factory in Elizabeth, and lived with his aunt and uncle, U.S. citizens who had come to this country in 1980, until he gained his own citizenship papers in 2002.

Sanchez quickly rose to the position of foreman at his job, and then graduated from law school, working as a young attorney in Elizabeth representing other immigrants and people of Hispanic heritage. He started to make himself known around local political circles as a young voice of the city's fledgling Hispanic community. Rumors were rampant about the circumstances under which he left Colombia – many whispered that he was involved with the Revolutionary Armed Forces of Colombia, better known by its acronym, FARC – the group of rebels which had, over a five-decade span beginning in the early 1960's before it called a unilateral cease-fire in November of 2012, engaged in battles which led to the killing of, according to some reports, more than half a million people. At the time of the cease-fire, undertaken during settlement talks between FARC and the Colombian government, the number of fighters was estimated to be over 9,000. It was well-known that Sanchez's father and uncle were Lieutenants in the organization, rising quickly up the ranks through their ruthless rampages and taking of innocent people's lives and lands in the name of the rebel forces. Whether or not his father had actually recruited Sanchez into the fold was the subject of some debate, but there were reports of his being present at various guerrilla-type training sessions and, therefore, the rumors about his involvement in the organization were thought to be factual. The mysterious disappearance of his father only weeks before Sanchez came to the United States only served to fuel such speculation.

Rumors also swirled about whether or not he had taken the lives of three unarmed civilians during one such training session; the tales grew to almost mythical proportions as they were recounted from person to person. One of the stories even had Sanchez ripping out one of the men's heart through his chest with his bare hands, as sometimes depicted in kung-fu movies. All of these stories, these tales of his activities while in the old country, only added to the mystique that swirled around Jesus Sanchez.

There were also numerous allegations of his being involved with Colombia's drug trade and the importing of cocaine for selling on the streets of Elizabeth, Union County's capital city, as well as other towns within the County and neighboring Middlesex County. None of the drug rumors were ever proven, however, at least not in a court of law. There was one charge for drug possession, marijuana and cocaine, several years ago. That charge, however, was quietly dismissed on an administrative technicality; some said due to the "friends" that Sanchez had within the court system or elsewhere. Word on the street was that Sanchez could make charges disappear with the help of his insiders, and clients across Elizabeth and the surrounding towns in Union County sought him out to work his magic with them.

Irrespective of the reason for the dropping of the charges against him, after that time Sanchez had escaped any additional police scrutiny. Sanchez did his best not to fuel the rumors as to his past, but neither did he ever completely deny them, instead choosing to respond to any such questions cryptically, as if to increase his "street credibility" and make his opponents fear him without ever admitting to any illegal activity. Those allegations and his tacit admissions, however, did lend an aura of power to the young Sanchez and he quickly raised in stature in the city's Democratic Party circles.

In 2010, however, an ill-fated attempt at gaining control of the party, which was met with resistance from county Democratic leaders, led to his virtual expulsion from local political circles. Sanchez claimed, publicly, that his ouster was due to the city leaders' fear of the growing Hispanic population, which was increasing exponentially, especially the number of undocumented non-citizens living within the city's borders. Those undocumented residents, until that time silent and living in the shadows of the city's lesser-affluent areas and predominantly in their teens and twenties, viewed Sanchez as their voice, and he was called by his Spanish moniker, *"voz de la gente,"* loosely translated as "voice of the people."

Over the past several years, Sanchez had become omnipresent in the Latino community; wherever there was a problem involving Hispanics, especially the Hispanic youth, Sanchez was certain to make an appearance to raise public awareness of what he professed to be the mistreatment of "his people." Detractors called him *"Hispanic Al"*, comparing him, and not in a nice way, to the Reverend Al Sharpton, who made a living feeding off of the public for decades in New York City. His fans, however, fawned over his every move, calling him not only *"voz de la gente"* but also *"Papi"* and *"Jefe."*

Sanchez had an insatiable thirst for publicity, which was matched only by his overwhelming desire for power. In fact, the event which precipitated his ouster from the local party's inner circle was when he mistakenly, and in a stupidly self-aggrandizing manner, compared himself to the "Tony Montana" character from the epic film, *Scarface.* While those who knew him understood the reasons for the self-comparison – the son of foreigners who comes to this country and ascends to a position of power – what Sanchez failed to realize in making his off-the-cuff remarks is that the film's overwhelming depiction of Montana as a paranoid, power-hungry drug trafficker would work against him. Some opined that his belief that he was similar to the title character would prove to be his ultimate undoing, and that Sanchez would end up like Montana, dead at the hands of his rivals; an eventuality which would be welcomed by some of Elizabeth's power elite. Despite this misstep, however, he was still adored by the people whom he called his own and professed to represent.

Within minutes after Eric and Wendi left the scene of the accident, Sanchez' dark grey Mercedes rolled up Elmora Avenue. Sanchez, seemingly relishing his role as the self-proclaimed voice of his people so much that he initially refused to appropriately recognize the gravity of the situation, waved and even blew kisses at his adoring fans as his car eased up the street. People seemed to move their cars out of the way on the heavily-trafficked roadway to allow him to pass, reminiscent of Moses' parting of the Red Sea in leading the Jews out of oppression in Egypt. Sanchez sat in the front passenger's seat of the car, his driver, Juan, at the wheel. Having his own personal driver made him the envy of his subjects. That he rode around in a car which cost more than most of his "people" made in a year, and did so with a personal driver, had no adverse effect on his popularity. His "people" were impressed with his glitzy lifestyle, his fancy cars and designer suits. These items were proof of his successes and, more importantly, were evidence of his power. The power that none of them possessed. He exhibited the power that, up until recently, no Latin Americans had possessed in their city, in their *ciudad*.

He was still the *"voz de la gente"* even if he did not act like one of them. They were too enamored of him to oppose or question his opulence. He represented the "American Dream" that they all shared when they or their ancestors were still in their home country. He represented what could be. They wanted to be like him, so they did not begrudge his penchant for excess.

When the car reached the intersection, Sanchez bounded out of the passenger's side door to the cheers and clapping of the Hispanics assembled at the scene where their *"niño"* had died minutes earlier. Sanchez was beloved by the entire Hispanic population. Colombians, of course, revered their countryman. He was also loved and respected, however, by the other Latinos - the city's Peruvians, Cubans, Venezuelans, Dominicans, Guatemalans, and residents of every other South and Central American nation. All put aside any differences which may have existed between their own countries, their neighborhoods, and even local gang memberships to unite in their support for Sanchez. He was a unifying force for them with respect to other ethnicities, against the white majority and the African-Americans alike. He shook hands with the men standing in between his car and the far corner of the intersection, where three of the local television camera crews awaited his statement, and paused to hug several women, all of whom had tears in their eyes or rolling down their cheeks as he consoled them, softly, in Spanish. *"Estoy aquí,"* he said to them, in a comforting tone, *"estoy aquí."*

Reaching the cameras, he paused and motioned to the cameramen that he was ready to make a statement, at least a statement that he wanted captured on video. Anything to be captured on film or video was carefully scripted by Sanchez to further not only the interests of his people, but also his own self-interests. He had to make sure that he was cast in the proper light, that his sound bites, the portions that he wanted, made the news that evening. The cameras were not to begin rolling, he cautioned, until he was ready.

He stood on the Northwest corner of Elmora Avenue and Westfield Avenue, his arm draped around the dead boy's friend, and began to speak.

"*Mis amigos and amigas,*" he began, "or shall I say, *mi familia ...*" He was interrupted by the cheering of the crowd which had drawn closer to hear his words. "*Mi familia, hoy ha sido un dia horrible. Hoy, hemos perdido a unos de nuestros hijos, uno de nuestros amigos, que forma parte de nuestro futuro.*" The crowd again erupted in applause. Sanchez raised his arms, and then lowered them slowly to urge the crowd to quiet. "Let me repeat myself in English for all of those who don't speak Spanish," he added with a hint of a smirk as he looked directly into the television cameras assembled on the corner, "My friends ... my family. This is a horrible day. Today, we lost one of our sons, one of our friends, part of our future." The Americans scattered throughout the crowd nodded in approval and clapped lightly, their verbalized agreements being drowned out by another roar from the Hispanics.

"*Te queremos, Papi,*" yelled two teenage girls, one of whom wore a jacket similar to that which was worn by the deceased Roselle Catholic Student.

"I love you too, girls," Sanchez responded. "*Las quiero mucho.* I love you all." He paused, and looked to the left to the mother of the deceased, who had just arrived at the scene. "And I loved Jose Gomez." He lifted his left arm to his face, and covered his eyes with his hand in what appeared to be an attempt to stifle tears. Clearing his throat, he stepped off the curb and took three steps toward the boy's mother, wrapping her in a warm embrace. "*Todos queriamos a Jose,*" he whispered to Maria Gomez. He then straightened up and turned back toward the cameras with a flourish. "We all loved

Jose," he shouted to the assemblage, his voice resonating well past the confines of the intersection.

"*Mi hijo está muerto,*" Maria Gomez cried, as she dropped to her knees.

Sanchez bent down beside her, got on one knee, and consoled her while the cameras continued rolling. For him, he could not have scripted her show of emotion any better, and it was his best publicity possible. "*No, señora,*" he said, looking up and with his voice rising with every word, making sure that his comments would be picked up by the cameras. "*Nuestro chico ha muerto.* Our boy is dead!" He stood and walked back toward the cameras. Looking directly into the Channel 7 camera, he bellowed, "Our boy is dead. And we will not stand for it!" He raced back to Señora Gomez. "This woman's son, our son, shall not have died in vain. We will insist on justice! I will be going to the County Prosecutor's office tomorrow morning and insist on an immediate meeting to discuss what action he will be taking!"

Some in the crowd applauded. Realizing that many did not understand his diatribe, which was delivered in English, he repeated part of it for the Spanish-speaking in the crowd: "*Hijo de esta mujer, no habrá muerto en vano. Vamos a inistir en la justicia ...*" The crowd roared, forcing him to pause. When the cheering subsided, he continued: "*Me reuniré con el Prosecutor en la mañana para discutir qué medidas va a tomar!*" The crowd roared anew, and several of the women rushed up to Sanchez and swallowed him in a group hug.

All the while, the cameras were rolling. Sanchez smiled faintly as he enjoyed his moment. His work at the scene done, he began to take his leave. Stepping away from the group hug, he went over to Señora Gomez one last time, wrapped his arms around her and whispered some additional comforting words in her ear. Signaling his driver that it was time to leave, he waved to the crowd and ducked into his car, motioning for Juan to slowly drive away from the scene, making a dramatic departure, all of which was captured by the news cameras. A few moments later, after the Mercedes disappeared from view, the camera crews packed up their gear, and several drove in an easterly direction, toward the center of the city, to question the County Prosecutor, Steven Crawford, about what action would be taken against Wendi Goldberg.

*****

Crawford, having heard about Sanchez's preening and grandstanding before the cameras and anticipating the imminent arrival of the news media, had already dispatched one of the senior Assistant County Prosecutors, Ben Kasper, to the front steps of the courthouse with specific instructions on what he was to say, and not to say, to the media. Earlier, as the camera crews began to arrive at the courthouse, Kasper had been sent to inform them that a statement would be forthcoming within the half hour. He then retreated into his office, met with Crawford and two others, preparing the office's first official statement on the accident. Twenty minutes later, Kasper, armed with his fresh set of instructions, took a deep breath, wiped his brow, and then again walked through the Courthouse's front door and strode down to the bottom of the marble staircase in the glaring sun. No less than seven camera crews were perched on Broad Street, at the base of the courthouse, when Kasper began his address:

"Ladies and gentlemen, thank you for your patience. My name is Ben Kasper, and I am one of the Assistant County Prosecutors here in Union County. I am here on behalf of Prosecutor Steven Crawford to discuss the events which took place earlier this afternoon. As you are no doubt aware," he continued, beads of sweat forming on his brow both from the afternoon heat and the added glare of the cameras as he recited his scripted remarks, "today there was an automobile and pedestrian accident at the intersection of Elmora and Westfield Avenues in Elizabeth, a few miles from this very courthouse, which resulted in a fatality. As you are no doubt aware, it is simply impossible for the Prosecutor's Office to comment on or take a position on an incident which took place only minutes ago." He paused, the heat beginning to make him feel slightly light-headed. Taking a deep breath to calm himself and clear his head, he continued. "As of right now, the matter remains under investigation and our office will have no comment about whether the driver will be charged with any summonses arising out of the accident. I can tell you that the County Prosecutor's Office will be working closely with local law enforcement and, should there be justification for any criminal or traffic charges to be filed, will do so in conjunction with and with the cooperation of city authorities."

Once Kasper stopped talking, the reporters tried to seize the moment to pose their questions. The voices of several reporters joined together in inquiry, none of which was clearly discernible to Kasper due to the various people all yelling at once as well as the noise of traffic which whizzed by on Broad Street. He struggled in vain to make out the voices, but his inability to do so was actually irrelevant since had no intention of answering any of their questions.

Kasper raised his right hand in an effort to stifle the questioning. The reporters quieted, with one exception. "Mr. Kasper," called a reporter holding a microphone emblazoned with the logo of the local CBS affiliate, "do you have any comment about the fact that the accident resulted in the death of a Hispanic high school student? Jesus Sanchez just gave a statement at the accident scene in which he seemed to indicate that the local authorities, including your office, would ignore the incident because it was a Latino boy who was killed."

Ben Kasper hesitated, and wiped some of the sweat from his forehead before answering. "As I said earlier, I cannot comment on that now, nor can the Prosecutor's Office comment on that topic. On a personal note, please note that I do not intend to comment about the inflammatory and improper rhetoric being advanced by Mr. Sanchez, other than to point out that, to the best of my knowledge, Jesus Sanchez does not currently work in the Prosecutor's Office, he has never worked in the Prosecutor's Office, nor does he have any legitimate ties to local law enforcement. So I am certain that you will all agree that he has no basis whatsoever for saying what this office, or any other law enforcement office, will or will not be doing." He paused, allowing his last sentence, purposefully demeaning to Sanchez, to reverberate before continuing. "His rhetoric aside, we have to make sure that any investigation is completed in a proper manner."

Several of the reporters thrust their hands in the air in an effort to gain Kasper's attention for a follow-up question, but he was not done speaking. Concluding his recitation of the verbiage discussed between he and his superiors before his appearance, Kasper continued. "The Prosecutor's Office and other departments and employees of the County of Union do wish to extend their deepest sympathies to the family and friends of the deceased student, and promise that we will be conducting a thorough investigation into the incident. And having said that, Ladies and gentlemen," he added, "I am not prepared to answer any additional questions at this time." Ignoring the groans which now emanated from the throng before him, he continued, "I have made my statement. Any further statements will be made by the Prosecutor's Office as events warrant. Thank you."

He turned and tried to walk back into the courthouse, but made it only three of the 21 steps before a female's voice, one with more than a hint of a South American accent, rang out.

"Mr. Kasper," called Lupe Espinosa, the local reporter for one of the New Jersey stations, "Lupe Espinosa. What exactly do you mean 'legitimate ties?' Are you insinuating that Mr. Sanchez somehow has illegal ties with the local police or authorities?"

The prosecutor stopped in his tracks. Turning back toward the group of reporters, he saw Lupe Espinosa standing in directly in front of him. The jacket of her pantsuit was unbuttoned, and the top two buttons of her white blouse were also undone. The lace edges of her bra provided a contrast to the blouse, and seemed to shimmer alongside her tan-colored cleavage. He stared at the reporter, noting not only her ample chest straining against the blouse but also the stiletto heels which left the hem of her pants legs hovering approximately six inches off of the Broad Street sidewalk. She appeared to be in her early-20s, he guessed, and she was clearly trying to make a name for herself on the local news.

Kasper took a deep breath, and continued to stare at his inquisitor. "I am not insinuating anything, young lady, and I would ask most respectfully that you refrain from reading anything into my comments. I believe that I was quite clear in my statement and that I have left nothing to interpretation." he answered in a clearly derisive manner. "To the extent that you are confused, however, allow me to clarify myself now. What I was doing was merely pointing out that Mr. Sanchez, to this office's knowledge, has no connection to the office and therefore is not equipped, in any way, to opine as to its intentions or procedures. And," he added, clearly deviating from his planned statement, "I am guessing that you are Colombian, is that correct?"

Now it was Lupe Espinosa's turn to pause, her face flushed with a combination of embarrassment and rage. "No ... no, I am not," she stammered, "I am Puerto Rican, and damned proud of it. But tell me, what is it to you, Mr. Kasper?"

He walked toward her until they were standing only two steps apart, and so that he could speak in a whisper and yet his voice would still be picked up by the various microphones being held by the curvaceous *Borinquen* native and the other reporters. "What it is, young lady," he said condescendingly, "is that I don't want to hear any questions from you about the fact that the deceased is Hispanic. I don't want to hear the Puerto Rican reporter talking about how the Colombian rabble rouser is yelling in Spanish about how a Latino boy was killed." The other representatives of the Prosecutor's Office who stood with Kasper began to squirm, as Lupe's face color deepened and her teeth clenched and Kasper continued to go off-script. Kasper moved even closer to her. "The office is not going to allow this situation to denigrate into a racial issue," he explained, "and you can go back to Mr. Sanchez, assuming that you will be bragging to him about how you stood up for him, and tell him that."

Lupe Espinosa stood, enraged, and began to shake with anger. She turned quickly to her cameraman, standing to her right, for assistance. As she turned, another button on her blouse popped loose, and the majority of her bra was now visible to those in front of her, most notably Ben Kasper. "And Ms. Espinosa," Kasper added, using her name for the first time in their conversation, "if you really want to be respected as a journalist, you might want to focus more on your lines of questioning than your appearance and dress a little more conservatively, because you don't want your manner of dress to detract from your skills." His voice turned to a sneer, as he leaned in and whispered, "Might I suggest a turtleneck next time?"

Lupe looked down, saw that her breasts were exposed, and quickly dropped her microphone. She grabbed the lapels of her jacket closed with her right hand, and raised her left hand as if to slap Ben Kasper in the face for his sexist comment. He pulled back, however, out of arm's reach, and her intended slap drew nothing but air. As the wind from her hand rushed past his face, Assistant Prosecutor Ben Kasper, smiling both due to the impromptu peep show and his ability to dodge being slapped, again turned toward the courthouse and began walking up its steps with the members of his office in tow, ignoring the reporters who continued to implore him to provide additional information. He did not look back as he ascended the steps, taking them two at a time to expedite his flight from the reporters.

When he reached the inside of the building he stopped and drew a deep breath, pleased to feel the wind of the door closing behind him.

His smug sense of pride in his performance, however, was short-lived. "What the hell was that all about, Ben?" asked Prosecutor Crawford, who had remained, hidden, just inside the doorway to monitor the events as they were unfolding. "Come on, Ben. We discussed staying on course. We did not discuss having you engage the reporters like that. You were supposed to say a few quick words, mention that we will not be bullied by Sanchez, and then come back in. What was with the ad-libbing?"

Kasper looked at his boss, the beads of sweat forming anew on his brow even as a large oscillating fan near the edge of the building's rotunda, a scant few yards away, turned its breeze in his direction. "Come on, Steve, relax," he pleaded. "She's nothing. She's little more than a pair of tits that some network wants to put on air to draw in viewers. She was an easy mark and no doubt a Sanchez sympathizer; and now, maybe, we can show Sanchez and his people that we're not fucking around with them."

"I hope so, Ben. I hope so. Because this shit is bad and is only going to get worse. Woodman called me from the scene. Guess who the woman driving the car was?"

"Do I even want to know?" asked Kasper.

"Probably not," replied Crawford. "The woman was Eric Goldberg's ex-wife."

"Oh, shit," Kasper cried. "You mean the one who slept with Doug Freeman and then divorced Eric? She was the driver? You have got to be kidding me." He paused and looked back to the front door, knowing that the reporters were still likely congregated at the bottom of the courthouse steps. "Please tell me that Goldberg, that pain in the ass, is not going to get involved in defending her when we do bring charges."

"You know the answer to that one, Ben. Of course he will be involved. She called him to the scene and Sarge let him take her away from there before Sanchez showed up. But assuming that he is going to be involved, I am not going to have you handle it. You know how Goldberg operates." He paused and smiled, although the curl of his lip made it more of a knowing smirk. "I'll put one of the young girls on it. That will distract him. We don't need this to be any more of a circus than necessary." The two men laughed an uneasy laugh, and then turned and walked back to their office, discussing the welcome sight of Lupe Espinosa's ample chest, debating whether it was real or filled with silicone, because, as Ben stated, "that's what the Hispanic women do," and how the sight broke up an otherwise lousy day.

From an office window several blocks away, Eric and Wendi Goldberg strained to watch the scene unfold on the courthouse steps. Wendi again began to cry. "That's all about me, isn't it, Eric? What am I going to do?" As the tears rolled down her face, she buried her head in Eric's shoulder.

He stroked her hair gently. "Don't worry, Wendi," he answered, "we'll take care of this." He again looked out the window, and wondered to himself how. He was pleased that Wendi had not shown the phone to the police at the scene, as was not certain that she was not talking on the phone or texting when she hit the pedestrian; he knew, however, that the prosecution could subpoena the phone records if they so desired, and he feared what those records would reveal. He certainly did not want to ask her to see the phone.

Chapter IV – Sanchez and His Plan

"The Prosecutor's Office said what about me?" asked Jesus Sanchez, "that *gringo* Kasper said that I have no legitimate ties to law enforcement? You've got to be kidding me," he said, a smile engulfing his face, "*Dios mio*. He's sitting there talking about me, instead of talking about the fact that the kid was killed? That's unbelievable. I clearly have gotten inside their *cabezas*." He lifted a glass to his lips, then paused and lifted it further upward in a triumphant pose before again lowering it to his mouth-level. He sipped slowly from the vodka tonic that had been prepared by his female companion, who sat on a chair next to where he was standing, the top two buttons of her white blouse unbuttoned and the slacks and jacket of her pantsuit laid neatly over another chair. She also was drinking vodka, with cranberry juice instead of tonic, and condensation from her glass dripped slowly and seductively onto her bare, tanned legs.

"Yes he did, *papi*," replied Lupe Espinosa from her position on the chair. "Between Kasper's talking about you and belittling me, I think we have plenty to use against the Prosecutor's office and how they disparage the city's Hispanic people. I didn't plan for my button to pop from my blouse, to be honest with you," she said, "rubbing her glass up and down the outside of her blouse, "but it could be the best thing that could have happened to me. It certainly got him to notice me, and no doubt he's going to remember me." She rose from her chair, her long legs still accentuated by her stiletto heels, and the bottom edge of her blouse barely covered the pink "boy shorts" underwear which framed her perfectly rounded posterior. "And you know something else, *papi?*" she asked, before answering her own question. "It was genius having me go there to ask him the question." She paused, and took her right hand, wet from the condensation which had gathered on the outside of her glass, and ran it through his thick, dark hair. "You never cease to amaze me, you know," she purred, removing her

43

hand from his hair and flicking her fingers so the remaining liquid sprayed on his face. "*Nunca dejas de sorprenderme.*"

Sanchez smiled. He walked over to a mirror which hung on the wall. He stood in front of the mirror, posing like a bodybuilder, and gazed at his own visage with an overwhelming sense of self-admiration. He was shirtless, and the well-toned definition of both his chest and stomach made him feel much less than his 36 years. Behind him, and also visible in the mirror, stood the lovely Lupe Espinosa, slowly and seductively unbuttoning the remainder of her blouse to reveal her perfectly rounded, and seemingly silicone-filled, C-cup breasts.

"*Mi amor,*" he answered without averting his eyes from the mirror, "I sometimes actually amaze myself. *A veces me sorprendo a mí mismo.*" He turned to her, and wrapped his arms firmly around her naked torso, his hands resting on the waistband of her underwear. He leaned in so that his head was alongside hers. "Things are going so well," he whispered into her ear, "*tan bien.* They are going so well." With his right hand, he slowly pulled at the waistband and lowered the fabric down her shapely legs. She smiled and kissed him softly on the cheek as the remainder of her clothing slid down to her ankles, and she slowly stepped up, right leg first, until she stood, naked except for her stiletto heels, with his hands cupping her rear end.

"Now, Jesus?" she asked. "I don't think that we have any time to fuck now." She looked over her shoulder to the clock which sat on the table to her left. "I thought that you have a meeting tonight? You'd better let go of my ass, because it's almost 5:30, you know. Look at the clock." Sunlight streamed in through the window of Lupe's apartment, its glare partially obscuring the numbers on the clock. "Don't you have to go home to change so that you look like a proper candidate?" She bit his left ear playfully.

Sanchez pulled his hands from her body and recoiled, his mood shifting in an instant and jolting Lupe with surprise. "A proper candidate?" he thundered at her, "*¿has olvidado?* Did you forget? Did you forget that we are not talking about that?" He paused and pulled her tightly again, but this time it was not a loving embrace. It was exactly the opposite, which frightened Lupe. She gasped in pain as he continued, "don't fuck this up, Lupe. *Estamos enfocados en el niño.* We are focused on the boy. Just the boy. *Sólo el niño.* This is not, I repeat, not, about me. *Esto no se trata de mí.*" He tightened his grip as she continued to squirm. "*¿Me intiendes?* Do you understand me, or do I have to spell it out again?"

Lupe Espinosa grabbed at Sanchez's hands and pulled away from his clutches. She bent over at the waist, coughing, her breasts convulsing against her face as she tried to regain her composure. "Calm the fuck down, Jesus," she yelled, again coughing before she continued, "*Estoy hablando contigo ahora. ¡Solamente contigo!* I'm talking to you now. Only you! We are the only people here!" She paused again, and cupped her breasts in her hands in a false moment of modesty as she stood before him. "I know what we are doing!" she yelled, moving to her right to retrieve her clothing. "I'm not some stupid *puta* you brought home." She hooked the clasp of her bra and then pulled on her blouse and stepped closer to him, sneering, "I'm a fucking college graduate, *una graduada de la universidad,* you fucking immigrant." She spit in his face, and snapped her head backward when he raised his right hand to block the saliva and, she thought, to strike her in the face. "And make sure to remember this, Mr. Sanchez," she added, "you have it backwards. *Usted tiene al revés.* You know what I mean, *papi. Sin mí, no eres nada.* Without me, you're nothing. I'm the one taking you to the Mayor's office."

"Oh, are you?" Sanchez asked. "You don't think I can do this without you? *¿Usted no cree que yo puedo hacer esto sin ti?*"

Lupe bent down and then straightened up, pulling up her pants, leaving her pink underwear on the floor next to the chair, and walked toward a mirror which hung on the wall. She quickly tucked her blouse into the pants, the silk of her blouse gently caressing her rounded ass, and fixed her hair while she admired her visage, and then quickly turned, her hair whipping around in a dramatic fashion. "Oh *papi, no creo, lo sé.*" She walked toward him and stroked his hair with her left hand. "I don't think, Jesus, I know that you're going nowhere without me." She laughed as he turned away from her. "Look at me, Jesus" she said quietly, to no response. "*¡Mírame!*" she thundered, grabbing him by the arm and turning him so they were again face-to-face.

"Listen carefully. *Eschuchame con atención.* You can't do this without me. You can't do this without all of the stories that I get done on the television and media coverage. You know it. *Usted lo sabe.* So cut out the macho shit."

Jesus Sanchez sighed deeply. He walked over to a chair and sat, his shoulders slumped. Lupe walked over to him, stroked his shoulder, and leaned down so that her mouth was alongside his ear. "I bet you want me to be reassuring and stroke your Latino macho ego now, right, *papi*? Well, that ain't going to happen. *Me voy.* I'm out of here," she added, "when you are ready to deal with me properly, you give me a call. *Llámame.*" She stood back up, out of arm's reach, as if she expected him to attempt to strike her. To her surprise, however, Sanchez did not move. He did not raise his arm to strike her, nor did he even turn to her in recognition of what she had just said. He did not even flinch from her venomous diatribe.

Lupe waited for a second and, seeing no response, turned and walked toward the door. "And Jesus," she added, "if you do call me, *tal vez voy a contester el teléfono.* Maybe I will even answer the phone. And lock the door behind you when you leave." She opened the door, walked outside, and slammed it behind her.

Sanchez never moved from his chair. For a moment, he did not even move a muscle. The first thing he did was reach to the table next to the chair, where his cell phone sat. He grabbed the phone, and punched some numbers. A deep voice answered. "*Tenemos un problema, amigo,* we've got a problem," Sanchez said, before clicking the phone off and throwing it against the wall.

Chapter V – Eric Starts To Panic

The next morning found Eric at his desk by 7:30, trying to do as much research as he could on the law regarding texting or talking on the phone while in an auto accident. He had read about the laws being enacted by the New Jersey legislature after two accidents, one of which resulted in the death of a pedestrian and the other which led to two motorcycle riders losing their legs. He suspected based on the comments made at the scene by the police officers that Wendi would be charged with vehicular manslaughter, since the boy died, and that the charge would also include aggravated factors due to the other boy's statement that Wendi was allegedly on the phone at the time of impact. He found an article on the internet which discussed the reasoning behind the law's passage as well as a recitation of the possible penalties for conviction:

"Under the law, if it is shown that a defendant made use of a hand-held wireless telephone while driving a motor vehicle, there is a presumption that the defendant was driving in a reckless manner while doing so. In such a case, municipal and/or County Prosecutors are permitted to charge a defendant who was allegedly making use of such a device with committing vehicular homicide or assault when such type of accident occurs from reckless driving. Vehicular homicide, normally, is considered a crime of the second degree, and is punishable by imprisonment of five to ten years, a fine of up to $150,000, or both. The lesser charge of assault by auto is a crime of the fourth degree if serious bodily injury occurs, and will be a disorderly person's offense if the accident results in bodily injury. The penalties for this lesser charge are, not surprisingly, less severe than the possible penalties for Vehicular Homicide - the fourth degree crime, for serious bodily injury, can result in a sentence of up to 18 months imprisonment, a fine of up to $10,000, or both. For the lesser version, which is a disorderly person's offense,

47

a defendant may be subject to imprisonment for up to six months, a fine of up to $1,000, or both."

Whether or not some injuries could be considered "serious" could be a source of negotiation with the Prosecutor's Office, Eric reasoned, and could mean the difference between a defendant facing actual jail time and a steep monetary penalty. Any ambiguity as to the severity of injuries meant that a defendant charged with the fourth degree version could likely plea bargain his case down to a disorderly person's offense, pay a $1,000 fine, and avoid prison completely. Additionally, since the court rules weighed against imprisonment for a first-time offender, any person charged under the lesser statute, for texting and merely causing injury to another person, even an injury which could be considered to be serious, would not likely be facing any jail time.

Here, however, there could be no such debate, and likely would not be treated in a manner where imprisonment would not be feasible. Jose Gomez was dead. There were no permutations of death, no way to haggle over whether the death was "serious" or not. The charge, by definition, would be vehicular homicide, a second-degree crime which was punishable, as set forth in the article, by a term of imprisonment for between five-to-ten years and fines up to $150,000. Eric, despondent over the possibilities, pushed his chair away from the desk and wiped his eyes, rubbing the backs of his fingers against his closed eyelids so hard that he thought his eyes would fall backward into his brain.

"Can't panic yet," he thought to himself, in an attempt to calm his nerves. "Just because an article on the internet says something does not mean that it is completely true," he reasoned, "I should probably look up the actual statute before I believe that an internet article is the gospel." Pushing the chair back to his computer desk, he clicked on the legal research icon on the computer and logged on with his username and password. Typing the statute number into the "search" box, he was able to locate the actual statute, and, to his chagrin, the verbiage of the statute only served to verify, if not amplify, his fears. The "death by auto" statute also dealt with alcohol consumption or drug use, not simply texting while driving – but the important part for Eric was limited to the cell phone portions. The relevant text of the statute read as follows:

N.J.S.A. 2C:11-5. Death by auto or vessel.

a. Criminal homicide constitutes vehicular homicide when it is caused by driving a vehicle or vessel recklessly... Proof that the defendant was operating a hand-held wireless telephone while driving a motor vehicle in violation of section 1 of P.L.2003, c.310 (C.39:4-97.3) shall give rise to an inference that the defendant was driving recklessly. Nothing in this section shall be construed to in any way limit the conduct or conditions that may be found to constitute driving a vehicle or vessel recklessly.

b. Except as provided in paragraph (3) of this subsection, vehicular homicide is a crime of the second degree.

c. For good cause shown, the court may, in accepting a plea of guilty under this section, order that such plea not be evidential in any civil proceeding.

d. Nothing herein shall be deemed to preclude, if the evidence so warrants, an indictment and conviction for aggravated manslaughter under the provisions of subsection a. of N.J.S.A.2C:11-4

As used in this section, "auto or vessel" means all means of conveyance propelled otherwise than by muscular power.

e. Any person who violates paragraph (3) of subsection b. of this section shall forfeit the auto or vessel used in the commission of the offense, unless the defendant can establish at a hearing, which may occur at the time of sentencing, by a preponderance of the evidence that such forfeiture would constitute a serious hardship to the family of the defendant that outweighs the need to deter such conduct by the defendant and others. In making its findings, the court shall take judicial notice of any evidence, testimony or information adduced at the trial, plea hearing, or other court proceedings and shall also consider the presentence report and any other relevant information. Forfeiture pursuant to this subsection shall be in addition to, and not in lieu of, civil forfeiture pursuant to chapter 64 of this title.

Now Eric began to sweat. He had heard about the statute when it was first passed, in the wake of great public outcry regarding cell phone use, whether talking or texting, by possibly inattentive drivers. He remembered reading the newspaper articles about the husband and wife, residents of Morris County, in western Jersey, several years ago, in the fall of 2009. In their accident, each of them had lost a leg in an accident caused by a pick-up truck driver more pre-occupied with texting than with properly keeping his eyes on the road and observing other traffic. He remembered hearing stories about elderly woman who was killed around the same time when crossing an intersection in Elizabeth, not two miles from his office and, eerily, only a few blocks away from where Wendi's car had come into contact with Jose Gomez. The allegation in that case was that the driver of the car who struck the old woman was on her cell phone at the time of the accident. He knew attorneys involved in that case, both for the criminal charges brought against the driver of that car, as well as those involved in a subsequent civil case.

He also knew of the various studies regarding cell phone use by drivers, which were reported time and again in the local newspapers and across the internet. Most studies did not show tremendous numbers of deaths due to vehicular cell phone use, but each was accompanied by disclaimers that most states simply did not indicate the fact that cell phones were in use at the time of the accident. Various insurance company studies showed increased cell phone-driving fatalities every year, but these studies also pointed out that most cell phone usage was not being properly reported. The National Transportation Safety Board, not long ago, had called for a nationwide ban on cell phone use by drivers.

Another study of over 1,000 New Jersey drivers, aged 17 through 25, was completed by an insurance company in response to raised concerns about drivers who were texting or talking on the phone. According to that study, an overwhelming majority of the youths polled had witnessed drivers young and old texting or holding the phone in their hands while driving; over half said that they saw their parents improperly talking on the phone without a Bluetooth device while driving, and seventy percent saw their friends do the same thing. More of a concern, perhaps, was that almost three-quarters of those polled had witnessed friends of theirs texting while driving. No doubt the same amount of people had seen their friends and parents eating while driving, applying makeup while driving, or turning around, distracted, to deal with their petulant children while driving. But the "hot-button" issue involved cell phone usage. All of the other distractions were not so prevalent that they, even collectively, proved to be of any consequence, nor did they merit any media attention.

But despite all of these studies and surveys, Eric had not heard of any actual prosecutions being made under the statute other than a bus driver who mowed down several people on a sidewalk due to his negligence while on a cell phone, at least any prosecutions under the "death by auto" law for an automobile driver who was using his or her phone at the time of an accident unless there were other circumstances.

As he completed his research, he was reminded of a case that came out of Somerset County. That case involved a boy, an 18-year old, who was not only texting and driving but was also drinking before the accident. The alcohol aspect made it different from Wendi's case. There was also a case out of Essex County where a woman driving on Routes 1 & 9 was texting while driving, veered from the express lanes into the local lanes, and plowed into a pick-up truck. The other driver was ejected from the vehicle, and the woman was charged under the statute because she was texting immediately prior to the accident. Reports revealed that her driver's license was suspended at the time of the accident, and, somehow, inexplicably, not only had her license been suspended on one occasion, but, rather, it had been suspended 65 times. According to a report in the local papers, she also had at least six speeding tickets on her record and a history of failing to pay court-mandated fines and motor vehicle surcharges. In short, she was a menace who should never have been on the road. Attempting to prosecute her was an easy decision, but her case never actually went to trial because she died from an accidental overdose of sleeping pills only four months after the incident.

For Wendi, on the other hand, this was her first potential traffic violation of any type. She was not drinking alcohol prior to the accident, like the kid in Somerset was, and she certainly did not have the checkered driving history of the woman charged in Essex. She would be, to his knowledge, the first person charged simply for being in an accident with the allegation of texting, with no aggravating circumstances such as alcohol or driving on the suspended list. Wendi would be the first automobile driver charged in Union County under the statute. And Eric certainly had no aspirations of being the first attorney to have a client charged as such, much less the first attorney who saw his client hauled off to jail for violating its provisions. More importantly, he did not want to be the first attorney to watch not only his client, but also his ex-wife, face the possibility of extended jail time for a crime which he believed, or at least hoped, that she did not commit.

The sweat was beginning to pour down his face, droplets ponding on his computer's keyboard. He felt tightness in his chest, making breathing difficult. He realized that he was suffering from a panic attack, something that had never happened to him before. He initially thought that he was having a heart attack, but soon realized that it was a panic-induced difficulty.

All the while, he had two thoughts. The first was his fear of having Wendi hauled off to jail, and the second was more personal, as he thought, over and over, "What have I gotten myself into?"

Chapter VI – Dealing With Fatima

The clock read 8:55 when Fatima arrived for her work day. She entered Eric's office and found him in his chair, back to the door. Even though Eric's back was turned to her, she could tell that his head was buried in his hands, shaking slowly from side to side. She walked slowly toward the chair and lightly placed her left hand on Eric's shoulder, startling him. He thrust his hands sideways, his reddened face looking to the left through watery eyes. Fatima looked down at Eric, intending to apologize for scaring him. When she saw the color of his face and the rivulets of red that coursed through his eyes, however, she gasped.

"What is wrong, Eric?" she asked, quickly scanning the papers strewn over his desk for a clue as to the reason for his dejected state. "Have you been crying?" She knelt down next to Eric, laying her left arm over his chest. She kissed him lightly on the forehead as another tear rolled down his cheek.

"I'm sorry," Eric answered, "I don't want you to see me like this." He looked at the clock. "I didn't think you would be here for another few minutes."

"Well, I am here," Fatima said, softly, "now tell me the problem." She looked to her left, at Eric's desk, and reached for the box of tissues that sat exactly at arm's length. Pulling one from the box, she gently dabbed at Eric's moistened eye and then handed the tissue to him.

"Thanks," he said, as he took the tissue and wiped both of his eyes, "but I don't even know if I can tell you the problem."

She stood and reached her right arm over his shoulders, leaning in and cradling his head against her ample chest. "Eric," she said, "we have been together for years now. Plus, we're not just co-workers. We're cousins, remember? You can tell me anything." She raised his head up and tilted it toward her face. "It's not like I haven't heard strange stories from you before, you know."

Eric cleared his throat and pulled his head away from Fatima's grasp. "Normally I would agree, Fatima, but this time may be different," he said, softly, reaching for another tissue and noisily blowing his nose before continuing. "It involves Wendi."

The mere mention of Eric's ex-wife's name sent chills up Fatima's spine. She stiffened and, through clenched teeth, asked Eric to elaborate.

Hesitatingly, Eric began to explain. "I think I made a big mistake getting involved in her case," he said, "if she is charged with the death by auto statute, she's looking at five-to-ten in jail and over a hundred thousand dollars in fines. How much pressure is that for me? If we lose, what will Jason say? That I let his mother go to jail? I'm a frigging idiot for agreeing to do this."

Fatima looked up at the ceiling and spoke, haltingly. "Normally," she said before taking a deep breath, "I would relish the idea of Wendi going to jail after what she did to you." She looked down at Eric, who looked back at her disapprovingly. "Normally, I said," she added, holding her arms outward with her palms facing Eric as if to explain her position. "But you don't even know if they are going to charge her with that, so why get all upset over something that may not even happen?"

"I see your point," Eric said, "but here's the problem. It's going to be very political, you know. Woodman said so at the scene, and I am beginning to think that he is completely correct. Think about it, Fatima, with that Sanchez guy having a press conference at the site and then that circus press conference at the courthouse," he added, turning and facing his computer as he scanned the internet for any articles about the accident, "I don't think that the Prosecutor will have any choice but to charge her with it. His political life may depend on it, what with all of the Hispanics in Union County."

"Well, you may be right, but until it happens I don't think you should worry." Fatima replied as she turned to walk to her desk. "And don't forget, Eric, this is a law office, not just the office of Wendi Goldberg. We have, well, you have, plenty of other clients to take care of here, plenty of other work to do, so you can't sit and obsess over one case, even if it is her." She lowered her voice, muttering under her breath, "plenty of clients who didn't cheat on you and try to ruin your life."

Eric did not hear her last sentence, muttered as Fatima passed through the door outside of her office. As Fatima sat down behind her desk, she heard Eric call to her, in a voice where she knew he was talking to her, but could not make out the words. She again stood and walked to his office, reaching for the door jamb with her right hand and leaning in so she could speak to him face-to-face. "Were you talking to me, Eric?"

"Yes," he replied as he leafed through the papers on his desk. Looking up, he asked, "can you do a favor for me?"

"Most probably," she said, hesitatingly. "What is it?"

Eric again cleared his throat before asking, as if he expected some resistance. "Can you, uh, can you call Wendi for me and tell her that I will come to the house Saturday morning to meet with her and go over the case?" His eyes widened and he took a deep breath as he awaited her response.

Fatima released her hand from the door jamb and took a step forward, such that her entire body was within the door frame to Eric's office. "Well, Eric," she replied, "you are my boss and, when we are within these walls, my job is to do what you ask."

Eric exhaled loudly and smiled. "Great, thanks. Please tell her I will be there by nine o'clock and I will stop for bagels so we can have ...."

"I didn't finish, though," Fatima interjected. Eric stopped talking before uttering the word "breakfast" and waited for Fatima to continue. "I didn't finish, so let me start again." She paused and took a deep breath of her own. Her eyes moistened as she began to speak. "Within these walls, my job is to do what you ask … usually. But, first and foremost, we are family. We are cousins. Family protects each other," she said as she again paused and a tear ran down her right cheek, her face turning red and her voice lowering to a whisper, "there is no fucking way that I am going to call that whore and tell her anything." As she said the word "anything," her voice began to rise. "You want to call that slut, feel free. But don't ask me to have anything to do with her. In fact," she added, "forget everything I said before. What I should have said is that you are a fucking idiot for representing her. She doesn't deserve any help from you, even if she is paying you. She cheated on you, Eric!" She wiped the tear from her face, turned, and walked back to her desk, grabbing a tissue from the box on her desk's edge and blowing her nose as she sat. Just so that her point was clear, she continued. "You call her, you idiot," she yelled to Eric, "I'm not going to do it."

Eric waited for a second before responding, to allow Fatima some time to calm down. "OK," he yelled back to her, "I will call her, thanks." He stood and hesitatingly walked out of his office and next to Fatima's desk. She was looking down at the papers stacked in front of her computer, and did not look up even though Eric knew that she sensed his presence. "Fatima?" he asked, "can I say something?"

"If you want to, because you're the boss," she answered, sniffling and reaching for another tissue. "But before you do, let me say something." She paused, continuing to look downward, and avoiding eye contact with Eric as she began to respond. "I am sorry for yelling at you. It wasn't right. It just upsets me so much that you worry so much about her. She certainly didn't worry about you, and doesn't worry about you, but now that she needs someone she is being nice to you. You know, it's actually a little funny, when you think about it. Usually you are the one using someone for your own gain, and for some reason I am able to deal with it. Now, though, when she is going to use you, it really bothers me."

"I was going to apologize to you, but I accept your apology, I think," Eric said. "I am sorry for trying to get you to speak to her, but remember, it is my problem, not

56

yours. She cheated on me, not you. And no, I am not past it. I am just trying to deal with it. So just deal with me, OK?"

"OK. I will," she replied. Eric came around the back of her desk, taking her left hand until she stood and hugged him as she began to cry again. "But I'm not going to be happy about it."

"Wouldn't want it any other way," Eric answered as he kissed her forehead before turning and walking back to his desk. Instead of calling Wendi, however, he texted her that he would come to her house, the house where he used to live, that Saturday morning to discuss her case rather than having her come in and have to deal with Fatima. Wendi texted back almost immediately, thanking him both for his offer to come to the house and for allowing her to avoid dealing with what was, and likely would continue to be, a sticky situation between her and Fatima. It was as if she had heard the conversation between Eric and Fatima, which Eric found strange but, knowing the women as he did, not overly surprising.

Placing his phone back onto his desk after receiving the text from Wendi, Eric tried to focus on the papers piled on his desk, papers from several other cases which required his immediate attention. He could not, however, get past the thought of Wendi being charged with the death by auto statute and facing up to a decade in jail. He did not think that she would be sentenced to such an extended term under any circumstance, but he really could not bear the thought of his ex-wife spending even one year, one month, or even just one day behind bars. He wanted to find out what the Prosecutor's Office was intending to do with her case. Only one day had elapsed since the accident, and the story and calls for Wendi's head were already intensifying. In fact, when he opened up his internet browser during the conversation with Fatima one of the main stories on the New Jersey news page focused on the young man's death and questions surrounding the Prosecutor's intentions with respect to charging the woman who was, in the writer's words (and no doubt greatly influenced by Jesus Sanchez's inflammatory comments) callously on the phone when she struck and killed him.

He had one friend in the Prosecutor's Office, Jim Parker. He and Parker had gone to Law School together, and, since they worked essentially across the street from each other due to the proximity of Eric's office to the county courthouse, they would meet for lunch or dinner at least once a month with a couple of their other classmates. On those occasions when Eric wanted to gain some insight into how the Prosecutor's Office was handling one of his cases, he would telephone Parker. Of course, Parker was bound by his ethical obligations to the Prosecutor's Office and would never actually answer any of his questions or provide him with any inside information that could help Eric in his case preparation, but, in light of the fact that the matter involved his ex-wife, Eric was hopeful that this call would be the exception.

Unfortunately for Eric, on this occasion he would be proven correct. Hearing Parker's response to his question, he thanked his friend, hung up the phone, and again leaned back in his chair, head in his hands. Parker's response was, to put it mildly, not positive. "They're going to charge her," he yelled to Fatima. "The pressure from Sanchez is too great. They're going to make the Elizabeth police charge her with the death by auto statute. It may not be today, but it is definitely going to happen." He paused. "How am I going to tell her?"

"Well," Fatima yelled back, "you have until Saturday to figure it out. I am sure that you will think of something." A small smile creased her face. "You always do."

Chapter VII – Eric Gets A Massage

That night, Eric drove to the health spa on Morris Avenue for his weekly massage. The spa where he went was a legitimate establishment, not one of those "rub and tug" parlors where patrons paid for and expected to receive "happy endings" from their masseuse. Eric had once accidentally wandered into one of those places. He was immediately freaked out by the clientele, as well as his fear that he would be caught in such a place and have his law license placed in jeopardy. It was the last time he ever went to a place that he even considered questionable in that regard.

This was not to say, however, that the atmosphere in this spa was entirely chaste. While all of the masseuses who worked at the salon, "*Let Us Rub You the Right Way,*" were properly licensed by the Board of Massage and Bodywork Therapy, as required by New Jersey statute, all of the women were residents of Elizabeth, all were Hispanic, and all dressed as they chose rather than in a standard uniform. Most of them were usually clad somewhat provocatively, while some of them dressed as if they were going out dancing for the evening. At other massage places, Eric recalled all of the masseuses wearing polo shirts and either yoga pants or sweatpants, or sometimes, like on cruises, polo shirts and long, thigh-covering shorts.

Not so at this establishment. Here, the women wore low-cut t-shirts, push-up bras, and while some did wear shorts, these articles of clothing were much more revealing than those worn at other massage places. Some of the shorts and skirts worn by the women were more reminiscent of large belts. At other massage places, the person receiving the massage was largely covered by blankets during the session, with only the part of the body being worked upon exposed. Here, the blankets were essentially optional, and the narrower tables made for more skin-to-skin contact between the masseuse and patron.

Eric had been going to this particular establishment for over five years, and had a standing appointment on Thursday nights at 8:30 for a ninety-minute massage. He found it particularly relaxing after a hard day at the office, and provided him with a respite from worrying about his clients, upcoming court appearances, and the other pressures of his everyday life. For the first two years, he had received massages by several different women, essentially being rubbed by whichever woman was available at that time. Three years ago, however, a new woman named Marisol gave him his massage, and he thought that she did such a great job that he insisted upon her becoming his steady masseuse.

Most masseuse/client relationships are superficial at best. There is a slight conversation in the beginning of the session, the two parties exchanging greetings and then some conversation about what aches and pains, if any, the client wants addressed. This is then followed by silence, with the exception of the sounds of the masseuse moving about the room and the new age music which plays overhead. The client, for the most part, remains mute after the initial conversation except to answer "yes" or "no" when asked by the masseuse if she is doing her job properly.

For Eric, however, such silence was simply not possible, nor was he content to have such a superficial relationship with someone who was rubbing oils and her hands all over his body on a weekly basis. Every week, he would learn more about Marisol, about her life, her family, her schooling, and her work. When she first started, she was 21 years old and attending the local community college, taking classes in both English and Spanish in an attempt to not only gain her degree, but also to increase her mastery of the language. She lived with her parents and two brothers, none of whom liked the fact that she was giving massages but, at the same time, none of whom objected to the income that she was generating for the benefit of the family. Her father had been hurt in a workplace accident, causing permanent injury to his leg and rendering him unable to work as a carpenter, his trade. While he did receive a monthly stipend from his last employer's workers' compensation carrier, those monies were insufficient to support and feed a family of five and all of the children did what they could to help pay the bills. Her mother spoke little English, and therefore was unable to work at most establishments. She did work on a part-time basis at two local restaurants - the salaries were meager, however, and the tips that she received helped - but neither, by any measure or standard, could be considered substantial.

At one point, a year earlier, Marisol had a serious boyfriend, the first one serious enough to merit mentioning to Eric. His name was Jose, and he was a waiter at one of the restaurants where her mother worked. He was 26; at the time she was slightly younger. They dated for almost six months, and Marisol would tell Eric about their dates and about her feelings for Jose, in a seemingly ironic manner, while she massaged Eric's body. Toward the end of the six months, however, Eric could tell that her enthusiasm for Jose had waned, and the two parted ways just before Marisol's 24th birthday. Since that time, she had remained essentially single. Eric joked, of course, that the two of them should date. Then, he reasoned, she could just massage him at home and he wouldn't have to pay for it. She would laugh and say that it would never work, that she was so tired of massaging people all day long that the last thing she wanted to do when she got home at night was to rub someone else.

The unwritten rule of legitimate massages, of course, is that the person being massaged does not touch the masseuse. At least there should be no voluntary touching, and certainly not in an improper way. Sometimes the masseuse would lift the person's arm in such a way that it would graze her, or the masseuse would lean against the table for greater leverage and the patron would find the masseuse's hip or some other part of her body pressed up against his arm or hand. It was expected that the patron would not reach out to grab the masseuse. Eric, however, liked to "push the envelope" and his conduct at the parlor was not much different from his usual code of proper conduct, or lack thereof. At first he might inadvertently reach out and touch Marisol's leg, or hip. He would do so in the small area where her shorts covered her body, so that he was not touching her skin. Over time, however, his wandering hands found their way to other parts of her body – one time, as she stood before him and bent over him to rub his back, he reached out with both hands and grabbed her ass. She jumped, startled, and reached behind her to remove his grasp. "Eric, really?" she asked, as she pulled her shorts a little lower, to the tops of her thighs, and resumed her work.

A month later, however, she was again standing in front of him, leaning over him to rub his back. He could feel her breasts lightly pressing against his back, and again reached out with his hands for her ass – this week, however, she was wearing a short skirt and, as she leaned over, her skirt rode up far enough that his hands grabbed nothing but her rear end, along with the wisp of fabric which constituted the back of her thong. And this time, he immediately realized, she did not jump. She did not scold him. Most importantly, she did not remove his hands from her body. She simply went about her massage, moving slowly from side to side as she alternately dug her hands and elbows into his shoulders and back. All the while, he caressed her rear end tenderly.

Chapter VIII – Returning "Home"

Saturday morning, Eric drove to his old residence to meet with Wendi. On the way, he picked up a half-dozen bagels, including two of Wendi's favorite, cinnamon raisin, along with a carton of orange juice, some cream cheese, and lox. He stopped at Dunkin' Donuts and picked up two large coffees, his with cream and sugar and hers with skim milk and Splenda. Pulling up the street where he lived for almost two decades during his marriage, he noted that a couple of the houses on the street had been freshly painted and the landscaping at several others had been changed. His old house looked the same; same color, same trees and bushes out front, albeit less well-maintained. The only thing missing was his "Parking for Yankees' Fans" only sign, the sign that hung from a tree directly next to the driveway. The side of the house somehow looked bare without the sign that had adorned the tree for years, so long that its navy blue color had faded several shades, to almost a powder blue, after years of exposure to the various forms of New Jersey weather - rain, heat, and snow.

He parked his car in the street, hesitant to use the driveway in recognition of the fact that he had no legal right to use it - the house, pursuant to the divorce judgment, was now solely owned by his ex-wife and, in this case, his client. He felt uneasy about acting in any way which would imply that the house, or property, was somehow still his. Exiting the car, he placed the two coffees on top of the car, opened the back door, and leaned in to retrieve his file and the aromatic bag from the bagel store.

"Holy shit," he heard a voice call from behind him as he stood, hunched over inside of the car, the bag of bagels and Wendi's file in his hands, "is that you, Eric?" the voice called. He recognized the voice, spoken with a slight Spanish accent, immediately.

Without even turning, Eric replied, "yes it is me, amigo. How are things over at *Casa Lopez*?" He placed the file and bag back on the seat and turned to see his old neighbor, Pablo Lopez, walking toward the car. "It's great to see you again, Pablo. It's been a while."

Pablo walked over to Eric, grabbed his right arm and then pulled him into a bear hug. "It's great to see you, Eric." He paused, and looked to the front of the house. "I really miss having you around here. It's just not the same here on the block since you moved out."

"I know man," Eric replied. "Believe me, I miss being here also. But not because of the neighbors, of course," he added, in a deadpan voice. His face broke into a smile, however, betraying the fact that he was joking with the last comment.

"What have you been up to, Eric?" Pablo asked, and then chuckled before adding a dig of his own. "I mean, what have you been up to, *amigo*," he said, with a lilt in his voice, "I mean, other than that shit that went down in Brazil?"

Eric laughed uneasily. "So you know about that, huh?" he asked, as Pablo nodded, smiling. "I guess I should be happy that it didn't end up in the *Ledger*."

"Come on, *amigo*, you know that I only write sports," Pablo answered, shaking his head and placing his hands on his hips in a scolding manner. Pablo Lopez was the Yankees' beat writer for the *Star-Ledger*, the largest newspaper in New Jersey. Over the years, he had provided Eric with tickets to see his beloved baseball team, and had even pulled some strings to allow both Eric and his son, Jason, into the Yankee clubhouse before a game about ten years earlier; the ball that the players signed for Jason that day still sat on a shelf in his old room in his mother's house, even though he now spent most of his time with his father. "What would I be doing getting involved with an attorney who allegedly killed his hot client's husband, possibly screwed her in his office, and then chased her to Brazil? Don't be silly. That's totally out of my league."

"Well," Eric replied, trying to deflect Pablo's comments and the information that he no doubt possessed about Eric's liaison with Bianca Rodriguez and his trip to

Brazil, "you know how it is. Just like you, amigo, I am just trying to earn a living." He paused and looked in all directions. "It is weird, though," he added, "not coming here anymore. I miss the old neighborhood sometimes. And you know what, I miss spending time with you guys and the others around here." His eyes grew misty. "It's tough to just completely change your life, you know. The transition from being a married guy to being a single or divorced guy is not always easy."

"I completely understand what you're talking about, and believe me, we miss you, amigo," Pablo said, putting his right hand on Eric's shoulder in a consoling manner. "It's just not the same without you around here." He lowered his voice to an almost inaudible whisper and leaned closer. "If it's any consolation," he added, "he doesn't come around here anymore either."

"He?" asked Eric, also in a whisper. "You mean ..."

"The guy," answered Pablo. "Your friend, the one that was, you know, the guy who with Wendi when you left." He smiled. "Let me tell you something, Eric, we never did like him all that much. Especially my wife. She couldn't stand him, probably just because of the fact that they hurt you. We all wish you were back for real." He paused and looked toward the house. "Maybe something is going on now, right? Why else would you be here early in the morning?" He inhaled deeply as the smell of the freshly-baked bagels emanated from the car's back seat. "Why else would you be here with such a delicious smelling breakfast?"

Eric broke into a deep laugh, bending with his hands on his knees as he gasped for air. "No, no, no," he sputtered. "I know what I just said about missing you guys, and I appreciate everything that you said, but Pablo, believe me, there is no way I'm coming back here."

"¿*Entonces por qué estás aqui, amigo?* Then why are you here?" Pablo asked, a faint smile creasing his lips.

Eric looked at his friend with bemusement. "*Usted sabe algo*," he said, surprising his old friend by speaking Spanish back to him. "You know something, Pablo," he said, "I can tell. Come on, fess up."

The smile on Pablo's face disappeared. "*¿Lo que sé?*" he replied. "What do I know? Since we're talking Spanish to each other, *Yo sé que usted esta representado a Wendi en ese case que involucra al niño muerto.*" He looked at Eric, whose face belied the fact that he did not fully understand what he had just said, so he repeated his response in English. "I know that you are representing Wendi in the case involving the dead kid," he said, softly. "And I also know that you're going to have problems because that idiot Sanchez is making noise. Anything else you want to know? *¿Algo más?*"

Eric looked down at his feet. "No, I think you've said enough, *amigo*. As always, it's nice seeing you. Even though I can't lie and say that I am happy to hear what you just told me. I certainly don't want to hear anything else now." He started to walk toward the house, but then stopped in his tracks as he reconsidered his earlier comment. He did want to hear whatever Pablo knew. In fact, he not only wanted to hear what other information Pablo might possess, but he had to know. Maybe it would help in Wendi's defense. He turned back around and walked back toward Pablo so that he could satisfy his curiosity. "OK, you know something that I don't know," he said to Pablo. "*Dime.* Tell me."

"OK, anything I know is unconfirmed, of course," Pablo said, trying to soften the blow of what he was about to tell Eric. "You know how it is at the paper. People talk. I rarely talk to the news guys, but I heard Wendi's name mentioned one day so, because I was concerned, I went over and listened to what they were talking about, and then I asked them for some details and where they had gotten their information." He looked toward the house. "*Yo no se lo he dicho.* I haven't told her yet, because I don't want to scare her." He paused. "To be honest, I am actually a little afraid of telling her because I don't want to hear her reaction."

"Oh shit," Eric said, shaking his head. "I don't like the sound of this."

"It shouldn't surprise you," Pablo said. "Here's what I heard. There's a lot of personalities involved her, very political, as you might expect. Sanchez is putting pressure on the Prosecutor's office to go after Wendi for what happened to the kid. He wants to be the next Mayor, you know. Well, you should know. All of the Hispanics know that he's gunning for that job. And, more importantly, the Mayor knows. So the Mayor, who doesn't want to lose his office to Sanchez, is also putting pressure on the Prosecutor to charge and convict her. He wants to save face, at least publicly, so that any prosecution does not become a campaign point for Sanchez. So he has to make sure and come out in favor of prosecuting her, because if he doesn't, then he won't get any of the Hispanic votes at the next election. He knows that Sanchez will get most of the Latin vote, but he thinks he can still win re-election if he gets some of them. If he loses them all, then Sanchez is a lock to win and he's out of a job. So, either way he looks, the Prosecutor is getting shit over this. And he has to do it. She's going to be charged with the death statute."

"That doesn't sound good at all," Eric said.

"Well, there is one good thing, though, depending on how you look at it. From what I hear, the Prosecutor doesn't like the shit coming down from either Sanchez or the Mayor, so he's going to try to stick it to them."

"Really," Eric replied, "In what way?"

Pablo chuckled. "Well, from my sources, I am hearing that instead of appointing one of the lead Assistant Prosecutors in the office to the case, like that guy who did the press conference on the courthouse steps, he is having some young girl do it. It's almost as if he is trying to lose just to piss them both off. They won't admit it, of course, but why else would they have someone without murder trial experience do it, right? It's like a boxer tanking a fight. He brings the charges and takes the case to court, but then loses. That way neither Sanchez nor the current Mayor can crow about putting Wendi away. Neither can use it as a platform point in the election. It's really fucking smart of him, when you think about it."

"Interesting," replied Eric. "What else can you tell me?" He reached into his pocket for a pen, but Pablo waved him off.

"No notes, *amigo*. You're going to have to remember it, but forget where you heard it. As for anything else, not much, really," said Pablo. "Word around the newsroom is that the Prosecutor is pissed at the Mayor, but more pissed at Sanchez and his theatrics. He wants to have the win for his office, of course, *pero* he is concerned that if Wendi is convicted, then people will think it was more because of Sanchez and his bullshit and that Sanchez will then be elected mayor in the next election." He paused, and lowered his voice. "And let me tell you something, nobody who is paying attention wants that. The Latinos on the streets may think he is the second coming of the *Christo*, but let me tell you, *aquellos de nosotros que estan pensado,* those of us who are thinking, don't want him anywhere near power."

"Really," Eric asked, "*¿usted no quiere un Latino por el Mayor de Elizabeth?* You don't want a Latino as the Mayor of Elizabeth, Pablo? Shouldn't you want him to win? With all the Latin people in the city, don't you think that the time is right for one of them," he chuckled, "for one of you, to take the reins? I mean, I don't have numbers, but I have to assume that Latinos are the majority in the city now."

"Absolutely, *amigo, es el momento.* It is time, and I would love it, but the question is not whether a Latino should be in power, the question is which Latino should be in power. The question is which Latino and which person. And it can't be Jesus Sanchez. You think those stories about him being in FARC are rumor, that they are some type of urban legend? Far from it, *amigo.* From what we're told, they are all true. *Todos son verdad, amigo.* He is ruthless. He is a killer. *Él es un asesino.* And many think that he won't change just because he gains an official title. That's not the way it works in Colombia, and that's not going to be the way it works if there is a Sanchez administration. And people are just fucking afraid of him."

Eric nodded as he listened to Pablo speak. When his friend finished, Eric asked a more probative question, at least a more probative question for his purposes. "Tell me, *amigo*," he asked, "is that the only reason that Sanchez has inserted himself into this situation, or is there something else? People are killed in the city every week; what about this one, other than the fact that Wendi is white, makes it so special to him? Isn't he better off attacking the gangs? You would think that would endear him more to the voters."

Pablo thought for a minute before responding. "You're right, that would make more sense. And to be honest, *no sé,* I don't know what else there is. But there has to be something, and I can keep an eye open for whatever comes across the newsroom, and an ear."

"I would really appreciate that, Pablo. You've got my number, and, of course, anything you tell me is off the record."

"Of course it is, *amigo*, because if anyone finds out that we've been talking, I will be forced to kill you. I have my own ties, you know, so don't mess with me." He laughed, but then grew stone-faced and leaned his head closer to Eric and lowered his voice to a whisper. "Seriously, *amigo,* you can't tell anyone anything," he explained, "aside from losing my job, I would have to face Sanchez's people, and from what I hear, it would not be a pleasant experience. I have a family to support, don't forget, and these people are really fucking scary. I just can't risk the chance, OK?"

"Wouldn't dream of it," replied Eric, "there's no way I am going to put myself, or you, or your family, in any danger with Sanchez or his people, so don't worry about it. Now let me go see Wendi. It was great talking to you, say hi to the family for me."

"You too, *amigo*," Pablo replied, shaking Eric's hand vigorously and slapping him on the back. "Do all of us a favor and win the case for Wendi, OK? We all think lots of her and don't want to see anything bad happen to her. And we believe she didn't do anything wrong, so when you are defending her you'll be telling the truth. It won't be like some of your other clients."

Eric laughed. "Like some of my other clients? They're all innocent, Pablo, you know that." He turned and gathered up the file, bagel bag, and coffees. He shut the car door with his hip, turned back toward the property, and began to walk up the driveway toward his old house. "Don't worry, Pablo," he said, turning back to his old friend, "I'll do everything I can for her." He then added under his breath, "I sure hope it's enough."

"*Será.* It will be, *amigo*," Pablo said quietly. "It has to be."

Eric approached the front door, placed the coffees on the ground, and reached for the doorknob with his free hand. He tried to turn it to the right to open the door, but the door was locked and the knob would not turn. He instinctively reached into the right front pocket of his pants for his keys, but then realized that he no longer had a key which would open the house door. Pulling his hand from his pocket, he reached out with his index finger and rang the doorbell. The sound of a dog barking echoed from within the house, which surprised him because he did not know that Wendi had gotten a dog; he had retained ownership of Peyton in the divorce, and thought that Wendi was just as happy to rid herself from the responsibility of taking care of a dog. Perhaps she was lonely rattling around the big house by herself, especially if, as Pablo had said, Doug wasn't coming around anymore. Part of him felt saddened by the fact that he was not told of the fact that she had gotten a dog, and part of him was saddened that he did not know that Wendi and Doug were no longer seeing each other.

A larger part of him, however, was heartened by the fact that she had protection in the house, and he was greatly pleased, perhaps too much so, by the fact that her affair, the one which, in large part, had led to their divorce, had ended.

After a few seconds, Wendi opened the door. She was clad in a pink tank-top and black yoga pants. She leaned in to kiss Eric on the cheek and then turned to go back into the kitchen, saying that she was in the middle of making breakfast for them. He could smell the aromas of coffee and cooking eggs wafting from the kitchen, smells which were once all too familiar for him within these walls. He glanced down at the coffees on the front stoop, coffees that would either go to waste or which would eclipse the liquids already brewing in the kitchen. Picking up the coffees, he walked, also carrying the orange juice and bag containing the bagels, lox, and cream cheese, into the kitchen. As he stepped onto the tile which ran the length of the house's entry foyer, a small dog leapt at him from her right side; it appeared to be some form of poodle mix, and looked like a 15-pound or so stuffed animal. "His name is Marmaduke," she called to him, in explanation as she stirred the cooking eggs around the edges of their pan, "you know, like the big red dog in the kids' stories."

"I see the irony, Wendi, very clever," Eric answered as the small dog continued nipping at his ankles and barking his staccato bark.

"Well," she continued, "those books were always Jason's favorites, so it holds a special place for me." She left the wooden spoon in the eggs, turned down the flame, and walked back toward Eric. She knelt down to pet the dog, and to pry him away from the bottoms of Eric's pants legs. "Not that he's ever going to get nearly that big, but he keeps me company," she said, as she rubbed the now prone dog's side vigorously. She paused and looked up at Eric. "It gets lonely around here now that Jason doesn't stay with me at all."

"Well, I am glad you have a companion," Eric replied. "I only have Jason around once in a while, since he's usually with his friends and crashes at their apartments, so I know what you mean by being lonely. As you know, though, I do spend a great deal of time in the office, more time there than at home, so it really doesn't matter all that much." Now it was his turn to bend down. "Hey, Marmaduke," he said, extending his hand for the dog to smell. "Do you smell my dog?"

Maybe not, but Eric certainly smelled Marmaduke – not just at his feet, but throughout the foyer and, he imagined, the smell would continue throughout the house. After he walked in the front door, Eric was hit not only by the smell of a fresh weekend breakfast, but also by another smell, one not so welcoming – the smell of dog, more particularly, the smell of a house where a dog resides. It was an aroma which permeated furniture, especially where the dog would spend his time, and one hated by all non-dog owners who entered any house where the stale odor wafted. It never smelled like that when he and Peyton were in the house, Eric thought, or was it just that he was used to the smell and nobody else was polite enough to tell him? He certainly was not going to say anything to Wendi. Let someone else be the one to let her know.

The smell of cooking eggs mixed with dog was turning to the smell of burning eggs. "Oh my God," Wendi yelled, "my eggs are overcooking." She wheeled around and ran back to the stove to take the pan off of the burner. As she turned, he caught a look at her rear end, wrapped tightly in the yoga pants. It looked smaller and firmer than he remembered.

Eric stepped further into the house, into the hallway which ran between the front door and kitchen. It struck him how different the house was. He had been in this hallway thousands of times when he lived in the house. It should have been a place of great comfort for him. Instead, it was almost unrecognizable to him, as if he had never been there before. He immediately noticed that the pictures hanging from the walls were different than when he had lived there. Gone were the pictures from their wedding and from family vacations long ago. They were replaced by pictures of Wendi and her parents; of Jason through the years, and of Wendi's siblings, nieces and nephews. One picture stood out from the rest. Eric stopped and paused to examine it. "Is this Kim?" he asked, "and who's the other woman with you?"

"Yes, that's Kim," she called from the kitchen," and the other person is Cary. I don't think you ever met her. She was another friend of ours from college. I saw the two of them a couple of months ago – we met at the South Street Seaport for lunch and that's a picture of the three of us together, the first time that we were all together in over 20 years." He could hear her sigh. "It was nice seeing them, you know, now that I have more time to do things like that. So much of our past we want to erase, but sometimes seeing people from the past, the people who we were most comfortable with, is the best thing we can do for ourselves."

"Erase?" Eric thought. "Meaning me, or Doug? Or does she want to erase something or someone else?" He thought it best not to ask for fear of re-opening old wounds for both of them, but that he should just agree with her statement without seeking clarification. "I know what you mean, Wendi," he said, then adding, "though I must admit, it is still a little strange whenever I come back into the house."

She laughed. "I would imagine it would be," she replied. "Many are the day it is weird for me, too, you know. There are actually days when I still expect you to come home at night, to come walking in through the garage door after a long day at work. In fact, it's funny," she said, chuckling lightly, "one night last year I actually began setting a table for the two of us, which was ridiculous because, well, you know, we almost never ate dinner together even when we were still married." She paused and then picked up the handle to the skillet which held the eggs, spooning the cooked eggs into a bowl. "Guess we are all still going through a period of transition." She smiled faintly, or was it more of a grimace?

"Guess you're right about the transition thing," Eric said, returning into the kitchen, "but if you don't mind me saying, you look great. Have you been working out?"

Wendi blushed and looked downward to avert eye contact with her ex-husband. "Yes, I have been," she said, hesitatingly. "I've been doing lots of yoga, trying to get this old body back into shape."

"Well, let me tell you, it's working for you." Eric said. "I don't recall you being in this good shape when we were still married." He immediately sensed that he had said the wrong thing.

Wendi's cheeks turned redder, but the color was now a combination of embarrassment and anger. "I would say thank you, Eric," she snapped, "but I am doing this for me. Not for you, not for anyone else. I'm finally doing something for me. That was one of the problems that I had when we were together, that I was always trying to do things for someone else, for you, for Jason, for whomever. Now, I do things for myself. It is much more satisfying. Plus, even if I had tried to get into shape to please you, you piece of shit, we both know that you wouldn't even have noticed during the last few years of our marriage."

Sensing a confrontation, Eric backed off. "Let's not fight, OK," he said, "all that I meant was that you looked good. Let's drop it. There's no need for name-calling or reading too deeply into what the other says. We can enjoy this breakfast and then talk about the case."

"OK, I am sorry for overreacting," she said, placing the bowl of eggs onto the table. "Let's forget about it and have a nice breakfast." She walked over to Eric and extended her arms, pulling him in for a quick hug. "I really do appreciate all that you are doing for me," she said, resting her head on his shoulder. "And I know this can't be easy for you."

Her embrace brought back a flood of memories, and he involuntarily returned her grip, pulling her closer to him as she spoke. The two almost fell over from the force of the embrace, and they both laughed slightly as they unlocked their arms. Eric pulled out the chair next to him and sat at the table, reaching for one of the coffees. "Think nothing of it," he replied, "it's not all that tough now, but let me tell you, it's going to be a lot worse for you as we go along, believe me."

Wendi walked over to the counter and reached into a drawer for a long knife to use for cutting the bagels. "I was afraid you were going to say something like that when you asked to come over today," Wendi said, "do you have any information for me?"

"Don't you want to eat first? " Eric asked, pensively, wanting to buy as much time as possible before discussing the possibilities.

Placing three sliced bagels on a large plate, she then reached for a knife to use with the cream cheese and carried the bagels and cream cheese tub to the table. "No, there is no need to prolong the agony," Eric," she said, "why don't you just tell me what's going on and we can figure out our strategy?" She turned and retrieved the orange juice container and two small glasses, placing one glass in front of Eric and laying one down alongside the plate located directly across from his seat.

Eric sighed. "If you insist," he said, taking a sip of coffee from one of the cups that he had purchased. "I spoke with a friend of mine in the Prosecutor's office, and he told me that they are going to charge you with Vehicular Manslaughter."

"Manslaughter?" she cried, "for an accident? Even if I was being negligent in the car, would that be enough for manslaughter? If I remember correctly, don't I need to have some intent involved?"

"Well, yes and no," Eric said, trying to maintain his composure and keep his own emotions in check so that he could stop her from becoming hysterical. "They are alleging that you were on the phone at the time of the accident, and that you are going to therefore be charged under the state's no texting or talking law. It's the new death by auto statute."

"But I wasn't on the phone," she said, exasperated, "I already told the police that."

"I know you did, but that kid eyewitness said that you were."

"Is that enough?" she asked, tears welling in her eyes.

"Honestly, he answered, "I would normally say no, but…" his voice trailed off.

"But what?" she asked.

"But this case is a little more complicated than a simple car-pedestrian accident and death, you have to understand."

"You mean because I hit a Spanish kid, right?"

"Exactly," Eric said, again sipping his coffee in a further attempt to calm the situation and slow down the conversation. "Jesus Sanchez is playing the role of community leader, more like community rabble-rouser, and has been raising all sorts of hell about the fact that the kid got killed. It's getting very political, and the Prosecutor's Office is reacting by pushing for the higher charge, due to pressure from both Sanchez and also from the Mayor's office." He reached for the other coffee, turned back the small plastic piece on its lid, and pushed it across the table to Wendi.

"Do you think we can beat it?" she asked, "and if we can't, what's the worst that can happen to me? Will I go to jail?" she asked, as tears began to flow down her cheeks.

There was no way to return the conversation to a calm level. "Not on my watch, Wendi," he said, as he rose from his seat, walked over to where she was sitting, and wrapped his arms around her shoulders. She buried her head in his stomach. "Not on my watch," he repeated.

"That's not the answer," she sniffled, as she pulled her head away from his stomach. "Tell me the truth. Can I go to jail if I am convicted of this charge?"

Eric took a deep breath and looked down at his sobbing ex-wife. He thought that he had to be honest with her. "It's considered a second-degree crime."

"You're kidding," she cried. "It's a second-degree crime?"

"Yes, a second-degree crime. The statute provides for the possibility of a jail sentence upon conviction," he said, quietly, "but since it will be your first conviction or plea to anything, I don't think that you will go away," he said, realizing that he was trying to convince himself at the same time that he was trying to calm her down. "I think that it will be probation, community service, and loss of license for a while. We can also try for PTI since you have no criminal record."

"Stop talking like I know these terms," she yelled. "I'm not an attorney, Eric. I know I've heard you say PTI before, but it doesn't mean that I know what the fuck that even means!" Her breathing grew more rapid as her voice rose, her face again turning beet red and her body beginning to shudder with anger. She stood and began pacing around the kitchen table like a caged animal, with her hands cupped tightly over her face. As she raised her arms to put her hands over her face, her shirt rose to reveal her midriff and the top of her yoga pants. Her stomach was flat, much flatter than Eric ever remembered.

Eric gazed at his ex-wife's flattened and toned abs, and then took a deep breath and motioned for Wendi to do the same. "OK, relax for a second," he said. There's no need to yell at me. Come back here and sit down, and I will explain. There's a lot going on here, a lot of information, and I don't want you to get the wrong idea because I did not tell you everything." He paused and took another deep breath, bringing his arms upward and then downward in a sweeping motion to exaggerate his need for her to remain calm.

Without looking at him, she exhaled deeply and closed her eyes tightly. When she opened them, she wiped the moisture from each with her hands and nodded to Eric, signaling that she was ready to hear his explanation. She returned to her seat, taking a cinnamon-raisin bagel from the plate in the center of the table and biting into it before taking a large gulp of her coffee.

He also took another deep swig of his coffee before speaking. "PTI is an acronym for Pre-Trial Intervention," he began. "It is a mechanism by which first-time offenders for certain crimes are allowed to essentially enter a Probation-like program. It's actually a little weird, to be honest with you. You don't plead guilty to the charge, but you don't plead innocent. What you do is apply for and, hopefully, get accepted into the PTI program. Basically, you need to do community service, you pay some fines, and you report to a Probation Officer for a period of time, say one year…"

"But I am not an offender," she protested as she again bit into the bagel, which by now she had covered in cream cheese. She then said something which surprised Eric, a comment which was so completely off-topic that he could not determine whether she was simply trying to deflect the conversation to a different topic or was going into a shock-like state where she simply could not process the information that he was providing to her. "And I can't believe you brought cream cheese," Wendi said to him. "It is so good. I have been avoiding cheese for months in trying to get back into shape. This breakfast is ruining my diet, you know."

Eric glared at Wendi in an effort to allow him to finish his explanation and in response to her comments about her diet, as he attempted, in vain, to determine the reasons underlying the cream cheese and diet comment. He was not, however, willing to stray from his explanation at this time. "Forget about a diet for a second. I already told you that you look great," he began, then adding, "and as for the PTI, which is much more important, you do the Probation for a year or however long the court tells you, and if you complete the program, meaning you do everything that the court says, then the complaint will be dismissed – no conviction, no jail. It's the best-case scenario for us, Wendi; all that you will need to do is complete the probation without getting into trouble again, which shouldn't be a problem for you." He widened his eyes, waiting for her response.

This time, however, the response was not immediate. Clearly Wendi was not able to deflect the reality of the situation any longer. Her face again dissolved into tears as she gently lay the bagel down onto her plate, and she then stood and walked, deliberately, to the kitchen counter to retrieve a tissue. She blew her nose loudly, wiped her eyes with her hands, and then bent over, hands on her knees, as she tried to collect both her composure and her thoughts. As she bent, her tank top sank from her body, affording Eric a view of her breasts. He hadn't even realized, until now, that she was not wearing a bra. And like her stomach, he did not remember her breasts looking so good, or so firm, as they dangled, vibrating, from Wendi's crying body. After a long minute, she looked forward, saw Eric staring at her chest, and stood. Trying to collect her thoughts, she walked back to the table, sitting back in her seat across from Eric.

Two deep breaths later, she was ready to speak, but, again, the subject matter of her comments was surprising to Eric. "Staring at my tits, huh?" she asked, "that's very professional of you, Eric."

Eric immediately did what he could to deflect her comment and the fact that she had, in fact, caught him staring at her body. "Don't give me shit, Wendi," he answered in anger, part real and part exaggerated so that they could move on from this topic without further discussion, "you're the one not wearing a bra. Don't give me shit or I will just get up and walk out of here. I am here for you, don't forget. I have plenty of other things to do on a Saturday morning than listen to you bitch at me." He really did not have anything else pressing to do, but she did not need to know that he was bluffing.

Now it was her turn to glare at him. She realized that she needed him to stay, so she would have to be nice to him, even if he was treating her like every other woman with whom he had come into contact during their marriage, like a sex object. In the past, she hated how he would do that to women, sometimes even in her presence. Even she was caught off-guard by the fact that it bothered her even more when his eyes were focused on her, like he was treating her like some cheap piece of meat. To avoid it from happening again, she vowed to herself, she would just make sure not to bend over like that again or to give him any reason to look at her in an improper way again. She made this promise to herself even though a little part of her was turned on by his lecherous look. There was also a small part of her mind that thought about the future, and about whether they could, or should, attempt to relive the past.

For now, however, she would suppress those thoughts. This was not the time. She sighed. "Let me see if I get this straight," she began, "and I am going to try to go step-by-step, to make sure I understand."

"OK, fire away," he said, silently pleased in his belief that he had dodged yet another bullet with her.

"We go to court," she began to explain, deliberately, "I can ask the court to be admitted into the PTI program. Can the court say no?"

"Yes, the court can deny it, but I don't think that would happen."

"Let's assume the court says yes, then," she said, calmly, taking another bite of her bagel and wiping some cream cheese from the outside of her mouth. "I apply, the court accepts the application. We go back to court a second time?"

"Yes."

"Then I am accepted into the program," she said, adding, "hopefully," as she crossed the index and middle fingers on both of her hands. "The court then sentences me to pretty much the same as probation, where I need to see a probation officer monthly, pay some fines, and do some community service, right?"

"Right" Eric said, taking the moment of relative calm to spoon some eggs onto his plate and take a plain bagel from the plate in the middle of the table, "although sometimes after a while you can just call the probation officer rather than show up."

"Will I have to pee in a cup?"

"I guess that's possible, but that's a small price to pay, don't you think?"

Wendi frowned and disregarded his comment. "And if I do it all properly, whenever the time for probation is up, then the case is essentially thrown out, right?"

"Yes. The fines can be around $1,000 or so, just so you know."

Wendi smiled. "I don't care about the money, Eric. I get plenty of alimony from my ex-husband, you know." She laughed, the first time that Eric had seen her laugh since the date of the accident. It made him smile, even though the joke was at his expense. He raised his coffee cup in recognition of her joke.

Then she stopped, and her smile disappeared. "But what if," she asked, "what if the Judge denies my application? Then what happens?"

He placed the cup back down onto the table. "Well, then we go to trial and take our chances."

"And our chances would be?"

"We've been through this already," he said, placing a forkful of eggs into his mouth in an effort to diffuse the potentially tense situation which would arise if he showed any weakness in his feelings about the case. "I think we have a good defense. To be honest, though, we need to do some more digging into what happened so that we can be sure."

A faint smile creased Wendi's face, a smile borne not of happiness but more of acceptance as she replied, "If you say so, Eric." She again began to think about the past, the distant past, about when they first met, were first married, and when they began to build their lives together. At this moment, she chose to ignore the later years, the years of isolation from each other, the isolation which drove her into the arms of another man. "I trust you."

"Seems odd, doesn't it?" he answered as he continued to eat the eggs along with half of the bagel, which was now covered with three pieces of lox.

Her smile broadened, as she tried desperately to keep out the thoughts of their bad times together. "I mean that I trust you with the case, you idiot." She paused, now thinking about those bad times, and said something that she thought accurately conveyed the pair's thoughts about each other. As it turned out, her thoughts were one hundred percent correct. "I don't really trust you otherwise, any more than you likely trust me. I think we both understand that, wouldn't you say?"

"Absolutely," Eric replied, as he again raised his coffee cup in mock toast. "Here's to ex-spouses who don't trust each other, except with respect to a little death by auto case."

"Jeez, we are fucked up, Eric."

"Yes we are, Wendi," he said. "I wouldn't have it any other way."

The two continued to eat their breakfast. Eric had eaten three more forkfuls of slightly burned eggs and the half a bagel before Wendi again began to panic.

"Eric," she asked, her voice rising with every word, "if this Sanchez person is pushing so hard for them to accuse me, then won't he also try that hard to have me locked up? And if they are so afraid of him, then won't they try to force us to a trial?"

Eric had forgotten just how intelligent his ex-wife was. "Your question is logical," he stammered, "but I think that the real prize is getting the Prosecutor to take action. It's all a publicity thing for him. Beyond that," he said, wishfully," I don't think that it really matters all that much to him." He did not tell her any of his conversation with Pablo Lopez. He did not want to give her any false hope.

"I sure hope so," she said, in a calmer voice. "I sure hope so. Peeing in a cup once a month for a year or two is definitely better than jail time."

The following Tuesday, Wendi received paperwork regarding the charges in the mail. As a courtesy, the Prosecutor's Office also faxed a copy of the summons to Eric at his office, so he had actually received it in the office late Monday, although he had not seen it until Tuesday because he was in Municipal Court on Monday afternoon and did not return to the office after court, instead meeting a friend to watch that evening's Yankees' game at a restaurant alongside City Hall.

The summons emanated from the Elizabeth Municipal Court, the very court where Eric had appeared that evening, and bore case number 2004-2014-12345. Although it was issued by the local municipal court, as was the custom, it commanded Wendi to appear at the Union County Court's central intake unit, also located in Elizabeth, but at the County Courthouse, rather than the court adjacent to the police station, for fingerprinting and processing. Afterward, she was to report to the jail building, across the street from the intake unit's office, and face her initial arraignment before criminal Assignment Judge Mary Turner. Wendi called Eric in a panic, asking if he would be with her at both destinations. He explained that attorneys were not usually present for the initial intake, and, in fact, their presence was frowned upon. After she begged him to accompany her, however, he reluctantly agreed to meet her that Friday morning at 9:00 for her intake appearance.

Chapter IX – Wendi's First Court Appearance

Friday morning, Eric arrived at his office at 7:30, checked and returned some e-mails from the prior afternoon and evening, and cleaned some papers off of his desk. He typed up some notes on a couple of cases and placed the notes, affixed to the top of the case files, on Fatima's desk, with instructions on what he needed for her to take care of on each case. At 8:40, well in advance of the scheduled intake time, he gathered up his faxed copy of the summons filed against Wendi, a printout of the statute language, a manila folder, and yellow legal pad. Placing the summons, statute printout, and pad inside of the folder, he took his suit jacket off of the chair in his office, straightened his tie, and made his way downstairs and then, once outside the building and on Broad Street, to the courthouse down the block. As he walked, he donned his suit jacket and acknowledged several other attorneys and court personnel whom he passed as he approached the alleyway between the court house and Revolutionary-war era church on Broad Street. Turning right after the church, he walked alongside its cemetery, dotted with tombstones hundreds of years old, until he reached the Union County Courthouse Annex building. He waited on its front steps, looking across the street at the Union County jail, and waited for Wendi. Silently he prayed that he would never have to visit her in the building across the street.

Wendi walked up to the annex building two minutes later. A couple of men clad in sports jackets and tan pants sat patiently on the steps across the street, the steps located directly in front of the jail. Each had a large badge dangling from the lapel of his jacket. One motioned to the other as Wendi walked toward Eric, and the two then stood and walked toward Wendi and Eric, their badges bearing the word "PRESS" gleaming in the sunlight. "Not now, boys," Eric called, anticipating the fact that they were going to seek an interview with him and Wendi and not wanting to engage Wendi in any such activity that morning, "we're going inside and have stuff to take care of. If there is anything to discuss, we will talk later." He waved his hand in their direction, and then turned and pushed Wendi inside of the front door to the annex building before they could respond.

"You've got to be kidding me, Eric - those reporters were there for me?" Wendi asked, innocently, as if shocked by the statement that Eric had made to them. "Is this something that we are going to have to deal with every time we are in court?"

"Don't know, to be honest with you. I hope not, but you never know. I guess I am not even really sure that they were here now for you," he added, looking out the front windows to see the two men now waiting on the steps of the annex building, "but I am pretty sure about it." He paused, and removed his wallet, keys, phone, and reading glasses from his pockets and placed them into a small plastic bucket on the table to the left of the building's metal detector. He then picked up the bucket and placed it on the metal detector conveyor belt along with the manila folder which contained Wendi's paperwork and the yellow legal pad. He undertook these tasks in a completely fluid and yet robotic motion, belying the fact that he had done identical motions countless times before. "Guess it depends on how slow a news day it is," he added. He walked through the detector without incident as Wendi placed her handbag on the belt and similarly walked through the detector without triggering any alarm.

They walked to the appointed room as Eric reminded Wendi to listen to the questions being asked of her, to keep her answers simple and not to volunteer any additional information. He reminded her that she would need to be fingerprinted afterward, which would no doubt be a demeaning experience for her but one which she could not avoid. She nodded in understanding, and then looked at him, her moistened and reddened eyes belying the concern that she had for the proceedings which lay before her, both that morning and thereafter. He placed his hand on her shoulder, pulled her closer to him, and whispered that she should not worry, that nothing bad was going to happen, especially not today. This was just a part of the process, he explained, a simple question and answer session. He would be with her and assist if needed, but he was confident that she would be fine as long as she listened to the questions and provided simple answers.

Opening the door to the room where Wendi would meet her inquisitor, Eric motioned for her to enter and then followed her inside. The woman behind the desk asked for her name, and then looked at Eric behind her, puzzled. Recognizing Eric, she asked, "Mr. Goldberg, what are you doing here?"

"Morning, Joan," he replied. "I am here to accompany Ms. Goldberg here for her intake."

"Mr. Goldberg," she replied, hesitatingly, "you know that attorneys don't usually come for this. It's just the intake. I don't even know if they will let you in."

"C'mon Joan," Eric said, quietly, "She's not just a client. Look at the name on her paperwork. She's my ex-wife. Give me a break and let me come in. I'll be good, I promise."

She looked at the two of them for a long moment, sensing Eric's discomfort at being present for the intake. After a pause, she realized that it was not worth battling with the attorney, and it was certainly not worth embarrassing him further in front of his ex-wife. She took a deep breath and shrugged. "OK, the two of you wait out here and I will get Ms. Jackson," Joan said, "She will be the one doing the intake for you."

Eric silently mouthed the words "thank you" to Joan, appreciative of her understanding and assistance. He then turned back and looked at Wendi and smiled. Wendi's face showed a faint smile, as she was silently pleased that his flirtatious manner may have actually worked to her advantage for once. The two then walked to their left and sat in adjoining seats along the wall, waiting for Wendi's name to be called so that she could begin her trek through the criminal justice system. As they waited, Eric sat, scanning his phone for the e-mails that he had forgotten to answer when he was in the office. Wendi, meanwhile, sat silently, staring straight ahead, expressionless, as her stomach churned.

Penny Jackson, clipboard curled under her right armpit, appeared in the doorway several minutes later. "Wendi Goldberg?" she called out, and then, upon seeing Wendi and Eric both stand in unison, motioned for the two of them to join her at her cubicle. When all three were seated, she briefly explained the process to Wendi and then asked Wendi if she had any questions. Wendi shook her head slowly from side to side, at which time Ms. Jackson began the process of obtaining information from Wendi before sending her for fingerprinting.

Initially Wendi answered the questions without hesitation, her crisp voice hiding the inner turmoil that made her want to either vomit or run from the building and hide, never to return, whether for this questioning, a trial, or for any other reason. After a few minutes, however, when the questions progressed past simple name, date of birth, and address-type inquiries, she began to grow testy, a change that did not go unnoticed by Eric. In an effort to diffuse the mounting tension, Eric attempted to answer one of the questions on Wendi's behalf, at which time he was cut-off by Ms. Jackson, who insisted that Wendi provide her own responses.

His attempts, it became immediately apparent, had exactly the opposite effect from his intentions. Instead of calming Wendi and giving her a chance to gather her thoughts, his responses, and the flippant response from Ms. Jackson, lit a fuse inside of Wendi. "What's the difference?" Wendi barked. "As long as you are getting the information, does it really matter who says it?" Her hands gripped the armrests on her chair so tightly that her knuckles whitened, and her body began to slowly, deliberately, rise from the chair.

Ms. Jackson, obviously no stranger to outbursts from indignant defendants, retained her composure even as Wendi began to tremble with anger. "Ms. Goldberg," she said, calmly, "I understand your point. I also understand that your attorney is here with you and, if I am correct, he is your ex-husband so he does know quite a bit about you, probably more than most attorneys know about their clients." Eric nodded silently. "But Ms. Goldberg," she continued, "There are procedures that we must follow here. One of those procedures is this intake of information. I have to get it from you. Not from him. That's just the way it is, that's the way that they make me do it. I am just doing my job," she said, motioning in Eric's direction, "I mean, I can't even write down information based on the papers in front of me. I need to ask you. And you need to answer the questions for me. If you don't, or if you want to create problems for me, then it will take that much longer. I'm just doing it the way they make me do it. So please sit back down, curb your attitude, and answer the questions."

Eric decided to stay silent at this point, like a cowering child caught in between two fighting parents. He knew he could not win in a three-way battle which included a strong woman and an overly-emotional woman. Far better, he reasoned, for Wendi to work this one out on her own. It was also the first test of her intestinal fortitude with the system, a test that Eric prayed she would pass. If she could not navigate her way through this step, he knew, every future step would be full of acrimony and fraught with potential disaster. At first, to his great concern, it did not seem like Wendi would be able to deal with Ms. Jackson. She turned even redder and gripped the armrests even tighter. "Are you threatening me?" she asked. "Eric, do you hear this?" She looked at Eric and then back at Penny Jackson. "I am not," she yelled, "a common criminal. Do not treat me like one."

Still calm, Penny Jackson replied, "if I were you, Ms. Goldberg, I would keep my voice down if I were going to use words like 'common criminal' so as not to insult anyone else in the building. They may not be as nice as me, you know." She paused. "And this has nothing to do with threats. I will be here all day, whether I am sitting and interviewing you or someone else. You don't want to be here all day, I am certain of that. So you'd best think about answering the questions so that you can get out of here." She turned to Eric, still sitting silently, and motioned in his direction. "Ask your husband here, he will tell you."

"He's my ex-husband," Wendi sputtered as she began to realize that she could not gain control of the situation, and that she was not going to win a battle of wits with Penny Jackson. She struggled to calm down as her face turned paler and paler by the second. "I just didn't understand why he couldn't give you information that he knew," she tried to explain, as her voice began to take a calmer tone. "If I need to answer," she said, compliantly, and, after taking a couple of deep breaths, added, "then I will do so. Go ahead, Ms. Jackson, ask the next question. I am ready."

Eric gave her a reassuring pat on the arm and smiled. Penny Jackson returned his smile, pleased that the situation had seemingly been diffused and was now under control. She looked down at her clipboard and continued her line of questioning – still trying to be a compliant subject, Wendi again began to answer the questions in a quick and forthright manner, and did not complain or create any disturbance when they walked across the street so that she could be fingerprinted afterward. Her next sign of emotion, in fact, was reserved for when she and Eric were released to walk to the jail building for her arraignment. As the two exited the police building, after all of the questioning as completed and the last vestiges of ink from the fingerprinting had been scrubbed from her fingertips, tears again began to form in Wendi's eyes. "They are treated me like a common criminal, Eric," she whispered to him, "I can't believe this is happening to me."

"It will be OK, Wendi," he whispered back. "The hard part for today is over. I will do all of the talking in front of the Judge. All that you need to do is stand there."

"I can do that." Looking around, she noticed that the two men from before were no longer in front of the building. "Plus, it looks like the reporters are gone, so that's one less thing to worry about."

Eric nodded silently. He knew that members of the press were often allowed into the building and might have been waiting upstairs for them, but he felt no need to make Wendi aware of that fact. No need to upset her further, especially since she had reacted so badly to the questioning. Perhaps they wouldn't be there waiting to ambush Wendi. Or was that just wishful thinking?

Chapter X – Arraignment and the Press

As Eric and Wendi walked past the metal detectors on the first floor of the jailhouse, it became immediately apparent that Eric's worst fears had been realized. Looking up to the second floor overhang, to the right of the open staircase, he saw not only the two men who were outside earlier, but that they had been joined by several others, including an attractive young woman whom he immediately recognized as local television reporter Lupe Espinosa. She stood at the edge of the balcony, leaning against the protective railing, her right shoe, with its five-inch heel, resting on the bottom rail. She shifted her right leg as Eric and Wendi ascended the staircase, causing the bottom hem of her already too-short skirt to rise further up her thigh. Eric found himself staring at her now mostly-exposed leg; upon shifting his gaze up further as Wendi spoke to him in words to which he was not listening, he caught Lupe's gaze looking down on him and a smile across her face. Lupe took her right arm and smoothed her skirt downward as she removed her foot from the bottom rail, and she motioned to her cameraman to move forward, toward Eric and Wendi, as they reached the top of the stairs.

Wendi continued to speak in a low voice as they walked, until Eric waved his hand in her direction and told her to look at the media members who loomed above. "Wendi," he said, stopping at the second-highest step and holding Wendi's arm until she did the same, "these people, the reporters, are likely all here for you. I need for you to stop talking until we are out of this building." He leaned forward and whispered into her ear. "Don't say anything. Don't talk to me. Don't talk to these guys. Don't talk to that woman over there," he said, gesturing toward Lupe Espinosa, "and don't even say anything in court."

"Don't say anything?"

"Right, say nothing. If you say anything, and I mean anything, whatever you say will be twisted by these people out here. The media needs a story, no matter how they get it or how much they need to twist the facts or your comments." He paused and pointed toward the courtroom door, continuing, "And in court, I will talk. You don't need to say anything. I don't care if the Judge asks you a question. Stay silent. I've got this." He looked at her, and noticed her eyes beginning to well with tears. "And don't cry, because you don't want to do anything that can be twisted or misinterpreted. You have to keep a stiff upper lip, OK?"

Wendi gulped hard and steeled herself to continue. "I got it. No crying and no talking. Let's go." She nodded her head in the direction of the courtroom. The two ascended the last steps to the second floor, at which time they dutifully removed all metal objects from their pockets, placed them on the belt to their right, and strode confidently through the metal detector. Once through the detector, they were accosted by the media assemblage, led by the preening Lupe Espinosa. Wendi found herself with three microphones thrust within inches of her face, and turned to Eric who waved a dismissive hand at the others. "My client has no comment," he said forcefully, "now let us go into the courtroom so that the court does not sanction us for being late." He looked at Lupe Espinosa and smiled. "And nothing will change on the way out, so there is no reason for you to wait here." He tugged slightly at Wendi's arm and eased her into the courtroom.

Wendi heard several voices calling out to her as they walked through the courtroom doors, but could not make out the words of any specific questions as they all blended into one another. Her heart was racing as her mind was consumed with feelings of dread. She did feel as though she had passed her first test by not talking to the media, however, and she exhaled deeply as the courtroom doors closed behind her. She also had even more confidence in Eric after how he had handled the media throng.

What she did not see, however, was that Eric also exhaled deeply as the doors closed. For a brief moment, he permitted his own feelings of self-doubt to be exposed. Thankfully, nobody was watching so nobody witnessed his moment of panic. Most importantly, his client was not watching.

Gathering his own emotions, Eric shrugged his shoulders and led Wendi to the third row of seats, motioning for her to sit. Seeing the camera to the right of the court officer's desk, he leaned down and whispered, "Look at the camera, Wendi. That's probably here for you also. I will make sure the judge doesn't read the charges against you out loud, to spare some embarrassment."

"Really?"

"Yes," he continued in a soft voice. "They are going to film your arraignment. Like we discussed out there, I don't want you to say anything, and if it goes as it should, we will be done in a couple of minutes." He paused. "Let me do all of the talking, OK?" She nodded her understanding and approval. Eric walked to the front of the courtroom, where the court officer and clerk stood.

"Madame Clerk," he said, then turning to the officer and adding, "Officer." He nodded to the officer, who returned his nod.

"Mr. Goldberg," the clerk said, "how nice to see you again." She looked over his shoulder at Wendi, who was now sitting in the third row and intently watching Eric's every move. "Is that your client?" She looked down at the list of defendants who were appearing for their arraignments that day, and saw the name "Goldberg, Wendi" as the third name from the top. She looked up at Eric and shook her head slowly. "Mr. Goldberg," she said, "your client's name is also Goldberg? Should I even ask?"

"No, don't bother," he answered. "She is my ex-wife. Please let the court know that we are here. I would like to see if we can get out of here as soon as possible to minimize the circus here, if you don't mind." He looked at the clerk and the court officer and smiled. "Maybe the judge can take our case first?" he asked, "you know, to get the camera guy out of here and let the others do their cases in peace?"

"Completely understood," said the officer. "I will go back and let her know that you are here, and we'll see what we can do for you."

"Thanks, Chuck," Eric said, calling the officer by his first name. "I assume you want us out of here also."

The officer nodded and turned, walking through the door to his left to alert the judge that Ms. Goldberg and her attorney were in the courtroom. Returning a couple of minutes later, he informed Eric that the Judge would be out on the bench within the next five minutes. Upon hearing this, the cameraman steadied himself behind the camera, so as not to miss a moment of the proceedings.

Eric sat in the first row, alongside two other attorneys. He exchanged pleasantries with them; he knew one well and he had never before seen the other. Neither of the other two acknowledged the circumstances of Eric's appearance in their midst, and Eric certainly was in no mood to discuss his case with them. Ten minutes passed with no sign of the Judge. All of the attorneys sat in the front row checking e-mails and social media on their cell phones, with Eric looking back to Wendi periodically to ensure that she was not becoming too concerned.

After another ten minutes, the door behind the bench opened and the Honorable Mary Turner, Presiding Judge of the Union County Criminal Courts, emerged. All of the attorneys and their clients rose from their seats in unison as a sign of respect for the Judge, who greeted them and asked everyone to sit. Turning to the court clerk, she asked, "What is the first case?"

"Docket number 2004-2014-12345, State v. Wendi Goldberg," called the court clerk.

Eric stood and turned back toward Wendi, motioning for her to come forward. As she reached him, he again reminded her to remain silent. She nodded her approval as she looked to her right, watching the cameraman assume his position behind his lens as the red light on top of the camera illuminated, evidencing the fact that the camera was recording.

"State v. Wendi Goldberg," repeated Judge Turner, "Mr. Goldberg, as always a pleasure to see you. Would you please enter your appearance?"

"Certainly, your Honor," Eric replied, "Eric Goldberg, G-O-L-D-B-E-R-G, on behalf of the defendant, Wendi Goldberg, who is standing to my left."

"Mr. Goldberg," the Judge stated, "your client is accused of …"

"My apologies, your Honor," interrupted Eric, "but my client waives the reading of the charges against her. I have advised her as to the charges and possible penalties, and we wish to enter a not guilty plea at this time," he added, as he looked at the cameraman.

The Judge also looked at the cameraman and shrugged her shoulders, in recognition of the fact that he was there to record an oral reading of the charge of death by auto which was now unnecessary in light of Eric's statement. "OK, Mr. Goldberg, thank you." She turned to Wendi. "Ms. Goldberg," she began as Wendi's face began to redden.

"Your Honor," said Eric, "I again hate to interrupt you, but in response to your next question, the address in the court's file, the Westfield address, is the correct address for my client. It is a single-family home so there is no apartment number, and that is the address where she receives her mail so the court notices should be mailed to her at that address, with copies to me, of course." He looked at Wendi and grinned as she nodded, her face returning to a more normal shade.

"Thank you, Mr. Goldberg," the Judge replied. "Ms. Goldberg, your attorney has entered a not guilty plea on your behalf and has waived the reading of the charges against you. Your next court appearance is three weeks from yesterday, before Judge Tompkins. I am sure that your attorney will advise you, but I will tell you now that his courtroom is not in this building. It is on the fifth floor of the building across the street, which is called the courthouse annex. 8:30 in the morning. Understood?"

Wendi nodded her understanding and then looked to Eric. "Yes, your Honor," said Eric, "we understand completely. Thank you."

"I am also going to give you paperwork regarding the county's PTI program. If this is your first criminal charge, you may be entitled to Pre-Trial Intervention." She paused, thinking about the presence of the cameraman and the possible media response to Wendi being granted what amounted to little more than probation. She decided it would be best to back off of her statement... "To clarify, you may be entitled. It will be up to the Prosecutor's office. Your attorney can explain it to you better."

"I already have, your Honor," added Eric, "but we will discuss it again. I can tell you that this is my client's first time in any court, so she is PTI eligible. Thank you for your Honor's indulgence."

Judge Turner nodded approvingly. "You're welcome, Mr. Goldberg. Please wait for a minute until the court officer hands you the required paperwork."

"Will do, your Honor, thank you," replied Eric. He and Wendi sat in the front row to await the court notice with the next appearance date. The red light on the camera turned off. The cameraman shook his head slowly as he dismantled the camera from the top of its tripod, no doubt concerned that he would not have any good footage for his bosses back at the station.

"Here you are, Eric," said Officer Chuck as he handed Eric the various pieces of paper which spelled out the next court date and information about the PTI program.

"Thank you, Officer Chuck, always a pleasure." He took the papers in his right hand and motioned to the door with his left, at which time Wendi stood and the two walked toward the door to exit the courtroom. The next case was called as they walked toward the door, and the court returned to its normal course of business, the largest case of the day having already been disposed of, albeit in a quiet, completely business-like manner. Both Wendi and Eric paused as they reached the door, however, sensing that their next few steps would be anything but routine.

As they walked through the door, they were greeted by three men, all wearing tags emblazoned with the words "press pass." Two held tape recorders and one held a notepad. There were no cameras, and, as Eric noticed immediately, no Lupe Espinosa.

"I told you before, gentlemen," Eric said, "we have no comment." He paused. "Let me change that. Here's our comment for now." He paused again, as the two tape recorders were brought closer to his face and the third reporter held his pen in his hand, ready to write. Eric continued. "Today was merely the first day in a long process."

The reporters waited for elaboration, but none was forthcoming.

"That's it, boys," Eric said, as he and Wendi walked down the stairs, out of the building, and made their way to Broad Street to go to Eric's office.

Chapter XI – Attorney-Client Friction

The ex-spouses, now joined by a bond of a different type, walked silently side-by-side until they passed the old church and turned left onto the sidewalk of Broad Street. Eric's office was a few short blocks away, and Eric believed that they could now speak freely. "OK," he said, "now we can talk. Any questions about what happened today?"

"Honestly, I don't know," Wendi said, "I think I understand, but it's all new to me." She stopped walking momentarily. "I know that we have a new court date and the Judge mentioned the PTI thing that you told me about. But I am more concerned with outside of the courtroom. Are those cameras going to be there every time we are in court?"

"That I don't know," he said, as he also stopped walking, "but let's assume worst case scenario that they are. All that you need to remember is to not say anything. That's the easy part. The harder part is not letting them get inside your head. We need to walk through the cameras, through the gauntlet, so to speak, as if they are not even there. That's the only way that we don't get ourselves into trouble. I know that I sound like an alarmist, but they'll do anything, twist anything, to get a story. And it won't be for our benefit."

"OK, but that's not easy."

"I know. That's why I gave them the little bullshit statement before. This way we can't be accused of ignoring them, even though we really are. I expect that there will still be articles in the paper tomorrow, and that the main focus, since we didn't give them anything, is that you are being represented by your ex-husband. So you shouldn't be surprised about that."

"Great, we're like a soap opera. Or worse, a Jerry Springer show."

"It could be worse. Jason knows and I assume you have told your family, so the important people know." He paused and again began to walk toward his office. Almost as an afterthought, he asked, "have you told him?"

"Who do you mean by him?"

"You know who I mean, Wendi. Have you told him?" Eric again asked. "I certainly don't speak to him anymore."

Wendi sighed deeply and shook her head. "You know," she said sternly, "I was really enjoying the fact that we have so many conversations lately, even about the case and working together, without ever discussing him." Her eyes began to well with tears. "I don't know why you're bringing it up now, as if I don't already have enough here to be upset about."

"I certainly have no need to mention him," Eric said, softly, "because he's dead to me. But I thought you might want to tell him that I am representing you. I assumed that you already did, but just wanted to make sure." Eric did not tell her about his conversation with Pablo, and that based on that conversation he assumed that Wendi was no longer seeing the man who had, in his mind, broken up their marriage. He assumed that Wendi was no longer seeing the man whom he had once considered a close friend but in whose arms Wendi had apparently found solace from the long nights when Eric was working. He assumed that Wendi was no longer seeing the man who had betrayed him. This was the perfect chance for him to confirm this assumption, and the fact that he could obtain such confirmation in such a backhanded way made it the perfect time to pose the question.

Wendi again stopped walking, and raised her hand to cover her eyes as she began to cry. "I really don't want to be discussing this now, Eric." Her voice began to rise. "Don't we have enough problems to talk about? Why even bring him up? And you do it out here on the street? Could we not do this in private, instead?"

Eric saw that she was crying, but wanted to follow through with his question. "I just wanted to make sure that you told him so that he would not be surprised if he read it in the papers, or heard it from another attorney. Is that so wrong?"

If that had been his true purpose, if his intentions had truly been noble, then no, she could not have possibly stated that his question was in any way improper. But that was not his true purpose. And, somehow, she knew.

"Don't fuck with me, Eric," she said, wiping tears from her eyes and still communicating in an overly loud voice. "You don't give a shit if I told him. He's dead to you, right? That's what you just said." She paused and looked for any sense of compassion in his eyes and, seeing none, continued. "You just don't care. You're just trying to get something from me."

"What are you talking about?" Eric asked, innocently, trying to cover up the fact that she had caught onto his real purpose for asking. "What can I possibly be trying to get from you?"

"You want to know whether or not I am still seeing him, of course," she cried. "Isn't that what this is all about?"

"No, it's not."

"That's bullshit, you asshole." She started to walk away from Eric. A few steps ahead, she turned to face him. "And the worst part of this is that you already know the fucking answer. I called you from the accident scene. I called you," she yelled, pointing her finger in his face. "I called you! Not him. And in all of the times that we spoke, and when you came to the house, has his name come up at all?"

Eric shook his head from side to side.

"You're damned right it hasn't! I haven't mentioned him, right? When you came to the house was any of his stuff there? Anything? Were there any pictures? Do you see any signs of him whatsoever?"

"No, I guess not."

"*You guess not?*" She mocked his answer. "What kind of a response is that, counselor? You would beat the shit out of a witness for an answer like that." She quieted, but her face reddened as she continued to fume at the topic of conversation.

Eric paused in a valiant, although vain, attempt at defusing the situation. After a short silence he spoke. "So you're not seeing him. All that you had to do was say so."

"You're a complete ass, you know that?" Tears again began to flow down Wendi's cheeks. "We have been broken up for months now. If you had even cared one bit, you would have known already." She paused. "You know something, Eric?"

"What?"

"You're a great attorney. That's why I asked you to help me. But as a man, as a husband, no, sorry, as an ex-husband, you're a complete piece of shit. Thanks for reminding me why I divorced you."

If that comment did not dig deeply enough into Eric, the next one did.

"In fact, thanks for reminding me why I cheated on you with him. If ever you doubted it, now you know. Are you happy now?"

"Can't say that I am," said Eric, quietly. "Are you?"

"Are you fucking kidding me?" she yelled. "Do I look happy to you?" Her eyes were now as red as her cheeks, and her cheeks were flushed with anger and stained with wetness from tears. "Do I look happy to you?" she repeated.

"Calm down, Wendi," implored Eric. "We are in the middle of the street. We don't know who is around us." He looked around, and saw no evidence of any members of the press who were witnessing the fight between him and his ex-wife-slash-client. "Pull yourself together and let's go to my office to talk some more."

She glared at him.

"And I am sorry for asking the question."

"No you're not, you asshole," she said, as she rubbed the remaining tears from her eyes and pulled a tissue from her purse to dry her face. "No you're not."

Chapter XII – The Women In Eric's Life

The two walked in silence for the rest of the journey to Eric's office. They remained silent even as Eric opened the door for Wendi, an act of chivalry that went unrecognized, and as they stood alone in the elevator, the two stood side-by-side; Wendi with her arms folded defiantly across her chest as she nervously and steadily tapped the heel of her right foot on the elevator floor. Eric, seeking any way to diffuse the tension of the situation, was again engaging in his custom of checking his phone for e-mails. He could tell that Wendi was still stewing about his intrusive question, and knew better than to enrage her further. Far better, he thought, to keep silent until they were within his office walls. Then they could speak on a pure attorney-client basis, avoid any personal chatter, and they could hopefully ignore the earlier conversation. At least he could ignore it, he reasoned. He knew that there was no way that she was putting the conversation behind her that easily. He knew that she would never forget, or even forgive him. It was, in a twisted way, like being married to her all over again.

His plan required an immediate change, however, once the elevator doors opened for Eric's office floor, because the dueling duo would need to join forces against an outside intruder. As he and Wendi exited the elevator and turned right to walk to the office, Eric spied two people loitering in the hallway. One was toting what appeared to be a television camera on his back, and the other was dressed in a suit jacket and mini skirt – Eric recognized those legs from earlier that morning, and as belonging to Lupe Espinosa. Wendi had not been paying attention when she first left the confines of the elevator, but when Eric stopped in his tracks she looked to the right and saw the two news people waiting to ambush her. She instinctively stepped behind Eric in an attempt to shield herself from their view, but they had already seen her and started to walk down the hallway toward the elevator, as if expecting that Wendi and Eric would try to avoid speaking with them by ducking back into the elevator, even though its doors had already closed.

Wendi began to panic as the cameraman neared her. "We're like caged animals, Eric," she cried, as she inadvertently dug the nails of her right hand deeply into his right arm. She was still trying to hide behind him, but she knew that she would be unable to do so. She started to cry again. Luckily, she noticed, the red light on top of the camera was not yet illuminated.

"It's OK, Wendi. Don't worry about them," Eric said with a slight chuckle, "I will take care of them. Just watch and learn."

Wendi peered around Eric's right shoulder and saw Lupe Espinosa and her cameraman continuing to walk toward them. The sound of Lupe's five-inch heeled shoes echoed through the otherwise silent hallway, and Wendi noticed not only Lupe's long, tanned legs, but also that her jacket was opened and flowing behind her in tandem with her long, brown hair. The top two buttons of Lupe's blouse were undone, and flashes of a lacy blue bra poked out from the edges of the blouse's cream-colored fabric. "You've got to be kidding me," she muttered under her breath as Lupe, emulating the Victoria's Secret ads which populate the television airwaves, with the models' flowing hair and clothing and exposed lingerie, approached her like a runway model. "I bet you will take care of them," she said to Eric, "especially the woman."

"Jesus, Wendi," Eric muttered under his breath so that nobody other than Wendi could hear him, "is this really the time for you to be jealous? It's not like I asked her to be here, or to dress like that."

"I didn't say that you set it up, only that you will like it. And how did you know that I was talking about the way she was dressed?"

"Whatever," Eric said, exasperated, "do me a favor and try not to be jealous now. Do you want me to handle this or not?"

"Of course I do," Wendi responded, "just try not to enjoy it so much, at least when I am here with you."

"Again, I am just doing my job. Do not act jealous." He paused. "Seriously, do not act jealous. If they see that you are acting at all jealous, we will have a whole new set of problems. Now come out from behind me and walk alongside me, so that we project a strong front."

"What if I don't have a strong front?"

"Then you are going to have to fake it. Let's go." Wendi moved alongside Eric, and the two began to walk toward Lupe and her cameraman, meeting them halfway between the office and elevator.

"Mr. Goldberg," Lupe began, "my name is Lupe Espinosa. We met earlier at the courthouse. I am a reporter for Channel 14 TV, and was wondering if you and your client would consent to a quick interview." She motioned to the man to her right, and added, "the handsome devil next to me is Steve, my cameraman. If you are OK with talking to us, I will have him turn on the camera." Her gaze never left Eric, and she subtly licked her lips after saying the word "camera," an action that did not escape Eric's attention. Nor, unfortunately, did it escape Wendi's eyes.

Eric cleared his throat before answering, and he made sure to note that the camera's red light was still not on. "Ms. Espinosa, I appreciate your need for a story, but as you can imagine this has been a difficult morning for my client and I would ask that you respect her privacy at this time."

Lupe ran her right hand through her long hair and her lips formed a slight pout. She moved her head downward and then looked upward, like an innocent child or dog, and asked, coyly, "*¿quiere decir que usted no quiere darnos una entrevista ahora?*" Seeing the look of confusion on Eric's face and realizing that she was inadvertently speaking in Spanish, she repeated her question. "Oh, sorry, I mean, you mean that you do not want to give us an interview now?" Her eyes still never strayed from Eric's face, although she could feel Wendi's stare burning through her head like laser beams.

Eric laughed. "That is correct, Ms. Espinosa."

"Please, call me Lupe."

"OK, Lupe. *Es correcta.*" He responded, using Spanish to show off a little bit for the attractive reporter. *"*That is correct. This just isn't the time. I am not saying that there won't be a time in the future when my client is willing to talk, but at least for now we need to say no."

"Mr. Goldberg," she said, smiling at his use of her native language. "Let me ask you *una pregunta,* one question."

"As long as we are off the record and that camera doesn't turn itself on," Eric said, motioning to the camera, "go ahead, I guess."

Lupe straightened her head, still staring at Eric, and lowered the microphone that she was holding to confirm that any comments would be "off the record." Motioning at Steve to lower the camera from his shoulder to ensure that there would be no filming, she asked, in a breathy voice, "Here's my one question, although I wish you would have let me ask it with the camera rolling. What I wanted to ask you is, what is it like, Mr. Goldberg, to represent your ex-wife in criminal court?"

"What?" Eric responded.

"Sorry, *quiero decir de una manera diferente.* Let me say it a different way." She arched her back and took a deep breath, and her chest seemed to expand by at least a cup size as the fabric of her blouse strained against her body. "*Mi pregunta es, oh, lo siento,* my question is, "what's it like representing your ex-wife in court, especially after you got a divorce due to her infidelity? More to the point, sir, *por qué,* why do you want to help her out after what she did to you?"

Eric was completely stunned by the question. Even as he had considered the ramifications of his representation of Wendi for the case, it had not occurred to him that stories about their marriage and breakup would become public knowledge. He was especially surprised by the specifics of the questions since the divorce had been based solely upon irreconcilable differences. Her infidelity was never mentioned in the court papers, so Lupe Espinosa could not have gleaned that piece of information from the public records. He certainly was not prepared to answer questions of this nature. He could respond to the ex-wife part of the inquiry, maybe, but not the other part of the question. Wendi gasped and began to speak, but Eric held his hand up in front of her mouth in order to ensure that she would not say anything that they would both regret later.

Composing himself, Eric began to answer in a robotic manner, slowly, deliberately, and devoid of any discernible emotion. He did not want to provide the reporter with any reason to twist his response. "Ms. Espinosa," he began, "*entiendo tu pregunta.* I understand your question and appreciate the reason for you asking it." Lupe smiled broadly at his continued use of Spanish and placed her hands on her waist, awaiting the response to the actual question. She continued to arch her back slightly, as if to distract Eric with her enlarged chest so that he would say something he might not otherwise offer to her. Her attempts, however, were futile, as she would soon discover. "Unfortunately, I am not sure that I can properly answer your question. Ms. Goldberg is not being afforded any special treatment from my office by virtue of the fact that she is my ex-wife. To the contrary, she is like any other client to me, and I will represent her, just like I represent all of the clients who retain me to represent their interests, to the utmost extent of my capabilities." He paused. "In fact, Ms. Espinosa, you can use that statement on the record, if you so desire."

"Mr. Goldberg," Lupe purred as she ran her hand through her hair, "as you can imagine, that's not the answer that I am seeking, but," she added as she reached out and touched Eric on the shoulder, "I can see that you will not be giving me anything today. Perhaps we can meet some other time for an interview." For the first time, she then looked directly at Wendi. "If you want, we can meet without your client. *Tal vez para la cena.* Perhaps we can meet over dinner." She slowly ran her right hand over the outside of her right breast as she spoke. "That way I can get some complete answers from you. This case can make you famous, you know."

Eric caught both Lupe's attempts at seducing him and Wendi's icy stares at both of them. "I am not in this case to get famous, Ms. Espinosa," he explained, "I am in it to represent my client. As I said before, it is no different from my representation of any other client."

"But be realistic, Mr. Goldberg," Lupe said, quietly, as she pointed to Wendi, "you and I both know that she is not just another client to you. She is special. Think about it. When is the last time that you heard of an attorney representing his ex-wife in what amounts to a murder trial? Never have we heard this, at least not around here. And that's the stuff that brings viewers, so that's the stuff that the media loves. Wouldn't some publicity in this case help you?" She paused and extended her hand to shake Eric's. He complied, and as the two shook hands, she added, "*que sin duda le dará una major publicidad que el desorden en Newark y Brasil.* It will certainly give you better publicity than that mess in Newark and Brazil, wouldn't you say?"

Eric tried to pull his hand from hers, but her grip was firm. "What do you mean by that?" Eric asked. "How do you even know about that?"

Lupe leaned closer to Eric and, when their heads drew closely together, she whispered, loudly, "Please, Mr. Goldberg. I am a newswoman." She then lowered her voice so that it was barely audible as she continued. "*Señor, lo sé todo sobre ti.* I know everything about you. If it makes you more comfortable, *me puede llamar,*" she paused, "you can even call me Bianca."

The mere mention of the woman who had accused him of murdering her husband and forced him to follow her to Brazil sent chills up Eric's spine. "I think this little meeting is over, Ms. Espinosa," he said, and removed his hand from her grip. "*Vamos,* let's go, Wendi," he added, pulling Wendi alongside him as he walked into his office. He did not look back at Lupe Espinosa as he walked, even as she apologized and beckoned for him to return. He reached his office door, turned the knob and swung it open, and then quickly walked through the threshold with Wendi and slammed the door behind him.

"Tough day, Eric?" asked Fatima.

"It was only tough for the last couple of minutes, believe it or not. Up until then it was fine. Court went the way that it should have, but then we were accosted by a newswoman in the hallway." He looked over at Wendi, whose face was again beginning to turn red as she thought of Lupe's last comments.

"Brazil?" Wendi exploded. "That shit's going to come up during this case? I can't do it, Eric," she cried. "It is bad enough that I am being accused of something that I didn't do, and that they know that we were married. I can even live with them calling me an adulterer. But now they are going to dredge up that stuff with you and the Brazilian woman to make my life even more of a living hell?" She buried her face in her hands and slumped down into a chair near the door. "And what was with all of that Spanish shit? Were you actually fucking hitting on that woman with me standing there?"

Eric was so deep in his own thoughts that he did not even realize that Wendi was discussing what had transpired in Brazil, nor did it even register with him that she clearly knew what had gone on between he and Bianca Rodrigues. Instead, he mindlessly looked over at Fatima, who could barely contain the grin that was forming on her face. "Oh my, Eric" she said, chuckling, "they brought up the Brazil thing?"

"Yes," Eric replied in a serious tone, again not even considering the fact that Wendi knew or did not know the story of what had happened the previous year, "the woman outside did. She even said that I could call her Bianca if it made me feel more comfortable."

"That's horrible," Fatima said as she began to laugh louder. "And you tried to talk Spanish to her?"

Even through her sobs and her hands, Wendi could hear Fatima's laughter. "How can you laugh at a time like this?" she cried.

"Oh, I am so sorry," Fatima replied in mock sympathy. "Is my laughing getting in the way of your little pity party?" Wendi dropped her hands and glared at Fatima, who was just getting started. "Yes, that's what I said, a pity party. Did it ever occur to you, Wendi, how this is affecting Eric? Did it ever occur to you that maybe this is also hurting him, and not just you?" Wendi stared at Fatima in silent horror. "Of course not," Fatima continued, "because all you ever think about is Wendi. That's the way it's been for years."

"That is so unfair of you," Wendi replied, turning to Eric and soliciting his support. "Eric," she implored, "please tell her that she's wrong." Eric looked back and forth between both women like a spectator at a tennis match, however, and opted to remain silent. Just like during Wendi's criminal intake session, he knew that he could not interpose himself between the two women. Such an action would prove to be, without a doubt, a recipe for disaster. He was smarter than that. Plus, he knew better than to blatantly choose sides between Wendi and Fatima. He was definitely smarter than that.

Eric remained silent long enough for Wendi to feel the need to speak to break the uncomfortable silence. "I … I don't always just think of myself," she stammered, "and I do understand how difficult this is for Eric. But you," she added, looking at Fatima, "you should not judge me. You don't know what I went through or what I am going through."

"I know some things, Wendi. I know what you did to my family," Fatima stated, matter-of-factly as she started to rise from her chair to confront Wendi eye-to-eye, "and that's all that I need to know. You have no idea how lucky you are that my idiot cousin here is even representing you. If it were up to me," she added as she looked over at Eric, still biting his tongue so as not to be berated by both women, "he would not have even taken the case, and you would not be here now. So consider yourself lucky, and do what you can to make his life easier." She again stared at Wendi and lowered her voice. "That means listening to him and not harping on what he has done since you cheated on him and left him, you catch my drift, slut?"

110

"Slut? Who are you calling a slut? You listen to me, you immigrant bitch," Wendi replied in an equally stern voice as she addressed Fatima. "I don't know who the hell you think you are, you bitch, but as long as the door here says Eric Goldberg and not Fatima Esteves, you had best learn to keep your mouth shut and not speak that way to me."

"Who are you calling an immigrant bitch?" Fatima yelled as she stepped from behind her chair, as if to come out from behind her desk and confront Wendi physically.

Finally, Eric had seen enough that he had to intervene. It was one thing to allow the women to spar verbally. It was quite another, however, to allow the situation to denigrate into a physical confrontation. "Ladies," he said, stepping forward to place himself in between Wendi and Fatima's desk, "that's enough. Both of you need to calm down." He looked at Fatima. "I appreciate your comments, but I am a big boy and can fight my own battles." Fatima started to respond, but then simply sighed and sat down in her chair. Eric then turned to Wendi. "And as for you, when you are here you are a client. You respect the office, you respect me, and you respect Fatima. If you can't do that, then find another attorney. OK?"

There was a prolonged silence. Fatima finally nodded her head in understanding. Both she and Eric then looked over at Wendi, who bowed her head and began to cry again. Struggling to regain her composure, she wiped her eyes and stared straight ahead, the whites of her eyes lined with crimson, and with mascara running down her cheeks. "I see," Wendi said, quietly, "and I am sorry." She looked at Fatima. "I am sorry to both of you. I will keep myself in check from now on. I just want you to understand what I am going through."

"We understand," Eric said, placing his arm around Wendi, "right, Fatima?"

"Right," Fatima said, begrudgingly. "I understand, and guess that I will also try to be sympathetic to your problems." She paused and wiped a tear from her eye. "I am sorry for snapping at you. This has been emotional for all of us, and I should have realized that it is the worst for you."

"Thank you," Wendi said, "it's been a very tough day.' She wiped her eyes and then motioned to Eric's office. "Eric, not that we've gotten that out of our systems, can we go talk about what happened this morning in court and what is going to happen going forward."

Wendi and Eric walked into his office and Fatima resumed her post behind her own desk. The next half hour was spent with the two ex-spouses discussing the Pre-Trial Intervention program, the possible evidence that the Prosecution could have against them, and how Wendi would dress for the next court appearance. They also discussed the need for her to steer clear of the media, should any reporters try to approach her, and how any talking to the press, if there was to be any, would be done by Eric.

They did not discuss Wendi's affair or how it had ended.

Chapter XIII – The News Broadcast

That night, Eric worked until after 9:30 before leaving for home. He felt exhausted from the day's events, and decided to jump into the shower while his two-day old pizza reheated in the oven. Emerging from the shower and returning to the kitchen at 10:10, he looked down at his cell phone, which he had left on the countertop, and saw that the light in its top corner was blinking; evidencing that he had received either a text message or e-mail. Pushing the top button on his phone to illuminate its screen, he saw that the icons for both texts and e-mails were lit. "Strange," he thought, "I had left the phone behind for less than 15 minutes." He decided to check his text first, and was surprised to find that he had received a half a dozen texts in that short time frame.

He checked the most recent text first, from Jon Grant, the attorney whose office was directly down the hall from his and with whom he had been friends since law school. "Dude, what the fuck did you do?" the text read, puzzling Eric because he had no idea to what Jon was referring.

The next text was from another attorney in Elizabeth, Mike Stevens. This one was equally cryptic. "What's with you and the hot Spanish woman?" Eric read the text twice, and still had no idea as to its possible meaning. Before he could read the other texts, however, he was provided with information which clarified the meanings behind the texts. The clarification took the form of a frantic phone call from Wendi.

"Eric, did you watch the local news?" Wendi quizzed in lieu of saying "hello." Without waiting for an answer, she continued, "apparently that Espinosa woman did a thing on the news about us, and from what I was told by at least two people, it wasn't overly nice."

"Well, at least that explains the texts," Eric replied.

"What the hell are you talking about?" she thundered. "Did you see the news or not?"

"No, I didn't," Eric replied in a sarcastic tone, "but I received a bunch of texts from people who apparently did."

"Well, what are we going to do about it?"

"What do you mean, 'what are we going to do about it?'"

"Isn't the question clear, Eric?" Wendi yelled. "You're my attorney. So you need to tell me, what are we going to do about the fact that this woman went on the news and, from what I've heard, not only discussed how I am guilty, but also said that you and I are back together again based on what she referred to as the 'chemistry' between us in court?"

Eric sighed. "Oh shit," he said, "is that what she said?"

"Yes, from what I was told. Now what can we do to stop her from saying that stuff?"

"Unfortunately," he answered, "nothing."

"What do you mean we can't do anything?" asked Wendi, her voice growing more exasperated.

"Exactly what it sounds like," Eric explained. "There is nothing we can do about it. She's a journalist. You are now in, and have dragged me into, the public eye. You are the defendant in a, let's call it a quasi- high-profile criminal case. I guess we have to get used to this."

"I don't want to get used to this," she cried. "It is so embarrassing."

"Which part upsets you more, Wendi?" Eric shouted back to her, "I mean, was it the part where she said that you were guilty of killing that kid or the part where she said that you were back together with your ex-husband?"

"Fuck you, you narcissist," she sneered in response. "This is not about you."

"Well, to be honest, it is about us. It's about you as the defendant and me as the attorney. Besides, it's not as if you and Doug are still together ..."

"This has nothing to do with him!" Wendi yelled into the phone. "I can't believe that you keep mentioning him, as if you get some perverse pleasure from hearing that we're not together anymore."

"No, that's not true, Wendi," Eric protested, although not overly convincingly.

"The fuck it doesn't!" She bellowed. "This has nothing to do with him! This is about me. It has to do with the fact that they are convicting me on television! I can't show my face out there now, Eric, people will be pointing and staring! What the hell am I supposed to do now? What the hell am I supposed to do now?" Eric could hear her begin to sob through the receiver.

He paused before speaking, trying to calm himself and to be as careful as possible not to upset her more. "Ok, let's calm down," he finally said, trying desperately to comfort her. "They will have another news report at 11:00. Let me watch that, see what she says, and then figure out if there's anything that we should be doing. Would that make you happier?"

"Ye... yes," Wendi choked out through her sobs. "It would. Please call me later. I'll be awake. In fact, I don't think I'm going to sleep at all tonight. Between her bullshit and your bullshit, I am beside myself with anger right now."

Eric thought it best not to respond to her comment about being mad at him, so as not to further inflame the situation. "OK, fine," he said simply. "Talk to you later." Eric clicked off the phone and scrolled through the rest of the texts and his e-mails. Every one of them referred to Lupe Espinosa and her report on Wendi's case. All of them, that is, except for the text from his friend Ray, one of the guys with whom he had grown up. Ray's text concerned a more tangential matter. It commented not on the case, but rather on the prodigious size of Lupe Espinosa's breasts. At least something could still make Eric laugh amidst all of the troubles.

A half hour later, Eric stopped watching that evening's Yankees game and turned to the local channel. The game was long since over anyway, with the Bronx Bombers on the short end of a 7-2 score as the game dragged into the bottom of the eighth inning. A half-empty bottle of beer sat on the table in between Eric and the television, directly to the right of two empty bottles of the same brand. It had been that kind of day and night for Eric. As the display on the cable box turned to 11:00, music emanated from the television and bright graphics filled the screen, signaling the beginning of that hour's news cast. When the graphics dissipated, the camera showed two people sitting at a desk, an attractive woman to the left, clad in a muted red jacket and white blouse, and to her right was a stereotypical anchorman, his blue and red striped tie providing sharp contrast to the stark whiteness of the shirt that peeked out from under his navy blazer. His hair was perfectly coiffed, and a thin, black and grey goatee framed his mouth.

"Welcome to the 11:00 news," the anchorman intoned as the studio lights illuminated. "Our top story tonight focuses on a case which is getting a great deal of attention here, a case which involves texting and driving, and the damages that can result from such activities. Our own Lupe Espinosa is here with a report on a case developing out of Elizabeth." He turned slightly to his right. "Lupe?"

Lupe Espinosa was dressed in a blue blazer which matched that of the anchorman. She was also wearing a stark white blouse, similar to his white shirt. But the similarities between their manner of dress ended there. Instead of a tie, Lupe had instead unbuttoned her shirt to right above where the fabric of her bra crossed her breasts. The resulting "V' made by the blouse revealed what Eric believed to be too much cleavage for Lupe to be considered a serious journalist, but he reasoned that perhaps the network allowed such provocative dress in order to attract and maintain viewership, especially, clearly, among the male demographic – at least those males with a pulse. Eric gritted his teeth as she began to speak, alternately admiring her beauty and

116

dreading the words that would emanate from her perfectly-formed mouth. His dread was not unwarranted.

Lupe: *Thanks, Brad. This case is drawing a great deal of attention, and for a multitude of reasons.*

"Multitude? That's a pretty big word for a newscaster to say," thought Eric with contempt. "She must have really practiced hard to be able to say that word correctly."

Lupe: *In fact, it is a case that involves not only texting and driving, but has also inflamed the Latino community of Elizabeth and, if that's not enough, there's also a possibly romantic component to this case.*

Eric bolted upright in his chair. "Shit, did she say 'romantic'?" he said out loud, to nobody in particular.

Anchorman: *Romantic? This case sounds interesting, Lupe, tell me more.*

The camera zoomed in on an obviously annoyed Lupe Espinosa, who pursed her lips slightly in response to the anchorman having interrupted her report. Actually, "zoomed" was not the most proper way to describe the cameraman's actions. Rather, the cameraman framed the shot, no doubt at the behest of his control room, so that the screen was filled not just with Lupe's face, but that the bottom part of the screen was just below her ample cleavage, cleavage which shook slightly from side to side as she delivered her report in an animated fashion. To the control room, no doubt, this shot was ratings magic as she again began to speak.

Lupe: *Well, Brad, here's the background for anyone who does not know. A week ago, a young Latino boy was killed on Elmora Avenue in Elizabeth when he was hit by a car while crossing the street. According to eyewitnesses and evidence collected by the police, the woman who was driving the car was sending a text message on her phone at the moment that she struck the teenager. Initially police did not arrest the woman, which caused an uproar in the Latino community because she is white and the killed* *pedestrian was Hispanic. Only through the efforts of local Hispanic leaders, who were led by Jesus Sanchez, did the County Prosecutor's office force the municipality to issue tickets to her for the accident.*

The main charge against her is for death by auto while texting, which, Brad, as you may recall, has been a very big issue in this state. In fact, the law itself, according to my research, is named in part after a woman who was killed by a driver allegedly talking on her cell phone – and that accident took place less than half a mile from where this accident took place.

The camera zoomed in more, forsaking Lupe's cleavage and focusing on her face as she managed a slight smile.

Lupe: *But there is more. The woman who was driving and texting and caused the accident is named Wendi Goldberg, a resident of nearby Westfield. Her attorney is named Eric Goldberg. Mr. Goldberg is well-known to the criminal court system in Union County, from what I am told. But he is even better known to the defendant. Much better known, and not necessarily in a way that you would expect. The attorney is her ex-husband. I did some research into this also, and could not find a prior example of an attorney representing his or her spouse or ex-spouse in such an important case.*

"Damn," Eric yelled. "This can't be good. She's going to kill me."

Anchorman: *Really, the ex-husband is representing her? You know, Lupe, there is an old saying that ...*

The anchor paused mid-sentence and his eyes moved slightly upward, betraying the fact that he was clearly straining to listen to the instructions being barked to him through the earpiece hidden by his hair and jacket. Seconds later, having received his instructions, meaning the remainder of his line, he continued.

Anchorman: *that 'he who represents himself has a fool for a client.' Do you think that will apply here, in the case of the ex-husband?*

The camera swung back to Lupe, who sat, silent, and clearly puzzled by the anchor's inquiry.

Lupe: *I'm sorry, Brad. I'm not quite sure that I understand your question.*

The camera panned back to the anchorman, whose facial expression showed to Eric that the two men shared the same opinion about Lupe's intelligence, or obvious lack thereof. "It's a good thing for her," Eric thought, "that she has those tits and face, because that brain isn't getting her anywhere."

Anchorman: *Well, Lupe, it means that an attorney would be stupid to represent himself in court because he is too emotionally invested in his own well-being. Do you think that would apply in the case of an ex-husband? I mean, it could really be the opposite, if you think about it. If the divorce was bitter, he may want her to be convicted and sent to jail.*

The anchorman and the woman seated to his left laughed. Lupe, still clearly not completely grasping the concept or the joke, sat, stone-faced, for several seconds before continuing.

Lupe: *In some cases, Brad, you may be right about your last comment. But here, I think it will be much different. I was at Mrs. Goldberg's arraignment in court today, and actually spoke briefly with Mr. Goldberg at his office, in her presence, after the court appearance. And believe me, these people do not act like they are bitter, or that they hate each other. To the contrary, Brad, it seems to me like they still think they are married. He is very protective of her, more than most attorneys would be for their clients, and she even held his hand this morning as they walked past people at the courthouse. I don't often see attorneys and clients holding hands as they walk into court, Brad, so I would say that the last thing that Eric Goldberg wants is for his client, his ex-wife to go to jail. He is going to work as hard as he can, in his ex-wife's defense. And Wendi Goldberg is no fool for hiring her ex-husband, because he will clearly do anything and everything to make sure that she does not go to jail and that should cause the Prosecutor's office some concern.*

Anchorman: *Thank you Lupe. Stay on top of this story and we look forward to your updates.*

Eric gulped down the remaining liquid from his beer bottle and waited for the call from Wendi. He struggled in vain to think of what he would, or could, say to her to diffuse the tension of his situation, and of the falsehoods and allegations set forth in the report. The phone rang seconds later. Cautiously, Eric looked at the screen of the phone to see who was calling. It wasn't Wendi, but, still to his chagrin, the picture on the screen was of someone else with whom he also did not want to discuss this topic. Staring at him from his phone was the social media profile picture of his son, Jason. The picture showed Jason and his latest girlfriend. Eric didn't like her much, but he had learned long ago not to meddle in his son's romantic affairs. This was especially true after his divorce.

He would have much preferred that Eric was still dating Leticia Alves' sister, to whom he had introduced Jason when his son came to join him a year earlier in Brazil. The long-distance relationship proved to be too difficult for Jason, however, and even when the young woman was able to obtain a student visa to come to the United States, Jason had made the decision to move on from that relationship. Luckily for Eric, even though the two split up, there were no adverse feelings between Eric and Leticia, or her soon-to-be husband, Steve, the nephew of Jon Grant. Those two had helped Eric through an extremely difficult situation in Brazil and had grown close in the process. The break-up of Eric's son and Leticia's sister was not enough to drive a rift through their friendship. In fact, Eric was in the process of making plans to return to São Paulo for a visit with Leticia and Steve to celebrate their wedding the following year.

Eric took a deep breath before clicking the answer button. "Hey Jason, what's up?"

"Dad, what the fuck is going on with you and mom? We had the news on at my friend's house and the lead story is about mom's case. I knew that you were representing her, but what's this stuff about you guys getting back together?"

"Jason, you know that you can't believe everything you hear in the media. We already told you about the case and that I am representing your mom."

"Yes, I know that. But the other stuff ..."

"Come on, son," he interrupted, "don't be ridiculous. There was a veritable gauntlet outside the courtroom today. Your mother was freaking out, so I led her out of there, through the people, while holding her hand. I assume that you would want me to do no less for her."

"I guess not."

"And then that Espinosa woman ambushed us in the hallway of my office, and your mother hid behind me to avoid speaking with her. Again, I assume you would want me to protect her. Rest assured we are not, under any circumstances, getting back together. I know she's your mom, but I'm pretty comfortable telling you that I'm not going down that road again."

Eric heard a deep sigh from the other end of the phone line, followed by the line of understanding for which he had hoped. "Of course, that makes sense, Dad. Now I understand."

"Good. Now I need to call her and make her understand, which I don't think will be as easy. Maybe you can stop by the house tomorrow and see her. I think it would cheer her up."

"Sure thing," Jason said, "and by the way, Dad, one question."

"What is it, son?"

"Lupe Espinosa. Is she as hot in person as she is on television?"

Eric paused. He was glad that Jason had shifted to a different topic and was not obsessing about his parents and the false possibility of their reconciliation. "Well, let's just say that if I could have any job right now other than being an attorney, I think I

121

would want to be the cameraman who is lucky enough to stare at her, and her chest, during the news reports – and get paid for it!"

"I agree completely, Dad. Maybe it's not too late for me to go to cameraman school," Jason said, laughing.

Eric also laughed. "Sure, Jason, whatever you say. But you are doing that on your dime. Let's just say that my days of paying for your education just ended, and I am not about to start again."

"I understand," Jason replied, still laughing. "Go call Mom, and I will try to see her tomorrow. And get some sleep, old man. I am sure that you need it."

Eric, still laughing, clicked off the phone, placing it down on the table next to the empty beer bottles. He turned off the television and sat in the darkened room, dreading the fact that he had to call Wendi and discuss the newscast with her. He knew that there was nothing that could be done about what Lupe Espinosa had said. There were no comments that could be considered slanderous. In fact, she had, in a back-handed way, almost complimented him. Maybe he could offer to try to sit down with Lupe Espinosa – if he offered her an actual interview, he would be able to give his perspective on the case and have that reported, which would no doubt, in his mind, help their case.

As he was steeling himself to make the call, his phone began to ring. Wendi's smiling face, along with her smelly dog, appeared in the phone's window. Eric knew that the Wendi on the other end of the line would not be the smiling Wendi in the picture. He picked up the phone, took two deep breaths, and then pressed the proper button to answer.

"Did you see the report? That slut is out of control, don't you think?" yelled a clearly agitated Wendi.

"Calm down, honey," Eric replied, instantly realizing that he had used a term of endearment that he had not used for Wendi in years, "it wasn't that bad."

"Not that bad? Are you kidding me? Can we sue her for libel or slander, or something like that?"

"No, we can't," said Eric, "now calm down. Here's my thought. Let me give her an interview. I can discuss the case and the fact that we are now just friends with each other, to try to clear up some issues. I just spoke to Jason, and he gets it."

"Oh shit, Jason! I forgot all about him. Did he see it?"

"Yes, but we talked and he's good," Eric replied. "Now, I can do an interview, without you because I don't want you saying anything, for the reasons that we discussed before. We'll get our side out, and try to minimize all of the publicity that that asshole Sanchez is getting."

"I ... I ... I don't know if that's a good idea," Wendi stammered. "I don't know if I like the idea of you having to tell the world that we are divorced and are not lovers anymore. I don't want our private life spilled out like that."

"Isn't it better to tell the truth than to have rumors about us? It's not going to get any better if we don't say anything. I learned a long time ago that silence can be taken as admission," Eric explained. "If we stay silent, then we are admitting that we are again a couple. And neither one of us wants that."

"But does that mean that we need to respond to everything that is ever said about me, or about us? Because I can tell you now, I won't be able to do that, Eric. It will be difficult to keep up with everything, first of all, but I don't have the stomach to keep fighting people. I can't do it."

"No, Wendi," Eric said, "I don't think we need to worry about fighting every comment that is made about you or us, because you are right, there may be too many to even consider responding to. But I think that we should address this one since it is the first. Give the media, to the extent that they even care about this case, the sense that we will not stand by and let rumors be spread about us. Maybe it will send a message that we won't take false allegations lightly, and they'll think twice before making them. Maybe."

"If you say so, then I guess you should do it," Wendi said, sighing. "But to tell you the truth, I also don't know if I like the idea of you being alone with her."

"Hmmm," thought Eric, "she still does care. Maybe Lupe isn't that far off – at least for her feelings. I have none for her." He paused, and then asked, "really, why?"

Wendi continued to talk as if she had not even heard Eric's question. "Not that I am jealous of you or anything. I just don't like it." Inadvertently, he believed, she had actually answered him. Her denial, in his mind, was telling and belied her actual feelings. He could not, however, confront her on the situation, at least not verbally, at least not now.

"I understand completely," Eric said. "But you don't need to worry. I will be completely professional."

Chapter XIV – Amanda Johnson, Assistant Prosecutor

Three weeks passed fairly uneventfully. Sanchez held another press conference and Lupe Espinosa did two more reports on the case, but other than the two of them, nobody seemed to care too much about the Goldbergs and Wendi's case. The next appearance on Wendi's case was scheduled before Judge Michael Tompkins, a fellow graduate of Seton Hall Law School. Judge Tompkins had been appointed to the bench only six months earlier, and Eric and several of his former classmates had attended his swearing-in ceremony. The two men were not close while in law school, but had several friends in common and had socialized at bar association events, and even some functions thrown by their other classmates since graduation, so he viewed this as a positive factor. He and Wendi appeared for the court date as scheduled, along with the 75 or so other people, defendants and their counsel, who filled the courtroom and sat, shoulder pressed against shoulder, in benches ill-equipped to handle that number of people.

This court appearance was for the purpose of the Prosecution making a plea offer to the defendant. If the defendant accepted the offer being provided by the Prosecution, then the case would end there. The defendant would plead guilty as agreed, and a date would then be set for his or her sentencing. If the offer was unacceptable to the defendant, or if the Prosecution did not want to make an offer, then the case would proceed to the county Grand Jury. There, the Prosecutor's office would attempt to obtain an indictment against the defendant on the delineated charges. As the Grand Jury is a completely one-sided affair, meaning that the evidence presented to the Grand Jury is solely from the Prosecution and no defenses are offered, nor is defendant's counsel even permitted to attend the proceedings, it is usually a foregone conclusion that the Prosecution will obtain its desired indictments. And, as the Prosecution will always say, the offer on that first date is the best offer that the defendant will receive; so many cases resolve themselves at that early juncture.

As the roll call for that morning was in alphabetical order, Wendi's name was the twentieth name of the 43 to be read by the court clerk. Eric stood and indicated his presence with Wendi, at which time Judge Tompkins looked up from the papers in front of him, peered down at Eric, and requested that both Eric, and the assistant prosecutor assigned to the case, Amanda Johnson, meet him in his chambers at the conclusion of the roll call. Both Eric and Assistant Prosecutor Johnson indicated to the judge that they would do so, and the court clerk continued to call those whose names ended in "h" through "z", a total of 23 additional names. Eric whispered to Wendi that he saw the Judge's request as a good sign, and gently held her trembling hand in an attempt to calm her nervousness. She squeezed his hand in response, smiled slightly, and leaned her head back against the top of the bench.

After the clerk called the last name, he asked if anyone's name had not yet been called and beckoned those who had raised their hands to approach his desk. Eric released his grip from Wendi's hand, told her not to worry, and stood. He picked up the file folder containing all of the papers related to Wendi's case, looked in the direction of Assistant Prosecutor Johnson, who was sitting at counsel table in front of the Judge's bench, and walked toward the clerk's desk. Amanda Johnson stood and offered her hand to Eric. She was one of the newer members of the Prosecutor's office, a fairly recent graduate of Rutgers Law School, and stood a statuesque 5 foot 10 in her four-inch heels, such that she and Eric stood eye-to-eye as they shook hands. Her handshake was firm, betraying the seriousness with which she sought to handle her interactions with opposing counsel, and her long, lightly-colored hair was pulled back into a tight ponytail. "It is a pleasure to meet you, Mr. Goldberg," she said, quietly, as the clerk seated to her right attempted in vain to locate the name of the person standing in front of his desk, "I suspect that Judge Tompkins wants to meet with us due to fact that your client has the same last name as you." Her face showed no expression.

"You're probably right, Ms. Johnson," Eric replied, smiling, "but please, call me Eric."

Amanda Johnson's face remained devoid of any expression. "OK, Eric," she said, without a hint of a smile, "and I insist that you call me Amanda."

Eric smiled wider. "Absolutely," he said, and glanced back to where Wendi was seated. "And in response to the question that you have not yet asked, she is my ex-wife."

Now Amanda smiled, or maybe it was a grimace. "Your ex-wife?" she asked, clearly surprised, as she pulled her hand from Eric's grasp. "That's, how shall I say, quite interesting."

"That's one way of putting it, Amanda," Eric said as he leaned closer to her. "I am more than a little intrigued as to whether Judge Tompkins will agree." His face was a scant few inches from Amanda Johnson's as they spoke. As he looked into her eyes, he could see that they were a sparkling blue color. He had not noticed her eyes until now. Nor had he noticed that he had inadvertently placed his hand on the small of her back as they were speaking. Once he did become aware of his hand placement, however, he became acutely aware of the fact that she had not made any effort to remove it.

"Perhaps we should go find out," Amanda said, as she looked down at Eric's arm, the crease of her smile increasing, "we don't want to keep him waiting." She turned to pick up her file from the counsel desk, and added, "I don't know if you know Judge Tompkins, but he is relatively new to the bench and likes to do things completely by the book, so we both want to make sure we are prepared."

Now Eric's smile broadened. "I have met him before," he said, without revealing the fact that he and the judge were former classmates, "so I have an idea of how things go in this courtroom." He pulled his hand from behind her and motioned toward the door to the judge's chambers. "After you, Madame Assistant Prosecutor."

Amanda laughed. "Why thank you, Mr. Goldberg," she replied, playfully, as she stepped in front of him and motioned to the court clerk that they would be going in to see the judge. The clerk nodded, and Amanda walked to the judge's door, knocked, called "Judge, it's Amanda Johnson and Eric Goldberg," and waited for a response. Hearing a muffled voice ask her to come in, she opened the door and walked in, with Eric close behind. She walked up to the Judge, who was standing behind his desk, extended her hand, said "Good morning, Judge. Always a pleasure to see you," and then sat down in one of the leather chairs in front of the judge's desk. As she sat, Eric could not help but notice that her suit jacket pulled up on her back, revealing a strip of pink which was emblazoned with the name of a familiar women's underwear company.

Eric looked back at the judge, certain that his old classmate had seen him eyeing the Assistant Prosecutor's rear end, and smiled. Extending his hand, he said, "good morning, Judge. Eric Goldberg, counsel for the defendant."

Judge Tompkins extended his hand, shook Eric's vigorously, and laughed. "Ms. Johnson, have you had the pleasure of meeting the world-famous Eric Goldberg?"

Amanda looked at Eric and grinned. "Have I had the pleasure of meeting him? For the first time just now, your Honor. I had no idea," she said, stressing the words "no idea," "that he was so well-known. It looks like I need to worry a little more about this case." She thought about what the Judge meant by calling him "world-famous," and was now strangely intrigued by the attorney sitting next to her.

"I wouldn't say that, Ms. Johnson," said Judge Tompkins, sitting down in the large chair behind his desk. "In fact, my hope is that this case can be decided rather quickly so that both of you esteemed counsel can go on to handle other matters." He looked directly at Eric. "Ms. Johnson, you're a Rutgers law graduate, correct?" His eyes never diverted from Eric, and he did not wait for an answer. "Mr. Goldberg and I went to Seton Hall law together. We have known each other for a long time, and I know that Mr. Goldberg does not want this case to drag out and most certainly will be looking for a nice, safe, plea arrangement. Am I correct in this assumption, Eric?" He asked, slowly nodding his head up and down as if to signal Eric that his answer would have to be in the affirmative.

Eric looked at Judge Tompkins and slowly shook his head from side to side. "Sorry, Judge," he responded, "but you are not correct. My client is innocent, and I do not think that we will be able to reach a plea agreement at this time. My hope is that the Prosecutor's office will realize that sometimes accidents just happen through nobody's fault, that their efforts will be in vain and that those trumped-up, reactionary, media-driven and politically-motivated charges will be dropped prior to trial," he added, looking at Amanda, "but if I must defend this case and continue what no doubt will be the pleasure of dealing with Ms. Johnson, then so be it."

Judge Tompkins scowled and leaned back in his chair, his hands clasped in front of him. "Ms. Johnson," he said, sighing, will you please do me the favor of allowing me to speak with Mr. Goldberg alone for a couple of minutes." He saw her face contort into a puzzled look. "Don't worry," he said, in order to placate her concerns, "nothing inappropriate. I just need to speak to Mr. Goldberg about a fellow classmate of ours. I don't want to forget to speak to him about this. When we are done, we will call you back in."

"I guess so, Judge," Amanda responded, hesitatingly. "I will be out in the courtroom." She stood and walked to the door, unaware that two sets of eyes were following the moves of her body from the time that she stood to the time that she stepped out of the room and closed the door behind her. Her exit was followed by a prolonged moment of silence, as the two men sat in their chairs to gather their thoughts.

"I'll tell you, Judge, it must be nice to work with her on a daily basis," Eric said, breaking the uncomfortable silence as he looked at a clearly exasperated Judge Tompkins. "She seems like a nice girl."

"Nice? Is that how you describe your fellow members of the bar these days?" the Judge replied. "Do you know her family history?"

"No, I can't say that I do."

"Do you remember that Elizabeth police officer who was shot and killed in the line of duty a couple of years or so after we graduated from law school?"

"Vaguely," Eric replied, "why do you ask?"

"Well," the Judge explained, "that cop was her father, and he was a damned good cop. So she was what, about six or seven when that happened?"

Eric looked toward the door, as if he could see Amanda Johnson standing on its other side. "So her father was killed when she was a kid. What are you telling me, that she is some type of superhero, trying to avenge her father's death by prosecuting the bad guys?"

"That's a little heavy-handed, don't you think?" Judge Tompkins replied. "I'm just giving you a little background. They never caught the guy, which, for a cop-killer, was pretty embarrassing for the Elizabeth PD. And even worse, after her father died, if you recall, word filtered out about an affair that her mother was having with one of the local councilmen. It was a little bit of a cause célèbre around here, you know."

Eric shook his head slowly, tacitly articulating that he had no memory of the scandal. "I assume that didn't go over too well with the daughter, then." His face curled, involuntarily, into a smirk. "Let me guess, Michael, she has daddy issues."

Michael Tompkins, the judge, was in no mood for inappropriate talk about Amanda Johnson. More importantly, Michael Tompkins, the man, was in no mood for such chatter. "Eric, let's forget about her for a minute, and let's talk about you," he responded, firmly, "what the fuck are you doing here?"

Somewhat taken aback by the vagueness of the question, Eric asked, "What exactly do you mean?"

"You know exactly what I am talking about," Judge Tompkins said, his voice rising. "What are you doing here representing your ex-wife on what amounts to a murder charge? Do you not think that you may be more than a little too interested in the outcome? Didn't you see the news report with that Spanish woman?"

"Yes, I saw the news that night, but no," Eric answered, sternly. "I believe that I am more than capable of handling this, Michael," he said, forgetting for a minute to properly address his old classmate in a manner more befitting his position as a jurist, "and she trusts me to handle it for her. Isn't that good enough for you?"

Judge Tompkins leaned forward. "I understand, but what happens when the case progresses? When it gets difficult?" His voice lowered so that nobody standing outside of the door could hear him, and grew much more serious in tone. "And what happens, Eric, pray tell, when she is on the stand, and the Prosecutor goes into her background, and, maybe, the shit with Doug comes out?"

Eric struggled to maintain his composure, but the look on his face belied his surprise at the last question. "How ... how," he stammered, "did you know about that?"

"Seriously, Eric," Judge Tompkins replied as he leaned back in his chair, arms folded across his chest. He pointed to the computer monitor on his desk and said, still keeping his voice barely above a whisper, "everyone knows, you idiot. Well, at least everyone we went to school with. Nothing is a secret these days, you know that. He kept it a pretty good secret for a while, but after their break-up, it seemed like everyone knew what was going on. I'm shocked that nobody has mentioned it to you."

*****

Douglas Freeman was, like Eric Goldberg and Michael Tompkins, a member of the Seton Hall Law School class of 1996. As their last names began with consecutive letters and classes were grouped alphabetically, Freeman and Eric were in the same classes during their first year of school. The two formed a fast friendship based, in part, on their mutual loves of baseball and the Yankees. It was not until years later that another form of mutual love proved to be their friendship's undoing.

The two men both went to work for mid-sized law firms following graduation, and each left their respective firms several years later to venture out onto their own. Eric started his own firm in Elizabeth, and Doug returned to his hometown of Westfield and opened an office on Elm Street, a couple of blocks from East Broad Street, in space that he shared with two other solo practitioners. The two met for lunch every couple of weeks, especially when Doug had to appear in court in Elizabeth, and they also had monthly nights out with their spouses for a period of time, until Doug divorced his wife in 2008.

It was a shock to Eric, therefore, when he found out about Wendi's affair with Doug. As she explained it to him, she had tried to talk to Doug about the fact that Eric was working such long hours and she felt alone, and thought that Doug could offer some assistance since he had gone through a divorce only a few years earlier. Her explanation turned more and more into a cliché as she continued to speak, to the point where Eric could barely even understand what she was saying other than the fact that she had gone to him for comfort and things had progressed too far between them.

Wendi continued to beg for Eric's forgiveness even as she began to file for divorce. He told her that could not provide her with such forgiveness, at least not then. Time had since dulled, but not erased, the pain of his wife and good friend betraying him. The pain still existed, at least in part. In Eric's mind, no lapse of time would completely eliminate those feelings. He could still deal with his ex-wife. He wanted no part of his ex-friend. Those feelings of betrayal would, in his mind, never abate.

*****

Eric had thought that the affair was a secret. He now knew that he was incorrect.

"So, Eric," Judge Tompkins said as Eric's eyes searched the ceiling while he remembered the affair, his eyes glistening with moisture, "explain to me how, with all of this information at the Prosecutor's disposal should the case somehow go to trial, with you having to sit there, at counsel table and not only to listen, but to actually defend Wendi not only for this case, but also, essentially, for cheating on you and breaking up your marriage, how you can possibly stay objective."

Eric sat silently, trying with great difficulty to reconcile his own thoughts so that he could respond intelligently to the Judge's multi-faceted inquiry. He looked out the window, and saw two birds sitting in the tree located several feet from the Judge's courtroom. They seemed happy together. Was it really so difficult for two people to stay together? Was it so difficult for two people to be happy together? For a moment, he wished he was a bird, or any other creature. Even another person so that he would not have to be sitting in Judge Tompkins' courtroom at that moment. Unfortunately, he was himself, he was in the Judge's chambers, and could not fly from the situation. He would have to address it head on.

He took a deep breath, and then began to address his old friend. "I can, but realistically, does it even matter? She will apply for PTI, be accepted into the program. You will sentence her to probation for two years, levy some fines, and you will sentence her to community service, likely in the Hispanic community to placate the masses. So does my objectivity even matter?"

Judge Tompkins leaned back in his chair and sighed. He then shook his head and reached for his reading glasses. "Eric," he said, perusing the file on his desk, "you know I can't give her PTI here."

"I don't know that, Michael," Eric, replied, in a confused tone. "What do you mean you 'can't'? Do you mean to say 'won't'?"

Closing the file on his desk, Judge Tompkins removed his glasses, wiped them clean with his tie, and looked Eric directly in the eye. "Can you imagine the shitstorm that I would be forced to endure if I let her get PTI? Every fucking Hispanic in Elizabeth would be coming after me. And I don't know if you have noticed from your office window, but this town has lots of Hispanics," he stated, as he pointed to the window in his office. "The fucking Prosecutor's office would skin me alive if I let her walk like that. We have to at least put on the show of prosecuting her, of making her pay for what she's done to that kid. I can't risk having them skewer me now. I've only been on this bench for six months; there's no way I could do it."

"Really, is that the truth, Michael?" Eric asked, concerned.

"Yes, it really is the truth, you asshole. Don't you get it? This is a political powder keg here. Certainly you've noticed. You said so yourself before, in your politically-motivated speech." He paused and looked at Eric, searching for some form of recognition of what he was talking about. Eric's face remained expressionless, so he pressed on. "You're right across the street. Don't you ever look out your window? Don't you pay attention to who is walking up and down these streets, especially late at night? They ain't Jews, I can tell you that. The city's Latin American population has grown by leaps and bounds the past couple of decades. They are replacing the other ethnicities. Look at where Wendi had the accident. It used to be an entirely Jewish neighborhood. Not anymore."

"I have no problem walking these streets."

"And you shouldn't. That's not my point. My point is that the city is largely Hispanic now. There are also strong Latin communities in surrounding places like Union, Roselle, and Roselle Park, don't forget. I'm not saying we should fear them, of course. I'm just pointing out that they are there. And this place will erupt, it will fucking erupt, if she walks now on a PTI. If a jury acquits her, so be it. There will be protests, but at least the blame will lay with her presumed peers, not with the actions of the white judge who let her walk. I'm not going to be that guy. I can't be that guy."

"Have you even discussed this with the Prosecutor?"

"They're having a pissing match over there between themselves, between you and me. Do you think that Amanda Johnson is the best they've got to try what may be the biggest criminal trial here in decades? Don't be ridiculous. Outside of these chambers I will admit she's quite a piece of ass, but she's not exactly the best and brightest in the office. Think about it for a second - she's just a kid. When did she graduate from Rutgers, a year or two ago? And they gave her this case? I don't know if they want a conviction for sure, but I do know that they are going to want a trial, at least to show the people that they care about them. Plus, I can't risk people saying that I did you any favors. You see how it is out there for judges now. I can't risk it, sorry."

Eric looked downward at his feet. "I thought that having you on the bench for this case would be helpful," he said slowly. "I never imagined that it would work against me."

"I don't see it that way. In any event, going back to my question, how are your going to maintain your objectivity as the case moves forward?"

Eric looked back at his old classmate, the sadness in his eyes replaced with anger as they continued to redden. "Judge, with all due respect, I find it offensive that you question my objectivity. I certainly haven't questioned yours," He rose from the chair, and wiped a tear from his right eye. "I am representing my client," he said, as forcefully as he could muster, "and I will do so to the best of my abilities. I will not run from my past, or from her past. Our past, especially our marriage, has no place in this litigation. You know that. I'm not running scared, Judge, and neither should you." He paused and turned to walk to the door to allow Amanda Johnson to return to the room. "Now, I will let Ms. Johnson back in, with your permission, and we can set a schedule for this case. I presume that I shouldn't even ask her about the possibility of PTI?"

"If you insist," replied Judge Tompkins, sadly shaking his head, "but let me say one more thing before you open the door. I worry about how this is going to go for you, Eric. The affair may not have destroyed you. The divorce didn't either. But this trial? Re-living the pain again and again? Seeing her daily and hearing about her problems? Worrying about whether she is going to jail? That may be too much for you. It would likely be too much for anyone."

Eric wiped his face with both hands and smiled. "Don't worry about me, Michael. Besides," he added, "we both know that you won't send her to jail."

"I am bound by the rules, Eric," Judge Tompkins said, quietly, "do not expect any favors from me on this one. You know that they will be watching me, and I can't risk any problems because of this case. So if you are thinking that you're going to get a better deal, or she will be walking away from this charge just because of our prior relationship, then think again. It's not going to happen. I can't, and I won't."

Eric nodded his head in understanding.

"Seriously, Eric, I don't think that you understand what you are up against. It has nothing to do with the, what did you call her, 'little girl'. Quite frankly, Amanda is a good Prosecutor, despite what I said before. But she's not that good, and you shouldn't be afraid of her in this case."

"What do you mean?" asked Eric.

"What I mean, Eric, is that you should be much more afraid of the County Prosecutor." He stood. "This is what I was alluding to before. Crawford has a bug up his ass about this case. He's being defiant against both Sanchez and the mayor now, but he's getting tons of pressure from the Hispanics because that kid died, and, depending on how long the pressure lasts, he may not be able to let it rest." He looked down to his desk. "You're dealing with Amanda now, but mark my words, if or when the case goes to trial, and depending on how much that asshole Sanchez and his supporters stay interested in this case and Wendi, you may be dealing with one of the more experienced guys from that office. I wouldn't even be surprised if Crawford himself sticks his fat ass into the case at some point." He sat back down, slumping into his chair, exasperated at the stubbornness of his former classmate. "Don't let this happen, Eric. You can't pray that something else happens to distract a suddenly united and vocal Hispanic community. Cut a deal and everyone can go away now. No ambiguities. No suspense of what may happen. No more anxiety. Have her plead to something and take the proper punishment. If you do it soon, at least I will have some leeway in sentencing."

"Like what?" Eric asked. "I assume that you know something."

The Judge smiled a knowing smile which betrayed the fact that he was well-aware of the Prosecutor's intentions. "They'll offer you a plea – first she'll want Wendi to plead guilty on the promise of a minimum sentencing. That's what she's going to start with today. When you say no, she'll back off to a Third Degree charge of something else, something which still seems pretty bad to the public and with a slight custodial sentence because of the politics involved here. Take that – they need it to be a crime, not just an offense, to placate the people, and I can change the sentence on that one to probation with some weekend lockup program and community service. That's the best that I can do for you, so you should take it and run."

"No way, Michael. We're not pleading to any crime, and definitely not agreeing to any jail time."

"You're going to tie my hands, you know."

Eric smiled, or, more appropriately, grimaced. "No, Michael," he replied, "you're trying to do that to me with this negotiation, if you can even call it that. What happened, by the way, to the presumption against incarceration for first-time offenders? Have you forgotten about that?"

The Judge sat upright. "You're absolutely right, which is why I mentioned probation and weekends instead of full-time jail. But," he admonished his old classmate, "I'm warning you, Eric, don't be too cocky. You may not get the result you want, you know. And it may not be in the best interests of your client." He paused. "Oh, and stop using words like 'we.' This is about her, not about you. It's the 'we' shit that is going to make people think that you two are together again, like that Espinosa woman said the other night."

Eric's smile disappeared. "So be it. I'm not afraid, Michael. You know I can do this. I need to do this. We're," he paused for dramatic effect, and then continued, "yes, I said 'we're,' still going ahead." He stood and walked toward the door. "I am going to get the Assistant Prosecutor now, so we can continue with this little charade." Opening the door, he beckoned for Amanda Johnson to return.

As she entered the room she noticed the red in Eric's eyes. "Is everything OK in here, Judge?" she asked, pensively. "I know that you said that you wouldn't be discussing the case, but has there been any movement from the defense? Do we have any resolution?"

"Ms. Johnson," Judge Tompkins said, matter-of-factly, as he stood and walked to retrieve some paperwork from the bookcase located to his right, "I told you that we would be discussing other issues. We did not discuss the case other than my telling him that his client would not be eligible for PTI in this case. My understanding is that Mr.

Goldberg is representing the defendant, who, as you may or may not be aware, is his ex-wife." He looked at Eric. "Both of you had better get ready for a circus."

"He told me outside," replied Amanda. "I feel like I have stepped into a TV movie." She looked at Eric and smiled. "But in a TV movie, the prosecutor would end up with the other attorney in some form of perverse love triangle, right? I think we can all be comfortable in the knowledge that's not happening here," she added, her lips locked in an almost imperceptible smile.

"Don't be ridiculous, Amanda," said Eric, "this is a woman's life and freedom that we are dealing with, not some schlocky made-for-TV movie. Now can we please set down a schedule for this case so that I know what I need to do and when to prepare?"

"Before we do that," Amanda protested, "I believe that I have a plea arrangement to discuss with you, one that I think your client will find very appealing. Perhaps we should step back into the courtroom to talk and let Judge Tompkins handle some of his other cases before he needs to break for lunch."

"Does it involve dismissal of the case, or a downgrade to a Disorderly Person's Offense instead of this obviously trumped-up charge?" Eric asked.

"No," Amanda responded, "I'm afraid not. I don't know why you would even think that either would be possible here." She thumbed through the papers in her file, looking for the witness' account of the accident. "I mean, really, Mr. Goldberg, this is a very serious charge and, no doubt, you know that my boss is under a lot of pressure on this case."

Eric shook his head slowly and stared at the Judge, even as he addressed Amanda Johnson. "Then the only thing possibly appealing here is you, Ms. Johnson, but rest assured that we," he paused and viewed a grimacing Judge Tompkins, who shook his head from side-to-side in disapproval at Eric's use of the plural pronoun, "I'm sorry, allow me to re-phrase. Rest assured, Ms. Johnson, and Judge Tompkins, that my client is not even going to consider pleading guilty at this time."

The Judge sighed and took out a form Case Management Order. He began to discuss dates as he entered them onto the form. Amanda Johnson dutifully copied the dates onto the legal pad which rested on her left leg. Eric did the same, and could not help but notice that Amanda Johnson seemed to be blushing. When she stopped writing the dates on her pad, she looked up and, catching Eric's watchful gaze, she turned a darker shade of red and quickly turned away. Running her hand through her hair as she leaned over to gather up the rest of her file, she stood and began to walk toward the door, thanking the Judge for his time and running her free hand over Eric's shoulder as she sauntered toward the door.

Chapter XV – An Affair to Remember (or Forget)

Amanda emerged from the Judge's chambers first, followed by Eric. Any tension which had existed in the judge's chambers disappeared as the reality of the situation sank into both of their minds, their mutual hopes of the case being resolved that morning having been dashed. The tension was immediately replaced with a common understanding of the fact that they would be working together for the near future, albeit with opposing goals in mind. Neither was overly displeased with the prospect of working with the other, although neither was yet aware that the other shared his or her feelings. The two walked closely together, and seemed to be sharing a laugh as Amanda approached the counsel table and placed Wendi's file into a large box which held the paperwork for that day's cases. "I will be in touch soon, Mr. Goldberg," she said, quietly, as Eric brushed past her.

"Just make sure to get me that discovery as soon as possible, please, Amanda," replied Eric. "I need to start working on this one in earnest as soon as I can, and I should have had the discovery before today, or at least this morning. Especially before the case goes to the Grand Jury, if that is the intention. I'm worried about losing witnesses," he added, "you know how certain people can be uncooperative when it comes to lawyers and appearing in courtrooms. You may have already lost that kid, you know. And without his testimony, I would urge, you may not have any case against my client." He looked at Wendi, who was staring back at him, a scowl across her face. He paused, puzzled by her look. "I have a very demanding client," he added, chuckling.

"I am sure that you do," Amanda said, joining Eric in laughter and glancing over at the scowling face of Wendi Goldberg, the defendant in the highest-profile case that she had been assigned to date. "But my case will be just fine, thank you. I will see

141

what I can do to expedite getting all of the paperwork to you." She leaned over the box, pulled out the file labeled "Gonzalez" and beckoned for the attorney who was appearing on behalf of John Gonzalez to come forward to discuss their case. As she spoke to that attorney, she looked over his shoulder and watched Eric walk away from her. "World famous?" she thought to herself, "I wonder what the Judge meant by that. Was he being serious, or was he just saying that as some kind of joke? I'd better ask around to see what I can find out about him." There was something interesting, if not oddly attractive, about Eric Goldberg.

In the meantime, Eric motioned to Wendi that their day in court was finished, and that they were free to leave. She glared at him as he approached, and then silently stood, still scowling, and walked out of the courtroom. Once the courtroom doors closed behind them, Eric made no attempts at masking his annoyance at Wendi's look of contempt. "Should I even ask what your problem is?" he asked. "Do you think that this is fun for me, coming to court to represent you? The least you could do is spare me that look."

"That look?" barked Wendi. "How dare you speak to me like that. It's bad enough that you are flirting with that little girl that they call a Prosecutor. Now you insult me?"

"What do you mean flirting?" Eric replied. He looked around to see if any members of the press were present. Luckily for him, the hallway was empty with the exception of some other defendants and Court Officers.

"I know that look on your face, Eric," replied Wendi. "You know the look, the flirting look. The one you always give to waitresses, to women in stores, and no doubt to your clients. I lived with it for years." She sat down on the bench in the hallway and shook her head. "I know that look," she said softly, "I just thought that I would never have to see it again."

Eric leaned in and whispered in Wendi's ear, so that nobody else in the hallway would hear him. "In case you forgot, darling," he said in a derisive tone, "we are no longer married. So even if I am flirting with someone, well, that is none of your business." He paused and stood up again, looking around to see if anyone was nearby. "And what I am doing, for your information, is trying to keep your ungrateful ass out of jail." His voice rose. "So let me do my job, or you're going to need to get someone else to do it." He paused and again looked around him before continuing. "You want to know what just happened in the Judge's chambers? Then listen up. There is no PTI, OK? They want you to plead guilty. I fought with the Judge about it. You know, Judge Tompkins, my old friend Michael. They're taking the case to the Grand Jury. Our only hope," he added, glaring at Wendi, "is to be nice to the Prosecutor, and, if necessary, to flirt with her to see if something else can be worked out, maybe. Possibly. In fact," he added, "it may not even make any difference. But we would never know if I didn't at least try." He stormed toward the elevator, leaving a crying Wendi sitting alone on the bench.

He was standing by the elevator, pacing as the lights depicting the various floors illuminated in order, when a contrite Wendi, still wiping tears from her reddened face, approached. "I am so sorry, Eric," she said, softly. "I am just so nervous about this whole thing." She looked up at him, her eyes glistening. "There is nobody I trust more than you. That's why I want you to handle it." She grabbed his arm with her left hand and squeezed it. "I trust you," she said, smiling faintly.

Eric pulled away, releasing his arm from Wendi's grip. Now he was scowling. "If you trust me, then let me do my job." He turned away, adding "this is not about our marriage. Let me do my job. You think it was easy for me in there? Did you forget that Judge Michael Tompkins knows me? Knows you? And that he knows Doug?" He stressed the word "Doug" so hard that his voice seemed guttural to Wendi.

"What does Doug have to do with this?" Wendi asked. "How did his name even get mentioned?"

"Well, the Judge brought it up," said Eric. "He asked how I would react if the Prosecutor asked you, under oath, about the affair."

"How does he know?"

Eric grimaced. "Apparently, everyone knows. All of the judges, the lawyers, and, for all we know, probably even the Prosecutor's Office. I certainly did not bring it up, trust me. How much embarrassment do you think I want to endure? Apparently Doug started telling people about it after you two broke up."

"Why should it matter in this case?"

"It shouldn't, but what if he lets the question stand? How are you going to look to a jury at that point? How will I look? And even if he doesn't allow the questions, maybe he was just making a point that there is going to be a tremendous discomfort between us moving forward. Like there is now." The elevator door opened, and Eric stepped into the empty box. Wendi followed. Neither spoke as the door closed and Eric pushed the button for the first floor, symbolically bringing that part of their conversation to a close as well.

The two rode the elevator in silence down to the first floor of the courthouse. When the doors opened, Eric saw some attorneys with whom he was familiar. He sighed deeply, and turned to Wendi. "Look, I'm sorry for what I said upstairs. Let's try to work together on this one, and not fight. Fighting won't help us." He looked to the right and nodded toward a couple of men seated on a couch in the courthouse's atrium. "Now please smile a little as I talk to these guys. You might recognize Steve Markerson. And he might recognize you, so please be nice."

"I've put on my happy face many times for you in the past, Eric," Wendi said, her face tinged with more than a hint of resignation, "it's a skill that I learned to perfect, so there's no reason that I can't do it again now."

Eric looked at her disapprovingly, annoyed at the tone of her comment, and went to speak for a few minutes with some of the attorneys gathered in the courthouse. Markerson did recognize Wendi, and they exchanged pleasantries; the topic of Wendi's pending case, thankfully, was not mentioned by anyone, nor did anyone seek to discuss the circumstances leading up to and surrounding their divorce. Eric then excused himself, and he and Wendi exited the courthouse and walked down the building's front steps to the street. They started to walk toward his office when Wendi spoke. "Do you mind if I come up to the office so we can go over what happened in court today?" asked Wendi. "Let's stop for coffee. I'm buying." She walked into the coffee shop on the corner of Broad Street and Elizabeth Avenue. Ordering coffee for the both of them, she looked back at Eric. "Do you think Fatima will want some?" she asked.

"Better get her something just in case," Eric answered, hoping that a cup of coffee would serve as a peace offering. "Make it simple. Get her a regular coffee, with milk and sugar."

"One more coffee please, regular," Wendi said to the man behind the counter. She handed him a twenty-dollar bill to pay for the coffees, and then placed a dollar bill in the tip jar from her change. She motioned to Eric to help her carry the coffee, and he placed the three cups into a carrier. Wendi picked up Eric's file, the one labeled with her name in bold letters, and the two exited the shop and walked along Broad Street to Eric's office. Eric saw one newsman parked in front of the courthouse, and since he did not react to their presence, Eric assumed that either he was there for a different case or that the reporter did not recognize them. Just to be sure, he instructed Wendi to walk briskly and to not answer any questions, should any reporters appear.

Arriving at the building, they took the elevator to the proper floor and luckily, this time there were no reporters waiting to ambush them in the office hallway. Their footsteps were the only sound filling the otherwise silent hallway as they approached Eric's office. As Eric was still carrying the coffee, Wendi opened the door to the office, allowing Eric to walk inside before her.

"How did it go, today, Eric?" Fatima asked, before realizing that Wendi was walking into the office behind him. "Oh, I'm sorry," she said, looking at Wendi. "How are you, Wendi? It's been a while."

"Yes, it has, Fatima," Wendi replied. Clearly both women were doing their best to avoid a repeat of their previous altercation, so much so that they spoke as if it had never even taken place. Wendi took one of the coffees from Eric's arms and handed it to Fatima. "How is everyone? How are the kids?"

"Everyone is fine, thank you. And thanks for the coffee, Lord knows I need it this morning," Fatima replied, hesitatingly, as she took the coffee from Wendi. "Bruce is really busy at work, and the kids are good. And me, you know, working for my cousin here is nothing but fun, right, Eric?" She looked at Eric to join the conversation, feeling a sense of potential tension rising in the office.

"Of course it is," Eric replied. "Now let me go and use the men's room really fast and then we will talk, Wendi." He turned toward the door. "You girls play nice, please." He exited the room, praying that nothing would erupt in his absence, and the women stood in silence, listening to his footsteps echoing as he strode, rapidly, to the men's room.

In Eric's absence, however, the détente quickly evaporated. "You hate me, don't you?" asked Wendi as she stood in front of Fatima's desk, her arms folded in front of her as her almost-empty coffee cup dangled from her right hand. "You hate me for what happened with Eric." She looked at Fatima, who stood, stone-faced and without any discernible reaction, as she spoke. "Hate me all you want," she said, "but you never know both sides of a story, so don't judge me."

"Don't judge you?" Fatima asked, her voice low and stern as she averted her eyes downward to avoid continued eye contact with Wendi, instead preferring to focus her gaze on the papers littering her desk. "How could I possibly not judge you? Do you know what you put him through? Do you have any idea how the divorce wrecked him? In fact, do you even care?"

"The divorce did not wreck him," interrupted Wendi. "He wrecked himself. He wrecked himself and our marriage, over a long period of time. He wrecked us."

"Spare me," said Fatima, mockingly. "I know what was going on. I am his secretary, so I know things. More importantly, I am his family. Don't forget, I am married to his cousin." She looked Wendi square in the eye as she stood. "You were at my fucking wedding, Wendi!" She yelled, glaring at Wendi. "Who the hell do you think he talked to when things got bad between you? Me! I was the shoulder that he came to cry on!" She sat. "You know something, I don't believe in hate," she said, shaking her head as her voice returned to a more normal volume. "But if I never saw you again, Wendi, it wouldn't bother me. And to be honest with you, bringing me a cup of coffee won't change that."

Wendi's eyes again welled up with tears as she searched for the proper words to say to Fatima. The two had once been so close. Wendi met Fatima the same time as Eric, and up until a couple of years ago, they had spent a great deal of time together, sometimes even alone when Eric and his cousin Bruce, Fatima's husband, would go to Yankees' games together. One time, when things with Eric got to the point where Wendi thought that her marriage could not survive, it was Fatima whom she went to speak with. Later, she discovered that speaking to Fatima was a mistake, as Fatima's allegiance was to Eric, no matter the situation. "I am sorry, Fatima," Wendi whispered as the tears began to flow down her face. "I considered you like a sister, you know," she cried, almost unable to speak due to her being overcome with emotion, "and not being able to see you has been one of the toughest things from the divorce."

Now Fatima's eyes welled with tears as she too was swept up in the emotion of the moment. At that instant, she tried to forget about Wendi's transgressions and instead recalled the many good times between them, memories that she had suppressed since she first learned of Wendi's affair with Doug Freeman. But the walls she had built up against Wendi remained strong, even as she began to cry. "Sometimes I miss you too, Wendi," she said, "but I can't forgive you. Maybe Eric can, but I can't. You cheated on him with his best friend. You cheated on us. I can't forgive that."

Wendi shook her head slowly as she dried her eyes with a tissue. "I understand," she said. "I wish that things were different, but I understand. I will try to stay away when you are here."

"Thank you," Fatima answered, "it will make things easier for me. This really is tough for me also, you know. And I don't know if it will ever be better again. I just don't know." She looked down at her desk as a teardrop fell on the lid of her coffee cup. "And I know what I just said, but thank you again for the coffee."

"It's the least I could do," said Wendi. "Maybe someday …"

The door to the office opened and Eric strode in, stopping when he saw that both women's eyes were red. "Did I miss anything in here?" he asked.

"Nothing at all," replied Fatima, wiping her face with a tissue as she sniffled deeply. "Everything is fine. We're just catching up on things."

"That's good, I guess," Eric said, with a disbelieving tone to his voice. He turned to Wendi. "Let's go discuss what happened today."

"You know what, Eric, I think I should leave," replied Wendi, also wiping the last remnants of her own tears from her cheeks. "I understand already, and I trust you. No PTI and going to the Grand Jury." She paused and looked in Fatima's direction. "I really should leave."

Eric turned toward Fatima, who did not protest Wendi's statement. "What happened here?" he growled.

"Nothing happened," said Wendi, as her eyes again filled with tears. She placed her coffee cup on Fatima's desk and turned toward the office door. "I just shouldn't be here. Call me when you get the paperwork for my case," she said, as she fled from the room, crying, and slammed the door behind her.

Eric again looked toward Fatima, who was staring blankly at her computer screen, her own eyes moistened with tears. He cleared his throat, at which point Fatima raised her hand and waved him away. "I don't want to talk about it," she said, "please just go into your office." A tear ran down her left cheek. Eric sighed, shrugged his shoulders, and slowly walked into his office, closing the door behind him to give Fatima privacy. Through the door, he could hear her crying.

Chapter XVI – The Second News Broadcast

Later that night, Eric returned home at 7:30 and settled in to watch the Yankees play against Boston. He sat at the desk in his spare bedroom, alternately watching the television located to his left and looking at his computer as he scanned the internet, looking for whatever information he could find on other states' texting and driving laws. Not surprisingly, there was a dearth of information on the topic, as he remembered that New Jersey was at the forefront of such legislation. Also not surprisingly, the Red Sox were providing the Yankees with a good, old-fashioned whipping, running the score up to 8-1 before Eric, in disgust, turned to the local news at 10:00.

He immediately realized that he should have kept watching the game.

Anchor: *Welcome to the 10:00 news, everyone. We begin tonight with an update on a continuing story out of Elizabeth, the story of a texting and driving prosecution. A woman named Wendi Goldberg, a resident of Westfield, has been charged with death by auto in the death of Elizabeth teenager and pedestrian Jose Gomez. Lupe Espinosa has been following this story for us and she is here with an update. Lupe?*

Lupe Espinosa's beautiful face and ample cleavage filled the screen. Her long, dark hair was pulled back in a ponytail, and she wore an off-white, scoop-necked blouse which contrasted nicely with her tanned neck and cleavage and which perfectly served to accentuate her chest. As was the case with the earlier broadcast, the cameraman framed the picture perfectly, so that the bottom of the picture ended just below her chest. Eric initially admired the view, but then, mindful of what was said during her prior appearance and conversation about the case, steeled himself for the report.

Lupe: *Thank you, Brad. The story of Jose Gomez, the Roselle Catholic Honors Student who was mercilessly run down and killed by Wendi Goldberg, continues to be a hot topic in the Union County Courthouse. Today, Ms. Goldberg and her ex-husband slash attorney, Eric Goldberg, were in court for her initial appearance before a judge, an appearance at which the defendants, we are told, are normally provided with a plea bargaining offer from the prosecution in an effort to avoid trial.*

The screen filled with an outside shot of the courthouse, and Eric could soon see video of him and Wendi walking out of the courthouse, angrily talking to each other, as they made their way to Broad Street. "Fuck!" he yelled as he slammed his left hand onto the top of his desk. "Where was the fucking camera? How could I not have seen that?" Meanwhile, Lupe's voice spoke over the voyeuristic video.

Lupe: *My sources tell me that there were no offers for Ms. Goldberg today, however, which may explain this heated exchange between the former and, we have reason to believe, current lovebirds outside of the courthouse. I spoke with a court officer afterward, who would not tell me anything other than that he believed that the case will be going before the Grand Jury, and that they will be the ones to decide whether or not Wendi Goldberg should be indicted for her role in the killing of Jose Gomez. According to the officer, it will be weeks, if not months, before the case reaches the Grand Jury, so we will likely not be hearing anything else from the court for some time unless, somehow, a plea arrangement is worked out between the prosecution and Team Goldberg.*

Anchor:*Thank you, Lupe. So should we assume that we will not be hearing from you for some time on this case?*

Lupe: *I wouldn't say that, Brad. Because of the sensitive nature of the case and the fact that the young honors student killed was Latino, there continues to be unrest among the Latino community in Elizabeth and Union County in general. Today I spoke with Jesus Sanchez, local community leader. And let me tell you, Brad, he had some interesting things to say about the case and how it is being handled by the prosecution.*

Anchor: *And we have a tape of that conversation, which we will show later in the program, so stay tuned. In other news ...*

Eric pressed the "mute" button on his television remote control, enraged at the teaser put forth by Lupe and the anchorman. "Here we go again," he thought, and waited anxiously for Wendi's call. Luckily, the phone did not ring in the first minute after the television started to show another reporter's story on violence that had erupted at a food store in Irvington, so he assumed that, thankfully, Wendi had not been watching the news that evening. The less she saw and read, of course, the better for her frame of mind and, therefore, his sanity. Not that he wouldn't get worked up on his own, but when she got frantic it made him that much worse. Anticipating the need for alcohol, he walked into the kitchen, pulled two beers from the refrigerator, and then returned to the room, this time sitting on the couch. He set one beer down on the table in front of him, unscrewed the bottle cap from the other, and began to drink in anticipation of what he knew would be a damning interview between the lovely Lupe Espinosa and the community rabble-rouser and resident asshole, Jesus Sanchez.

His phone began buzzing with texts, which he knew were undoubtedly all related to the news report; either people were going to tell him what was already said, or warn him about the upcoming interview. But he already knew about both. He heard how Lupe Espinosa use the words *"mercilessly run down"* and *"killed"* to describe the death of Jose Gomez, a media conviction of Wendi if ever there was one. He heard how she twice referred to him as an *"honors student,"* clearly in an attempt to make him even more of a martyr and to further cast Wendi as a villain. And, of course, he had heard Lupe Espinosa refer to Wendi and him as *"current lovebirds."* Again, he was forced to consider, what kind of a mess had he gotten himself into?

Ten minutes later, the mess got worse.

Anchor: *Earlier in the broadcast, we heard from Lupe Espinosa about the on-going prosecution of Wendi Goldberg with respect to the death of a young pedestrian, Jose Gomez. The allegations against Ms. Goldberg are that she was texting at the time of the accident, and that her inattention to driving is what resulted in Mr. Gomez's death.*

Today Ms. Goldberg appeared in court to face a judge with respect to the charges against her and, based on what Lupe was told by a court officer, nothing has been resolved and the matter is heading to the Grand Jury in the near future. After that court appearance, Lupe spoke with local community leader Jesus Sanchez. She is here now with a report on that conversation. Lupe?

Lupe: *Thank you, Brad. Yes, today was a court appearance for Wendi Goldberg. As I reported earlier and as shown on the video that we aired earlier in this broadcast of her and her husband, I mean ex-husband, attorney leaving the courthouse, things did not go well for Ms. Goldberg in court. Most defendants who appeared in court this morning were offered at least some form of plea arrangement, which would have allowed them to end their case at this time. From what I was told by one court officer, however, Ms. Goldberg was offered no such deal and the case is being sent to the Grand Jury. The likelihood is that she will be indicted by the Grand Jury and will then face trial. Her case is now in limbo, and whether or not she will be formally charged can take weeks or months. Afterward, I sat down with a person who has shown great interest in this case, Jesus Sanchez, who has been at the forefront of the local Latino push for prosecution of Ms. Goldberg and who has also acted as a spokesman for the Gomez family. Let's watch the interview now.*

The screen changed from the news set to an office, no doubt the faux law office of Jesus Sanchez, the office which served as the home for his political aspirations and front for his other non-legal related activities. Two diplomas hung on the wall behind Mr. Sanchez, who was seated at a table which contained three miniature flags to his right – the one closest to him was that of New Jersey, and the one furthest from him was of his home country, Colombia. These two flanked the United States flag. All were approximately four inches in height, and all stood in small, gold-colored bases.

To the other side of the table, crossed legs barely encased in a skin-tight, short, black skirt and ample cleavage accentuated by yet another low-cut, cream-colored blouse, sat Lupe Espinosa. The skirt's hem rested a scant few inches from the bottom of her crotch, Eric realized. If she were to uncross her legs or shift more toward the camera's watchful gaze, he would be able to find out if his guess that she was concealing a dark blue, lace thong beneath her skirt was correct.

It was apparent from the outset that there was certain congeniality to the interview, a palpable spark and energy between Lupe Espinosa and Jesus Sanchez. Eric wondered if Lupe was merely being her usual flirty self with Jesus Sanchez, or whether there was something else between them. Hell, she accused him and Wendi of being involved, why couldn't he think the same about them?

Lupe: *I am sitting here with local Elizabeth attorney and community leader, Jesus Sanchez. Mr. Sanchez has been a vocal advocate for the Gomez family in the wake of the death of pedestrian Jose Gomez. We thank you for taking the time from your schedule to speak with us, Mr. Sanchez.*

Sanchez: *Thank you, Lupe, but please call me Jesus. All of my friends call me Jesus. It is my privilege to be sitting here today in my office, a proud American citizen of South American descent, and be able to express my feelings to your viewers.*

He looked directly into the camera and smiled, his pearly white teeth practically illuminating the television screen. Eric did not remember Sanchez's teeth being so sparking white the last time that they saw each other in court. He must have had them whitened, no doubt in anticipation of all of the free press that he was trying to generate from the accident. And what a self-serving piece of shit he was, even from his first comment.

Lupe: *The privilege is all mine, Mr. Sanchez, I mean, Jesus. Please tell our viewers why you have become so involved with the Gomez matter.*

Sanchez: *Lupe, to be honest, I have become involved involuntarily. It was never my intent to be anything more than an interested bystander while I trusted the local law enforcement authorities to do the right thing with respect to the woman who killed Jose. I was simply counseling the Gomez family, especially his distraught mother, and really, Lupe, truly did not think that I would need to take any public position other than my little speech immediately after the accident took place.*

"What a load of bullshit," Eric thought to himself. Sanchez appeared to be grinning as he delivered his completely self-serving statement, quite the opposite of showing the emotions of a man who was mourning the loss of a teenager. He was not being dragged into the situation. It was almost as if he had manufactured the death of Jose Gomez to serve his own political purposes.

Sanchez: *The problem, however, is similar to the problem that we have seen time and time again when dealing with the police and minorities. And that is why I have to be involved. Whether the victim is black, tan, or brown simply does not matter. If you are not white, the response of the police is just not the same. So the problem, Lupe, is that local law enforcement is showing, again, that it cannot be trusted to do the right thing here, and many people have urged me to speak on the Latino community because they believe that justice will not be done here because the victim of this horrible crime was Hispanic.*

Lupe: *Can you explain what you mean? As I reported earlier on tonight's news program, the case is being sent to the Grand Jury and, if I understand correctly, it will be up to that group of citizens, presumably people of all races, not just Caucasians, to determine whether or not Ms. Goldberg will be charged with the crime of death by auto. The reason why it is even going to the Grand Jury is because the Prosecutor's office, as I was told, was not offering the Goldberg family any plea bargain in court today. So I guess the question on people's minds now will be- what else should they be doing?*

Sanchez: *I completely understand why you and others would ask that question, but don't forget, Lupe, I am an attorney ...*

"Using the term quite loosely," Eric said aloud. He was impressed with Sanchez's manner of speaking, however, as his command of the English language and use of inflections definitely sounded much better than he recalled. Still, he had not seen Sanchez in court for some time, nor had he heard anything about Sanchez actually practicing any form of law in months. Clearly the "attorney" job was just a front for something else, but what?

154

Sanchez: *And as an attorney I am aware of certain laws and procedures that must be followed, or at least should be followed. Let's just say that I know my way around the courtroom (winks at camera) and the procedures leading up to this point have not been done properly. To tell you the truth, Lupe, it's as if the prosecutor's office may get an indictment, but if they do, it will almost be in spite of their own actions.*

Lupe: *I don't want to say that I am confused, but can you please explain what you meant by those last couple of statements?*

Lupe, looking puzzled, shifted in her chair. She uncrossed her legs and re-crossed them, right over left, as she turned slightly toward the camera. Eric realized that he was incorrect – white lace.

Sanchez: *Of course, Lupe. The death by auto statute is relatively new in New Jersey, don't forget, and it seems like the police don't really know how to properly handle these cases. The same is true for the Prosecutor's office. First off, they have charged the driver of the car with death by auto, pero, I mean, but, they have not charged the person who sent her the text that she was reading at the time of the accident with any crimes. They should also be charging that person, who I believe was her mother, with a crime for sending the text to someone who she knew was driving.*

Lupe: *You mean that the police can charge you with a crime if you send a text to someone and if you know that they are driving a car?*

The answer, of course, was no. There was a New Jersey appellate court decision which indicated that the sender of a text could be held liable for sending the text to someone driving – as part of the husband and wife case, the one which led to the actual texting while driving law. After that, however, the couple decided to not even pursue the sender of the text for damages, and, more importantly, a bill was introduced into the state legislature, which clearly did not agree with the court's decision and wanted to take immediate steps to preclude the decision from being used to hold innocent people responsible for the actions of others, to provide that the sender of such a text could not be held responsible for another's injuries.

As a self-professed practicing attorney, Jesus Sanchez, no doubt, was well aware of all of these facts. But Jesus Sanchez, apparently, was not one to let the facts get in the way of a good diatribe – especially when the facts could stand in his way. In his mind, he could say what he wanted, because the public likely wouldn't know the difference. As was stated long ago by Dame Edith Sitwell, "[t]he public will believe anything, so long as it is not founded on truth." Sanchez seemed to adhere to that maxim, as evidenced by his answer.

Sanchez: *Yes, they can. The courts are still debating whether the police have to do so, but at least a couple of court decisions say that they can. And they haven't done that here. No charges have been filed against Wendi Goldberg's mother. The mother has not been called to appear in court, nor is she facing any penalties for what she has done. No charges have been filed, even though they should be. There is no reason for the police's failure to charge Ms. Goldberg's mother with abetting her crime by texting her.*

Lupe: *That's shocking. What else?*

Sanchez: *Well, according to another recent law, they have to test all people involved in fatal accidents for alcohol, to see if they were driving under the influence at the time of the accident. That was not done here, even though it is now standard protocol.*

Lupe: *Really? Why not?*

"Softball question," Eric thought. "No doubt they cooked this one up ahead of time." He took a large gulp of beer and then, remembering something critical, bolted from his seat. "That fuck! He knows that law never passed. That's total bullshit." He had remembered the push for what was to be called "Michelle's Law," which was proposed by a member of the New Jersey legislature in 2013 following the death of a high school senior pedestrian at the hands of a drunk driver. The law would have required all people who were in fatal accidents to submit to a blood test to determine if they were under the influence of alcohol at the time of the accident, even if they showed no outward signs of alcohol use. The proposed law, however, was eventually defeated and never made it to the statute books. In order to force the driver to submit to drunken driving tests, the actual protocol required that the officer have a reasonable suspicion that the driver was under the influence at the time of the accident. The driver would have to be slurring his or her speech, driving in an erratic manner, possess blood-shot eyes, or smell of alcohol. Eric knew that none of those factors were present when Wendi was initially spoken to by the police. None of these factors were present when he got to the accident scene, and the police report was devoid of any such factors. More importantly, Sanchez was well aware of the fact that there was no legitimate reason for her to be forced to submit to an alcohol test, especially when the "law" that Sanchez was citing was not even a real law.

No doubt even Sanchez, a fake lawyer, would have known that. He was, as usual, just grandstanding. And Lupe Espinosa wasn't calling him out on it. No doubt they had concocted parts of the interview before they went in front of the cameras, and there was no way that she was going to question him, especially not in front of a television audience. Eric, resigned to the fact that Sanchez had this free forum not only to improperly accuse the police and prosecution of misconduct, but also as to crucify him and his client, shrugged his shoulders and slumped back down onto the couch. He raised the bottle to his lips, took another swig of beer, and nervously waited for the answer. His nervousness was not without cause.

Sanchez: *Well, Lupe, there could be many reasons. My belief, and the belief of many people who I have talked to, is that the police at the scene did not do that test for two reasons. First, as you have already hinted at, because the driver was white and the person who she hit and killed was Latino. I know that this may sound shocking to some, but it reflects today's culture here in the city. Even though Elizabeth is populated by many people of Hispanic heritage, Lupe, the reality is that we are still treated like second-hand citizens. People tell me that they are still looked down upon by white people when they talk to each other in Spanish. People tell me that others tell them to go back to their own country if they don't speak good English. Teenagers tell me how people turn the other way when they walk past them in the street, as if they are all gang members. It's the same complaint that you hear from the African-American community, Lupe. The Latino community of this city, and, I believe, of this country as a whole, have*

157

the feeling that they are being profiled due to their coloring and their heritage. So these people tell me that they do not believe that the police care about them, and that the death of another, you'll pardon my use of this word, another spic, means nothing to them.

Still drinking, Eric nearly spit out a mouthful of beer when Sanchez used the word "*spic.*" "This is really bad," he said, to no one in particular, but even he could not anticipate that it would get even worse in the next few minutes.

Lupe: *That is so very sad, Jesus. Being a Latina myself, and being from Elizabeth, I would like to think that we, as a people, are being treated equally here. My parents came here and could not speak any English. They taught themselves some of the language, but they still prefer to speak Spanish, because they are more comfortable speaking in their native language. They made sure that I spoke both languages from an early age, though, and pushed me to go to school, to college, and to better myself. They value education, and just because they can't converse with everyone in English doesn't mean that they are uneducated. My father was an attorney back home, but he knew he could make a better life in this country for his family, even if it meant taking a physical job rather than being an attorney like you. And I know that he is not alone.*

She had turned to the camera while making her speech, and right after she began the sentence about her parents valuing education she uncrossed her legs and sat, squarely in front of the camera, with both legs on the ground. Her face was stern, but Eric, and likely every male viewer, was focused not on her face or her voice, but rather on the large patch of white lace which rested between the tops of her thighs. Eric did not even hear what she said after "*my father was an attorney.*"

Sanchez: *Lupe, you are correct. There are so many people like your parents. As you are aware, I came here from Colombia. I have taught myself the language and, I think, speak it good. And I was lucky, Lupe. I was lucky that an attorney named Greg Preston took a chance on me, gave me a chance to work at his law firm after I graduated from law school. So many people do not have that chance, Lupe. There are many like me who receive college degrees, graduate degrees, and, despite achieving these levels of* *education, the people of this country, meaning the white people, and even some of the blacks, still look at us as foreigners. They look even worse at the older generation, the ones like your parents, who are not comfortable speaking English to strangers and instead prefer to speak in Spanish.*

My parents never came to this country. My father, Jose Sanchez, worked two jobs to make the money to send me to this country for a better education and a better life. My mother, Sonia Ortiz, stayed home with my sisters and me and made sure that we always had a clean house and food on the table. Sometimes I think that her work was harder than his. She would sit with us and try to teach us what little English she knew so that we would know something when we first came here. Here's the ironic part, Lupe. The people of this country seem to completely forget that their families were all immigrants at one time, and that their parents, their abuelos y abuelas, and before had to learn to speak English. They forget that.

Lupe: *(shaking her head in agreement and turning back toward the desk, again concealing her crotch) You are so right, Jesus. So many people forget. They need to be reminded, which is why we need people like you to raise awareness. I owe you, no, the city of Elizabeth owes you a big gracias, a big thank you. In fact, the entire Latino community in this country should say gracias to you, because hopefully, whatever you can accomplish here in Elizabeth will make things better for our Latino hermanos and hermanas across the United States. People will begin to see us as more than just immigrants, more than simple Mexicans, more than wetbacks, to use another common derogatory term. We will be Americans, and not spics.*

Sanchez: *Thank you, Lupe, and I appreciate your kind words. But I do not do this for thanks, Lupe. I do what I do for one reason. I do it because it is right.*

Lupe smiled as the camera panned back to her. Eric could not tell if she was smiling in response to Sanchez's last comment, or whether she knew something about what he was going to say next.

Lupe: *Jesus, you said earlier that there were two reasons why you think the Prosecution is not handling the Goldberg case properly We already discussed the first. What is the second?*

"Shit, she knows something else," Eric said aloud, "what the hell else can he say?"

Sanchez: *Well, Lupe, as you are aware, this is not a normal case. The defendant, the person who hit and killed poor Jose Gomez, is named Wendi Goldberg. She is being represented in this case by a local attorney named Eric Goldberg.*

"Fuck." Eric buried his head in his hands and again slumped backward into the back of the couch. As bad as their little Hispanic *tango de amor* had been, now it was going to get more personal for him. Realistically, it was about to get more personal about him.

Sanchez: *Mr. Goldberg is well-known to the judges and other attorneys, me included, here in Elizabeth. He is also, because he does a large amount of criminal defense work, well-known to the local police. My belief, Lupe, is that the local police, once they realized that the driver of the car was their friend Mr. Goldberg's wife, purposefully did not do the tests that they were supposed to do and allowed her to leave the scene without even being properly questioned. People have told me that she left the scene with Mr. Goldberg almost immediately after the accident. I can tell you it was quick, because I arrived at the scene only shortly after the accident took place and both of them were already gone. You can draw your own conclusions, Lupe, but I think it is pretty obvious that they let her go because of her husband. Also, no tickets were issued at the scene. Only after I and Mrs. Gomez arrived and demanded justice did the police and prosecutor's office do anything. Why? Because they didn't want to do anything, even though a high school honors student was lying dead in the street, because he had been struck and killed by her car. A dead Latino boy lay in the street, dead. And they did not want to do anything about it. Instead, they wanted to protect the wife of their own, of their attorney friend. That's why. And that's wrong.*

"Fuck," Eric said again, "I can't fucking believe he is saying this."

Lupe: *Those are some pretty strong allegations, Mr. Sanchez. (Takes a deep breath, eyes wide open as if surprised by Sanchez's comments)*

Lupe Espinosa was, at best, an adequate news person. If not for her face and large chest, the chest that she had no problem showcasing for the camera, there was little doubt in Eric's mind that she would not be anywhere near a television studio. But even her minimal abilities as a news person were still far better than any talents that she may have possessed as an actress. She was feigning surprise, and was doing it poorly. Eric was sure of that. She knew exactly what Sanchez was going to say. This was all a big set-up.

Lupe: *(following a dramatic pause) So you're saying that the police and Prosecution have actually not been doing their jobs correctly because of their relationship with the driver's attorney? The man who is her ex-husband? That is also pretty shocking.*

Shocking to most, but it was clearly not to Lupe. She knew exactly what Sanchez was going to say, Eric was sure of that. Plus, there is no way that she could have processed all of that information in that short a period of time. The camera then cut back to Sanchez, who was smiling, smugly, as he leaned forward, elbows on the desk, and spoke in a lowered voice.

Sanchez: *Shocking? Sí, pero there is more.*

"*Pero?*" Eric said aloud. He was acutely aware of the fact that many of his Spanish clients, even when speaking to him in English, would pepper their sentences with Spanish words like "*pero*" instead of "but" and "*entonces*" instead of saying "then." He was used to it, but he assumed that most people watching the broadcast would not understand what he had said.

Lupe: *More? (another mock-horror gasp) ¿Que más?, I mean, what more could there be?*

Sanchez: *Well, Lupe, this one may be the most amazing one of all. It goes to the "old boy network," as they call it, which exists here in the New Jersey courts. First, let me correct myself. I earlier referred to Eric Goldberg as the defendant's husband, when he is actually her ex-husband. I don't think that it makes that much difference, but I want to be, as always, as correct as possible. What I can also tell you that Eric Goldberg, the defendant's ex-husband and attorney, graduated from Seton Hall Law School. And guess who else graduated from Seton Hall Law School, in the same class as Eric Goldberg?*

"Please no, please no," Eric muttered to the television, anticipating that Sanchez was going to say and imploring him, in vain, not to go any further.

Lupe: *Who?*

Eric saw the smirk on her face. Again, she knew the answer already. Eric also knew the answer. Most people watching the show, however, did not yet know the answer. They would momentarily, however, and Eric knew that a shitstorm would be kicked up once Sanchez said the name. He closed his eyes and waited.

Sanchez: *Michael Tompkins, Judge Michael Tompkins, graduated from law school in the same class as Eric Goldberg. The same Judge Michael Tompkins who Wendi Goldberg appeared before today, and the same Michael Tompkins who will probably be hearing the trial, should the case go that far, was a law school classmate of her attorney.*

Lupe: *You mean that the attorney and the judge went to Law School together? Wouldn't that be a, como se dice, I mean what do they call it, a conflict of interest?*

Sanchez: *It absolutely would be. And yet, there it is. No wonder the Latino community is worried. Think about this for a second, Lupe. You can't possibly make this up. It's like a novella. Think about it. A Latino boy is killed by a driver. He is killed by a white driver. The driver is represented in court by her ex-husband, who, as I have taken to saying, is acting in his ex-wife's defense. That attorney also just happens to be an old classmate of the Judge. I might expect this type of closeness back in Colombia, but not* *here. That's one of the reasons people leave our home countries and come to this country, because of the alleged fairness of our systems, including the judicial system. But in this case, we have reason to be concerned. This case will be anything but fair, because of the closeness of everyone involved.*

By now Eric was again up off of the couch, beer bottle in hand, and pacing in circles around the room. "I can't fucking believe this!" he yelled, throwing the bottle against the wall, where it smashed into little pieces, streaks of beer running down the wall to the carpet below. "That fucker! He knows that there are only six criminal judges in Union County and that three went to Seton Hall! This happens all the time! It's fucking New Jersey, for crying out loud. Half of the attorneys and judges here went to Seton Hall or Rutgers!" He was no longer watching the television, so he failed to see Lupe Espinosa wrap up the interview, and he also did not see her brief conversation with the news anchor thereafter, although if he had been watching he no doubt could have guessed what they were saying to each other.

The cell phone on the table began to buzz. Eric feared who was on the other line, but when he looked down, he did not recognize the number. It was a local number, though, so he answered, tentatively, as he watched the last drops of beer trickle down his den wall. He had barely croaked out a "hello" before the caller yelled into his ear.

"Eric, what the fuck is going on?"

He immediately recognized the voice. He had listened to that voice for three years in law school, at many alumni and Bar-related functions since his graduation, and had heard that voice numerous times both while the speaker was seated behind a large bench or in his office, most recently that afternoon. The voice was that of his old classmate, Michael Tompkins. Judge Michael Tompkins.

"Michael, I mean Judge," Eric replied, "is it fair to assume you were watching the news tonight?"

"You're damned fucking right I was watching the news tonight," Judge Tompkins yelled. "What kind of a fucking circus is this?"

"I had nothing to do with it, Michael. I think those two are somehow working together. No other person would have let him get away with that shit."

"I don't give a shit who's working together," Tompkins yelled, still irate. "That fucking scumbag and his whore reporter are putting my balls in a vice here. What the fuck am I supposed to do with this shit? I'm a fucking judge, god damn! I can't get involved in a pissing match with Jesus Sanchez!"

As frustrated as Eric was with the situation, he could tell that his old classmate was much more concerned about the baseless allegations being made by Jesus Sanchez, and understood that he, as a Judge, unquestionably had more to lose due to the misrepresentations. Both men knew that the comments were all contrived and erroneous. Sanchez's attempts at citing laws were incorrect, and his allegations regarding the judge were completely wrong. But both men also knew that the truth was irrelevant, at least as far as the public at large was concerned. Facts and truth meant nothing. Allegations of impropriety were what made for good television. And Sanchez's sensationalist comments about Eric, Wendi, and the Judge were just the kind of rumors that would, in many people's minds, no doubt transcend their malicious beginnings and be construed as fact, not fiction.

"I don't know what to tell you, Michael," Eric replied, struggling to maintain his calm demeanor so as not to inflame the Judge any further. "I would assume you should somehow respond to it. There must be some way that a Judge can respond to bullshit, so that nobody will think that it is true."

Eric's attempts at trying to calm his old friend, however, failed miserably. "I can't do that, you idiot." Tompkins bellowed, even more enraged. "I can't comment on his statements. It's beneath the position. I'm not just an attorney anymore, Eric, I'm a fucking Judge! If I respond to that little piece of shit, the Administrative Office of the Courts will have my ass." He paused, sighed audibly, and then, realizing that he was taking out his aggression on the wrong person, apologized in a softer tone. "I'm sorry for calling you an idiot, Eric; I'm just totally bent out of shape over this. Tomorrow I'm no doubt going to hear from Trenton, and there's nothing I can do about it. I am totally fucked because of that piece of garbage. I don't need this shit."

"Do you think they'll take you off of the case?" Eric asked. He was having trouble understanding everything that Judge Tompkins was saying, or yelling, because his phone kept making clicking noises, indicating that someone else was calling him on the cell phone. Someone was calling him incessantly.

"I don't think so. I mean, come on, I went to Seton Hall, as you are aware. If I had to recuse myself, remove myself from every trial where the attorney was from Seton Hall, I'd have a great deal of free time on my hands. And then, the same would be true for the Prosecutors. If I can't sit on a trial where the Prosecutor went to the Hall, based on a theory that I would be overly biased toward them, then realistically, they have no need for me on the bench. They would have to appoint only people who went to school outside of Jersey – and what kind of message would that be sending to the bar?"

"True. I guess you'll have to do nothing. But I keep hearing one of your fellow judges in my head. He told me years ago that if you remain silent when someone accuses you of something, you're making a mistake. If you don't respond at all, then your silence to the accusation is the same as admission. Assuming that's true, then you, or someone else on your behalf, will at least have to address it. If you can't, do you think that the higher-ups will say something?"

"I guess that I hope that they do just to cover my ass," Judge Tompkins said, wishfully. His demeanor remained calm as he continued to speak. "Maybe the Office of the Courts will issue some type of statement. But let me tell you something, Goldberg, I am not looking forward to going to Elizabeth tomorrow. And I'm blaming you. You should have taken that fucking deal today, you asshole. I told you to take it. Look at the crap you've allowed them to stir up."

"Judge, I understand completely," Eric replied, in an apologetic tone. "Believe me, I wish that it hadn't happened either. But," he added, "we both know that even if we had done some type of deal today, no matter what type of deal, you know that they still would be talking about us this way, you included. These two people are making my entire life into a circus."

"Speaking of life and circus …"

"No, Michael, Wendi and I are not back together," Eric said, anticipating the Judge's question. "You can't believe everything you hear on the news, you know."

Eric could hear Tompkins laugh through the phone. He immediately knew that he had guessed correctly.

"That's true, Eric," the Judge said, still laughing, "You certainly can't. Now let me go, because I need to muster all of my judicial talents for my toughest task, trying to calm down my wife. I would suggest that you call your ex-wife and do the same, because I wouldn't want to be in your shoes when she finds out about these allegations."

"Well," Eric said, "that's true. Have you heard the clicking sounds during this conversation? She's only tried to call me four times over the past few minutes. I'd better deal with it, although I am certainly not looking forward to it. Night, Judge."

"Good night, Counselor. Good luck."

Eric heard the phone disconnect and sighed. He could not talk to Wendi immediately and instead decided to have another beer to calm him down a little. He put the phone down on the table and walked to the kitchen. The phone began to vibrate and dance on the table almost immediately after he left the room. He knew it was her. He did not rush back to answer.

While reaching into the refrigerator to grab his next drink, he spied a small box which contained two slices of pizza, the leftovers of dinner three nights ago. He wondered if the pizza was still good to eat, and decided that it did not matter. He was suddenly hungry, and placed the slices on a paper plate and threw them into the microwave. Two minutes later he was sitting at his kitchen table, eating reheated pizza and drinking his third beer of the evening. As he ate, he pored over that day's newspaper, which sent his spirits even further down as he read of the continuing failures of the Yankees, as well as the winning streaks being put together by two of the team's division rivals. There was still much baseball to play, but the team was falling further and further out of playoff contention. Eric read the players' quotes, the commentary which included cliché after cliché about playing one day at a time and expressing optimism for a good result, even in the face of seemingly insurmountable odds. He leaned back and took a long swig of beer. "Are we any different?" he asked, aloud. "Is my optimism about the case no different from these ballplayers?"

He hoped not.

The phone began to vibrate again, the noise of its movement echoing off of the glass table. Eric could hear it from his seat in the kitchen. He knew that he had to call Wendi. More importantly, however, he knew that he had to keep convincing Wendi to be optimistic. He had to convince her to remain optimistic even if, deep down, he was beginning to believe that this optimism was misplaced.

Chapter XVII – Protection For Judge Tompkins

NOTICE FROM ADMINISTRATIVE OFFICE OF THE COURTS

Last night, a local news broadcast contained a taped interview with a member of the New Jersey bar. During that interview, certain unfounded accusations were leveled against the Honorable Michael Tompkins with respect to his handling of an ongoing matter in the Union County vicinage. Such accusations, especially when made without any basis, are improper and are contrary to that counsel's responsibilities as a member of the bar. This office, as a result of these accusations, is forced to release this notice in support of Judge Tompkins, and clarifying that Judge Tompkins' conduct with respect to this matter has not, in any way, created an appearance of impropriety that had the potential to weaken public confidence in the integrity and impartiality of the judiciary.

Judge Tompkins has been instructed by this office to remain silent on this issue, as it would be equally improper for a sitting member of the judiciary to engage in any such conversation regarding an attorney admitted to practice law in this state. Discussions between the Judiciary and counsel, especially when those conversations are based on or emanate from baseless and clearly politically-motivated origins, cannot and should not be carried out in any public forum.

Judge Tompkins is a valued member of the judiciary and the Administrative Office of the Courts is satisfied that his handling of the subject matter has been, and will continue to be, exemplary.

Eric recognized the language at the end of the first paragraph – he had read a similar version in the newspapers when a lawsuit was filed against a pair of Judges. He was pleased to see that the Administrative Office was backing Judge Tompkins, and hoped that the office's swift and unequivocal rebuke of Sanchez's allegations would cause Sanchez to think twice before making up any such false statements in the future, including against him personally. At the same time, however, he knew that Sanchez would be unable to move his subversive political and personal agendas forward without such fiery rhetoric, so he realized that more allegations would be on the horizon. All that he could do was ignore Sanchez and his people as best as possible, and go about his business of representing Wendi, and his other clients, to the best of his abilities.

Chapter XVIII – Ms. Johnson, I Presume?

The next week, Eric was appearing in Judge Tompkins' courtroom on behalf of a new client, a teenager who was accused of assaulting a fellow student at Westfield High School. He met with his client and the youth's mother in the hallway, and explained that day's process to the nervous pair. The boy was sweating profusely, his hair matted to his scalp. The mother tried in vain to calm her son, and she seemed on the verge of tears as the trio stood and walked into the courtroom. As he entered the room, Eric saw several familiar faces, including a certain young Prosecutor who was seated at the counsel table, thumbing through her files.

He walked up behind the Prosecutor's table and leaned down behind the woman seated in the rickety chair, whispering, almost inaudibly, "Ms. Johnson, I presume?"

"Just a second," she replied, clearly unaware of who was addressing her. "I need to finish something and then I will be right with you."

"Do I really have to wait," Eric said, quietly, "I would have thought that you could take a break and talk to me. I'm world famous, you know."

Amanda Johnson stopped reading the file in her hands, and slowly placed it onto the table. "Oh, the world famous Mr. Goldberg, I presume," she said, without turning. "I didn't know that you were going to be here today. To what do I owe this surprise?"

Eric immediately launched into flirtation mode, which, in reality, was his most comfortable manner of dealing with people, especially in dealing with attractive young

171

women. "Sorry to disappoint you, Madame Prosecutor," he said, softly, his mouth a scant few inches from the back of her ponytail so Amanda could feel his breath on the nape of her neck, "but I'm not here to see you."

"You're not?" she replied, coyly, clearly playing along, "how disappointing. But tell me, Mr. Goldberg, if you are not here to see me, then what are you doing whispering in my ear, counselor? I don't see you breathing on the other Prosecutors' necks."

"Damn," he thought, "I am busted." He had to think of something else to say. Luckily, he had an ace hidden up his sleeve. "Well, Ms. Johnson, I'm still waiting for my discovery, you know. We had discussed it over a week ago, if you recall. None of the other Assistant Prosecutors here owe me anything. Believe me, if Mr. Howard over there owed me paperwork, I would be breathing down his neck much harder than I am doing to you now." He paused and then spoke in a softer voice. "And you should thank me, you know. I didn't want to embarrass you by saying, out loud," he lowered his voice even more, "that you're not doing your job properly."

"Not doing my job?" she cried, causing Eric to recoil. She stood and faced Eric, crossing her arms in front of her chest. "No, that just won't do. We can't have anyone saying that I'm not doing my job right. No," she added, shaking her head from side to side, "we can't have that. I will tell you what," she said, her eyes looking up and down and her voice taking on a more friendly tone, "in order to show that I am, in fact, doing my job properly, I will personally hand-deliver the paperwork after work today. Will that be acceptable to you?"

"Y-y-yes," Eric stammered, surprised by her offer and also for what he perceived to be her efforts at checking him out. "That will be fine. My last appointment is at 4:30 and I figure I should be done by five or so, but I will stick around to wait for you."

"Then it's settled. I will be by later. I just don't know when for sure," she said, brushing her hair away from her face with her left hand as her right hand fiddled with the buttons on her blouse. "I do have a retirement thing after work for one of the secretaries here in the department that I have to go to, so I assume that should be to you by six or so. Unless, of course," she said, smiling, "I drink a bit and then I might be there a little later. If that happens, however," she added, reaching out with her right hand and touching his arm lightly, "then it will certainly be more interesting."

Eric stood, stunned at the last comment. He was unsure of how to respond to her last statement, not wanting to make too much of it but at the same time not wanting to make it seem like he did not hear what was unquestionably a flirtatious come-on. "I like interesting," he finally said, tentatively, "so let's see how it goes later." Amanda smiled in response, at which time Eric tried to think of something witty to add, but then realized that he should quit while he was ahead. He simply returned Amanda's smile, then turned and returned to the row of benches to sit down with his client and the boy's concerned mother. He sat alongside his client, opened the boy's file and read his notes, presumably to prepare for speaking with Steve Howard, the Prosecutor handling the boy's case. Instead of reading, however, he thought of Amanda Johnson, and again smiled.

The other Prosecutor arrived ten minutes later, and Eric pounced on him in an effort to ensure that his case would be resolved quickly. As this was the young man's first offense, the Prosecutor informed Eric that the charge against his client was going to be downgraded to a disorderly person's offense, and would be sent back to the Westfield Municipal Court for disposition rather than being handled at the County level. This meant that the case would not be addressed that day, and that Eric and the client would receive any future notices to appear from the Westfield Municipal Court, where the charges and, therefore, the potential penalties, were lesser than if the case was going to be handled by the Union County Prosecutor's office. Eric thanked him and looked to his right, where Amanda Johnson stood, rifling through her own files for that day.

She must have sensed his presence, because she looked up almost immediately to catch him staring at her. "You see, Ms. Johnson," Eric said, when he saw her eyes lift and look into his eyes, "this is how it's done."

"Unless that young kid killed someone, Mr. Goldberg," she responded with a lilt in her voice, "then don't even bother talking to me." She looked in Steve Howard's direction and smiled. "It is clear that you are trying to accomplish the proverbial comparison of apples to oranges, Mr. Goldberg," she added, "but let me explain something to you. I don't work that way."

Eric laughed. It was time for him to engage in a little more foreplay with the young, attractive, Assistant Prosecutor. "Touché, Madame Prosecutor," he said, and walked closer to her.

Amanda Johnson could not be bothered with any such repartee at that moment, not when she had to deal with a courtroom full of defendants and attorneys, all of whom wanted a piece of her time. At the same time, however, she could not forego another chance at flirting with Eric. "I am busy, sir," she said, stopping him in his tracks and so as not to annoy the other attorneys patiently waiting to speak to her about their clients' cases. Then she leaned closer to him and whispered, "But don't worry, I will see you tonight."

****

Eric's 4:30 appointment arrived 15 minutes late, and was still in the office with Eric at 5:15 when Fatima went home for the day. The retainer agreement for the man's divorce case was officially signed at 5:20, and the men spoke for 25 additional minutes, with Eric taking notes on his background, personal information, and reasons for the divorce, before the new client left. It was now 5:45. Eric had approximately 15 minutes until Amanda Johnson was expected to arrive. Wanting to rid himself of the day's grime and clean himself up, he grabbed the toothbrush from the top drawer of his desk and walked down the hallway to the bathroom to brush his teeth and wash his face. While walking back from the bathroom, he noticed that the light was on in Jonathan Grant's office. Opening the door, he called out to his old friend.

"Come on in, Eric," Jon replied, "I am just cleaning up some shit before I leave for the night. What are you still doing here?"

"Seriously?" asked Eric, "it's only 5:45. You know that I never leave here before 6:30."

"That's it?" Jon said, looking at the clock on the wall. "I thought it was later. Amazing how time seems to drag when you're not having fun, wouldn't you say?" He sat down and shuffled some papers into a pile. "This is how I clean now. What's up with you?"

Eric smiled. "Let me ask you a question, Jon."

Grant dropped the papers from his hand. "I don't like the sound of this. Whenever you start with that, I know that it's not going to be good." He paused, and looked at Eric, who was now smiling broadly. "What is it this time? It's not going to get you into trouble, is it?"

"Don't know," Eric replied. "You do much more criminal stuff than me. You're in Elizabeth pretty much every week, right? What do you know about a Prosecutor named Amanda Johnson?"

Jon laughed. "Amanda Johnson? She's a young one. I hear good things about her. She knows her way around a courtroom and according to my friend who works with her in the office there have been some rumors that she also knows her way around the bedroom, if you know what I mean."

"Yeah, I think I do," Eric answered, "let's face it, it's not like you're subtle."

"I've heard that she got her job because of some family connection. Her father was a cop, you know, who was shot in the line of duty. Anyway, if I recall correctly, her mom was shacking up with one of the local politicos and that's who got her the gig with the Prosecutor. From what I hear, she's popular with the older guys in the office." He paused, noticing that Eric was now smiling. "Should I even ask why you are asking?" Grant asked, as his right eyebrow arched.

"She's the Prosecutor on Wendi's case," Eric said, as Grant's eyes widened. "But that's not why I am asking." He paused and looked over his shoulder to make sure that there was nobody else in the office, or at least nobody else who could hear the conversation between him and Grant. "Listen to this, Jon. I was busting her about getting me the discovery on Wendi's case when I was in court today, and she told me that she would bring me the discovery tonight."

"Tonight?" Jon asked, his eyes widening until they reached an almost impossible size, "What do you mean she is going to bring you discovery tonight?"

"Exactly what it sounds like," replied Eric. "We were talking in court today and she told me that she would come to the office tonight and bring me the discovery for Wendi's case. Isn't that strange? Or am I over thinking this one?"

Jon stared at Eric for a minute before responding. "Very strange," he said. "But I really don't think it is possible to over think this one, because I've never had a beautiful young Prosecutor who seems to like older guys offer to hand-deliver paperwork to my office after normal business hours. What time is she supposed to be here?"

"She said about 6:00. That gives me five minutes to get there. And not that anything is going to happen between us, of course, but please tell me something, is there a rule against something happening between me and a Prosecutor? You know the ethics rules better than I do."

"Oh my God, Eric," Jon exclaimed, "That's really not saying very much. I think it is safe to say that everyone knows the ethics rules better than you do. Or at least everyone knows them enough to follow them, everyone, that is, except for you. And to use the phrase 'of course' when discussing anything that involves you, my friend, is a tremendous leap of faith. We both know that."

"You're a funny guy, you know that?" Eric replied. "Let's just play Devil's Advocate for a minute. Tell me, is there an actual rule against being involved with the Prosecutor in the rules of professional conduct, or is it just common sense?"

"You've got to be kidding me," Grant said, chuckling to himself. "Do you even listen to yourself sometimes? Your question to me, if I understand it, is whether there is a rule against you and an Assistant Prosecutor, on a case that you are handling, having an affair?" He paused, waiting for an answer to his seemingly rhetorical question. When he did not receive any response, he continued. "Yes, there is, you asshole. And wait, let's make this even better. Is there a rule against having an affair with the Prosecutor when your client is your ex-wife? I would assume that would be a definitive fuck yes, as if you even needed a rule to know that such an affair could only get you into deep trouble."

"I thought so," Eric said, shaking his head sadly. "But now let me ask you this question. Have you seen her? She's really hot."

"I can't believe that we are even having this conversation, Eric. Yes, I have seen her. She is attractive, very attractive. She is also very, very young." He paused and looked Eric in the eyes. "What is she, about five years older than Jason? Come on, Eric, you're not in your 20's anymore."

"I know, I know," Eric said. "But it never hurts to imagine what could be. You can't get in trouble with the ethics committee for your thoughts, can you?"

"To tell you the truth, I don't want to find out." Grant said, shaking his head in disbelief at the fact that he was even engaged in this conversation. "Now I am going to leave for the night so I don't get caught up in any of your adventures. I don't want to be here and be a pseudo-accessory to your violation of the ethics rules. I thought you got that out of your system last year, but, you know, I've been wrong before." He looked down at the clock in the bottom corner of his computer screen. "It's 6:00 now. Go back to your office, get your paperwork, and send young Amanda on her way. Don't do anything stupid."

"You know something, you take all the fun out of it, Grant. I don't even know why I come to talk to you," Eric said.

"Well, let's see," Jon answered as he gathered up a handful of papers and placed them into his briefcase to take home for the evening, "Let's start with the fact that you're a fuck-up, and that, just last year, my nephew and I saved your ass in Brazil. But more importantly, Eric, and I can't stress this enough, I am your moral compass and, not surprisingly, one of the only people on this earth who will listen to your shit. Is that good enough for you?"

"You're my moral compass? That's pretty sad, but I guess that you're right," Eric replied, sheepishly. "That's why I come to you. And by the way, Jon, I'm not a complete moron. I know you're right, you stupid fuck. I just like messing with you."

"Then go, get out of here," Grant said. "I am going home to my normal, boring life." He wagged his right index finger at Eric in an accusatory manner. "Don't be stupid. You may say that you're just messing with me, but something in those eyes of yours tells me different. Do yourself a favor, Eric. Say hello, get your paperwork, and then say goodbye and send her home or out to play with the other kids. Just make something up so you can get her the hell out of there before you do something that you're either going to regret or that is going to get you into a heap of fucking trouble. Tell her you need to go home for the dog or something like that."

"OK, Jon. I have heard you, and I understand completely what you're saying. Have a good night and, seriously, don't worry about me," Eric added, "I won't do anything stupid. At least not until the case is over." He stood and walked toward the door. Turning before he exited the office, he added, laughing, "but once the case is done, all bets are off."

Jonathan Grant shrugged his shoulders, knowingly, and shook his head. He knew that no matter what Eric said to him, the night was going to lead to trouble for his friend.

Chapter XIX – The Chair

Eric noticed that the door to his office was closed, even though he remembered leaving it slightly ajar when he left for the bathroom 15 minutes earlier. That meant that someone was in there, and he suspected that his expected visitor had arrived early. He quietly opened the door and walked past Fatima's desk to his office room, where he spied the rear of his high-backed chair facing the doorway. A bare arm extended from behind the chair, and its hand picked up papers from the folder labeled "Wendi Goldberg".

Eric loudly cleared his throat, causing the arm to jump as the person in the chair was startled by the sudden noise. "I don't think you should be looking at those papers, you know. I'm sure that there is some rule against you looking at them," he said to the woman in the chair. All that he could see was the top of her head, topped with lightly-colored hair, and her bare left arm, which still clutched some of the file's contents.

"Why can't I look at the papers?" the woman asked, her voice taking on a seductive tone. Eric was shocked at the sound of the woman's voice. It was not the voice of Amanda Johnson, the voice that had whispered to him earlier that day. Rather, the voice that came from the chair was a voice that he had heard on an almost daily basis for the past two and a half decades.

"Wendi?" he cried. "What are you doing here?"

Wendi swung the chair around. She was clad only in a black lace bra and panties, and her hair was dyed a dirty blonde color instead of its usual brown. "I am looking at my file, silly. And I hate to even ask this question, but who did you think I was?" She ran her right hand through her hair, extending a lock as if to show off its new, bottle-provided brightness. "Did my new hair color throw you off?"

Eric's mind was racing. Amanda could be arriving any second. Certainly she could not find Wendi there. That would be a real problem for him. More importantly, Wendi could not know that Amanda was coming by that evening. She was jealous enough in the courtroom. Even though they weren't married anymore, he knew that it would be cataclysmic for Wendi to even think that anything was going on with Amanda Johnson. "Honestly, I didn't know," he lied, "I went out to the bathroom, stopped at Jon's office, and then came back to find you here. I didn't expect anyone to be here, and I had no idea that it was you because of your dyed hair." He paused. "Don't forget, all that I could see was the top of your head, with the different-colored hair, and one arm. It's not like I could pick you out of a lineup based on your arm, you know."

"You were at Jon's? How is he?" Wendi asked, ignoring his comment about why he did not recognize her, and as she twirled her newly-dyed hair with her left hand. "I haven't seen him in years."

Eric could not help but stare at his wife's almost-naked body, the body which he had not seen for almost a couple of years now and the body which clearly had shed a great deal of weight since he last saw it undressed. After a prolonged pause, he again cleared his throat and looked away. He needed to get rid of her, and quickly. Not just because of Amanda, but also because nothing could happen between he and Wendi. Crossing the line with any client, as he had learned all too well the previous year, was a violation of ethics requirements and, of course, simply wrong. Crossing the line with her, his ex-wife, as a client, he realized, could be an even worse idea than his illicit thoughts about Amanda and could lead to any variety of long-term misconceptions between them. "Wendi," he said softly and deliberately, "you can't do this. You have to leave."

"What do you mean, Eric?" she asked in a seductive tone, as she released her grip on her hair and ran her left hand up and down the inside of her right arm. "I don't *have* to do anything." She paused. "I am here because I *want* to do something." She reached out and took Eric's belt buckle in her hand.

Eric pulled her hand away from his buckle and stepped backward. "No," he said, "you don't want to do this. No good can come from this. You need to go home now."

Wendi's face hardened. "I *need* to go home now? Is that what you just said to me?" Her fists clenched and her face reddened as she stood, the curves of her legs accentuated by her heels. "I can't believe this shit. How dare you tell me what to do? I am not your property." She moved closer to Eric, and he could detect a slight smell of alcohol as she snorted in his direction. She raised her hand to slap him, but stopped in mid-motion when he raised his hand to catch it. "I can't win with you, Eric. You get mad at me when I question what you say in court, and now you get mad at me when I am trying to be nice." She moved both arms behind her and began to unhook her bra when Eric again raised his hand and waved it for her to stop.

"You're not my property," Eric answered, "but nor are you my wife, and nor are you my girlfriend or someone who should be getting undressed here in the office." He lowered his hand and reached down to retrieve Wendi's clothes. "I smell the liquor on your breath, Wendi, and trust me, you don't want to do this," he added, as he handed her a pair of jeans and blouse that were sitting, folded, on a chair in his office. "You need to go home, so you don't regret this tomorrow." He looked at her and pointed to the door, so that she knew that he was serious. "Are you OK to drive or should I call you a cab?"

Wendi looked away as she pulled her blouse over her shoulders and began to fiddle with its buttons. "I am fine," she said, sheepishly. "To tell you the truth, I ... I just don't know ... I don't even really know what I am even doing here."

"Don't ask me," Eric answered, "I can't figure it out."

Wendi sat back in Eric's chair as she slid her well-toned legs into her jeans. "I think," She said, "I think that I was just a little jealous of that woman in court the other day. I guess that's what it is. I mean, look at me. Look at my hair. What was I thinking dying it?" She took a lock of her hair in her left hand and shook her head slowly as she pulled her hand in front of her face so that she could see her newly-lightened tresses. "You know, Eric, I know that we're not together," she added, as her eyes moistened, "but it still bothers me to see you with someone else, which I know sounds really ironic after what I did. I need to get over that." A tear fell down her left cheek.

Eric paused. At least Wendi was correct about one thing. She had no right to be jealous of Eric and Amanda, or, quite frankly, to be jealous of Eric and anyone else. He was never unfaithful to her when they were married. Rather, she had cheated on him. She cheated on him with someone whom he also trusted, which to him was an even more severe betrayal than a simple affair or one-night stand with someone unfamiliar to him. She could not now plead jealousy, or try to make him feel guilty, if he moved on with his life.

But he also knew that this was not the time to pick a new fight with Wendi, and his best move was simply to move her along so she could go home and he could wait for Amanda to arrive. "I am not with her, Wendi," he said, calmly, handing her a tissue from a box on his desk. "And you shouldn't be jealous of anyone, whether now or in the future. It's not a productive use of your time."

"I know," Wendi said, shaking her head. "I know that I shouldn't be jealous, and know that I have no right to be jealous of anyone, whether that young girl or anyone else. I don't even know what I am thinking sometimes anymore." She looked down at the arms of the chair, slowly stroking one its arms with her left hand, and then looked back up at Eric. "I do have one question, though, even if it does sound a little jealous," she said, "this is where it happened, right?"

"It?" Eric asked, quizzically. "What do you mean, it?"

"You know exactly what I mean," Wendi said, pulling her hand from the chair, "this is where that Brazilian woman and you had sex, right? It was in your chair."

Now it was Eric's face which began to redden, as it occurred to him that, other than the other day, Wendi had not been in the office, and therefore in the presence of the chair since the incident with Bianca Rodrigues took place a year earlier. "How … how?" he stammered, "how did you know about what happened with her? Who told you?"

Wendi started to walk toward the door, brushing Eric with her left hand as she passed him. "Just because I never mentioned it doesn't mean that I don't know what happened with her, stupid." She paused and turned back toward Eric, her mood turning sour. She never was a happy drunk, Eric thought. "You know what, stupid?" she added, "I think this is very similar to what happened in court. You know, the fact that 'everyone,' as you said, knows about the affair between me and Doug. I would venture a guess that everyone also knows about you and her." She paused, and looked back at the chair again. "In fact," she continued, "I know everything about her, what was her name again? Oh yeah, Bianca. I know everything. I know about the blow job in the chair. I know about how you went to Brazil."

Eric slumped in that very chair, the chair where Bianca had performed oral sex on him the year before, and ran his hand through his finely-cropped hair. "Wow," he said, almost absentmindedly. "I guess I never thought that you knew about what happened. In fact, for some reason it never even occurred to me. Why, I don't know. Guess I was just being stupid."

"Stupid?" Wendi asked. "More like ridiculous. The woman accused you, my ex-husband, of killing her husband and you went to Brazil to find her. Somehow, through some fucking miracle, you did find her and got her to confess that she was lying. Is that about right?" Her eyes narrowed. "Do you really think that nobody was going to tell me? The police, the goddamned Newark police, came to my house looking for information about where you might be after you disappeared. They came to me looking for you. How much of a joke is that? And then, to add insult to injury, several other people told me all about it. You think this is a secret? Guess again," she added, chuckling. She walked toward the door, but the 'mean drunk' part of her was not yet done. "You know something," Eric, she said, running her hands down the sides of her

183

chest, "you could have had this again tonight. You could have had the new, improved version of me. And you blew it. Guess I will just go home."

"Yes, please," Eric said, "go home."

"Oh, that's right," she said, as icily as possible. "As usual, Eric, get back to work. It's what you do best anyway," Wendi mocked, "and, Eric," she added as she now ran her right hand up and down the back of her thigh, "remember that you could have had this tonight," she repeated. She laughed again and walked out the door, closing it behind her. Eric remained slumped in his chair, and leaned forward, laying his head on his desk.

Eric sat, with his head on his desk, for the next five minutes. He did not move until he heard the door open again. "Oh shit," he thought, "what does she want now?" He stood and walked into the next room, ready to withstand another barrage of commentary from Wendi.

For the second time that night, however, he was wrong about the identity of the person in his office.

Chapter XX – Amanda Johnson Delivers Paperwork

Amanda Johnson stood in the doorway. She wore the same outfit that she had worn in court earlier that day, a navy blue suit with a skirt that reached down to the tops of her knees, and an off-white blouse with navy buttons. Eric guessed that her heels were at least four inches high, and her hair, unleashed from the ponytail which confined it earlier, was loose, flowing over the shoulders of her suit jacket. In her left hand was a brown folder, seemingly stuffed with papers. "Mr. Goldberg, I presume," she said, stretching her left arm and pushing the folder forward. "I have a delivery for you from the Union County Prosecutor's Office." Her words were slightly slurred. "I think that it's some kind of paperwork," she added, laughing, "I mean, the folder has the name 'Wendi Goldberg' on it, so it's probably about someone named Wendi Goldberg. Hey, wait a minute," she said, laughing, "this is the same last name as yours. What a coincidence, wouldn't you say?"

"Ms. Johnson," Eric replied, choosing to ignore the last sentence in an attempt to avoid discussing his ex-wife, "I had completely forgotten that you were coming by tonight." He looked at her, running his eyes down her body, perhaps for a little too long. "This is indeed a pleasant surprise." He extended his arm and beckoned for her to enter the office and hand him the folder.

"Forgot?" she asked, quietly. "For some reason, Mr. Goldberg," she said, handing him the folder and touching her hand to his *a la* Hannibal Lecter and Clarice Starling from *"Silence of the Lambs"*, "I sincerely doubt that you forgot that I was coming over." She looked around the office, noting that nobody else was present. Peeking quickly into his room she noted that his desk was devoid of any strewn paperwork other than a folder which seemed to bear the same name as the one that she was delivering, indicating that he was not actively engaged in any work prior to her arrival. "Why else would you be here this late?"

Eric laughed. "Late? Ms. Johnson, I am not a government employee. I often work into the night." He looked down at her legs. Much like his ex-wife earlier, her heels accentuated the curves of her lower legs. He thought that he remembered her wearing pantyhose earlier in the day, but now her legs were clearly bare. "The bigger question is, what are you doing here so late?"

She placed her hands on her hips in mock anger. "So late? Government employee? I take great offense to that comment, Mr. Goldberg. In fact," she slurred, "I will have you know, sir, that I often work late." She paused and lowered her voice to a whisper, "that's why I have no personal life, you know. All work and no play, blah, blah, blah." She took a step closer to Eric and adopted a more serious, sober tone. "As for the time now, I know that I said about six o'clock and I am pretty close, no?" She searched in vain for a clock, to confirm the actual time. "I am sorry for being here late, Eric, but I was at a retirement party, like I told you, and it ran longer than I expected. I tried to leave, but it would have been bad politically so I had to stick around." She reached out for his arm and pulled him into a weak embrace. "Do you forgive me?"

Eric smelled alcohol on her breath. It was the second time tonight. "Déjà vu," he thought to himself, but this time he did not intend to shoo the woman away so quickly, even though that would have been the action taken by a smart man. "Of course I do," Eric replied, pulling her closer to him. "The important thing is that you are here now. It's not often that I have discovery for a case delivered personally, and I can tell you unequivocally that I have never had such an attractive courier deliver any paperwork here."

Amanda smiled in response to his comment, and then kissed him gently on the cheek to further show her appreciation for his recognition of her beauty. After she kissed him, she then brought her head back and thanked him for his kind comment. Leaning her head close to Eric's afterward, she whispered in his ear. "I want to see the chair, Eric. Is it in that room?"

Eric pulled back, with a surprised look on his face. "The chair? What do you mean?" he asked. His sense of déjà vu was again returning.

"The chair," she repeated, cryptically. She searched Eric's face for some sign of understanding, but saw none. "Come on, Eric, you know, where it happened," she added, shaking him slightly in an attempt to jar his memory; but there was still no discernible reaction from Eric. This required her to expound further on her request. "Eric, listen to me carefully," she said, sternly, the smell of alcohol continuing to emanate from between her lips, "because you know exactly what I am talking about. I want to see the chair where it happened." She paused. "And so there is no confusion with this question, by 'it' I mean the thing with the Brazilian woman."

Now Eric could not maintain his poker face any longer. For the second time that evening he was forced to confront that dark chapter from his personal history, and for the second time that evening he was genuinely surprised that his inquisitor even knew about the existence of Bianca Rodrigues and what had transpired between Eric and Bianca. "Dare I even ask how you know about that?"

"Well," Amanda answered, again drawing her face close to Eric's, "when the Judge referred to you as 'famous' I was intrigued." She giggled. "To be honest, it made you more than a little enticing, you know, sexy, because I have never heard him use that word to describe anyone, so I asked around the office." Her breath was warm on his cheek as she spoke, and he could feel her chest brushing up against his arm. He was growing ever excited.

"And what were you told?" he asked, breathlessly.

"I was told that you had gotten involved with one of your clients," Amanda said, pulling him even closer so that her mouth was mere inches from his. "I was told by a couple of the guys that you had sex with this crazy woman in your chair, well, that you were seduced by her, and then she told the police that you killed her husband even though she had done it."

"Is that it?"

"No," she said, again in a whisper. "After she told the police that you killed her husband, she apparently went to Brazil, where she was from, to escape the law and to collect insurance money. Then you followed her to Brazil and somehow, although this part is a little fuzzy, not only found her, but even got her to confess to the crime so that you were cleared of any culpability. Like a Prosecutor."

Eric sighed, surprised at the recitation and at the breadth of knowledge possessed by Amanda. Trying to avoid truly discussing the matter, he said, "very interesting, but that sounds like a strangely implausible story, Ms. Johnson, wouldn't you say?"

Amanda looked at Eric and pursed her lips. "That does sound very strange, Mr. Goldberg. But it is so strange that it must be true, and sexy." She paused and smiled. "I mean, think about it. Especially the part about you going to Brazil, finding her, and getting her to confess. Nobody could make that up, I would think. It's just too perfect." She again grabbed him in an embrace. "You're kind of an urban legend around the office, you know. Well, you are a legend to anyone who knows the story. You're the guy who got blown in his office. You're the guy who went to Brazil and somehow forced the slut to confess. It's quite an aphrodisiac, at least I think so." She leaned in and again kissed him on the cheek. "Do you think so?"

The stirrings in his pants belied the fact that Eric agreed. He pulled his crotch away from her so that she would not feel its bulge, and said "no, not really. To be honest, it was an incident that I would rather forget. Trust me, being forced to defend myself like an animal was not fun."

"Well, you can tell me all about it," Amanda answered, "in a minute. I must use the ladies' room." She looked at the door. "It's in the hallway, right? I will be right back." She lowered her right hand and lightly brushed it over the still-growing bulge in his pants. "Don't miss me too much," she said, chuckling. She turned and walked out of the office door, the clicking of her heels echoing through the hallway.

188

Eric went to his desk and sat in the chair where Bianca Rodrigues had, apparently famously, seduced him a year earlier. He leaned back and muttered, to nobody in particular, "What a strange fucking night this has been. What the hell is going to happen next?"

It would not take long for him to find out. A scant few minutes later, He heard the outer door office open and close, and the clicking of Amanda Johnson's heels were joined by another familiar sound, of the dead bolt on the door turning. Eric did not move from his chair. Soon thereafter, he saw the bottom half of Amanda's right leg, bare except for the shoe still wrapped around her foot, thrust through the doorway. "Are you in there, Eric?" she called out. "Are you actually sitting in the chair?" The top half of her leg came into his view. To his surprise, it was as bare as the lower leg. Amanda had removed her skirt, and as she walked into the room, he could see that she had also removed her jacket. She stood in the doorway, hands on her hips, clad in her white blouse, a blouse which extended low enough in front to cover her crotch but which was cut high enough on the sides to expose the black straps of her thong. The top three buttons of her blouse were undone, and the top of her black lace bra peeked out from the pale fabric. She lifted her hands in an upward motion, as if to beckon for a response.

Eric took in the sight of Amanda Johnson standing in his doorway, her perfectly-formed body bathed in light from the adjoining room. "Uh, yes," he stammered, "I am sitting in my chair."

"That's not what I asked you," she cooed. "I didn't ask if you were in your chair, counselor, I asked if you were in *the* chair."

"If you want to be technical, I guess yes," he said, quietly, "this is the chair."

"So this is the chair where you had sex with a client in clear violation of the attorney ethics rules. Tsk, tsk, counselor," Amanda said, in a scolding manner. "What a bad boy you were," she added as she walked closer. "But let me ask you something else."

"Uh, OK."

189

Amanda lowered her voice to a whisper. "Other than her, has there been anyone else?"

"What do you mean?"

"You know exactly what I mean, Eric. Did you have sex with anyone else in the chair? You know, maybe with your secretary, or another client?"

Eric gulped. He was shocked by Amanda's moxie. "No, the answer is no," he said.

"Really?" she asked, as she moved closer still. She walked around the side of the desk so she was standing to his left, in exactly the same place where Bianca Rodriguez had stood a year earlier. Leaning forward so that Eric could see completely down her open blouse, she again whispered, "how about your wife, Eric? I mean your ex-wife? You know, Wendi. The woman whose file is sitting there on top of your desk. Did you ever have sex in your office with the woman that I am prosecuting?"

Moxie did not even begin to describe her, Eric thought to himself. He intended to answer, "No, I never had sex with my wife in the office, to answer your question." But he said nothing. He did not mention the fact that she had been there just minutes before, and had been sitting half-dressed, in very similar lingerie, in the very chair where he now sat. No words were forthcoming. He merely lowered his head and shook it from side to side.

"Too bad," she said, "how cool would it have been for me to fuck you in the exact chair where you had fucked a defendant that I am prosecuting?" She again lowered her voice to a whisper. "I don't know for sure, but I have to think that it would be a first-time event, an unprecedented lay. It would be the ultimate slap in her face, don't you think?"

"Well," he said, as nervous sweat began to form on his forehead, "I guess that it would be, but since I would never tell her, or anyone else, if that was to happen I don't think so." He paused, and again studied her taut, young body. Feelings of guilt

190

were beginning to overwhelm him, as well as the knowledge that any such relations with the Prosecutor would run completely afoul of any ethics rules.

"You don't think so? Well, Eric," she said, undoing another button on her blouse and pulling the blouse slightly upward to expose the front of her black, lace thong, "I'm not sure I know that that means. So, pray tell, what do you think? What are you thinking now?"

He started to answer, and then saw that she was staring at his crotch, his erection evident within his pants. He crossed his legs and turned to the side to block her vision of his manhood, and decided, at that moment, to forego his urges for what he believed to be the more proper action. "Well, since you asked, what I am thinking, Amanda, is that despite the fact that you are a gorgeous young woman and that any man would be lucky to have you, that this is wrong." He paused and then gazed again at her, fearful that the remainder of his answer would result in her leaving the office, never to return again. He wanted to make sure that he would remember her body. "Surely there is some rule against us being here together, doing this, being here now."

Amanda gasped and stood upright. She crossed her arms in front of her chest, pulling the fabric of the blouse up again, this time so high that her entire thong was exposed. "What is wrong about me being here with you now? I'm a Prosecutor, Eric, so believe me when I tell you that I know what is right and wrong. It's what I do for a living. Remember, you are the one who defends wrongdoers." She laughed, and continued in a sarcastic tone, "and I show them the path to righteousness."

"I know, Amanda," he replied, trying unsuccessfully to avoid gazing directly at her black lace-covered crotch and disregarding the sarcastic wit behind her final comment, instead focusing on her position as a Prosecutor. "That's exactly why it is wrong." He stood, seemingly oblivious to the fact that his cock had swelled to such a large size that it almost struck the underside of the desk as he stood. He turned to her and continued. "You are a Prosecutor. I am defending a person whom you are prosecuting. I believe that there are multiple ethics rules that would say that we can't be involved with each other."

Amanda sighed and looked downward. "Your little head certainly doesn't seem to agree with your big head," she said, giggling. "Besides, Eric, you know as well as I do that it is only wrong if someone else knows about it." She reached out and grabbed Eric's bulging crotch in her right hand. "And I'm not going to tell anyone. Will you?"

Eric recoiled, took a step backward, and again sat down in his chair to avoid having her grab him again. "No, I certainly would not tell anyone." He felt light-headed, a combination of the blood rushing from his head downward and his moral compass spinning out of control. He was beginning to lose control, and was incapable of resisting her.

Amanda seemed to have no such difficulties controlling her thoughts and actions. "I thought not," she said. Looking down at Eric, she said, "so this *is* the chair." She slowly removed her shoes and then ran her hand up and down the leather back of the chair as she stood alongside Eric, her chest hovering tantalizingly at his eye level. "Tell me, how did it happen? I heard she seduced you." She moved her hand from the chair to his shoulder. "Was she standing here?"

"I am really uncomfortable with this," Eric said, still trying in vain to extricate himself from what promised to be a compromising position.

"Perhaps you should loosen your pants and let that monster breathe," she said, looking at his crotch as she swung his chair to the left. She was now standing directly in front of him. "That would make you more comfortable, don't you think?"

"I meant that I am uncomfortable talking about this."

"Come on, don't be such a baby, Eric," she replied, curtly, "I find this discussion very sexy. It's certainly much more so than talking about law shit."

Eric sighed, in recognition of his realization that this was a battle that he was incapable of winning. "Do I have to?"

"Yes," she replied, smiling, sensing his feelings of defeat and advancing forward, like a lioness playing with her prey. "Now tell me, was she standing here?"

"Yes."

"What was she wearing?" Amanda continued. "Was she fully dressed while she was standing here or was she already undressed?"

Eric looked up at Amanda. As she stood there in her blouse and underwear, her hair set free from her ponytail and dangling over her shoulders, he could not help but think back to Bianca Rodrigues. About how exciting she was to him, and about how he had been weak when she stood in that very spot. He felt identical feelings of weakness in the presence of Amanda Johnson, who was younger and more attractive than Bianca. He stared at Amanda's chest. Bianca's was much larger, he remembered, but Amanda's mid-20's body was in better overall shape than was Bianca's 30-year old body. How could he not have sex with the young woman throwing herself at him, especially when she would also be afraid of telling anyone? She had as much to lose, both personally and professionally, as he did. She could not tell anyone about their escapades. It was a strangely perfect scenario. It was fate. How could he resist?

Now, having accepted the inevitable, actually, having happily accepted the inevitable, Eric decided that he would play along as a willing participant. Staring up at Amanda, he said, "It was a lot like now, to be honest," he said, "she started off fully dressed but then took her clothes off piece-by-piece as she walked over to where you are standing now."

"Very interesting," Amanda said, as she knelt down next to Eric and again placed her hand on his crotch. This time she moved her hand over his bulge in a slight motion, gripping him through his pants as she did so. "So by the time she was next to you, was she dressed like I am now, or had she gone further?"

Eric looked down at the hand grasping his stiffened cock, and then looked left to see Amanda's face a scant few feet from his. "I guess further. If I remember correctly, by the time she was next to me, she was only wearing her thong."

"Then I am doing it wrong," Amanda said, disappointed, "I feel so embarrassed. This is a re-creation of the incident, counselor. We need to strive for correctness. Why didn't you tell me that I wasn't doing it right?" She stood and began to undo the remaining buttons of her blouse. "Let's be clear about this so I don't fuck it up again," she said, her smile growing in size. "You mean that her blouse was already off? I want to do this as properly as possible, you know."

Eric appreciated Amanda's enthusiasm and effort, even if he found her desire to identically replicate the events of the prior year strange, if not oddly creepy. "She was actually wearing a tank top when she came to the office, not a blouse like yours, but yes, by the time that she came around here it was already laying in a ball on the chair across from my desk."

"You mean like this?" she asked, as she removed the blouse from her shoulders, curled it up into a ball, and tossed it onto the chair.

"Yes."

"And her bra, that was also off?"

"Yes. It was lying on top of the blouse."

She began to unhook her bra, but then stopped. "Tell me something before I go any further, Eric," she said, standing up as straight as possible and looking down at her chest, "were her tits bigger than mine? I want to know if I measure up or not. And I must warn you," she cooed, "I hate losing." She moved closer to him, so that her bra-encased breasts were now directly next to his eyes.

Eric quickly realized that this was a question that could not be answered honestly, because Amanda's B-cup breasts were no match for Bianca's large chest, as far as size was concerned, and he certainly had no intention of upsetting her. Plus, Bianca's chest was saline-enhanced. Amanda's seemed natural. Details would only muddy the waters. "It's hard to say," was all that he could muster.

194

"Well, maybe it's not a fair question yet. You know how some women's breasts look larger when they are not harnessed. I think mine are like that," she said, as she unhooked the bra and slipped the straps over her shoulders, allowing her breasts to swing freely next to Eric. "Do you agree?"

He had to agree with her statement. Her breasts definitely looked bigger now – but they were still not as large as Bianca's. "Yes, you are correct," he said, as she leaned forward and brushed them against the side of his face. "They definitely look bigger than when you had the bra on."

"Well, whose are bigger, then?" she asked, as she brought her arms to her sides and pushed them inward in an obvious attempt to make her chest seem more ample.

Eric paused and thought about his best answer. He decided that lying was better than incurring Amanda's wrath with an incorrect response. "Yours are bigger," he said, simply, "and much firmer."

"I was hoping you would say that," she said, as she leaned over, wrapped her arms around his shoulders, and slowly kissed his left ear. "Is this what she did?"

"No, she climbed into the chair and sat on top of me."

Amanda looked down, puzzled by the logistics of such positioning. "How did she do that while facing you? Where did her legs go?"

"She was facing away from me, like a lap dance," Eric explained, eagerly anticipating Amanda's next move.

Amanda maneuvered herself closer and turned the chair so that it faced her. "I can do that, if that's what turns you on." She began to writhe slowly, as if to imaginary music, and backed herself onto Eric, her thong-clad rear resting atop his hardened cock. "I think you are enjoying yourself, Eric, and that is great," she said, "but I know that there was more, so I need for you to tell me," she lowered her voice to a barely inaudible whisper, "in detail, what happened next."

195

The sight and feel of Amanda gyrating her hips on him was almost too much for him to handle. It was getting closer to payoff time. "She knelt down in front of me and blew me."

"That's pretty forward of you, Mr. Goldberg," she said, laughing at the irony of her statement in light of her line of inquiry. "Are you asking me to blow you?" she asked, as she continued to move her almost bare ass up and down on his crotch. "I don't recall ever saying anything about oral sex."

"I am not asking you to do anything, Ms. Johnson," he replied, his breath growing heavier as she continued to gyrate on him, "you asked me a question and I merely told you the answer."

"Well, it's a good thing for you that I am not morally opposed to oral sex," she said, standing up and turning around so that she was facing Eric. "But to be honest with you, Eric, there's a big problem here."

"Really? There's a problem?" Eric asked, breathlessly, while enjoying the continued sight of an almost-naked Amanda Johnson in his presence. "What's the problem?"

"Well," she said, as she pulled her hair back from her shoulders and wrapped it in a ponytail with a rubber band from Eric's desk, "you still have your pants on, silly."

"Details," Eric laughed, as he undid his belt and pants, stood, and let his pants slide down to his ankles, where Amanda carefully slid them over his feet and then, similar to her own blouse, balled them up and threw the pants onto the chair across the desk. Reaching her hand down the waistband of his boxer shorts, she pulled the shorts down to the top of Eric's thighs and gently took his stiffened cock in her hands.

"Are you ready?" she asked, licking her lips as she leaned her head closer to her hands.

Eric took a deep breath. "Yes, Amanda," he said as she began to kiss him, his erection growing even larger. He was careful not to incorrectly say the name "Bianca." Or, even worse, he was extremely careful not to use the name "Wendi."

*****

An hour later, a naked and exhausted Eric Goldberg lay, panting, on the carpeted floor of his office. Next to him, an equally naked and exhausted Amanda Johnson lay, snoring quietly as Eric ran his hand up and down the small of her back. Her eyes fluttered open, and she squinted as she tried to remember where she was. "Oh, my head," she said, "I've got to cut down on the liquor."

"If you want, I can go make coffee in the other room," Eric's voice said from behind her. "That will help with the headache."

Amanda rolled onto her side, and propped herself up with her right elbow as she looked at Eric. "No thanks, Mr. Goldberg. I never drink coffee at night, because then I won't be able to sleep no matter how tired or physically exhausted I am," she replied. "Besides, I've got a better idea." She looked down at her naked chest, smiled, and then looked over at Eric. He was also lying on his side, and Amanda's eyes drifted from his face down to his chest. She began to rub her own chest with her free left hand, and slowly moved her gaze down Eric's body, stopping at his again-growing member. Her smile widened. "Looks like you've got the same idea, Eric."

"Maybe, but not right now," he protested. "I need to catch my breath. I'm old, you know." He laughed. He enjoyed her company, and thought that he would like to spend more time with her – and that additional time with Amanda could possibly lead to an easier path to resolution of Wendi's case.

"Not that old," she said, licking her lips and smiling.

"I feel it now, believe me. Just let me rest a little." He lay back down, his half-erect cock listing at a 45 degree angle. He suddenly thought of an easy way to ask Amanda out for a date. "Let me ask you a question. Do you like classic rock music?"

"Classic rock music? You mean like the stuff my parents listened to?" she responded, smiling.

"That hurts a little, you know."

"Just kidding, silly," Amanda said, laughing. She moved closer to Eric, pressing her breasts against his chest. "Yes, I do like that old person music, like the stuff my dad listens to. Why?"

Eric looked at her with a disapproving look, still displeased, although not totally surprised, with her comparison of him to her father. "One of my favorite bands is playing tomorrow night in West Orange. Do you want to come with me? I've seen them so many times that it's as if I am friends with the band. I promise it will be a great show."

She pushed herself off of Eric and sat up, her breasts swaying as she spoke. "Wait a minute," she said, "Is this a *date*, Eric?"

"No, Amanda," Eric tried to explain, speaking in what amounted to a half-truth, "it is not a date. It is a show that I was going to see alone but thought you might want to come along."

"Well, as long as that is clear," she said, lying down next to Eric and draping her arm over his chest and moving her leg so that it rested against his growing cock, which now was listing at a 75 degree angle, "lucky for you I had no plans for tomorrow night. I was just going to catch up on work, you know, being the government employee that I am, but, oh well, it's just trying to put away bad guys and girls," she said, sarcastically, chuckling, "and that can all wait. I would love to come along with you on our non-date."

"I look forward to it," Eric said, "but now," he added, looking down at his crotch, "I am looking forward to something else." He rolled to his right and grabbed Amanda in an embrace. "I think I am ready for round two."

Amanda took her hand and gently stroked Eric's manhood, which was now at full attention. "OK," she said, in a whisper, "but then I've got to go home. I do have some work to do, you know, on these silly criminal things, and then I have a date for a concert tomorrow night."

"It's not a …" Eric began to say, but Amanda thrust her tongue into his mouth before he could finish his sentence.

Chapter XXI – Two Friends Go To a Concert

At 7:00 the next evening, Eric drove up Morris Avenue, past the illuminated buildings of Kean University and the Union Train Station, toward Amanda Johnson's rented townhouse in Union. She met him at the street corner, climbed into his car, and gave him a long kiss before settling down into the passenger's seat. She was clad in a denim miniskirt and a pink tank top, and a light sweater was draped over her shoulders. Her long hair was loose, and framed her face as it cascaded down to the top of her sweater.

"I'm really excited for this concert," she said as Eric pulled the car away from the curb and drove toward the Garden State Parkway. "I'm really excited to listen to a bunch of music that was made before I was even born." She smiled when she saw Eric grimace in response to her comment. "But I have to tell you, I got home late last night, as you know, and thankfully was able to fall right asleep. You really tired me out," she added, as she gently caressed his right leg with her left hand.

Eric smiled as he looked down to see her hand on his leg. He was still somewhat surprised by, but clearly enjoyed, her flirtatious manner. "I was pretty tired myself. It's not often I have sex in the office, especially twice in one night."

"Well," Amanda said, smiling coyly, "I would hope not. As best as I know, the last sexual encounter that you had in that office resulted in a multi-continental chase to avoid prosecution."

Eric's smile disappeared. "Can we please change the topic and not discuss her?" he asked.

"Well," Amanda replied, "we can talk about how I spent two hours this afternoon preparing for an inevitable Grand Jury presentation for your ex-wife, if you'd prefer."

"No, not really," Eric said with a deep sigh. "Can we find another different topic, please?"

Amanda laughed. "I was just kidding, silly," she said as she took his right hand in her left. "How's this for a topic? What's the name of the band again?"

"The name of the band is 'George Glass Rocks'," he answered. Looking to his right, he saw Amanda's puzzled look, as if she did not understand the origin of the band's name. Trying to explain, he added, smiling, "they are named after the fictional boyfriend in the old '*Brady Bunch*' episode, you know, the one where Jan invents a boyfriend."

"I never watched the show, to be honest with you," Amanda said as her face brightened with recognition, "but I do remember something about a 'George Glass' in the '*Brady Bunch Movie*' that I saw when I was a kid, so I assume it's the same, right?"

"Yep," Eric sighed as his smile again vanished, "but now I am feeling a little old again."

Amanda laughed and placed her left hand on Eric's lap. "Don't be ridiculous, Eric. If anything, you proved last night that you are not *that* old. In fact, you're not old at all, if you ask me." She ran her hand up and down Eric's right leg, bringing her fingers to rest atop his crotch. Changing the topic, she asked, "Eric, you said that you know one of the guys in the band, right?"

"That's right," he replied. "I'm friends with the lead singer. I met him a couple of years ago at one of their concerts. I've seen them about a couple of dozen times since then, and we've had some drinks together, so we've gotten to know each other pretty well. He's from Westfield, and he's only a year younger than me. We have some mutual friends, guys whom he grew up with and I know from work or Law School. Sometimes,

I will even run into one of them at one of the shows. You probably even know a couple of them. So it's always kind of cool seeing him."

Amanda pulled her hand away from Eric's crotch and her voice took on a serious tone. "Let's keep it quiet who I am, then, when we get there. On the off chance that we do have any mutual friends, it probably wouldn't be great for them to find out that I was out on a date, uh, you know, I mean a non-date, with defense counsel on one of the cases that I am prosecuting; especially *the* case that I am prosecuting." She paused and looked out the window. There was no need for her to elaborate on what she meant by the phrase "*the* case," as she clearly meant Wendi's pending prosecution. "Not that I think I am doing anything wrong," she added, "but I just don't need the drama. And there's already enough drama at the office." She shook her head disapprovingly. "You wouldn't believe some of the shit that goes on there. It's simply incredible."

Eric looked over at her as he eased the car off of the entrance ramp from Route 78 and onto the Garden State Parkway. He did not know what to say in response to Amanda's last comment, especially because he also continued to have some doubts about the propriety of this relationship, or whatever it was, that was forming between him and Amanda. He could certainly see how it might look to others. He had thought about it, but had not seriously considered it before he asked her to accompany him. All of a sudden, her word made the specter of being seen in public loom larger than he had originally thought, and now, for the first time, it worried him also. He pondered for the first time what his friend Jon Grant would have said had he told him of his intentions for that evening. He knew that Grant would disapprove, and likely for valid reasons.

For a few moments, the two attorneys, so well trained in the art of articulating their positions and in looking into the souls and minds of others as they honed their craft, sat in silence as they engaged in their own private introspections.

Amanda continued looking out the window as the houses of Irvington seemed to whiz by. Traffic was unusually light for the hour, and the three-mile drive on the highway took only a couple of minutes, due also to Eric's penchant for driving in excess of the speed limit. As the car passed through the toll booths at Exit 145 and then went left to merge onto Route 280 West, Eric, finally, cleared his throat and then tried to break the uncomfortable silence. "Just so I know when we get there, what's your drink of choice?"

She looked back at Eric for the first time since they first entered the Parkway, and ran her hand through her hair as she sighed, clearly trying to get past her internal conflict of being with Eric, of wanting to be with Eric, at the same time that she was charged by the government with prosecuting the woman who was both his ex-wife and client. Reaching a positive resolution, at least for the moment, that she would enjoy the evening and Eric's company, she answered, in a seductive voice, "My drink of choice? I would have to say 'Sex on the Beach.'" She turned toward Eric, her left leg resting comfortably against the car's center console as her denim mini-skirt rode up to the top of her thighs. "I prefer vodka drinks," she added, "You?"

"Honestly, not a big vodka fan," he replied. "It's going to make me sound like an old man, again, but I like Scotch - over ice." He paused and looked to his right, where Amanda sat, smirking as she visualized him nursing a glass of scotch. Recognizing the reason behind her expression, he continued, "Yes, you're right. I look very refined when I drink scotch." He laughed. "But I don't wear a smoking jacket, smoke a pipe, or wear slippers when I drink it. And my dog does not lie at my feet in front of a roaring fire, so get that scenario out of your head." She smiled, and reached out with her left hand and placed it on his right shoulder. Eric knew that her internal crisis had passed, at least for the moment. He drew the conclusion that she was a very tactile person, as indicated by her various ways of touching him, even if only since she got into the car. She touched his leg, then his crotch, and now his shoulder. He admired her brazen nature.

Now if he could only get past his own internal trepidation about what others would think if they were seen together in a social setting.

He wanted to be out with her for several reasons. First, he still thought that he might get a better deal with Wendi if things went well with Amanda. At the same time, he was enjoying her company. He liked the attention. He had not had anyone show that much attention or any form of interest in him since the Bianca fiasco. Amanda was attractive, she was funny, and she was smart. She also had a very straight-forward manner about her, which no doubt was partially a defense mechanism for her own internal insecurities, but he found her manner very refreshing. He did know that any relationship could only progress so far, especially as the case was still active, but he had made the decision to just ride it out and see where things led between them. If things got too heavy, he would just bail out. He had done it before.

A couple of minutes later, Eric pulled the car into the parking lot of Smiley's Bar, the venue at which the band was performing that evening. Parking the car, Eric exited and walked over to the passenger's side. He opened the door and took Amanda's hand, helping her exit the vehicle. As she stood, he took her in his arms and kissed her, a kiss which lasted several minutes and which left them both with racing heartbeats. "Alright, Eric," she said as she pulled her face from his, "we should go inside. The night is still young, relax." She pushed his hands off of her body and stepped backward. Turning to walk into the bar, she made sure that nobody familiar was nearby and then, satisfied that they would not be discovered, took Eric's right hand in her left as they strode through the parking lot. Entering the bar, Eric paid the cover charge for the two of them, over Amanda's mock opposition because they were "not on a date." They then walked over to the nearest bartender, where Eric ordered two drinks – a "sex on the beach" and a scotch on the rocks.

"To a nice concert with a friend," Eric said as he raised his glass and pushed it lightly into Amanda's. She smiled, nodded approvingly, and then slowly sipped her drink, her hips slowly swaying with the music emanating from the speakers overhead.

"Eric!" boomed a voice from behind him, "always glad to see you back here." Eric turned and was immediately engulfed in a bear hug – courtesy of Jim Spinner, lead singer of "George Glass Rocks." Eric, taken by surprise, fumbled with his glass, being careful not to spill any of his scotch. "You're still drinking scotch, old man?" Jim said, looking down at the glass and slowly shaking his head from side to side. "Obviously you are making too much money, Mr. Lawyer. We've got to get you to drink like us little people."

"Us little people?" Eric asked, incredulously, as he poked at Jon's ample midsection. "I don't know what you consider to be 'little,' but our definitions clearly differ. And I couldn't possibly drink as much as you, Jim," Eric replied as he broke free from the singer's grasp and motioned toward Amanda. "I'd like you to meet a friend of mine, Amanda," he said, gently taking her hand in his. He was careful not to use her last name, based on their conversation in the car. "She's a fan of the tunes, despite her obviously tender age, so I brought her along to enjoy your music tonight."

Jim extended his right hand, and Amanda returned the gesture. As the two shook hands and exchanged pleasantries, Jim subtly looked Amanda up and down, admiring her young body, clad only in a tank top and denim shorts, her sweater now wrapped around her waist, and smiled. Turning back to Eric, he mouthed, this time not so subtly, "a friend?" Eric looked toward Amanda, hoping that she had not seen Jim's comment. He could tell by her smile that she had. He motioned to Jim that he wanted to buy him a drink, and led him to the other side of the bar. Amanda could see the two talking and laughing as the bartender poured Jim a beer, and the two continued to talk as they walked back toward her. "It was nice meeting you, Amanda," Jim said as they reached her, "I hope that you enjoy the show tonight. My regular keyboardist is out so we're trying out someone new, but I am sure he will work out well enough." Jim then pointed to the stage, indicated that he had to go prepare for the show, and walked away. As he walked toward the back of the bar, he turned around one time to again look at Amanda. Watching her standing next to Eric, with her arm wrapped around his, Jim sighed and continued on his way.

Amanda, seeing Jim again checking her out, laughed and grabbed Eric tightly. "Looks like I'm your arm candy tonight, old man," she whispered in his ear. "I think I could get used to this." Just as she had thought while watching Eric walk away from her in court, there was something about him that she found very attractive. Her thoughts were accentuated by the atmosphere in the bar, and also by her relative anonymity in his presence. "And you know something," she added, "being somewhat incognito is a bit of an aphrodisiac. If they don't know who I am here, then we can do whatever we want and there are no consequences," she said, inserting her tongue into the outside ridges of

Eric's right ear and gently swirling it around. "Yes," she added, "I could get used to this."

"Shit," Eric thought to himself as he pawed at his now moistened ear, her brazenness had suddenly kicked into overdrive and he was more than a little hesitant to reply in kind. "Better be careful with this one," he murmured to himself, but his need to be cautious, however, was more of a long-term plan. Swept up in the moment, he threw such caution to the wind. "Me too," he whispered back, as he pulled Amanda tightly and kissed her again. He grabbed with such force that some of his scotch did spill, droplets of the brown liquor falling onto Amanda's skirt. "I'm sorry," he said, as he realized what had happened.

"No problem," she replied, again taking her alpha-female forthrightness to a new level, "you can clean the skirt later ... with your tongue."

It was 9:45. The band was not scheduled to begin playing until 10:00, which meant that they probably wouldn't begin their first song until at least 10:15. The bar was beginning to fill up with people, most of who, surprisingly, seemed to be in Amanda's age range. Some of the men had wisps of grey hair, but the overwhelming majority of those in attendance were likely born after the music that they would be enjoying that evening was first written and recorded. The true meanings of the songs of the 60's and 70's would likely be lost on this new generation of listeners, but they were there that night to hear Jim and his band's rendition of those past hits, not for discussions or political discourse. A few of the kids wore retro-rock t-shirts, shirts emblazoned with the logos or pictures of bands which stopped making music decades ago. It was kitschy, apparently, for them to wear the shirts and listen to the music of their parents' generation.

Eric and Amanda found two stools at the end of the bar and sat, waiting for the show to begin. Each was in the middle of their second drink when Amanda asked the question that she was dying to ask since the night before: "so what ever happened to Bianca?"

Eric nearly choked on his scotch when he heard the question, at the mere mention of that name. "Excuse me?" he croaked out, the only answer that he could muster.

Amanda looked into his eyes, noting his discomfort at the topic. It was a look that she had seen numerous times before, most often on the faces of defendants as she was grilling them on cross-examination during trials or plea hearings. It was a look of someone who clearly did not want to address the topic, a look of someone who would rather be anywhere else than to be subject to that line of questioning. In the context of a case, she would not let the defendant off that easily, and would press on with her inquiry. And this was no different to her. She liked Eric and was greatly attracted to him, but for now, her curiosity about his past trumped any feelings that she might have had for him. "I said," she repeated slowly and clearly, "what happened to Bianca? You never told me."

Eric pondered the question for a second, and took another gulp of scotch. He did not want to talk about that woman here, at a bar where people could hear his response, especially because he would have to raise his voice in order for Amanda to hear him over the din of the music in the bar. He also most definitely did not want to talk about that woman with this woman; while it was kinky the night before to discuss the sex between him and Bianca, he did not want to discuss the specifics of the case itself. "I would rather not talk about it here, OK?" was his evasive answer, given as he looked her straight in the eye, his attempt at conveying that he was serious and that he would not be changing his position.

Amanda grimaced like a petulant child whose parent had refused her request for a toy, even though she understood and, to a certain extent, appreciated his reluctance to discuss what was clearly a bad time in his life. A moment of uncomfortable silence followed, at which time Amanda realized that it was best not to discuss Bianca at the bar, especially with the show about to begin, and decided to move on instead of ruining their night. "You know what, Eric, I understand completely," she said, as she leaned forward, placed her hand on Eric's leg, and kissed him on the cheek. "Another time, maybe," she stopped and paused before continuing, "then we can discuss it when you're ready. Let's talk about something else."

Eric smiled, glad that he had dodged that topic. "How about the Yankees?" he asked. "That's another topic that can depress me if that is your goal."

"Really, Eric, you want to discuss baseball? I know absolutely nothing about it. There's nothing else that we can talk about?"

"We can talk about how nice you look tonight."

Amanda smiled. She swiveled her stool so that she was facing Eric, her legs spread just far apart enough to expose the pink thong underneath her denim skirt. She pulled the sweater from around her waist and placed it on the back of the chair behind her, and arched her back slightly so that her chest stood a scant few inches from Eric's. "Now that's a topic that we can discuss, sir," she answered. "Go ahead, continue. Tell me how good I look." She tossed her head backward in an exaggerated motion, causing her hair to whip around in a faux modeling pose. She laughed, then licked her lips and added, "and please make sure to use details. Details are critical."

The mood lightened, Eric began to describe, in great detail and through the eyes of a great inquisitor, his appreciation of Amanda's body and beauty that evening. The two then discussed a couple of meaningless topics, having moved their chairs closer together so that the stools themselves were touching and Eric's arm was wrapped around Amanda's waist. The bottom of her tank top was pulled up along the small of her back, and he placed his hand inside the waistband of her skirt, running his fingers along the top of her thong and playing with the tag which pointed upward from its fabric. The banter between the two continued for the next 20 minutes, until the lights dimmed and the band took the stage.

Jim and his band mates needed no introduction to the crowd. They immediately launched into their first song upon stepping under the stage lights, and did not stop playing until after their fourth song was completed, effortlessly segueing from song to song, clearly to the crowd's delight. The crowd was raucous, most people

209

singing along with Jim; the younger crowd members danced their way through the songs, while the older people, like Eric, alternately clapped and put their hands into their pockets as they rhythmically moved a leg forward and back. Amanda, like the other twenty-somethings, began to dance with the opening chords of the first song and did not stop moving until after the initial round of songs was completed. Beads of sweat dripped from her hair as she whipped her head around, and she tried, in vain, to get Eric to dance by grabbing his waist and trying to shake his feet from their locked position on the ground. Even when Jim ventured off the stage and into the crowd during the third song, Eric stayed put. Amanda rushed, with others, toward Jim, and Eric could hear her voice singing a few words of an old Kinks' song as Jim passed the microphone among those clustered around him.

The end of the fourth song resulted in a sustained round of applause. As the crowd showered the band with adulation, Jim waved the other members of the band off to the side of the stage. "Take a rest, guys," he said, "I'm going to do something special for a friend of ours." He picked up a stool from alongside the drums and placed it on the front of the stage. He then retrieved an acoustic guitar from behind the keyboards, placed its strap over his right shoulder, and sat on the stool, in front of the microphone. The crowd roared its approval, and several of the women shrieked about how they loved Jim. Raising his hands to quiet the crowd, he responded, "I love you ladies, too." Pushing his hair back, giant drops of sweat falling down his face, he took a guitar pick from the top of the guitar strings and began to strum a few chords.

"I hope that you will indulge me a bit tonight," he said into the microphone, as the crowd again began to clap and cheer. "We've got a lot of familiar faces here tonight," he continued, "and those of you who have been with us for some time should know that we like to stretch ourselves a bit sometimes. And some of you may not even know this, but I can play guitar." The crowd noise grew louder as he contorted his face into a mock grimace. "And some of you just thought I was a pretty face," he said, sarcastically, to the delight of those in the crowd.

"Play us something nice, Jim," called a woman from the back of the crowd.

"Of course, my dear" he answered, "I wouldn't dream of doing anything else." The crowd again roared, forcing Jim to again raise his arms sideways in an attempt to quiet them. When the noise lessened, he again began to strum a chord. A lone spotlight shone on Jim as he sat, reflecting off of the bald spot on top of his head as he leaned forward while strumming the guitar."This next song is one that I haven't played live before, so I hope I get it right," he said, almost apologetically. He looked to the side of the stage, where some of the band members stood, drinking and using towels to remove what appeared to be buckets of sweat from their heads. Jim smiled at the sight. "And the band doesn't know it, so I am going to try it alone because I don't want to embarrass them." The crowd roared its approval. "It's a request for an old friend. It's a song that was originally recorded around 1980, if I remember correctly, and wasn't actually released until years later. It's a dedication for a special someone who, if my guess is right, wasn't even born when the song was released, and definitely wasn't around when it was first recorded."

The crowd roared as he continued to tune the guitar. "Well," he said, "here goes. Like I said before, I hope I get it right. This one, actually, is for a friend of a friend. I hope you all like it." He began to strum the guitar again, this time with a familiar melody. The crowd hesitated, many sensing that they recognized the song but unable to immediately place its title.

Amanda, standing next to Eric, looked at Jim as he began and then looked over at Eric. "I know this song," she said, "what is the title again?"

Jim continued to strum the guitar, the spotlight now illuminating the guitar and his hands. Seconds later, another light shone directly on his face as he moved it closer to the microphone. He began to sing quietly, almost in a whisper, "Babe, tomorrow's so far ..."

"Oh my God!" Amanda shrieked. "That's my song!" Her voice was so loud, and so much louder than Jim's amplified voice, that half of the people in the bar turned in her direction. Her face turning red, she buried her head in Eric's chest as she continued. "It's *Amanda*, by Boston. My dad used to sing this to me all of the time."

She looked up at Eric, as her eyes moistened and a single tear fell down her right cheek. "You asked him to play this for me?"

"Maybe," he replied, softly.

She reached up and grabbed his head, pulling his face to hers as she kissed him as hard as she could without breaking his teeth. "This is the sweetest thing anyone's ever done for me," she yelled, "you are amazing!" She again kissed Eric, and then looked toward the stage to listen to the rest of the song, especially the part where she would hear her name, over and over. Jim sat, still playing and singing, and as he played he looked up and over in Amanda's direction. Seeing the smile on her face, he also smiled and winked.

"Thank you," she mouthed to him.

After he completed the next verse, Jim paused and said "you're welcome," and then played the last two verses so strongly on the guitar that Amanda feared he would bloody his fingers. When the last chords of the song echoed through the bar, Jim stood, took an exaggerated bow, and said into the microphone, "that's for you, Eric. And it's for your friend, whatever her name is." The crowd cheered and laughed at the last comment. Amanda stood, tears running down her face, as she grabbed Eric and held him as tightly as she had ever held anyone before. At that moment, she did not care who saw them together, even if someone knew who they both were. It was a release of pure emotion for her – the exact opposite of how she had to act for so many hours each day, suppressing her emotions while she went about prosecuting the underbelly of Union County. She had to be a cold, calculating machine to do her job properly. Too often, this coolness carried over into her private life, where she refused to allow her emotions to take hold of her. Now, she was completely overtaken by her emotions, and it felt good, almost as good as being wrapped up in Eric's arms.

The rest of the evening was a whirlwind for Amanda. It was filled with more music, more dancing, a couple of more drinks, and then back to her apartment with Eric. When she awoke the next morning, however, she was alone in her bed. She did not recall when Eric had left. Sunlight poured into the apartment, filling it with a warm, welcoming glow. Yet, as she lay in her bed, bathed in the warm sunlight, she felt lonely without him being there, and the feeling concerned her greatly. She had never felt lonely before. She really barely knew Eric, and, despite his amazingly thoughtful gestures of the previous night, she still wondered why his absence pained her so.

She also knew that her budding romance with Eric was ill-fated, at least for as long as the prosecution of Wendi Goldberg continued. That knowledge, however, was not enough for her to derail the relationship, at least not yet.

As Amanda fretted over the prior evening's events, however, Eric was already in his office, trying to validate his own feelings. He spent the better part of an hour poring through some of the dusty, formal-looking books that had sat, untouched, for years on his office bookshelves. Closing the last book, and satisfied that he had done appropriate research on a specific topic, he typed the following e-mail to his friend, Jon Grant:

"Jon – just for the record, I checked them all. I went through the ABA Canons on Professional Ethics. I read through the 1984 NJ Rules of Professional Conduct, as well as the 2002 amendments. I even went through the now-obsolete NJ Disciplinary Rules – and none of these contain any provisions that say, or even suggest, that some form of relationship with a Prosecutor is taboo. Not that I'm planning on doing anything, mind you, but I just wanted to let you know."

He received Grant's response a few minutes later – *"Eric, I will take your word for it. But logic should tell you that it's wrong, and perhaps it is so wrong that the writers of these various codes didn't think that anyone would be stupid enough to think that it would be OK, just because it is so blatantly obvious. You're a complete ass, my friend. Please just be careful."*

Eric smiled. He would be careful, or at least he would try to be.

Chapter XXII – A Morning With Jesus and Lupe

Several miles away, on the other side of Elizabeth, Jesus Sanchez awoke in a bed which was bathed in the same warm sunlight. He opened his eyes slowly, adjusting them to the daylight, and the first item he saw was a framed 4x6 picture on the night table next to him. It was a picture of Lupe Espinosa's parents, the parents whom she had described in their television interview only days before. Her father did look sophisticated, Jesus thought, and his piercing eyes were the eyes of an attorney, the eyes of a man who could make others quake through his stare. They were also the eyes of a man who had endured years of struggle, the difficulties of his people reflected in his pupils. Jesus pondered whether the old man would be a worthy addition to his machine, the group that would one day catapult him to the Mayor's seat in Elizabeth, just one of the stops on his way to political grandeur.

Sanchez could hear Lupe's heavy breathing as she slept next to him. She was facing away from him, and as he sat up he pulled the bed's light blanket with him, so that it was now bunched up around his waist. Lupe's bare bottom faced his legs as he sat, and, for a moment, he was able to forget about his overwhelming desires for political greatness, the thoughts which constantly pervaded his mind, and he was also able to simply appreciate the perfect form of Lupe's posterior. This was a moment to be treasured, one to be imprinted in his memory. That ass was a perfect ass. As for the rest of her, sometimes he wondered. His concerns mainly focused on her mind, her thoughts, and, most importantly, her loyalty to him.

He decided to get out of bed and make a cup of coffee, so that he could begin his morning routine of scanning local news broadcasts for any information about the city of Elizabeth, Union County, or any other information that he could spin to his personal or political benefit. He slowly turned, so as not to wake Lupe, and placed his feet quietly on the wooden floor. He slid his boxer shorts on, and then attempted to

215

walk, quietly, into the hallway and then to the kitchen. The apartment's creaky floorboards, unfortunately, betrayed his efforts and Lupe was awakened by his third step on the old, noisy floor.

"*A donde vas, Jesus?* Where are you going?" Lupe murmured in both Spanish and English as she buried her head in the pillow to spare her eyes from the morning sunshine. "*Es muy temprano,* it's so early, and neither of us have anything to do until the afternoon." She took her left arm and patted the area where he had been laying only seconds before. "*Por favor, vuelves a la cama* (Please come back to bed). *Sólo vamos a mentir aqui por un tiempo. Nunca llegamos a hacerlo* (Let's just lie here together for a while. We never get to do that)."

"I was just going to make us some coffee, *mi amor*," he replied. "Let me start it and then I will come back to bed."

Lupe sat up, leaning her back against her pillow. She initially pulled the blanket up to cover her large, bare breasts as she sat, but as she began to speak she let go of the blanket and gravity took over, dropping it to her waist level. "*No, no lo hare,* no you won't," she protested as Jesus' stare went directly at her bare chest. "*Te conozco demasiado bien* (I know you too well). You will go into the kitchen and start the coffee."

"And?" he asked, his eyes never diverting from her naked body.

"And," she said, again grasping the blanket a pulling it up to her neck, "*Café es solo una forma para que usted pueda salir de la cama* (the coffee is just a way for you to get out of bed)."

"*No, mi amor,*" he protested.

"*Sí.* Then, once you are done with that, you will go into the next room and turn on the television so you can see what's going on in the world or, more importantly, what's going on in Elizabeth."

"*Tu eres equivocas,* you're wrong," he answered. "That's what I was going to do." He paused. "Besides, even if I was going to leave, is it wrong to want to know what is going on in the world?"

Lupe's face immediately turned a bright shade of red, showing her anger, the anger that results when one comes to the realization that one is being patronized. "No, you asshole. It is not wrong. *Pero puede esperar.* It can wait. Especially because once you know what is going on, then your phone calls start to your fucking people, so that you can figure out how to best benefit from any bad stuff that is going on within a ten-mile area!" By now, her voice was raised. "And then, once that happens, I have completely lost you!"

"Just calm down, Lupe, *calmarse,*" Sanchez said, extending his palms forward and slowly moving them up and down in the official "calming" position. "*En realidad solo iba a hacer café.* I really was just going to make coffee. Once you woke up, I decided I was going to come back to bed. *Te lo prometo, mi amor. Estaré de vuelta en pocos minutos.* I promise, I will be back in a few minutes." He winked his eye and continued. "Maybe we can take some of your anger and tension and use it to our advantage."

"The fuck we will!" a still-angry Lupe responded. She dropped the blanket, again exposing her breasts. "*Quieres éstos?* You want these?" she asked. "You think that I will change my tension into some form of pleasure for you? Think again, *muchacho.* And take a nice look at my *chi-chis,*" she added, rubbing both of her breasts with her hands, "*porque esto puede ser la última vez que los vea durante un tiempo* (because this may be the last time you see them for a while)!" She stood, turned, and raced into the bathroom, closing and locking the door behind her. "*Cabrón!* (Asshole!)," she yelled from behind the door.

Sanchez shrugged. They had been through similar scenarios before. Yes, she was correct. He wasn't planning on returning to bed. He was going to check the local news immediately after making coffee. And clearly she knew that. His singular focus on his political aspirations had been the source of tension between them for some time. But it was exactly that focus, that drive, that had drawn Lupe to him in the first place, he knew. She had a similar drive, a desire to be a news anchor on her network. He knew that it would never happen. She just wasn't good enough, and that lovely smile and great pair of tits could only get her so far.

His role, however, was not to make her face those limitations or realities. No, he could not tell her those things. Rather, he was better off encouraging her. He knew that. And part of this encouragement was walking her through these times, when her hot Latina blood took over and she lost sight of the big picture, the picture that included both of them achieving their goals. Together, he would preach to her, together they would both attain their desires. Together, they would rule both the city and the local airwaves. Together, he had convinced her, they were unstoppable.

Apart, however, was a different story. He knew, deep down, that he would still one day be Mayor. He could taste it, and he was convinced that it was within his grasp. At the same time, however, he also knew that she would never be anchorwoman without his help. And his hubris prevented him from not reminding her of those two facts at times, at least the first one.

Now, however, he would need to act conciliatory. For now, at least, she served far too important a purpose to him and his political aspirations, and there was simply too much at stake at this moment to lose his media mouthpiece. He still believed that she could be controlled, and he knew how to push her buttons to make her fall back into line. He walked slowly toward the bathroom, from which he could hear the sounds of Lupe's anger: a hairbrush thrown onto the sink area; a slamming door to the medicine chest. The thud of the door against its jamb as she attempted to open it, even though she had forgotten it was locked. As he reached the door, it flung open. Lupe, dressed in a t-shirt and shorts, emerged from the bathroom like a woman possessed, ready to continue her battle with her lying and manipulative suitor.

"*Mi amor, estaba llegando a conseguir que* (I was just coming to get you)," Sanchez said as Lupe crossed the threshold between the bathroom and bedroom. He opened his arms as if to hug her as he stepped closer.

"Fuck you, Jesus!" she screamed. "*Usted miente mierda!* You lying piece of shit! You don't care about me at all. It's all you, you, you. I'm sick of it." She began to cry, and sat on the edge of her bed with her head in her hands. "*No puedo seguir con esto.* I can't do this anymore."

Sanchez shrugged his shoulders, realizing that he would have to smooth over yet another crisis in order to keep his plan in motion. He also realized that the current situation was the most severe and extreme crisis that the two of them had faced together, and he could not let it escalate any further. Walking over to the edge of the bed, he stood alongside her and placed his hand on her shoulder. He gently caressed her shoulder, and said, in as calming a voice as possible, "*Lo siento.* I'm sorry, Lupe. I really was going to come back to bed. *Yo no quiero pelear.* I don't want to fight."

At first, however, Lupe was not falling for what she perceived to be his continued lies. With her head still down, she peeked in between her fingers and saw that he was standing directly next to her, to her right, with the top edge of his boxer shorts at her eye level. Without warning, she flung her right arm in an outward manner, with her hand balled up in a fist, and struck him directly below the top of his shorts, barely missing his cock. "You fucking *puta!*" he yelled, as he doubled over in pain. "You could have really fucking hurt me." He took a few steps back, out of her arm's reach, as he lightly massaged the area, trying to dull the pain caused by her punch.

Now Lupe looked up. "I just thought you would want a blow of a different kind, you fucking asshole!" she yelled as she rose from the bed and took a step toward him, "how does it feel to be hit hard? *¿No se siente tan bien, lo hace?* (Doesn't feel so good, does it?)" She balled up her fist again. "And you'd better not ask me to kiss it and make it better, *a menos que quieras que yo muerdo* (unless you want me to bite it off)," she sneered as she stood just outside of striking distance, ready to fight the still doubled-over Jesus Sanchez.

"*Puta loca* (you crazy bitch)!" he yelled as he also stood and raised his hand to slap her. She quickly recoiled at the sight of his movement, turned, and raced to the other side of the bed. Sanchez's eyes were watery from the pain caused by being struck, and he then pawed at them with his left hand while holding himself in his right, as sort of a delayed form of protection. "You almost hit me in the fucking dick! Are you out of your fucking mind?" He slowly began to walk around the bed, toward Lupe.

She raised her beautiful right leg in a kicking-style motion as he approached her, the looseness of her shorts giving him a clear view of her crotch and betraying the fact that she was not wearing any underwear. The lovely sight momentarily distracted Sanchez. "*¿Qué vas a hacer, papi chulo?* Come on, tough guy, what are you going to do to me?" she asked as she caught his stare. "*¿Lo mismo que le hiciste a esos chicos en Colombia?* (The same thing you did to those guys back in Colombia?)" She lowered her leg and lowered her voice. "Are you going to kill me also, just like those guys?"

Sanchez released his grip on his throbbing crotch and, with both arms outstretched, leapt at Lupe. His leap fell short, however, as she hopped onto the bed and dashed across to the other side. "You fucking *puta*," he repeated, "who the fuck do you think you are? We've been through this. *No eres nada sin mí.* You're nothing without me. You need me. You think that those tits are getting you the anchor desk, without my help? Then you're fucking crazier than I thought you were."

Lupe grabbed the alarm clock from the night table alongside her bed. "If you come any closer, I am going to knock you out, you fucking dick!" she yelled. "And then you can explain to your fucking people how you ended up knocked out, naked, on my bedroom floor. *¿Cómo va a buscarte? Dime!* How's that going to look for you, *papi chulo?* Tell me!"

Sanchez stopped and stood on the other side of the bed. She was right, he realized. They needed each other. He needed her. They needed to work through this – now.

He sat on the side of the bed, the sunlight cascading over his shoulders, ironically, like an angelic aura. "You're right, Lupe, *tienes razón,*" he said, quietly. "*Nos necesitamos unos a otros. Podemos ayudarnos unos a otros* (We need each other. We can help each other)." He sighed deeply and stood, back facing Lupe, as he stared out the window into the sunlight. "Look at that sunlight, Lupe," he said, in a voice barely above a whisper, "*mira lo que hace brillas nuestra ciudad.* Look how it makes our city shine." He turned to face her, smiling. "Our city, Lupe. *Nuestra ciudad.* We can run this city. *Pero tenemos que trabajar juntos.* We need to work together." He paused, and then repeated himself. "*Es importante que nosotros trabajar juntos.*"

Lupe slowly put the clock back on the night table and looked at Jesus. Her eyes began to water and a tear fell, moistening her left cheek. "*Tu haces que sea muy difícil,* Jesus. You make it very hard. *A veces no sé si puedo confiar en ti* (Sometimes I don't know if I trust you)." She did not realize the irony of her statement, and that the real trust issue lay with Jesus and his lack of trust in Lupe.

"*¿Confiar en mí? Mi amor,* you know you can trust me," he said, and began to walk around the bed, toward Lupe. She stood, unmoving, as he approached her. "Now, can we put this behind us? I am sorry for the names I called you. I promise you. It won't happen again. *Te lo prometo. No va a suceder de nuevo.*"

Lupe began to sob as she stepped toward Sanchez and wrapped her arms around his shoulders. "I need to know that I can trust you, Jesus. *Necesito saber.* I need to know."

"*Usted puede, mi Corazon. Usted sabe que.* You can, sweetheart. You know that. And," he added, in what amounted to little more than a complete lie, "*recuerdes, confío en ti* (remember, I trust you)."

Lupe looked up and smiled. "*Eso me hace feliz.* That makes me happy," she said, as she kissed him on the cheek and gently rubbed his crotch with her hand. "I hope you're feeling OK," she said, as she motioned to the kitchen. "Let's go have some coffee, sit in the other room, and watch the news."

Sanchez looked down at his crotch, feeling and seeing its bulge growing under Lupe's caress, and nodded. "OK, let's go. But if you keep rubbing me," he said, "*no vamos a llegar a la cocina* (we're not going to make it to the kitchen)."

221

"Well then, I will stop," she said, *"Necesito café ahora.* I need coffee now. I just woke up and already I am exhausted. Certainly too exhausted to deal with that," she said, pointing to the bulge beneath his boxer shorts. "Let me make the coffee. You go turn the television on and I will be right in."

Sanchez nodded, turned, and walked toward the couch in the next room, where he sat, reached for the remote control, and turned the television to the local news channel. Within minutes, he could smell the aroma of coffee from the kitchen. Hearing Lupe call his name, he looked to his right and saw her in the doorway between the kitchen and the room where he was sitting. She had removed her t-shirt, and was standing in the doorway wearing nothing but a pair of shorts.

"Tengo una pregunta de seguimiento. I have a follow-up question, Mr. Sanchez," she said. "Just so we are clear, these tits can get me lots of things, don't you agree?" She placed her hands on her hips and moved her right hip outward in a pose, her lips pursed and her breasts thrust forward.

The sight of those breasts still excited Jesus. He felt his still-tender crotch again begin to grow, and he quickly tried to formulate a witty response. All that he could come up with was *"sí,"* however, which he stammered out into four syllables before finishing.

"Ya me lo imaginaba. I thought so," Lupe said, as she turned and walked back into the kitchen. As she walked, she slowly shook her head from side to side in a knowing manner, her lips curling upward into a broad smile.

Sanchez admired the vision of Lupe's shaking backside passing into the kitchen, and then turned his attention back to the news. A couple of minutes later the anchor mentioned that, after a commercial break, they would be talking about the Goldberg case. Sanchez called to Lupe to come in to see the report, and she answered that she would be in momentarily, after she poured their cups of coffee. She appeared shortly thereafter, and, much to Sanchez's chagrin had again donned her t-shirt. She handed one of the coffee mugs to Sanchez, and then sat alongside him, draping her leg over his. She playfully stroked his crotch one more time, and then pulled her hand away, stating that they should focus on the news.

When the news show returned from commercial, a split picture appeared to the left, behind the reporter's head. One side of the picture showed Wendi Goldberg exiting the court after her last court appearance. The other side of the picture was Jesus Sanchez. "Look at you, *papi, mírate,*" Lupe cooed, "you're on another news program." She moved closer to him and wrapped her arms around his chest and shoulders. "I guess you don't really need me anymore."

"Not now, Lupe," he said, despite the fact that he was thinking the exact same thing and had been debating that issue for quite some time. "Let's listen to what they're saying."

The two watched the remainder of the report in silence. It lasted all of ninety seconds, during which the reporter simply stated that the case was on-going, and that Sanchez had been acting as spokesman for the family of the deceased teenager. The reporter indicated that the case was going to the Grand Jury, and that, pending the outcome of that Grand Jury hearing or a resolution in the interim, that there would likely be no news to report on the case for some time.

"Seriously? ¡*Usted debe estar bromeando!* You must be joking," Lupe cried. "It's as if she just watched my report and copied it!" She looked at Sanchez for his agreement.

He looked over at her and, seeing that he would have to support her, nodded his head in agreement. "You are right, Lupe, *tienes razón.* And I owe you thanks, then, because your reporting is getting my face on other channels. We just need to stay in front of the cameras long enough for me to get enough people behind me. Then, I run for Mayor and, let's say, hopefully win."

Lupe kissed him on the cheek as she stood to retrieve a napkin from the kitchen, having spilled some coffee on the table as she was watching the news reporter essentially steal her story. "*Que sin duda ganar.* You will definitely win, baby.

Especially if that Goldberg woman gets convicted," she said, "then you will be the *hombre* who got it done."

"*Me gusta.* I like the way that sounds, Lupe."

"And she will be, I think, based on the evidence against her," Lupe said, as she started to walk into the kitchen. "You just need to make sure that little delinquent stays around to testify. You know, the kid who claims she was on the phone."

Sanchez reached out and grabbed Lupe's arm. This was not, however, a soft touch. To the contrary, it was a move borne of anger, and his left arm squeezed Lupe's right arm with all of his strength, causing her to cry out in pain and try to escape his clutches. Her efforts were in vain, however, as he somehow tightened his grip even more and pulled her back down alongside him on the couch.

"What's your problem?" she cried as she continued to struggle to free her arm. "*Me haces daño.* You're hurting me," she said, as she began to cry again. "*¿Por qué haces esto a mí?* Why are you doing this to me?"

Sanchez's eyes were red with anger as he refused to release her, almost as crimson as hers as she continued to cry out in pain. "*¿Por qué llamas a ese chico un delincuente?*" he bellowed, "what did he ever do to you? Why did you use that word? Why did you call him a delinquent?"

Lupe, still crying, could barely speak through her sobs. "What … what does it matter to you?" she gasped. "*¿Qué te importa a ti?*"

Sanchez's face was turning redder by the second, its color matched only by the red rivers running through his pupils and the discoloration of Lupe's arm as he continued to cut off its blood supply. It was the angriest that Lupe had ever seen him; perhaps this is how, she wondered, he was able to kill those people in Colombia and not care about what he had done. "I was called a delinquent when I was younger," he yelled in response, "and I hate that word. *¿Me entiendes? No me gusta esa palabra.*" He then began to ease the pressure on her arm slightly, but still kept it in a fairly tight grip.

Lupe looked at him, puzzled, through her tear-covered eyes. "Jesus, what the fuck?" she yelled. "Yes. I understand you. *Entiendo.* But seriously, you're hurting me because someone called you a name when you were a kid? *¿Cuando usted era a niño?"* She gritted her teeth. *"Eso es ridículo.* That's ridiculous," she sneered. "Let me the fuck go now." He relaxed his grip and she pulled her arm free from his grasp. She stood, stepping several steps away so as to be out of his arm's reach. "I've never seen you that mad before, Jesus. In all the fights we had, you've never hurt me this much. *Nunca me has hecho daño tanta."* She turned and ran, crying, to the bedroom, slamming the door behind her and locking it so he could not enter.

A still-enraged Jesus Sanchez remained, sitting on the couch. He was not mad, however, because he had been called a delinquent when he was younger. He had fabricated that story. He was mad, rather, because she had insulted the witness. She had insulted someone close to him.

Chapter XXIII – Amanda and Her Boss

"Please come in, Amanda." County Prosecutor Steven Crawford said as he beckoned Amanda into his office. "Thanks for coming in to meet with me this morning. I want to discuss something with you."

Amanda walked through the doorway. "Sure, Steve, what can I do for you?" she asked as she strode toward the big desk situated near the far wall of the office and sat in the chair directly across from it. Amanda and the other Assistant Prosecutors were instructed to call Crawford by his first name. He had been an Assistant Prosecutor for fifteen years under his predecessor, John Blank, and worked with many of those who still toiled in the office, people whom he considered friends from their decade or more time spent together. Whereas Blank had insisted upon being called "Mr. Blank" by everyone in the office, including his senior Assistants, Crawford ran the office in exactly the opposite way; each person who worked in the Prosecutor's Office, from his highest-ranking Assistant Prosecutors down to the man who ran the mailroom, was instructed to call him "Steve." Those who mistakenly called him "Mr. Crawford," except when there were outsiders present, were fined one dollar per infraction. The monies were collected and, at the end of every month, Crawford would use the monies to purchase pizzas for lunch on a Friday afternoon. If there were insufficient funds in the till to pay for all of the pizzas, then Crawford would pick up the rest of the tab himself. It was no surprise, therefore, that morale in the office was high and everyone wanted to do their best for Crawford, Amanda included.

This was not to say, however, that Crawford was soft. In reality, he was a skilled and tenacious litigator, one of the best ever to pass through the Prosecutor's office, and with a reputation as being extremely tough on defendants and their counsel.

The stories of his cross-examinations of defendants were legendary. He had an almost 100 percent conviction rate during his time in the trenches, and Prosecutors and defense attorneys alike sang praises of his courtroom acumen. At six foot-three, and well over 200 pounds, he also was a large and dominating presence, both in the office and in the courtroom. When Blank announced that he would be stepping down as Prosecutor two years earlier, the choice for his successor was easy. Crawford was originally appointed on an interim basis, but quickly established that the job should be his to keep.

"Well, Amanda," he said, standing behind his desk and placing two books from his desk back to their proper places in the office's bookshelves, "I want to talk to you about your cases."

"You want to talk about my cases?" Amanda queried, nervously, "why? Am I doing something wrong?"

"No, not at all," Crawford quickly answered in order to assuage any fears she had regarding her performance, his normally booming, deep voice seemingly softened to just a reassuring whisper as he sat down in his chair. "I just want to make sure that we are not overworking you." He looked down, rummaging through some papers on his desk before picking up a thick manila folder. Quickly thumbing through its contents, he looked back up at her before continuing. "Take, for example, the Goldberg case."

Amanda stiffened in her chair, her right hand tightly clenching the chair's arm. Suddenly, she was panicked by Crawford's seemingly innocuous statement. She had been as careful as possible to conceal her dalliances with Eric. Aside from the night in his office and their attendance at the concert, they had two other outside "non-dates," one time going to the movies and another dinner. They took great pains to avoid being seen by anyone they knew, however, traveling south to Menlo Park for the movie and choosing a restaurant in Hackensack, about 25 miles from Union and Elizabeth, for their dinner. Any other time they saw each other was at her apartment. Was it possible that someone had seen them together and had told Crawford?

Luckily for Amanda, the answer was no. Sensing Amanda's concerns, he placed the folder back on his desk and leaned back, so as to make his posture as non-threatening as possible. "I don't want you to take this the wrong way, Amanda. I just fear that the Goldberg case is taking up too much of your time," he explained, standing and walking toward her, sitting on the edge of his desk, directly in front of her. Even sitting, he still cut an imposing figure due to his large size. "I know you have many other cases to handle," he continued, as he fiddled with the stapler from his desk in what appeared to be a somewhat nervous manner, surprising to Amanda as she felt that she should be the one who felt nervous, "believe me, I understand the pressures of working in this office and the overwhelming caseload as much as anyone. I don't want you to give your other cases less attention because I have given you the high-profile case to handle as well. It's an issue of time allocation more than anything else, something that we've all grappled with during our careers. To be honest, it's something that I still grapple with today, even just administrating here. I just want to make sure you're handling things properly." He paused, and then again spoke before Amanda could answer. "Wait; let me rephrase that, because it sounded wrong as I was saying it. I just want to make sure you're not feeling completely overwhelmed."

Amanda, trying desperately to exhibit false confidence and showing steely resolve, looked Crawford directly in the eye as she answered. "Don't worry about me, Steve," she said, "Yes, to be honest with you, the Goldberg case isn't really taking up a great deal of my time, especially because the main witness has been largely unreachable. We do have the phone records which seem to show that the woman was on the phone and texting right before the impact, but that's all the work we need to do other than get the kid to cooperate. There were no other witnesses, at least not any who spoke to the cops at the scene." She paused. "But rest assured I have not been avoiding any of my other files. All of the cases are moving along at their normal rate, and I have been able to settle some recently that I never thought would resolve themselves without trial. We've gotten some good results."

Crawford smiled, and returned to his chair behind the desk. "That doesn't surprise me, to tell you the truth," he replied. "Let me ask you something," he said, as he picked up a pen from his desk and twirled it between the fingers on his right hand. "Did you turn the phone records over to her attorney?"

"To be honest, no, I haven't. We had given the discovery to him before we got the records, and since we're just at the Grand Jury stage I figured there was no reason to give them to him until after we got the indictment." She paused, before adding, "It's not like he could do anything at this stage anyway."

Crawford again smiled, placing the pen down on his desk and leaning forward so that his face loomed over the mid-part of the large desk. "I have been hearing some very good things about you, Amanda." He chuckled. "I did hear that the witness is being difficult, and has been dodging our investigator and your calls, but I am not worrying at all about your abilities. In fact," he said, trying to further stroke her ego through a contrived story, "one person told me that you're probably the best young Prosecutor since me, but I don't really know if that is a good thing or a bad thing."

"From what I have heard," Amanda said, "that is a large compliment for me."

"Don't believe everything you hear, my dear," Crawford said, leaning forward in his chair. "Oftentimes I think that the stories about my 'prowess,' for want of a better word, while I was prosecuting cases was greatly exaggerated." He pointed to a plaque on the wall, which bore his name and the inscription "*Top Assistant Prosecutor 2005-2010.*" "Look at that plaque," he said, "do you really think that I could have possibly been the best one in the office for six consecutive years? Not possible. But at some point the legend of you, the myth of you, begins to outweigh the reality. And then it is up to you as far as how you handle it, much like with actors, or musicians, or professional athletes. How many careers have been derailed by overly-inflated egos? More than I can even count. You can't let that happen to you."

Amanda nodded her understanding. "Over-confidence has never been my problem, Steve. If anything, I am insecure about my abilities, which I think sometimes makes me work more efficiently and better." She smiled. "Besides, I am a long way from even approaching the possibility of thinking of being over-confident."

"A pretty girl like you?" he asked, incredulously, "I would have thought that you were oozing with confidence."

Amanda's smile quickly evaporated into a grimace. She was taken aback by Crawford's last comment. The Prosecutor had, up until that time, always been unfailingly professional with Amanda. She had never even heard him utter an expletive, much less such a sexist, patronizing term like "pretty girl." Unsure of what her proper reaction should have been, she began to turn red, a combination of blushing and anger, and tried, in vain, to sputter out an objection to his use of such a derogatory term.

Seeing her turning red, however, Crawford quickly realized his error in judgment and addressed his prior comment. "I apologize for what I said, Amanda. I should not have called you a 'pretty girl.' Not that you're not, of course, because you certainly are lovely. But this is not the place for such talk."

"That's true," she replied, now a little confused as to how to react by his pseudo-apology and his now calling her "lovely," no less offensive in a workplace setting, but at the same time seeking to keep the peace at work so as not to get herself into trouble. "Thank you for your apology. I think we can move past this now. If you are willing to forget about this conversation, then so am I."

"Agreed," Crawford said, "but Amanda, before you go, there is another reason why I mentioned this topic." He pointed to the diploma on his wall, the one which bore the seemingly omnipresent logo of Seton Hall Law School. "I don't know if you were aware that I am a Seton Hall law graduate. In fact, I graduated a couple of years after your adversary, Eric Goldstein. I assume you met him when you were before Judge Tompkins?"

Amanda was beginning to perspire, as her nerves were beginning to get the best of her and she again began to fret about what Crawford knew or may have known about her and Eric. Not betraying her concern, she responded in a calm voice, "yes, I did meet him that day. He seems like he knows his stuff, but he's in a very tough situation, you know, what with him representing his ex-wife."

"He is a good attorney, but I've dealt with him numerous times in the past and he's an ass, Amanda." Crawford said, bluntly, his eyes narrowing. Seeing a look of surprise on Amanda's face at the terseness and crudity of his comment, he went on to elaborate. "I mean, think about it, Amanda," he explained, "what idiot would possibly want to represent his ex-wife, or, I should better say, what idiot would take the chance of representing his ex-wife in a murder case? It's going to end badly for him no matter how it plays out."

Amanda was starting to relax, growing more confident that Crawford had no idea of the goings-on between her and Goldberg. "You're probably right," she answered, "it does seem to be a no-win situation for him, especially if our witness testifies against her. But why are you bringing this up now?"

Crawford paused before answering, and when he did, he spoke slowly and deliberately, much more so than at any time before, as if he was choosing his words with extra care. "Well, Amanda," he began, "one other thing that you should know, that you have to know about Eric Goldberg if you are going to be dealing with him is that he is a ..." he paused, clearly searching for the correct word, "he is a, well, let's put it this way, he fancies himself as a ladies' man."

"I'm sorry, Steve, did you say 'a ladies' man'?" Amanda asked, smirking. "That's not a term that I have heard in this decade, Steve." She laughed. Unknown to her boss, her laughter was more of a nervous laughter, not due to the use of such an old-timer's out-of-date phrase, but more so for the fact that she had become involved with Eric, and, in fact, was becoming quite infatuated with him.

As Steve did not know the reason for her laughter and assumed that she was laughing at his use of an antiquated term, it was his turn to take offense at Amanda's actions. "Laugh all you want, Amanda. Ask your father. He will tell you what it means," Steve barked. "But here's the skinny. Goldberg thinks he's the shit. You're a pretty young woman." He stopped, realizing that he was repeating a phrase that had gotten him into trouble earlier, and chose to diffuse the comment immediately. "I say that objectively, not to offend or harass you, by the way. Since you are a pretty young woman and he is, well, he is himself, I think that you can probably throw him off his game pretty well when you are in court together."

Despite his attempts, Steve was unable to prevent Amanda from reacting in an adverse way to his last statements. "Whoa, Steve, stop right there," Amanda interrupted. "I am an Assistant Prosecutor here in the County." She leapt from her seat, making sure to close the lapels of her jacket tightly against her chest as her voice began to rise. "Are you saying that you want me to glam it up just for defense counsel, so that he will be so distracted that he won't be able to properly represent his client? I find that suggestion offensive." She paused and carefully considered her next sentence, aware of the fact that she was treading into dangerous waters and trying desperately to hide her body from Crawford in an attempt to minimize the very sexiness that he was promoting. "I'm not on the vice squad, you know," she concluded, "I am an attorney. I am an Assistant Prosecutor. You know, like you were."

Of course, she neglected to mention to Crawford the remarkable irony in his suggestion, that her youthful beauty had already worked its magic on Eric Goldberg. She did not intend, however, nor did she know if it had affected his representation of his client, but it had certainly affected his performance in the bedroom and office, in a positive way. But there was no way that she was going to tell Crawford anything of what had been taking place between her and Eric.

"I know you are," Crawford replied, "and you're a damned good attorney and Prosecutor at that. But you need to understand the following," he added, standing, this time so that he again towered above Amanda in a tacit show of power, "We're also in a very difficult situation here. I don't really give a shit if that woman is convicted. Of course, any conviction helps our office, but in this case, I just don't care. This is not a prosecution, at least in the purest sense. It's a political war, as I assume you have noticed. That piece of shit Sanchez has all of the fucking Spanish people worked up. That means that the goddamned Mayor, that milquetoast piece of shit, is pressuring me to get a conviction so it looks like he is doing his fucking job. So if there is a conviction, each of those two assholes will claim it is because of their efforts, certainly not because of the efforts of you or our office. And in case you haven't figured it out, I can't stand either one of those fucking guys or their fucking pressure. Or, for that matter, I can't stomach the pressure from all of those Hispanics who keep talking about justice for their people. I'm sick of this garbage already." He began to walk back around his desk, shaking his head slowly as he sat down in his chair. "On the other hand, however, if we lose, we will look like shit. So there is some element of importance here, and if you can distract her attorney, then I am all for it."

Amanda's face again began to turn red, but this time with anger, as well as shock at both her boss' comments and his use of heretofore-unheard of profanity. "Tell me one thing, Mr. Crawford, because now I need to know," she said, being careful to use his proper name and disregarding the monetary penalty which would result, "If it is such a difficult case for this office, then why am I handling it? Was I selected to be the prosecuting attorney on this case because of my abilities, or because, as you said before, I am a 'pretty young girl?'"

Crawford leaned back in his chair, exhaled deeply, and then leaned forward, elbows on his desk. "Ms. Johnson, what is one of the first things you learn in law school when it comes to questioning witnesses?"

Amanda's heart sank. His question essentially supplied the answer to her inquiry. "If you mean that you should never ask a question of a witness unless you already know the answer, yes, I remember that. And if I correctly understand what you are saying," she added, standing up, "then it is not the answer that I wanted to hear. I think our conversation here is done." She turned and stormed out the door, leaving a speechless Steve Crawford sitting behind his desk. A speechless Steve Crawford who, thankfully, was blissfully unaware of the budding relationship between the pretty young Assistant Prosecutor and the attorney for the defendant, a relationship which could lead to much greater difficulties, and a public relations nightmare, in what was unquestionably his office's highest profile case.

Chapter XXIV – Eric Meets With the Prosecutor

It was 10:00 when the phone rang in Eric's office. Fatima answered the call on its second ring, and Eric could barely make out her voice as she asked the identity of the caller. After a brief conversation, Fatima placed the caller on hold and, cupping her hand over the phone, beckoned Eric to come out to her desk. "It's Prosecutor Crawford calling for you," she said, barely audibly, even though the caller could not hear her. "Should I tell him that you're not here?"

Eric stopped in his tracks, wondering why the Union County Prosecutor himself would be calling rather than Amanda Johnson. A quick wave of dread overcame him, as he began to consider the possibility that Amanda had told Crawford of their activities together; worse, that she told him of improper activities and her unwilling participation, as if she had been forced to engage in relations by Eric. He knew, however, that he would have to face any such allegations of impropriety immediately. If she had said something to Crawford, it was best dealt with now, rather than allowing such claims to fester and cause further problems for his ex-wife's defense. "No, I will take the call," he answered, tentatively, as he could feel beads of sweat forming on his furrowing brow. "Just tell him to hang on for a minute and I will be right with him."

Fatima eyed Eric curiously, noting the perspiration forming on his forehead. She ascribed his obvious nervousness to concerns over the case itself, however, as she was still completely oblivious to the goings-on between Eric and Amanda Johnson. She looked back down at her phone, pushed the "hold" button, and informed Prosecutor Crawford to wait a minute and that Eric would pick up his call.

Eric slowly walked back to his desk, sat down with an audible sigh, more a sign of his advancing age than his exasperation, and reached for the phone's receiver.

Picking it up, he pushed the flashing light on the phone's console and raised the receiver to his ear. "Hello, Steve," he said, "to what do I owe the pleasure of this call?" The confidence in his voice was in sharp contrast to his inner turmoil, a level of concern that was belied by the sweat which was now pooling on his forehead.

"I wish that it were a pleasure," Crawford replied, causing Eric's blood pressure to rise even further as he imagined all of the possibilities of Crawford's next sentence. Luckily for Eric, however, the reason for the call was not the reason that he was dreading. "I need to see you regarding your wife's case. Now."

"But Steve," Eric replied, "first of all, she's my ex-wife. And you need to see me? What about Ms. Johnson?" He wanted to make sure that this call had nothing to do with his dalliances with Amanda, and thought that by invoking her name he would force Crawford to reveal if their interactions were at all the root cause of Crawford's insistence on a meeting. "I have been dealing with her on this case. Shouldn't I continue to deal with her directly?"

Eric heard an audible sigh through the phone. "Look outside your window, Eric," he said quietly.

"Outside my window?" Eric replied. "OK, hang on a second." Eric stood, walked around his desk to where he could raise the blinds which kept sunlight from entering the window facing Broad Street. Pulling the cord to raise the blinds, he looked to the left, toward the courthouse, and saw what appeared to be approximately two dozen people, all of whom appeared to be of Hispanic heritage, milling about in front of the courthouse steps. Some held signs; due to the distance between his office and the courthouse, he could not make out the wording – but clearly one was dominated by a picture of a young man, who he surmised was Jose Gomez. "Shit," he muttered, barely audibly.

Apparently his murmur was loud enough to be picked up through the phone, however, because Crawford immediately replied, "yes, Eric. Shit. Now please get your ass over here. Now. Thank you."

"Yeah, I will come over now," Eric replied. "Give me a few minutes."

"That's all I've got before I've got a real problem, Eric," Crawford said, his voice almost a whisper. "Really, just get here, please." Eric heard the phone click off, lowered the received back into its cradle, and dropped into the chair located on the other side of his desk. Peering out the window again, he watched as the numbers gathering outside of the courthouse began to grow. Clearly it was going to be some type of demonstration. What he could not determine is why his presence with Steve Crawford was demanded. He had no choice, however – he had to walk over to the Prosecutor's Office, but he was heartened by the fact that he could sneak in through the rear of the courthouse plaza, and avoid moving through the gauntlet of Latinos who would no doubt not be pleased with his presence in their midst.

Eric walked out to Fatima's desk, informed her that he was going to meet with Prosecutor Crawford, and then walked out of the office as her face contorted in a look of disbelief and surprise. He strode to the bathroom, his footsteps echoing, as usual, through the otherwise empty hallway, and splashed his face with water from the rusty sink in order to remove any last remnants of sweat from his forehead and face. He knew that he would begin to sweat anew during the walk from his office to the Prosecutor's Office, especially with the hot morning sun beating down on his balding head, but wanted to "freshen up" and gather his thoughts together before meeting with Crawford. He had seen the group outside of the courthouse. No doubt that was the reason that Crawford wanted the meeting. But what could be accomplished between the two of them? Crawford was not going to parade him in front of the Latino masses, and he no doubt knew that he would not be able to convince Eric to accept a guilty plea for Wendi. The uncertainty regarding the meeting's intent weighed heavily on Eric. He noticed that the sweat had already begun on his forehead as he walked out of the bathroom. By the time he exited the elevator on the building's first floor and walked out of the front door onto Broad Street, it was if he had not even stopped to wash his face in the bathroom.

The walk to the Courthouse seemed to take forever. Eric's feet felt heavier and heavier with each step, and he did not know if it was due to the oppressive New Jersey heat, made worse by the fact that he was wearing a suit, or if it was increasing dread at what awaited him in Steve Crawford's office. What if Amanda was in the room with Crawford? Would the two of them be able to act completely professional? Would even the slightest of emotion on behalf of either of them signal Crawford as to the situation between them? Crawford was a superb Prosecutor, and one of the tools required for that reputation was, of course, the ability to read a person's face and try to decipher their thoughts and emotions. While Eric certainly did not fear Steve Crawford, he realized that he was genuinely afraid of meeting with him that morning. The fears and trepidation only increased as he approached the throng gathered on the courthouse steps, and he deftly turned right before reaching the building in order to duck down the alley to Elizabethtown Plaza. By now, he could feel the sweat covering the entire top of his head and forehead, and felt beads of sweat falling down his shirt, uncomfortably running down his sides and back. At least his jacket would hide the sweat stains that were no doubt forming on his shirt, he reasoned to himself.

When Eric reached the Prosecutor's Office, he was quickly ushered into the meeting with Crawford. To his immediate relief, he noticed that Amanda was not in the room. He did, however, note three other people in the room with Crawford, all clearly of Hispanic heritage. He recognized one – the man seated in the chair directly to the right of the door, across from Crawford's large mahogany desk, and clad in a crisp navy blue suit with light tan shoes. As he entered the room, the man in the chair turned to see him, his bright teeth glistening under the office's fluorescent lighting. The man rose to greet Eric, extending his right hand.

"I trust that you remember Jesus Sanchez," Crawford said, as the man neared Eric.

Eric looked directly at Sanchez. "Of course I do," he said, extending his right hand and clasping Sanchez's. "It's been a long time, Jesus. What an unexpected pleasure."

Sanchez smiled and placed his left hand on Eric's right arm. "The pleasure is all mine, my friend," he said, smiling broadly so that his obviously whitened teeth continued to glisten. "It has been so long. I guess I haven't been spending much time in the courtrooms anymore," he added, laughing. "How are things going for you, I mean, other than avoiding the press on this case?"

Eric scowled. "I'm not avoiding the press, Jesus," he answered, coldly. "I just don't look for a camera every time I leave the house."

Now it was Sanchez's turn to frown. His smile immediately disappeared, and he removed his left hand from Eric's arm at the same time that he released his grip from their handshake. Taking a step back, he motioned toward the other two people in the room. "Mr. Goldberg," he said, sternly, "you may recognize Maria Gomez. She is the mother of the child that your ex-wife killed." Eric's face reddened as he turned to Crawford, who quickly motioned to him to keep his calm so that the tension in the room did not escalate. Eric bit his lip to avoid saying anything in response as Sanchez then turned to Ms. Gomez and said to her, in Spanish, *"Senora Gomez, esto es Eric Goldberg. El es el abogado de la mujer acusada de golpear a Jose."* She nodded slowly and stared at Eric, without saying anything in response. Eric understood what Sanchez had said to her – that he was the attorney representing the woman accused of hitting Jose. He was relieved that Sanchez used the word "accused" rather than saying that she had actually done it, although the woman's icy stare clearly showed that she had already convicted Wendi in her mind.

"Ms. Gomez," Eric said, *"mis condolencias"* (my condolences). Her stare did not waver, however, and her face showed no hints of amity. Eric felt new drops of sweat begin to form on his forehead. The man seated to Ms. Gomez's right shook his head slowly. Eric was not introduced to this man, but since he was holding Ms. Gomez's hand in his Eric surmised that he was either her boyfriend or a relative. No introduction was necessary. It could only lead to further discomfort.

"Eric," Crawford said as he walked back around his desk and settled into his chair, breaking the uncomfortable silence, "you're probably wondering why I have asked you here today." Eric, returning his gaze to Crawford, nodded. "Well, you probably noticed the people out front."

"That I did," Eric replied, "but I don't know what that has to do with me being here now." He looked down to his right, where Sanchez had again sat back down, taking Ms. Gomez's left hand in his right, and was slowly massaging it with his left hand. Her face, however, remained in a scowl.

"We are trying to defuse a situation here, Eric," Crawford said, "and I know that it is unorthodox to have you here now, and I don't have Ms. Johnson here with us today because I am trying to keep this meeting as low-profile, with as few people, as possible. Mr. Sanchez has called for what he says will be a peaceful rally outside of the courthouse today." Turning to Sanchez, he added, "no police needed for this, right, Jesus?"

Sanchez nodded slowly. "No *policia* needed today." He turned to Ms. Gomez and gently took her left hand into his right hand. She squeezed his hand slightly. Turning back to Crawford, "I don't think so," he said, the glint of his whitened teeth betraying the smirk that was forming on his face, "but you never know how people will react to situations, right, *Senor* Crawford?"

Crawford grimaced, clearly less than pleased with Sanchez's answer. Turning again to Eric, he continued. "I wanted to make an effort today to see if we can work out a resolution of this case, Eric. Amanda is a fine Prosecutor and I have no doubt that she is handling the matter properly, but she does not have the ability to make things resolve quickly, at least not to the level that I can do so. Maybe we can discuss a reduction in the charge, to something less, something that will still placate Ms. Gomez and Mr. Sanchez so that we can all move forward," he looked over at Maria Gomez. Sanchez was whispering in her ear, he presumed translating what he was saying, and he immediately realized that his last comment would come off as flippant and uncaring. "I mean something that will bring justice to Jose's death but without resulting in extended incarceration for your wife, I mean ex-wife. I know that his whole meeting is unorthodox, but given the circumstances, I believed it to be necessary in light of the surrounding events." Sanchez continued to translate for Maria Gomez, whose face somehow continued to show a more sour expression with each passing word.

Eric also grimaced, his face belying both his disbelief at being called into such an improper meeting with the Prosecutor, the victim's mother, and her mouthpiece, as well as his lack of understanding of what Crawford was truly seeking. "I'm not sure that I understand, Mr. Crawford," he replied, "are you suggesting that you can offer Wendi a plea bargain here that will somehow be palatable to her and yet at the same time be acceptable to both Ms. Gomez and Mr. Sanchez?" He turned to his right, watching Sanchez continue to softly translate to Ms. Gomez, whose face continued to contort as she slowly shook her head back and forth. "Without even thinking about how I can even consider doing this on my client's behalf, I should note that based on what I perceive to be Ms. Gomez's reaction to Mr. Sanchez's translation, I sincerely doubt that this will be possible."

"Mr. Goldberg," Sanchez said, "allow me to interrupt for a brief moment." He turned to Ms. Gomez and mumbled something to her in Spanish, but which was inaudible to both Eric and Crawford. She nodded slowly in comprehension, her face still betraying her utter contempt for both the men in the room and the situation. "It is wrong to assume that Ms. Gomez will not entertain a potential plea bargain in this matter." Sanchez continued, as the man seated to the other side of the deceased boy's mother softly translated in her other ear. "Nothing that happens here will bring back her son." A tear ran down Ms. Gomez's cheek as that sentence was translated to her. "But there must be some penalty for Ms. Goldberg. Not just for Ms. Gomez, but also for the Latino population of Elizabeth. They will not stand for anything less."

"Hold on, there, Jesus," Crawford interjected, loudly. "This is not about a political discussion. That is not the reason that we agreed to have Mr. Goldberg come here this morning. It is not my intention, as the Prosecutor of Union County, to browbeat him into taking a deal for his client based on what you claim your people, I mean, what you claim the people want. That's not my job here. So let's get that straight."

"Mr. Crawford," Jesus replied, with more than a hint of condescension in his voice, "I understand your job, but clearly we have had a misunderstanding about my job, my position here. I am not here, as you will recall, as the attorney for Ms. Gomez."

He stood. "Let there be no confusion, Mr. Crawford. I am here," he said, his voice rising and his arms outstretched in a camera-ready pose, "for the people of Elizabeth." He turned back to Maria Gomez. *"Estoy aqui,"* he said to her, his voice still booming, *"para la gente de Elizabeth."* For the first time, Ms. Gomez's face registered a positive response as a small, faint smile appeared. The man seated alongside her also smiled as he clapped his hands furiously.

Eric waited a moment after Sanchez's grandstanding to respond. "Mr. Crawford," he said slowly, "it appears that we are at an impasse here. Mr. Sanchez's theatrical performance clearly shows that he is not looking to negotiate, to the extent that we can even call this meeting a negotiation, and obviously I am not here to agree to any plea bargain that will result in my client seeing any time behind bars." He looked toward the window of Crawford's office. "And while I empathize with and understand your trepidation about the continued public outcry and demonstrations, I do not share those concerns, at least not to the detriment of my client who is," he slowed the pace of his voice as he looked down to Jesus Sanchez and Maria Gomez, "who is, was, and will be found to be innocent of the charges against her."

The second part of Sanchez's grandstanding and preaching was about to begin, and both Crawford and Eric knew it. Sanchez slowly rose from his chair, placed his right hand on Ms. Gomez's left shoulder, and then took a few steps closer to Crawford's desk so that he was now standing equidistant between the two men. "Gentlemen," he began softly, "this meeting is an outrage." He looked down at Ms. Gomez. *"esta reunion es un ultraje,"* he continued, his voice beginning to rise, *"me ofende que estamos discutiendo aqui el hijo de esta mujer como si fuera un pedaszo de carne, y no una creature viva, cuya vida fue quitada por las acciones imprudentes de client del Sr. Goldberg respirar."* He turned back to Steve Crawford. "It offends me that we are here discussing this woman's son," he continued, reaching down with his right hand, which Ms. Gomez immediately grasped in her hands, "as if he was a piece of meat, and not a living, breathing creature whose life was taken away by the reckless actions of Mr. Goldberg's client."

Crawford began to reply, but Sanchez quickly cut him off. "In fact, there is nothing that we can do here today that will satisfy Ms. Gomez and, more importantly, there is nothing that we can do today that will ease the suffering of the Latino population of Elizabeth. I will go outside now and spend time with my people in what I will try to keep as a peaceful demonstration." He knelt down and kissed Maria Gomez's left hand, translating what he had just said to her, "*de hecho, no hay nada que podamos hacer aquí hoy que va a satisfacer la señora Gomez y, más importante aún, no hay nada que podemos hacer hoy que aliviará el sufrimiento de la poblacion de Elizabeth. Voy a salir a la calle ahora y pasar tiempo con mi gente en lo que voy a tratar de mantener como una manifestación pacífica.*"

Now it was Maria Gomez's time to make a scene of her own. She dropped to her knees, still clutching Sanchez's hand, and began to sob uncontrollably. "*Jesus elogios,*" she said again and again through her wailing, which Eric mouthed to Crawford meant "praise Jesus." Neither man knew if she was referring to Jesus Christ or Jesus Sanchez. At that moment, however, as she knelt before Sanchez and began to kiss his hand through her tears, it appeared that to her, they were one and the same.

The melding of Jesus Sanchez the man and Jesus Sanchez the deity was the very belief that concerned Crawford the most. Both he and Eric were acutely aware of that fact. It was also the eventuality that Jesus Sanchez relished the most.

A smiling Sanchez looked alternately at both Crawford and Eric. "Gentlemen," he said, bending down to assist Maria Gomez in standing, and then providing her with a handkerchief to wipe her darkened face, moistened all over with her tears, "our work here is done. I am going outside. I will call for peace." He started to lead Ms. Gomez out of the office door. As he passed through the door's threshold, and without attempting to shake the hands of either Crawford or Eric, he turned back and added, "I will call for peace. But I make no guarantees. The longer that this goes unresolved, the more difficult it will be for me to keep these people calm." He paused. "Or as you said, Mr. Crawford, for me to keep *my people* calm," he added, in a mocking tone. He turned back around, gently kissed Maria Gomez on her forehead, dabbed at her still-moistened cheek with another handkerchief, and led her out of the office, to the street, and around to the front of the courthouse where they were greeted with cheers from the still-growing throng on the courthouse steps.

Crawford and Eric remained in Crawford's office, silently. Both shook their heads slowly at the events which had just transpired, until Crawford admonished Eric for making comments that exacerbated the situation. "You've got to be kidding me, Steve," Eric protested, "there was no way that this little love-fest of yours was going to accomplish anything. Did you see him? Did you watch the way she looked at him? He thinks he's the messiah, and these people believe it. The fact that his name is actually Jesus just makes it even more of a *fait accompli.* He is going to deliver them from their oppression, Steve. He's the one. He's the fucking Latino deliverer. At least he's the one in his own mind. The sick thing is that other people believe it."

Crawford slumped in his chair, his face showing defeat. "Fuck, Eric," he said, "you may be right. This is going to turn into a total shitstorm, you know."

"It already has been, Steve," replied Eric, "you just haven't been in the middle of it until now." He turned to walk out of the office. "And even though it was misguided, I do appreciate your efforts this morning and I'm sorry for you that I couldn't play ball. Tell Ms. Johnson that I was here and that I spoke highly of her. These young kids need some encouragement now and then, you know."

"I will tell her," Crawford answered, "but Eric, just so you know, it's clear that I need to take a more active role in this case now." Eric nodded, knowingly. "Now get out of here so I can prepare for the media onslaught that I'm going to be facing today. And please don't go around the front of the building. I don't want you encountering those people today."

"Way ahead of you, Steve, there's no way I'm going that way. I was already planning to just schlep down Elizabethtown Plaza and maybe cut quietly up the alley to Broad Street, and then dash, out of the camera's eye, back to my office. Remember what former New York Mayor Ed Koch said when someone dared him to walk in

Central Park at night back in the 70's? Something like 'the Mayor is not afraid. The Mayor is also not a schmuck.' The same is true here. I'm not going near them."

Eric moved toward the desk and shook Crawford's hand, both men clearly resigned to the fact that their lives would continue to be dominated by this case for some time. He exited the office and quickly made his way down the hallway to the outside, wary of coming into contact with Amanda Johnson. As promised, once he returned to the sunlit street known as Elizabethtown Plaza, he continued along his way until he reached Caldwell Avenue, in the shadow of the Christian Bollwage Parking Garage, and turned right. He strode quickly along Caldwell Avenue until he reached Broad Street, stopping briefly to turn to his right and survey the situation which was unfolding in front of the Courthouse. The number of people gathered had increased, seemingly doubling or tripling in number, and some were standing in the lane of traffic closest to the courthouse steps, blocking traffic, as they jostled each other for a chance at hearing their self-appointed Messiah speak.

He could see two news vans parked in the area, and watched as a woman clad in a navy blazer and oh-so-short skirt bounded from one of the vans, moving in a rapid manner that seemed impossible for someone wearing what appeared to be six-inch high heels. "No surprise," Eric said to himself, quietly, as he watched her chest bounce up and down with her every footstep. Even from this distance, he could clearly see her curvy silhouette. "There's Lupe Espinosa. I'd like to see that asshole Sanchez say a word without her being there, as if that is possible."

That night, as expected, Eric and others were treated to yet another Lupe Espinosa report about what she termed "the on-going situation in Elizabeth." Several snippets of Sanchez's fire and brimstone oration, during which he mentioned the failed meeting with the Prosecutor and the defense attorney, were included in the broadcast, and the cutaways to Lupe, with her blouse barely covering her breasts, also revealed the look of admiration, if not awe, in her eyes. Something was going on between them. He was sure of it.

He was also certain that Steve Crawford must have come perilously close to having an aneurysm during Sanchez's speech and its broadcast, especially due to the mention of what he had clearly hoped would be a clandestine meeting, and worried about how much Crawford would be interjecting himself into the case going forward. What he was unsure of was how Crawford's involvement would impact his interactions with Amanda Johnson, both in and out of the courtroom.

Chapter XXV – Fatima Reviews the File

An interesting thing happened to Eric after Lupe Espinosa's news reports aired. Business started to pour in; he was meeting at least one or two new clients each day. The maxim that "any publicity is good publicity" appeared to be holding true for him, and some people told him that they decided to use him as their attorney just because of the fact that he was still so close with his ex-wife that he was willing to represent her. "Mr. Goldberg," one woman who hired him to handle her divorce told him, "if you can stand in a courtroom next to your ex-wife, and represent her even though you are divorced, then you are the compassionate, fair, and honorable attorney that I need."

The benefits of the increased exposure, of course, also had a detrimental result. Due to his increased caseload, the workdays became even longer for Eric. He was struggling to keep up with the newly-beefed up work load, and logging twelve and thirteen-hour days became the norm. He was simply unable to leave the office before 8:00 at night on weeknights, and coupled with the additional hours that he was putting in on the weekends, he was beginning to tire more easily as the days dragged on. He was also seeing Amanda one or two nights per week, sometimes staying at her apartment until the wee hours of the morning before driving home, bleary-eyed, for three or four hours of sleep before beginning his work day.

"Eric," Fatima said to him one Wednesday morning, "you look exhausted. Why don't you take a day off? There's nothing on the calendar tomorrow except for one client meeting to go over interrogatory answers. I can do it for you. Take a day and rest. Stay home. Just sleep. You clearly need it."

Eric looked at Fatima through eyes colored by rivers of red lines, the marks of exhaustion, as well as eyes framed by discolored, puffy growths. He was also eating improperly, in addition to drinking more alcohol, and he had gained almost ten pounds over the past month. "Thanks, Fatima," he said, "but I don't think I can take a day. We're too busy here. I appreciate the offer, but I'll be here tomorrow." He stood and walked over to her, placing his arms around her in a light hug. "Thanks for worrying about me," he said, "here's what we can do. I will let you do the interrogatories with the client. And I promise that I will leave here tonight by 6:00."

Fatima rested her head on Eric's shoulder as she returned his hug. "I just don't think it's worth killing yourself, Eric," she said. "I understand we're busy with the new work, but I think that you're spending too much time looking over the paperwork for Wendi's case. I've seen you looking over the stuff at least a dozen times, and who knows how often you've looked when I haven't been looking. It's not going to change, you know. The facts are what the facts are."

"Fatima, don't start on Wendi …"

"No, Eric, this has nothing to do with her personally," Fatima interrupted. "You shouldn't spend this much wasted time on any case. The papers say what the papers say. Nothing is going to change. How about this? Give me the papers. I will look them over and see if anything catches my eye. If so, I will tell you. If not, you agree not to look at them until the next court appearance." She lifted her head and looked him squarely in the eyes. "We got a deal?"

Eric looked at her suspiciously. He wondered why she wanted to look at the papers, but at the same time, maybe she was right. He had reviewed the file dozens of times. Nothing seemed strange enough to merit a proper defense other than the question about time and phone usage. He decided to agree. "OK, Fatima," he said, warily, "you've got a deal. Tomorrow you spend the morning looking at the paperwork and I will let you tell me what I am missing, if anything."

"Don't be silly, Eric," Fatima replied. "Give it to me now. That way there is no temptation for you to look at it again this afternoon, or tonight after you leave at 6:00."

Eric winced. Fatima was half-right. He had intended to go through the paperwork that afternoon, especially the medical records of the dead teenager. He would not have time to look at anything after he left the office, however. He was going to leave the office at 6:00, just as he had promised Fatima, but he was not leaving at 6:00 in order to appease her or to get some rest. He had already been planning to leave at 6:00 – and he was driving straight to Amanda's to have dinner with her before they both settled in to watch that evening's Yankees' game. "You know me too well, my cousin," he said, reaching under the file in front of him and pulling out the sheaf of paperwork. "You caught me. Here's the discovery that we got from the Prosecutor's office. Have at it."

Fatima laughed as she took the papers from Eric's grip. "OK, now you focus on something else and I will go through these papers." She turned and started to walk back to her desk. Turning and looking behind her, she added, "and I guarantee you that I won't find anything else. You're very thorough, Eric. I can't imagine that you would have missed anything."

For reasons that he could not explain, Eric felt somewhat liberated as the file left his office in Fatima's capable hands. For weeks now, Wendi's file, or some part of it, had occupied a space on his already overly-cluttered desk. The papers called to him, they beckoned him, and demanded his attention to the exclusion of the other files. Now, with the file and its contents gone, he was able to better focus on the remainder of his cases. He spent the next three hours going through the other files and mail on his desk, returning e-mails and phone calls, and, for the first time since he could remember, was able to reduce the number of papers in the "inbox" on his desk by half. It was easily the most productive day, paperwork-wise, that he had in what seemed like weeks or months, or at least since Amanda first brought the discovery on Wendi's file to him.

After some time passed, he was, however, intrigued by Fatima and her review of the file. He wondered if she had located any inconsistency in the files, or whether anything had appeared odd to her. An hour after she first began her review, Eric walked out to her desk. Without even looking up at him, she shooed him away with a wave of her right hand. Eric retreated to his desk, silently, and did not bother Fatima again until she reappeared in his doorway two hours later.

"Well?" Eric asked as she stood, silently, holding the contents of Wendi's file in her right hand, clutched against her chest.

She sat down on the chair opposite his desk and opened the file. "Well, I went through the entire file," she said, thumbing through its pages. "Overall it's pretty boring stuff, to be honest with you," she began. "There were, though, two things that I noticed. One that I think you already saw, and one that may be nothing but to me it leapt out."

Eric leaned forward, intrigued by Fatima's comments and pleasantly surprised that she had read the file carefully enough to notice anything that he may have missed. "OK, first tell me the one that you think I already know, and then let's discuss the other."

Fatima thumbed through the file until she reached Jose Gomez's medical records. On the third page of the medicals, there was a section which had already been noted with a blue pen, presumably by Eric. "I assume that this pen mark is yours, Eric," she said, holding up the piece of paper and showing it to him. He leaned forward and strained to see the page, and then nodded in agreement when he realized that the mark was, in fact, previously made by him. "In looking at these records, most of the injuries seem to be consistent with what we, as laypeople, would think would happen in a car accident. But one entry was interesting, and I think it is the part that you had noted with your mark – the wound in his back that appeared to be straight and deep."

"Yes," Eric said, "I did find that interesting. I don't know how that could have happened from the accident as it was described by Wendi, or even by the other kid."

"Unless some part of the car that was long and sharp punctured his back, I don't see how it could have happened. And if he fell into the car, then Wendi hit him on his side so there would be no way for that type of injury to take place in his back, unless when he rolled he fell directly on top of something; but then the police would likely have found something at the scene, I would think."

"So do you think that there was something else?"

Fatima stared at the ceiling. "I can't say for sure, and I am certainly not a doctor or an investigator, but I would have to assume that there was something else that caused that wound. The only question in my mind is what, and I have no answers for that."

"I agree completely," Eric said, "that's one of the things that have caused me the most concern about this case, and one of the reasons why I keep reading. I want to understand that better."

"Understood. Now do you want to hear my other point?"

"Absolutely," replied Eric. He reached for a pen and pulled the legal-sized yellow pad on his desk closer to him so that he could take notes as Fatima spoke.

"Well, you are going to have to forgive me a bit on this one, but I need to give you a little bit of background. One of the quirks in the Hispanic community, as I am sure you are aware, is the use of two last names. White people, you know, Europeans and Americans like you have a last name. Sometimes you have a middle name, and sometimes that middle name can be your mother's maiden name. Also sometimes, but not often, people hyphenate their last names. That's pretty rare, though."

"I think I know where you are going with this," interrupted Eric, "but please keep going so I can see if I am correct."

"Anyway, white people have one last name. Most Hispanics, however, have two, which they hyphenate. And the interesting part is that when they hyphenate, often their father's last name is first and their mother's second, which is the opposite of what white people do when they keep both last names."

"Right," Eric said, as he finished scribbling notes on his legal pad and looked up at Fatima. "I have heard of that. It's something we have had to deal in the past with some of our clients. But why is that interesting?"

Fatima smiled. "I was hoping you would ask me that question," she said, laughing. "Here's why it is important. Sometimes, the people do not want to use the fully-hyphenated last name, so they use just the second name, which is their mother's maiden name. So even if people are siblings, they can have last names that are different depending on which of the last names they decide to use, or which name their parents decide to use for them."

"And that is important here because?"

"Well, the witness, the one who said that Wendi was on the phone at the time of the accident, is identified in several sections of the papers as Ramon Lopez. In one other area, though, he is identified as Ramon Lopez-Ortiz. If I know you, then you have already done some form of background search for Ramon Lopez, which, since there are no notations to the contrary, I will assume revealed nothing bad. Perhaps if we did a search on a Ramon Ortiz, the outcome would be different. Likely not, but you never know."

Eric smiled. "That's true, Fatima, you never do know." He wrote the name "Ramon Ortiz" in large, block letters on the pad in front of him. "Normally it is hard to get any kind of bad records on kids, but it's certainly worth a shot."

Fatima beamed, with a sense of self-satisfaction from having found something in the records that Eric had overlooked. It may not lead to anything, but it was still nice to be complimented. "But Fatima," Eric said, "now that you did find something, I don't have to put the file away. We had a deal, you know." He reached out with his right hand. "Hand it over."

"Eric, honey," she replied, "I don't want you to put it away." Silently assenting to his statement, she carefully placed the file back into its customary place on his desk.

"I want you to look into this," she said, a faint smile creasing her face, "and if it turns into something, then, believe it or not, I will be happy that I was able to help."

Eric contorted his face into an exaggerated expression of surprise. "Well, my dear," he said, "I'm glad to know that you want to help Wendi. That makes me feel good."

"Don't feel too good, cousin," Fatima said, shaking her head and her smile disappearing as she stood. "Don't misunderstand me. I'm not doing this to help Wendi. Not at all. I'm doing this to help you." She turned to leave the room as she continued. "We've been through this before. I want you to succeed, that's all I have ever wanted for you, especially since I began to work here with you. And if she benefits, I guess that is good for her. But my efforts are expended for you, my dear, not for her. I never work for her." She paused. "Nothing that I will ever do will be to benefit her, not after what she did to you. I don't forget, and I don't forgive."

Eric sighed. He was pleased that Fatima was so loyal to him, which was expected in light of their close relationship. He was, however, disappointed in her continued animosity toward Wendi, although he realized that her feelings toward Wendi were, to a large extent, also expected. "Thanks, Fatima," he said, as he turned toward his computer and began to check his e-mails.

"Eric?" he heard Fatima ask, seemingly still from the doorway. He turned and was surprised to see that Fatima was still in his office, with a concerned look on her face. "You know that she's guilty, right?"

"What do you mean, Fatima?"

"Well," she answered, "what I mean is, no matter what evidence we find, I think we can pretty much agree that she was texting while she was driving and that's why she hit the kid."

Eric's face no doubt betrayed his disbelief at the conversation. "What do you mean, agree?" he asked, "we don't know for a fact that she is guilty."

Fatima scowled. "Don't play word games with me," she said, coldly. "Let me ask you this question. Have you asked her, point blank, if she was texting right before or during the accident?"

Eric leaned back in his chair. "When I got to the scene, she told me that she wasn't."

"Oh did she?" Fatima asked in a mocking tone. "So in the heat of the moment, as you attorneys would say, she denied causing an accident which killed a teenage pedestrian. That's not a surprise. Have you asked her since? Have you asked her since she calmed down?"

Eric looked away, out the window to the courthouse. "Have I asked her again?"

"Yes, Eric. My question is, counselor, have you asked Wendi even once if she is guilty?"

"No," Eric replied. "I have not. But Fatima, you know as well as I do that we never ask such a pointed question."

"You know she killed him, right?"

Eric turned back around and stared Fatima squarely in the eye. "It doesn't matter."

Chapter XXVI – Watching the Yankees' Game

Fatima left the office that day at 5:10. Before she left, she poked her head into Eric's office and admonished him to make sure that he left before 6:00, as he had promised, and that he should go home, relax, maybe watch that night's baseball game and then try to get a good night's sleep. "Under no circumstances," she scolded, "are you to bring any work home with you tonight. It will be here when you get back here tomorrow. Especially Wendi's file. Make sure it stays on your desk."

Eric gasped in mock horror. "Yes, mom," he said, "I will leave at 6:00. I will watch the baseball game later. I will not bring any files home with me, not even Wendi's." He did not promise to go home or relax, of course, nor did he promise not to "work" on any files. He also did not mention the fact that he was going to Amanda's apartment, of course. He had already formulated an idea of how his new friend may be able to help him get some information on Ramon Ortiz, using her powers as a Prosecutor. He did not share those thoughts either. Satisfied that she had convinced Eric to go home and rest, Fatima smiled, blew him a kiss goodbye, and then turned and left the office. Once she was out the door, Eric immediately swiveled his chair and began to search the internet for people named Ramon Lopez, Ramon Lopez-Ortiz, and Ramon Ortiz.

The middle selection, the one with the hyphenated last name, revealed nothing, other than the generic "we find people" websites that inevitably pop up whenever a search is performed on a person's name. The other two searches, since the names provided were both somewhat common, led to thousands of results. Eric then tried to narrow down the choices by also including "Elizabeth New Jersey" in the searches – which still led to numerous sites, including hundreds of social media pages. The search with the last name Lopez also revealed entries regarding membership on the Honor Roll at Elizabeth High School; these were the same sites that he had located when he first searched the name, and the entries were recent enough that Eric surmised that the Honor Roll student Ramon Lopez was the same Ramon Lopez who was now accusing his ex-wife of murdering Jose Gomez.

The name "Ramon Ortiz" did not yield any such possibly productive results, at least not for anyone with that name who resided in Elizabeth. Eric tried to scroll through some of the social media pages that appeared, but, sadly, so many looked exactly the same that he gave up after a couple of dozen. He did not know how many teenagers were named Ramon Ortiz, but his conservative guess, based on the number of social media pages, was approximately ten thousand. And at least half of them, it appeared, resided in the greater Elizabeth area. He could never wade through all of them. Even if he were to try to go through them all, he had never really gotten a good glimpse at the kid, so he would likely not even know if he was even looking at the right page. It was, clearly, an exercise in futility.

He looked at his watch. It was 5:50. He was scheduled to arrive at Amanda's at 6:15 for dinner. Given the normal amount of traffic on Morris Avenue on weeknights, he would have to leave within the next five minutes in order to get there on time. As he turned to retrieve his keys and wallet from his desk drawer, the office phone began to ring. Normally he would not even consider answering the phone after 5:00, but with the sudden surge in new work following his television exposure, he was more apt to do so, thinking it could be another person calling about possible representation. Despite the fact that he had to leave within minutes, he decided to risk being late for Amanda's in order to speak to a potential new client, and picked up the receiver.

He immediately regretted answering the phone. The caller was not a potential new client, but rather, the exact opposite. Eric found himself speaking to a man whom he had represented for a divorce; the matter had settled over three years ago. The ex-client was calling to complain about something in the property settlement agreement that he and his wife had signed before the divorce was finalized. He was calling to complain three years after the document was signed and the divorce finalized. He was calling to complain even though the document had been negotiated over a three-month period between him and his wife, through their respective counsels and on their own. Despite the fact that the man had agreed to the terms of the agreement, had ensured that he fully understood them, and even enlisted the advice of an accountant with respect to the financial terms, now, three years later, he had a problem and somehow, inexplicably, it was Eric's fault.

Eric had no time for this kind of garbage now. "Listen to me, sir. We did this agreement three years ago. I don't remember the specifics, and you can't possibly expect me to remember what on earth we discussed three years ago. What I do know is that you agreed to it then. You can't argue with me about it now."

The former client would not back down that easily. "Yes I can, Mr. Goldberg. Just because you clearly still get along with your ex-wife does not mean that the rest of us don't have continuing problems with ours, problems that our attorneys should have taken care of for us when we first got divorced," he stated, emphatically, "that's what I paid you for!"

"What does my ex-wife have to do with this?" Eric asked, his voice also rising as his level of anger was increasing by the second.

The man chuckled. "Well, from what I hear you are not only representing her in court, but are also having what I guess we would call an affair with her. Aside from not being very professional of you, it kind of makes me wonder about your ethics and, then, whether or not you were really properly representing me. Now, I have to deal with the fallout, but if it was because you fucked up, then you need to deal with it also."

Eric was growing more irate by the second, and was completely offended by this last set of comments and the former client, whom he now remembered was an asshole to deal with from the beginning, questioning his ethics or job performance. And he did not want to deal with it any longer, especially since it was not benefiting him in any way. "Are you paying me for this phone call?" Eric barked.

"Why would I pay you to fix your screw-up?" the man yelled back.

"You're not!" Eric yelled. "You're not, because I didn't screw anything up and this call is over!" He slammed the receiver back into its cradle. "Fuck you!" he then yelled, although he knew that the caller would not hear him. The phone immediately began to ring again. Still hot, Eric went to reach for it, but then thought better of engaging in further arguments with his unreasonable ex-client and decided to let it ring until the voice mail picked up. Once the voice mail engaged the caller hung up, and then the phone rang anew. Again Eric let it pass directly into voice mail, and again the caller hung up. Eric did not know whether either or both of those subsequent calls were from the same person, but he assumed that they were. He did not know if the man would never call again, and hoped that he would not, but, regardless, this was not the time for argument.

It was now a few minutes before six o'clock. He was going to be late for Amanda's. He certainly did not want to go there, however, in the bad mood caused by the phone call. He gathered up his wallet and keys, turned off the monitor to his computer, and sat in his chair for a second. Trying to calm himself, he took several deep breaths and closed his eyes. After a couple of minutes, the mood seemed to pass. His heart rate slowed. The color of his face lightened. He was ready to go.

As he walked down the hallway to the elevator, he was struck by an unnerving thought. Perhaps, he suddenly realized, the publicity from Wendi's trial could actually work against him with some people. This ass was the first person to refer to Eric's representation of Wendi in a negative way, but he wondered if others would feel the same way. Would clients whom he had represented during the divorce argue that he was ineffective as their counsel because he was too pre-occupied with his own divorce to properly handle their cases? Would current clients complain that he was distracted by his representation and alleged romance with his ex-wife, and that he therefore did not handle their cases properly? Was this asshole simply the tip of the iceberg?

The elevator door opened. As Eric stepped inside, he began to seethe again. The ex-client had put the germ for thoughts of self-doubt in his head. Now, as the door closed and the elevator began to descend, he began to wonder if clients would call him in a few years, complaining that he had not handled their cases properly, because he was too focused on his ex-wife's case. Or because he was too busy romancing the Prosecutor who was handling his ex-wife's case.

He wondered which was worse.

As he approached the parking lot where his car was located, he could see that the westbound traffic on Broad Street was even more congested than usual. He decided to alert Amanda that he would be a few minutes late, so that she could slow her cooking to coincide with his arrival. He reached for his cell phone, and carefully punched out the numbers of her home telephone. He was loathe to use her cell phone, and was especially careful not to text her – he worried that the Prosecutor's office monitored the phones given to the Assistant Prosecutors, and was concerned that their texts were being monitored as well. There was simply no reason to give those spies any reason to suspect anything.

Amanda picked up the phone on the second ring, and clearly recognized his cell phone number on her caller ID. "I'm not going to like this call, am I?" she asked, with more than a hint of sadness in her voice. "Dinner is almost ready, and I've been studying the Yankees' website so I know the players for tonight's game. You can't cancel on me now."

"I'm not canceling," Eric said. "I'm just running a little late. Some asshole called me to ream me out about a divorce we did three years ago and I couldn't get off the phone. Now I'm walking to my car and the traffic here looks bad. I assume it's the same on Morris Avenue, so I figure I will be about ten minutes late. I just wanted to let you know."

"Well, isn't that considerate of you?" Amanda said, her sadness turned to an upbeat tenor. "Don't worry about it; dinner won't be ready for a while anyway." She laughed. "I'm not much of a cook, if I haven't mentioned it before, so my timing of things leaves a lot to be desired. I have a feeling we won't even be eating until the second inning or so."

"I'm sure it will be fine," Eric replied. "I'm looking forward to it."

"I'm looking forward to seeing you," Amanda said. "No, let me rephrase that - I'm really looking forward to seeing you. I had a bad day and the only thing that got me through this shit was the knowledge that I was going to be able to see you tonight. Knowing that we would be eating together and watching the game. But drive carefully and don't speed. Neither of us knows any good defense attorneys."

Eric was taken slightly aback by her effervescent recitation of the evening's events, especially her repetition as to her joy at seeing him. Could she be getting really serious about their relationship? If she were, would that be a bad thing? He was having the same feelings for her, right? Eric struggled to clear his head, knowing that he had to say something in response to her before he hung up the phone. "Very funny," he said as he took his keys out of his pocket and unlocked the car doors. "No, neither of us knows any good defense attorneys. I guess that we are lucky that the Prosecutors in this county suck so much that the defense guys don't even have to be that good." He laughed, and laughter that was joined, on the other end of the line, by Amanda. "I just got to the car," he said, "see you in a little while."

Eric pulled his car out of the lot and turned right onto Broad Street. As he approached the Elizabeth train station, he could see that there was a stopped car underneath the train trestle. Cars were going around the stalled car, but at a slow pace. From what he could see from his vantage point, the cars were moving at a proper clip after passing that obstruction. His car, like the others in front of it, moved at a snail's pace; once he was able to edge over to the right, directly under the railroad trestle, however, he was able to accelerate to a more proper 25 miles per hour as he approached the next light. When that light turned green he quickly turned left in front of oncoming traffic, and proceeded along that road until making a right at the next light, onto a similarly heavily-trafficked Morris Avenue. His slow progress west continued until several minutes later, when he was able to make a left turn into Amanda's condominium development and find a parking space.

Bounding from his car, he strode quickly to Amanda's building and, when he reached its front door, dialed her number on the intercom system so that she could unlock the front door for him. "Hello?" she called through the intercom.

"I'm here, can you buzz me in?"

"Do I know you?" asked the voice through the intercom, clearly Amanda. Her playful demeanor excited Eric. He was definitely falling for her, and he believed that she was no doubt feeling the same about him. The concept of them having mutual feelings for each other both excited and frightened him.

"No, you don't," Eric answered, "because if you knew me, and the trouble that I bring, there is no way you would let me up."

He could hear Amanda laughing through the speaker. "Well, in that case," she said, still laughing, "come on up. This sounds interesting." The buzzer on the door sounded, and Eric pushed open the door and then walked the two flights up to Amanda's apartment rather than talking the elevator, which was notoriously slow. Approaching the door to her apartment, he saw that she had left it slightly ajar.

Pushing the door open and poking his head into the apartment's hallway, he called, "I'm here. Can I come in?"

A voice called from the kitchen. "That all depends. Is this the mystery man from downstairs who I wouldn't want to let in if I knew him?"

Eric could smell the dueling aromas of cooking marinara sauce and of baking bread. "Guilty as charged, Madame Prosecutor."

"Well then," she said, "come on in. But I must warn you," she said, "you can't stay long. I have a friend coming over soon for dinner, a special friend, and I don't know if he will like you being here with me."

The phrase "special friend" lingered in Eric's ears. In a positive way.

"Did you say he? It must be a man friend." Eric said, closing the door behind him. "Tell me about this man friend." Despite Amanda's use of the word "special," he was still a little uncertain of his exact status with her so he was careful not to use the term "boyfriend" for fear of her reaction. He was also a slight bit unsure as to whether he would want her to be happy or upset with the use of such a term, although he was beginning to feel more and more like he would want her to answer in the affirmative should he invoke the term.

"Let me see," Amanda replied. "How can I describe him? Well, he's pretty old. His hair is getting really gray, he keeps telling me how out of shape he is and, perhaps worst of all, he listens to really old music." She giggled and then gasped as if she remembered something important. "Oh! I almost forgot, he's a criminal defense attorney and a divorce attorney, and you know how they can be."

"That I do," Eric replied as he walked the short hallway, toward the kitchen. "Can you tell me anything positive about him?"

"Yes I can," Amanda said, laughing. "I am positive that when he comes into the kitchen, he will like what I am wearing."

Eric was two steps from the kitchen entry when she made that declaration. He paused just before he reached the opening, and asked, "He will? Are you really positive?"

"Oh, absolutely," Amanda replied. "If he's not, then it's not for my lack of trying. You know all of those movies when the guy comes into the kitchen and his woman is in there wearing nothing but an apron?"

Eric began to sweat. "Yes. Are you just wearing an apron?"

"No, silly," she said. "That would be too cliché. We need to improvise, you know. We can't just do the expected. An apron was too simple."

"Well, now my interest is really, uh, really piqued. He, whoever he is, is quite the lucky guy. And I guess that I am also, also, well, also lucky since I get to see you first." Eric stammered. "Can I come in to see?"

"Of course you can. As I told you, I've been waiting for someone, and if my other friend isn't coming here, then I guess that you can come in and see what I had prepared for him. It will just be his loss, even though I've been really looking forward to seeing him all day."

"OK, then," Eric answered, "I'm coming into the kitchen." He was eager with anticipation as to what Amanda had concocted for him. He peeked around the corner and, seeing Amanda, gasped audibly. She was not wearing an apron. She was, however, wearing what was once a Yankees' jersey. It was one of the female-style jerseys, the ones that accentuate a woman's curves rather than hanging limply like the men's versions do. It was clearly too small for her, and she had cut the sleeves off, along with parts of the sides, so that he could see the sides of her braless breasts when she turned to the side. Also, the bottom of the jersey came to just below her navel, and she was wearing navy and white pinstriped underwear. "Wow!" was all that he could say. "You look fantastic!"

She turned to him. The top three buttons of the jersey were undone, showing off her cleavage. "That's the word? Fantastic?" She unbuttoned another button, and moved the right side of the jersey front to the side so that her entire breast was exposed. "Well, how about now? Do I still look fantastic?"

"More than fantastic, I would say. You are downright sexy. How's that for an analysis?"

She pulled the jersey slightly inward so that it again encased her breast, and then buttoned two buttons so that more was left to the imagination. "Do you like the boy shorts?" she asked, rubbing her hands along the back of her pinstriped underwear. "I ordered them a week ago. I didn't know that baseball teams made such kinky things for women."

"Neither did I," said Eric, "but I like. And I have to tell you, this friend of yours who's coming over is one lucky guy." He paused and scratched his chin. "Let me ask you a question. No, forget that. Let's pretend."

"Pretend?" She asked, in a voice barely above a whisper. "That sounds kinky."

"Yes, pretend," he answered, as he took another step toward her. "How about you pretend, just for the moment, that I am him, you know, the other guy." He laughed. "It may be hard for you to imagine looking at what a fine physical specimen I am," he said, his hands moving up and down alongside his torso, "but imagine, if you can, that I am the old, gray, fat guy that you described. Now, assuming that I was this man friend and I walked into the kitchen and found you dressed all sexy in that uniform, wait, I'm sorry, I'm not really a big baseball fan. What team's jersey is that, anyway?"

Amanda chuckled. "My man friend would know right away. I don't know how I can even think of faking that you are him if you don't know what team this is for."

"Shit," Eric said. "You're going to make me guess, aren't you?" He wiped pretend perspiration from his forehead in an exaggerated motion. "That's a lot of pressure for me. But I can probably guess. Let's see," he said, "we're in New Jersey. There are two teams in New York, if I recall properly. The Mets wear blue and orange, I know that; I remember someone telling me that they wear those colors to honor the two New York teams that went to California in the 1950's. Pretty impressive that I know that, don't you think so?"

"Impressive … and sexy," Amanda purred. She did not know if what Eric had said was correct, of course, but she loved what he was saying, and the way that he was playing along with her little game. His feigned ignorance endeared him even more to her.

"I thought so," Eric continued. "Maybe I know more about baseball than I thought. So if that shirt, I mean jersey, isn't the Mets, then that team must be," he held up his hands in front of his chest and crossed the index and middle fingers on both as his voice turned to a questioning and hopeful tone, "the Yankees?" He opened his eyes wide as he waited for her response.

She took a step toward him. "Yes, mystery man, this is a Yankees' jersey. Now I can pretend that you are my friend." She stopped and looked at Eric, her gaze running from the floor to the top of his balding head. "Let me think," she began to say as her eyes moved up Eric's body, "like I said, he is pretty old, and he drinks, get this, scotch. So what I would probably be doing if you were him would be to walk to the table over there," she pointed to her right, "and tell him that he can help himself to some of the scotch that I bought for him today. I would also need to pray that I bought the right kind, because, let's face it; there aren't a lot of women my age who buy scotch, except maybe for our daddies." She reached up with her right hand and grabbed a handful of her hair, twisting it between her fingers like a schoolgirl. "There's a little ice bucket there because, get this, that's how he likes it. Scotch over ice. He's not even man enough to drink it neat." She paused for dramatic effect. "Neat. That's a bar term, in case you didn't know."

"Well," Eric interrupted, "very few people drink scotch without ice, so I understand him. And as for bar terms, I am also an attorney, I will have you know, so I know a little something about the bar."

"Oh do you?" Amanda asked. "That makes one of us. Anyway, I would tell him to make himself a scotch, and when he turned his back, I would sneak up behind him and give him a big hug." She ran her left hand up and down her backside. "And while I was hugging him, I would let him take his arm, reach behind me, and rub my little Yankee underwear."

"Well, I don't want to be overly forward, but I can do that, I mean, especially since he's not here," Eric said, wishfully.

"Nope," Amanda immediately responded as she removed her hand from her own butt and crossed her arms in front of her chest. "Now that I think about it, I'm not big into pretending. I think that I will just wait for him to get here. As I told you before, I was really looking forward to seeing him tonight, and I don't want to spoil things by getting involved with someone else, especially someone whom I just met." She looked at Eric and her face broke into a smile. "But tell you what, sir," she added, "since he's not here, I am going to keep cooking for him. Why don't you fix yourself a scotch?"

Eric sighed. "It's not as exciting, but OK. You keep cooking. I'll make myself a drink." He walked over to the table where the bottle of scotch sat, turning his back to Amanda. Picking up a glass, he reached for the ice bucket, grabbed three pieces of ice, and dropped them into the glass. He was reaching for the Scotch bottle, which was of a high quality, when he felt Amanda grab him from behind.

"Change of plans, mystery man. Looks like my boyfriend's not coming, at least not yet," she purred. Eric smiled happily at her use of the word "boyfriend," although she could not see his grin since she was still behind him. "So I guess you will have to do. Do me, that is." She took his arm, lowered it so that the glass came to rest on the table, and then pushed the arm so that Eric turned around, his face still in a smile, and the two were facing each other. "Dinner's almost ready," she said, returning his smile and hoping that it was because she had used the word "boyfriend" to describe him. "I hope you like spaghetti and meatballs. I know it's a messy meal and not proper date food, but since we're not really dating I have no real need to impress you with how neatly I can eat." She looked down at her jersey. "Besides, if I get some sauce on my clean white jersey, I will just have to take it off."

"You're going to make me throw sauce on you while we're eating," Eric said as he grabbed Amanda and pulled her closer to him in a strong embrace. Suddenly a bad smell permeated the air. "I think something's burning," he said. He looked over Amanda's shoulder, to the oven, and saw smoke curling out of its top edge. "Are you cooking something in the oven? It smells like something seems to be burning."

"Shit!" Amanda yelled, breaking free of Eric's grasp. "I was making garlic bread to go with the spaghetti." She dashed over to the oven and turned the knob to "off." Opening the oven door, she allowed the smoke from inside to billow out and envelop the entire area. The smoke alarm began to chime, so Amanda and Eric opened every window they could reach so that the smoke would dissipate. The alarm abated seconds later, and when the building superintendent arrived a few minutes later Eric went to the door to tell him that everything was under control, rather than have an almost half-dressed Amanda give the super a thrill.

"Well, that was a little excitement," Eric said as he scraped the tops off of the burned garlic bread. Amanda pulled two bowls from the cabinet above her countertop, and filled them a little more than half-way with spaghetti that would, true to her statement of being unable to properly time food preparation, turn out to be slightly al dente. She then took a wooden spoon from a drawer to the right of the oven, scooped up some small meatballs hidden in a pot of sauce, and placed them atop the pasta in each bowl.

"Here's dinner, actually done before I expected," Amanda said as she handed one of the bowls to Eric. "I hope it's good." She looked down at the bowl in Eric's hand, examining its contents as if it were the first time she had made them. "To be honest, I've never been much of a cook … but this is something that I think I can make. At least something I have made before." She took the other bowl in her hand and carried it over to the small table located on the other side of the kitchen. Two napkins were already laid out on the table, each covered with a full set of utensils. Looking back over the counter, she said, "Eric, don't forget your scotch. I'm going to pour myself a glass of white wine, if you don't mind."

Eric walked back over and took his scotch. He had already consumed most of it, and finished it in one gulp. "Wine sounds good to me," he said. "Is it cold? If not, let me get some ice from the freezer, if you don't think I am being too forward." He retrieved a half-dozen ice cubes and placed them into two wine glasses that sat on the table. Amanda reached for the bottle of wine and poured, filling each glass to just below the top rim. "Looking to get me drunk, I see," commented Eric. "I hope you're not planning on taking advantage of me."

"Of course not, silly. I just like wine." She waited for Eric to take his first taste of the meatballs, and then waited for his assessment of her cooking prowess.

A framed 5x7 photograph stood sentry on the window ledge located next to the kitchen table. From inside the frame, the smiling faces of a police officer and a woman stared in Eric's direction. Looking at the photo and then at Amanda, Eric asked, "nice picture, Amanda. Who is it?"

Amanda gulped down a large sip of her wine. "Those are my parents," she said softly. "My dad was a cop here in Elizabeth, and that picture was taken when I was about five years old, a couple of years before … before he …" Tears welled up in Amanda's eyes. Eric already knew what she was having difficulty saying, even though she did not know that he was aware of his murder.

"It's OK," Eric said, reaching out and taking her hand in his. "We can talk about it another time." He looked down at the bowl of pasta in front of him. "Now, let's eat this food and get ready to watch the game."

"Thank you," she said softly as she wiped the moisture from her eyes. She watched Eric take a forkful of the food. "What do you think?"

"This is really good," Eric said after he swallowed that initial taste. And he meant it. He rarely cooked for himself, and, especially since Jason was almost never home with him now, his opportunities to cook for someone else had waned. Even when he cooked, it was nothing too exotic, but he appreciated a good meal. Wendi was a decent cook, and he had learned to appreciate her abilities more after he moved out, when he could no longer eat her offerings. The meatballs, he believed, were actually better than most of the food that Wendi had cooked for him during their marriage. Eric's delusions of Amanda's cooking acumen quickly waned, however, when he took some of the pasta. He found the pasta to be little too al dente, meaning a little too crunchy, for his liking. He saw no need, however, to tell Amanda of this problem.

She soon figured it out herself, as Eric could actually hear the crunch of the pasta as she took her first bite. "Oh my god," she cried, "this spaghetti is so hard. Why didn't you say anything?"

"I didn't see a need, to tell you the truth. Mine isn't so hard, and the meatballs and sauce are so good that it doesn't even matter."

Amanda smiled. "You are so sweet," she said, "and such a good liar." She cautiously maneuvered her fork around the bowl so as to pick up only a meatball, and no pasta. Changing the topic, she asked, "Eric, do you want to brief me on the game before it starts so that I understand it better?"

Eric looked across the table. As expected, a spot of sauce glowed from the white of her Yankees' jersey, just above her left breast. "I can do that if you want, but of more pressing concern is that you seem to have gotten some of that tasty sauce on your Yankees' jersey." He motioned toward her chest. "You might want to put some water on it right away."

"I knew this would happen," she said. She stood and walked over to the sink. Pulling a paper towel off of the roll standing to the left of the sink, she folded it twice so that it was now reduced to one-fourth of its original size. Running it under the water to make it wet, she then dabbed at the spot carefully, trying not to increase the size of the potential stain. "Is it gone?" she asked as she continued to dab at the sauce, trying in vain to look downward. "I can't really see too well from up here."

Eric strained his eyes to see due to the distance between he and Amanda. The stain appeared to be gone, replaced with a large wet circle. "From what I can see, you're good," he said, "come on back and finish your dinner. The game starts in a few minutes. But let's eat. We can talk about baseball when the game is on, and it will be easier to understand if we talk about it as it is happening." He paused, and then laughed. "In fact, I can brief you during the game, and then, if you're good, I can debrief you after the game."

Amanda looked at him and smiled, enjoying his use of double entendre. "I think I would like that. Let's finish eating so we can watch the game. I never knew baseball could be so sexy and exciting."

The two finished the meal in relative silence. Eric thought about asking her whether she would be able to obtain some information on Ramon Ortiz, but he did not know how to broach the topic. He did not want to upset the ambiance of the dinner by talking about work-related topics. He also worried that she would recognize the name from Wendi's file and refuse to help him, whether in her role as Prosecutor or jealous woman. He decided to wait until they were watching the game, when her guard would be down more, especially after she polished off her second glass of wine.

A half an hour later, the Yankees were already on the short end of a 1-0 score. Eric had spent the better part of the game's two innings explaining the game to Amanda, who seemed a willing student as she lay on the couch, her head resting against Eric's shoulder. Her jersey rode up on her side as she lay there, and her perfectly-formed behind was staring Eric in the face when he looked to his right. As the game progressed, he took to rubbing that ass with his right hand for good luck during certain key at-bats. She did not resist nor complain. Sadly, however, the Yankees did not draw any luck from his actions.

Eventually, the game ended as so many had during this lost season for the Yankees, with them falling by a 5-2 count. Eric and Amanda were unaware of the final score, as they had turned the game off during the middle of the seventh inning when the visiting team scored their fourth run, seemingly putting the game out of reach at that time. Amanda's Yankees' jersey had found the floor by the fifth inning, and shortly thereafter her pinstriped boy shorts joined it. What started out as foreplay on the couch progressed to the bedroom when Eric could no longer focus on the game, not that he wanted to, in the company of his attractive aggressor.

When Eric left the apartment to return to his home later that evening, he did so without ever asking Amanda about Ramon Ortiz. The reason he did not ask her was simple. As he enjoyed her cooking for dinner, as he enjoyed the sight of her laying there, half-naked and asking him questions about baseball and the Yankees, and as she showed a distinct lack of morals in the bedroom, he realized something critical about Amanda Johnson. He was, confirming his earlier thoughts, beginning to fall for her. He was also thrilled by her use of the terms "special friend" and "boyfriend" to describe him. The fact that she felt strongly about him was exciting; he had not felt this way about someone in quite some time, at least since his marriage had soured.

He just could not bring himself to ask her to help him defend the case that she was prosecuting, especially since he would have to do so in an underhanded manner.

What had started off as flirting with an underlying purpose had morphed into an actual relationship, with actual feelings toward Amanda. Real, amorous feelings. He did not want to continue to deceive her, and he did not want to use her anymore in the hopes of obtaining a more favorable result in court for Wendi.

The good news was that he did not need to deceive or use her anymore. He genuinely wanted to be with her. He knew that to continue doing so would be dangerous to and could even jeopardize both of their careers, but he did not care. His desire for her, for Amanda Johnson, the person, was too great. He dared to think it, but he thought that he might be in love with her.

Chapter XXVII – Seeking Information From Other Clients

Having decided that he was not going to seek to obtain any information from Amanda, Eric set out on an alternative fact-finding mission. He was going to take a more grass-roots approach to his search for incriminating evidence as to Ramon Ortiz, also known as Ramon Lopez. What better way to find out about a teenager and his activities, Eric figured, than from other teenagers? Kids would know the activities of others and, most importantly, they knew about such activities even when those actions were not known to their own parents or the authorities. Eric sat down the following Monday morning with Fatima and the two of them brainstormed while reviewing his master list of clients, making notes on every client in the Elizabeth area who had teenaged, more particularly, high school-aged children. They then divided the list in half, so that each could begin contacting the clients to see if their children possessed any information about either Ramon Ortiz or Ramon Lopez. They also decided to ask about Jose Gomez, and therefore included in their inquiries other clients who sent their kids to Roselle Catholic or other local private schools.

At first, the results were terrible. Many of the clients had moved and left no forwarding address or telephone number, which was bad on two levels – first, because they would be of no assistance to Eric and, perhaps more importantly, it was possible that some had sold their residences and purchased new ones, or maybe gotten divorced before moving, without using Eric to do the legal work for them. The specter of lost revenue and the possible, actually probable, lack of client loyalty disturbed him, and made an already difficult mental situation even worse for Eric. One client's son did know Ramon Lopez, but did not have any information on him other than that there were rumors of him being involved in a street gang, which simply made him similar to the overwhelming majority of the boys in his class. Fatima did get to speak with someone whose daughter was in the same Roselle Catholic class as the deceased boy, but the daughter had nothing but nice things to say about him so it seemed as though his reputation would remain untarnished.

On Wednesday, though, Eric was in court when he received an interesting text message from Fatima. He was waiting in a courtroom waiting for a judge to come out and begin a divorce hearing for his client, and he had just warned his client of the ills of having a cell phone on in the courtroom. If the phone went off when the Judge was conducting a hearing, he explained, it would be confiscated for the entire day. He had taken his phone out of his jacket pocket only seconds before, and was in the process of changing it to "silent" mode when it vibrated with the text. Seeing that it was from Fatima, he went to the texts page – which read as follows: "Eric – just received call from Ana Perez. Her daughter goes to R.C. and knew Gomez; and it turns out that he wasn't a choirboy. Will explain when you get back."

Eric's heart began to beat faster. He was elated by the text, but at the same time completely frustrated at the vagueness of Fatima's comments. He turned to his client and indicated that he would be back, and stood to walk out into the hallway to call the office. As he approached the door, however, the Judge came out from his chambers and the court officer indicated that it was time for the divorce hearing. Eric begrudgingly tucked the phone back into his pocket, turned, and walked back to retrieve his file from the bench. He motioned to the client, and the two of them walked to counsel table so that the hearing could begin. The two men stood. Eric announced his presence to the court and his client was sworn. They then sat, and the Judge began to question the plaintiff both as to the factual background leading up to the filing of the divorce complaint, as well as questions about the fairness of the property settlement agreement that he had signed the week before with his soon-to-be ex-wife. Eric was thankful that the Judge did the questioning, because he was unable to focus on the case, instead thinking about the specifics underlying Fatima's text.

After the Judge was done questioning the plaintiff and rendered his judgment codifying the parties' divorce, he asked the man and Eric to wait patiently for the executed Judgment. His staff was short-handed, he explained, so it would be a few minutes before the paperwork could be properly processed. Eric wanted desperately to make his phone call or run back to his office for details, but he was forced to sit and speak to his client, who was suddenly full of questions about the aftermath of a divorce judgment. The next ten minutes were pure torture for Eric, who tried as best as he could to answer all of the client's questions, even though his mind was clearly on other matters. Eventually the clerk produced the final judgments – one for the client and two for Eric. "I will send one to your ex-wife," Eric explained, and then said, jokingly, "now let's get out of here before the Judge changes his mind." They walked out of the court house together, and Eric walked to Broad Street while his client turned and walked the other way to the parking deck by Elizabethtown Avenue.

As he reached the corner of Caldwell Avenue and Broad Street, the light turned red for traffic on Broad. Eric quickly sprinted across the street as the cars on Caldwell started to turn onto Broad, and then went to his left and, still running, made it to his office. He raced up the stairs, eschewing a wait for the elevator, and, panting heavily, pushed open the door to his office. "My God, Eric," Fatima said from her desk as she saw Eric, doubled over and sweating, in the doorway. "Did you run all the way here from the court?"

Eric picked up his head as he steadied himself against the door, which he pushed closed with his hip as he removed his suit jacket and tossed it onto a nearby chair. Still gasping for breath, he sputtered, "yes, yes, pretty much." He coughed twice, wiped the sweat from his forehead with his shirt sleeve, and straightened up. "OK. Your text was cruel," he said, "what's going on with the Gomez kid?"

Fatima laughed. "I wasn't trying to be cruel, silly," she replied, "I just thought it was too much to put into one text."

"Well, I am here now. Tell me." He walked over to the chair where his jacket lay, crumpled in a mess. He picked up the jacket, smoothed it out, and sat, laying the jacket neatly across his lap. "What did you hear and from whom?"

Fatima reached for a pad of paper on her desk. "I want to make sure I get this right," she said. "Do you remember Mary Graham?" Eric looked at her, puzzled. Realizing that he did not, she continued. "You did her divorce three years ago. Her married name was Mary Weathers." Now Eric nodded, and Fatima smirked in response. "Anyway, I remembered her. I also remembered that her son was a senior when we did the divorce, and that her daughter was in eighth grade. When you negotiated the agreement for her, she made a big deal about private school and her ex-husband having to kick in for the tuition at Roselle Catholic, so I figured that the girl was going there now."

"That's great, Fatima," Eric replied. "At least one of us has a memory."

"Very funny," Fatima continued, shaking her head, "luckily, I was right. The girl is a junior there now. I talked to Mary on Monday afternoon, and the girl was already home from school. She said that she did not know him personally, but would ask around a little bit and get back to me if she could find anything interesting. Well, Mary called me this morning."

"OK, now I am very intrigued. Keep going."

"Well, the daughter knows a boy that they call Paco. That's not his real name, but Mary couldn't tell me what his real name even is. This Paco told her daughter that Gomez was an honors student, like we knew, but that he was beginning to get in with the wrong crowd near home in Elizabeth. His mother was having some money troubles, according to this kid, and the uncle was helping them out. But when money started getting tight again, Gomez wanted to help out. He couldn't find a job that paid enough, so he began talking to some kids about buying and selling drugs. He told Paco that he had some big-time dealer who he was going to be getting weed and cocaine from, and that he wanted Paco to help him sell it."

"He was a drug dealer?" Eric asked, incredulously. "You've got to be kidding me."

"No, I am not," Fatima replied. "Paco also told the girl that Gomez was going to look to get into one of the gangs in Elizabeth, because then he would be better able to sell the drugs and make more money."

"When did this Paco allegedly hear all of this shit?"

"From what Mary thinks, it wasn't that long ago," Fatima said, looking at her notes. "But let me ask you a question, Eric. Does it even matter? The kid got hit by a car. Whether he was an angel or a devil is not a factor in crossing the street at the wrong time."

"Maybe," Eric said, standing and starting to walk toward his office. "Maybe it doesn't matter. But, now we know something about Gomez. Who's to say that we won't find out something about Lopez-Ortiz? He was in a gang, right? Maybe there was something going on there."

"And?"

"I don't know, Fatima," he said, "I'm still piecing this together." He passed through the threshold of his office. "Maybe he pushed the kid in front of the car."

"And what, Wendi was so busy texting that she didn't notice?" Fatima asked, sarcastically.

Eric poked his head out of his office. "Maybe she was texting. What if she were?"

"Well, then she would be guilty, right?"

Eric pondered the question before responding. "Maybe, maybe not. Like I said," he said, again turning away, "I am still trying to figure this out."

Eric knew that the information about Jose Gomez, in and of itself, meant nothing. He had to get something on the witness. But how could he get such information? He could not ask Amanda. Actually, he did not want to ask Amanda. His relationship with her was too important to him for him to possibly ruin it by asking her to help him sabotage her case. Meanwhile, none of his clients seemed to know anything substantive about him, other than a vague reference to him being a gang member, like any other kid at the school.

He had to find something else. He decided to call Jim Parker, another old friend of his. Parker was an Assistant Prosecutor in Union County, working in the same office as Amanda, and, therefore, had access to the same resources as she did.

As usual, Parker was not in his office. Eric left him a voice mail message and asked if they could meet for drinks after work that day. Parker texted back about an hour later that he could not talk but that meeting later was fine, and that they should meet at the bar down the street from Eric's office at 6:30 that evening. Eric replied that he would see him there.

*****

Eric arrived at the bar at 6:25. He walked in the front door, looked around, and saw Parker waving his arm from a table located all the way in the far corner. He walked over to the table, greeted his old friend with a hug, and wasted no time in stating his purpose for the meeting.

"I need your help, Jim," he began. "I need for you to check into someone for me."

"Come on, Eric," Parker replied, "you've got to be kidding me. Is this a Union County matter? You want me to use my office's resources to help you on a case?"

"You know you can do it, Jim. Just look up a kid for me and see if anything turns up." He looked around to make sure that nobody else could hear their conversation. "You know how hard it is to get information on teenagers. I can't do it, and it's really important."

Parker also looked around before responding. Satisfied that he would not be heard by anyone else, he continued, "Eric, a teenager? Please don't tell me that this has something to do with Wendi's case?" He paused. "I'll be honest with you; our office

278

isn't even spending tons of time on it. It's like we're prosecuting, but at the same time it's a relaxed, laid-back form of prosecution, like shit's just going to fall into our laps. I know that Amanda Johnson is doing her thing," he said, not noticing the faint smile that crossed Eric's lips when he mentioned Amanda, "but I haven't heard of our investigators really doing anything in-depth so far, other than trying to track down this witness of theirs. So I don't even think they have really even followed up on the kids involved there."

"I understand," Eric said, the smile gone from his face. "I just need for you to look up this witness kid for me. Nobody will trace it back to you, I promise. Something's fishy there, and I need to find it out."

"Fishy? With all of the reporting in the papers and on the news, don't you think the media would have uncovered something by now?"

"If they wanted to, maybe," Eric said. "Or if they had the correct name."

"What do you mean the correct name?" asked Parker.

"Check this out," Eric answered. "The name of the kid is Ramon Lopez. But at one point in the paperwork, it lists him as Ramon Lopez-Ortiz. You know how the Spanish people are with their last names, right? Some use both of their parents' names and they hyphenate."

Parker nodded his understanding, even though he had never heard this before.

"Nothing will turn up under Ramon Lopez, I assume. But I want you to check out Ramon Ortiz, if you can. Just look to see if there are any juvenile records or anything else under the name Ortiz and let me know. I promise that I won't ask you for anything else, and, again, nobody is going to know where I got the information if you can turn anything up for me."

Parker sighed and looked at his old friend. "You're putting me in a bad spot, Eric," he said, shaking his head in disbelief at what he was going to say next, "I will do it for you just this once. But you'd better not tell anyone, because I am essentially working against my own office by helping you. And most of all, you'd better not say anything to Amanda Johnson. She'd kill me."

Eric laughed. "Be serious, Jim," he said, adding, "when would I see her to tell her?"

Chapter XXVIII – Other Clients and Another Massage

The next day brought no news from Jim Parker. Eric tried to focus the bulk of his energies on one of his problematic divorce cases; there was a mandatory mediation taking place the following week, and there were numerous issues between the parties, mostly financial, which needed to be addressed at that time. Eric had not even opened the file since the last court appearance, which was five weeks earlier, and his client, Paul Aarons, had called no less than a dozen times over the past week trying to discuss the issues with him. Today, Eric thought, would be the perfect day to organize the file and, more importantly, organize his client's positions for the upcoming mediation.

As was the case with so many of the other cases, however, the large file sat on his desk, unopened, for the entire morning. There were numerous phone calls to return and e-mails which required responses; most were largely unimportant, but Eric realized that he had better respond to them all because several were follow-ups on prior unanswered messages. Still, he remained acutely aware of the time. As the clock ticked past noon, Eric began to panic that Parker was not going to assist him. He spent the next hour trolling the internet, searching for news regarding "Ramon Ortiz." Much like his previous search, however, all that he was able to find was a bunch of social media pages; as he did not know what Ramon Lopez/Ramon Ortiz looked like, he was unable to even focus in on any of the pages as belonging to his alleged witness.

He was staring at his computer screen, trying to figure out a different way to search for Ramon Ortiz, the Elizabeth High School version, when he heard the office phone ring. Fatima answered, and he could hear her speaking to the person on the phone, explaining that he was busy and had been busy for the past few days. He heard her exasperated explanation continue, and finally her uttering a terse "hold on for a second, I will see what I can do."

Seeing a light on his phone blinking, signaling that Fatima had placed someone on "hold," Eric called out, "who's on the phone?"

He did not realize that Fatima had walked over to his office and was standing in the doorway, so the volume of her response surprised him. "It's Paul Aarons. He says he's called you a hundred times this week and you are completely ignoring him. He doesn't want me to take a message, and he doesn't want to leave you a voice mail. Can you please just talk to him?"

Eric sighed. "I will pick up in a minute. Just please pick up and tell him that I am finishing something up and will be right with him." Fatima looked at him like a wounded puppy, afraid to incur the client's wrath just by telling him that there would be another short delay. Eric ignored her attempts at having him simply pick the phone up and not involving her further. After a brief, silent pause, he added, "Thanks," without even looking in her direction. He heard her walk to her desk and exchange a few quick words with Paul Aarons, at which time the light on the phone began to blink again.

After another minute, Eric prepared himself for what he considered to be an unavoidable verbal onslaught and picked up the phone. Taking a deep breath and then clicking on the button below the blinking light, Eric spoke to the client in a voice which disguised the fact that he had no intention of talking to him but for the fact that he was forced to do so. "Hey, Paul, how are you?" he asked, brightly.

"How am I?" thundered Paul Aarons on the other end of the phone. "You tell me, Eric. I've been trying to reach you for a week, and we have the mediation next week. I am starting to get worried about things, and not being able to reach you doesn't make it any easier." Eric could tell that Aarons, not surprisingly, was quite agitated about the fact that he had not returned any of the prior calls.

"Calm down, Paul," Eric said in a soft voice, so as not to irritate the client any further. "There's nothing for you to worry about. I have the file right here on my desk and will be going through it this afternoon."

Despite Eric's efforts, however, Paul became more agitated by the patronizing response. "For some reason, Eric," he replied, coldly, "I don't believe you. All that I know is that we have a mediation to do next week. There are so many issues that we haven't been able to talk about, issues that are really important to me, and I have no confidence whatsoever going into the mediation without first sitting down with you and going through each one. This is my life, Eric. Do you hear me? It's my life. I have to care about it."

"Of course you do, Paul."

"And so do you, Eric," he continued. "You are my attorney. I am paying you a pretty decent fee to represent my issues, so you need to care about it also." His voice was, somehow, growing even louder as he continued to berate Eric. "I know you have other cases," he yelled, "but to tell you the truth, I don't give a shit about your other clients. I only care about my file. That's the one you should be focusing on. The others will have their times, some other time."

"But Paul," Eric answered, still calmly in an attempt to diffuse his client's anger, "I do have other cases and I have to work on all of them, all of the time. Sometimes that means that yours gets put aside. When I am at the mediation with you, no doubt others will complain that I am not working on their cases. It's a juggling act, you know."

Again, the client was not buying the excuse. "That's a load of crap, Eric," Paul replied, his voice still raised and obviously agitated. "It's Thursday. The mediation is next Wednesday. We need to meet before Wednesday to figure out our plans. You know that. You told me that after the last court appearance. Well, when were you planning on meeting?" he asked, the tone of his voice taking on a mocking tone. "You have to call me to set it up, right? It's Thursday. We need to meet by Tuesday. When were you going to call me to schedule a meeting?"

Eric was trapped, and he knew it. He decided to come clean, hoping that telling the truth would placate the still hot Paul Aarons. Still speaking softly, but now in a more apologetic tone, he replied, "You got me, Paul. I am sorry. I did put the file on my desk first thing this morning, but have been tied up with shit all day long. Let me hang up with you and I will start right now, and I'll put you on with Fatima so you can schedule a time to come in next Monday or Tuesday. That work for you?"

Thankfully, Eric's honesty was well-received by Paul, whose tone grew softer as he responded. "Yes it does, Eric," he replied. "That works for me. Just be honest with me. That's all I ask. But we need to be prepared for next week, OK? I don't want to hear about how you were too busy, because I want to pound the shit out of them next week. I don't want my wife coming out of there thinking that she has any kind of advantage, and the only way to prevent it is through preparing properly. I'm counting on you."

"You got it, Paul. I've got the file in my hand," Eric replied, as he eyed the actual file sitting across the desk from him. "Hang on a second and I will put Fatima on."

"OK, Eric, see you next week. E-mail me with any questions or comments and that way I can do whatever is needed before I come in."

Eric pressed the "hold" button and called to Fatima to pick up the phone and schedule the appointment for early next week. He looked at the file labeled "Aarons" which sat on his desk, to his left, and then looked to the right, at the glowing computer screen with a series of web pages purporting to belong to someone named Ramon Ortiz. He realized that he could not waste any more time searching for the elusive student, and knew that he had to wait to hear back from Jim Parker. He used the computer's mouse to move its arrow to the top right-hand box of his internet explorer and clicked on the "x", thereby closing out the search. When his home screen picture appeared, the picture of his dog, Peyton, he shrugged and began to take the papers out of the Aarons file.

He spent the next hour reviewing the file. He pored over the correspondences between the attorneys, each posturing as to their client's relative positions on the contested issues. He again reviewed the parties' financial records, and also reviewed his notes following the last court session, when the Judge to whom the case was assigned had weighed in on several of the still-unresolved issues. The sum total of this review was that each of the parties was simply acting unreasonably. This standoff, and the resulting acrimony, was exacerbated by the fact that his adversary, the attorney for his client's wife, was an asshole. Eric looked again at some of the letters that he had sent to the other attorney. This was one of those cases where the attorneys could not even be civil to each other; in fact, Eric thought that he detested his adversary even more than his client despised his soon-to-be ex-wife.

Eric's positions as to the contested issues were pragmatic and, if the other attorney had even an iota of intelligence, the case could have been resolved long ago. Would his client have gotten everything that he wanted? No, but the reality is that clients never do. As the old maxim goes, the best compromise leaves nobody happy. If only his adversary understood that concept.

Eric put his thoughts as to the various issues on paper – the points where Mr. Aarons would likely prevail, and those issues where they would have to seriously consider either abandoning or compromising their positions. He then typed all of these notes in a more orderly and coherent fashion, and sent his final version to the client via e-mail with instructions for him to review and respond if he had any questions or changes that should be made before their meeting. After he was sure that the e-mail was sent, he printed out the confirmation and turned off his computer. He did not want to wait for an answer, nor did he want to see any other e-mails, for that matter. He did not want to deal with any other client bullshit for the day.

He was physically exhausted. Somehow, he was even more spent mentally. He could not remember a time when he more needed a massage to relax him. Luckily, as he looked at his watch, he realized that his scheduled massage was only a half-hour away. He cleaned some papers off of his desk, grabbed his keys and wallet from his top desk drawer, and left the office, fleeing the aggravations that plagued him as he sought even a moment's peace. That peace would shortly be possible, under the gentle touch of his favorite masseuse, the lovely Marisol.

It was 6:30. His massage was scheduled for 7:00. Eric walked to the bathroom in the office hallway to wash his face. The hand soap above the sink, like in so many office buildings, possessed an offensive odor. Momentarily forgetting that he never used the hand soap for that reason, Eric placed his left hand under the dispenser and pushed the button with his right. As the soap landed on his outstretched palm, Eric's nostrils sensed that he had made an egregious error. He tried to rinse the soap off of his hand before placing his hands to his face, but was unable to completely eliminate the soap's aroma and it again permeated and offended his sense of smell when he raised his contaminated left hand to his cheek. "Shit," he thought to himself, "that's what this smells like." Five more minutes of vigorously running his hands under tepid water from the sink did the trick, at least for the most part. There was still a slight lingering smell from the soap, but nothing that could not be cured by the application of a little alcohol-laden hand sanitizer. Thankfully Eric had a container of such sanitizer on his desk, and even though it was unscented, the alcohol smell masked that of the soap when he placed a silver dollar-sized dollop, certainly more than needed, on his palms upon his return to the office.

Satisfied that he had overcome the aroma problem, Eric gathered up his keys, phone, and that day's newspaper which he had not yet perused. He strode out into the hallway and locked the office door behind him. He then walked to the stairwell and down the building's steps, eschewing the elevator in a half-hearted attempt at getting at least a modicum of aerobic exercise, until he reached the ground floor. Once outside the building, he walked toward the parking lot where his car was located, retrieved his car, and hopped in the car for the short drive to the massage parlor. He arrived there at five minutes before seven o'clock, and several minutes later Marisol appeared and beckoned him to join her in room number four. Marisol was clad in a white polo shirt, with the three buttons undone, and the same short skirt that she had been wearing for his last appointment. Clearly, Eric thought, Marisol was ready not only to give him a massage, but to be on the receiving end of some rubbing as well.

Even more surprisingly, Marisol was in a chatty mood. Things started off as usual – Marisol led him into the room, told him to get ready and then left the room for a couple of minutes. Eric stripped down to his boxer shorts and lay down on the table, underneath the towel which he placed, as expected, over his boxers. When she reappeared, Marisol instructed him to roll over onto his back, which he did, and as he turned the towel fell to his side. Neither one of them attempted to place it back over his crotch. Marisol then began to work on his shoulders, as Eric closed his eyes to better enjoy the massage. Standing behind Eric's head, Marisol leaned over, rubbed oil on his left shoulder, then right, and then proceeded to massage his upper right arm. She stopped momentarily and Eric could hear her moving towels or something onto the chair that sat to his right. She quickly returned, and then took his right elbow into her hand as she continued to rub his upper arm. She maneuvered his arm so that the back of his hand was resting against her hip.

Suddenly, he realized that he could feel the thin strip of what he perceived to be her thong on her hip – and nothing else. Turning his head to the right, he slowly opened his eyes and could see Marisol standing next to the table and massaging his arm, wearing only her bra and thong. He realized that she was not throwing towels onto the chair moments before – those were her clothes! Looking down, Marisol saw him looking at her body. She turned slightly so that her crotch was now facing his gaze, the white lace of her thong shimmering in the mostly-darkened room. As she turned, his hand moved as well, so that the tips of his fingers were now resting on her thigh, just to the right of where the fabric ended.

"*¿Tienes una problema, papi?*" Marisol purred as Eric moved his fingers slowly to the left. Marisol pivoted her hips slightly, so that his fingers were now resting directly over the triangle which formed the front of her thong. "Is there a problem?" She smiled.

"No, no problem, *tengo no problema ahora*," he responded as his fingers grazed over the lacy fabric. He felt a sensation run through his body in the next moment, however, which surprised him. Looking down, he expected to see the fabric around his crotch rising. He expected to become aroused, as he thought anyone would, due to the fact that his hand was exploring Marisol's body in an even more intimate manner than she was rubbing him. The feeling that washed over him, however, was not one of eroticism. It was, rather, a feeling of guilt. A feeling like he was somehow cheating.

He had a feeling that he was cheating on Amanda.

He moved his hand back to the top of Marisol's thigh. She still had his elbow in her grasp, and attempted to move it back to her crotch. *"Estoy confundido, papí,"* she said, "I am confused. Is something wrong?" He saw her looking disappointingly at his seemingly lifeless crotch.

Eric pulled his arm out of her clutches and rolled over on to his side. "No, Marisol. It's me." Even he could not believe that he was rejecting her clear advances, especially as she stood there before him, pouting, with her breasts barely encased in a white bra which matched her wisp of a thong. "I just can't."

"¿Por que la amas, sí?" Marisol asked, bending down to retrieve her shirt from the chair and providing Eric with a spectacular view of her ass. *"Is it because you love her?"*

Eric was taken aback by her comment. He began to consider whether he loved Amanda. He did not think so, although she was taking up a great deal of his thoughts and he did feel guilty stroking Marisol's crotch, a movement he had imagined, even dreamed of, for months. All of the flirting between he and Marisol had led to this moment, and now he refused to allow himself to enjoy it? Perhaps he did love Amanda. He knew that he had strong feelings for her. He had vowed, however, never to love another woman. He knew what his divorce from Wendi did to him. He saw, on a daily basis, what divorce did to his clients. If he could prevent himself from becoming so emotionally involved in the future, he reasoned, he would never feel that kind of pain again. And yet, here was Amanda, giving him reason to become emotionally involved. Again.

"Wait a minute," he thought, realizing that he had never mentioned Amanda to Marisol. How could she possibly know about Amanda? He had to find out. "Marisol," he asked, as he watched her lift her skirt around her waist and zipper its side, "what do you mean?"

"Oh, I'm sorry, Eric. I didn't mean to make you sad."

Eric moved a little backward and patted the other edge of the table, motioning for Marisol to sit and talk. She slowly sat on the table's edge, her right leg bent atop the table and her left off of the side. Her skirt was so short that it rode up as she sat, again exposing her thong's crotch as she steadied herself on the table with her right arm.

"I'm not sad, Marisol," Eric replied. "I just want to know who you are talking about when you said something about me loving her."

Marisol again looked down at Eric's crotch. "I just thought that you would like touching me, like before. But look," she added as she reached out and rubbed the top of Eric's boxer shorts, "you don't."

Eric recoiled slightly, almost falling off of the back of the table, to avoid Marisol's touch. "It's not that I don't like it, Marisol, believe me. *Me gusta. Me gusta mucho.*"

"Pero tienes una otra mujer," replied Marisol. You have another woman. *"Yo sé. Te vi en las noticias."*

Eric could not fully understand what she said. "Wait a minute," he said, "you saw me where?"

"Lo siento. I saw you and her on the news."

Eric struggled with her words. How could she have seen him on the news with Amanda? It was not possible. "Me and who?" he asked.

"Con su esposa, Eric. Su ex-esposa." Marisol said. "You know, Eric, your ex-wife. You were outside of court. That woman said you were *juntos de nuevo,* you know, together again."

Eric laughed with relief at the thought that Marisol thought that he and Wendi were back together. "No, Marisol," he said. "Not her."

"*¿Tienes una otra mujer?*" she asked, "another woman?"

Eric began to blush. "Not important."

"I know that it isn't the reporter, Lupe Espinosa. She was here *la semana proxima* (last week). She was here with that guy," Marisol said, "you know, the one called *'la voz de la gente.'*"

Eric leapt off of the table excitedly, and then placed his hands on Marisol's upper arms as he pulled her closer to him. "You mean she was here with Jesus Sanchez?"

"*¿Es que su nombre?*" Marisol asked, "*yo no le presto mucha atención a la noticia.*"

"You don't pay much attention to the news?" Eric asked, chuckling, "you paid enough attention to see me and my ex-wife, right?"

Now Marisol blushed. "*Debido a que era usted ... y me gustas.* Because it was you," she said, "and I like you. *Tu eres más guapo de Jesus Sanchez.*" She moved closer to Eric, so that they were only inches apart. She slid her left leg outward, so that she was now sitting spread-eagled on the table and her knees dangled over the edge. Her still-exposed crotch sat immediately next to Eric's boxer shorts. She pulled him closer so that the fabrics of the thong and boxer shorts were touching.

Eric felt her body against his. He felt her breath on his neck, and felt her breasts pressed against his chest. He still felt uncomfortable and that he was being unfaithful to Amanda, but he also did not want to upset Marisol when she could provide him with some information on Jesus Sanchez. So he did not pull himself from her grasp. Not yet. "Marisol, they were here together?" he asked.

"*Sí, Eric,*" she whispered, "*estaban aqui el pasado Miercoles por la noche.*"

"Last Wednesday night?" he repeated. "And you're sure that they came here together?"

"*Creo que sí*," she replied. "I think so. I did his massage for him. He's like you. *Le gusta hablar mucho.*"

Eric smiled. "He likes to talk a lot also? What did you talk about with him? *¿Lo que hablan con él?*"

Now Marisol smiled. She loved when Eric tried to speak Spanish, even though his tenses were often incorrect. The effort itself was enough for her. It was exactly the opposite reaction that the locals had to the Spanish-speaking immigrants who tried, desperately, to communicate in broken English but who continued to be vilified by people who looked down on and belittled their efforts. In fact, it made Eric even sexier to her. And even though it hurt her that there was another woman in his life, she was more than happy to help him out. "*El habló conmigo de cómo él quiere ser el alcalde de Elizabeth.*"

Eric tried to break down the pieces of her explanation. "You mean he talked to you about wanting to be something in Elizabeth? What is '*alcalde*'?" he asked, "that is a new word to me."

She apologized. "*Lo siento, 'alcade' is, como de dice,*" she thought for a moment, "*el hombre que gobierna la ciudad.*"

"It means the guy who runs the city? You mean the Mayor?" Eric barked, "Jesus Sanchez wants to be Mayor?" He lowered his voice. "Guess that shouldn't surprise anyone. I have heard that before." He reached out and placed his hand on Marisol's leg. "Did he say anything else?"

"*El me tocaba*, he was touching me, like here," she said, as she took Eric's hand from her leg and slid it over her thong. "*Le pregunté acerca de su novia, y él me dijo que no es su novia.*"

"OK," Eric replied. "You asked about he and Lupe and he told you that Lupe was not his girlfriend, right?"

"*Sí*, so it was OK to touch me, *él me dijo*," she said, still holding Eric's hand over her now-moist crotch, "*él me dijo que solo estaban trabajando juntos.*"

"He told you that they were just working together?" Eric asked. "What did he mean, working together?"

"I asked him," Marisol said as she moved Eric's hand slowly up and down her crotch, "*él me dijo que ella trabajando con el television y es possible que ella ayuda el para el alcalde.*"

Eric's knowledge of Spanish was being put to the test tonight, especially since he had the additional distraction of his own hand moistening from its contact with Marisol's ever-wetting nether regions. "You mean she is helping him be elected Mayor," he asked, "Like by putting him on the news?"

"*Sí, mí amor, es correcto,*" she answered, "*Pero* I did not believe him. I think they are together. They were acting like *novio y novia*."

Eric now had the information that he needed – with the possibility that Lupe Gonzalez and Jesus Sanchez were actually having some form of fling, just as he had suspected while watching the bogus interview between them on television. He knew it!

He realized that he could not just run away from Marisol, however, so he took his hand from her crotch, placed it on the small of her back and wiped the moisture from his fingers, and gently kissed her on the cheek. "*Gracias, mija,*" he said, "thank you." He glanced down at his watch. He still had twenty minutes for his massage. It would be better, he thought, to forego the time and see Amanda. He couldn't share this information with her yet, but, at the same time, suddenly had the urge to see her. He again thanked Marisol, told her that he was going to leave, and quickly dressed.

Walking out the door, he took a twenty-dollar bill, handed it to her as a tip, and again wrapped his arms around her and kissed her in gratitude. She thrust her pelvis against his as she returned his kiss, and slowly gyrated her hips. *"Para la próxima vez,"* she said, "for next time."

Eric smiled as he pulled himself away from Marisol. They both looked down at the same time, unknowingly, and Marisol grinned as Eric placed his hand on his crotch to adjust his growing member. This was the response that she had been seeking earlier. Perhaps there was hope, she thought. Eric, slightly embarrassed by his involuntary reaction to her movements, hustled out the door, thinking about other topics so that he would return to his flaccid condition – at least until he saw Amanda.

<u>Paragraph XXIX – Doughnuts and Amanda</u>

As he pulled out of the parking lot, Eric reached for his cell phone and called Amanda. "Hey, thought I would come over if you're not busy. I just finished my massage and am feeling extremely soothed. It's a perfect time to just chill on the couch with you." He made sure not to mention what Marisol had told him about Lupe Espinosa and Jesus Sanchez, especially because he and Amanda had made a promise to each other weeks ago not to mention the case.

"I don't know, Eric," she replied, sounding tired. "I've had a really long week and have some heavy matters to deal with tomorrow. Maybe I can see you over the weekend."

"You sound exhausted," he said, "how about I pick up some sushi and bring it over? We can eat, chill a bit, and then I will leave so you can get to bed early."

"I already ate, to be honest with you," she replied.

Eric really wanted to get to Amanda's that evening, but realized that he was beginning to sound desperate. He decided to try once more. If she said no, then so be it. "Then how about this," he asked, "how about I stop by Dunks, pick up some coffee and doughnuts, and bring them over? I'll even make sure to get decaf so that you're able to sleep tonight."

He could hear Amanda sigh through the phone, as she was clearly engaging in an internal battle over whether or not to see Eric. "Would it be a Boston crème doughnut?" she asked.

"If that's what you want, my dear, of course," he answered, "you know that my sole aim in life is to please you." He laughed, and was pleased to hear her chuckling on the other end of the phone. "A Boston crème it is. I will be there in about fifteen minutes."

"OK," she said, "and I apologize for sounding so negative. I'm just tired." She paused. "But I really am happy that you're coming up … and not just because you're bringing doughnuts, although that does make it even better."

"Doughnuts and coffee make everything better," Eric replied. "I'll see you soon."

Playing the role of dutiful and chivalrous suitor, Eric purchased several Boston crème doughnuts to go along with his cruller and two large decaffeinated coffees. He drove to Amanda's apartment and then, carrying the bag of doughnuts and coffee tray, used his elbow to push the buzzer. "Who is it?" Amanda's voice asked through the intercom.

"No time for games tonight, Amanda, I'm going to drop these doughnuts any second," Eric replied as he struggled to keep his grip on everything, "or worse, I may drop the coffee. Your coffee."

"Really, Eric, you have no time for games?" Amanda asked, sighing audibly, "well, then I guess I had better buzz you in. Hang on a second."

Eric waited for the buzzer to sound. He waited, and waited. A couple of minutes later, he was still waiting. He placed the coffee carrier on the ground and again pressed the buzzer. "Well, do you have time for games now?" Amanda asked.

"Come on, Amanda, I'm too old for this shit. Just let me up," he pleaded. "The coffee is getting cold."

"I'm not going to worry about a little cold coffee, Eric. I can warm it in the microwave," she replied. "Say you're sorry for being mean to me."

"Being mean?" Eric thought. "She's got to be kidding." Realizing that he would have to do so in order to be invited upstairs, however, Eric did what any other intelligent, or even barely intelligent, man would do. He immediately apologized. "I'm sorry, Amanda," he said. "I'm sorry for being mean to you."

She laughed. "That was too easy, you sissy. Come on upstairs." The buzzer on the door sounded, and Eric was able to pull the door open and, balancing with his right leg inside the door, reach back to pick up the coffees and walk inside the building with all of his purchases. He pushed the button for the elevator with his elbow and, upon entering the elevator, did the same for Amanda's floor. As the elevator door opened and he exited, he could see that her door was, as was usually the case when he arrived, ajar. Something, however, was different. Amanda's mood was much different than the usual.

As he closed the door to the apartment behind him, he could see that its only light was coming from the kitchen. He walked to the kitchen and found Amanda sitting at the kitchen table, with files strewn over almost the entirety of its surface. Her head was buried in her hands, and when she looked up at Eric, the lines of make-up streaming down the sides of her cheeks gave clear indication that she had been crying. "I'm sorry, Eric" she said as she dissolved into sobs. "I was trying to clean up for you. I just wanted to clean the kitchen and myself up for you. Guess I didn't do a very good job."

Eric placed the coffees on the countertop to his left and walked over to the table with the doughnut bag in his right hand. Laying the bag on the table, he put his right arm around Amanda's shoulders and pulled her closer to him so that her head was resting against his stomach. "It's OK, darling," he said, "too much work and messy files is how I make my living, don't forget."

She sniffled deeply and raised her head from his stomach. "That's not it, Eric." She reached for a tissue from the table and, turning away from Eric, blew her nose. "I need to tell you something."

Now Eric sat down, taking the seat directly to her left. "Go ahead, but do you want your coffee or Boston crème first?" He picked up the bag, opened the top so that the delicious aroma filtered its way through the room, and placed a doughnut on the table in front of her.

"Thanks, but in a minute," she said. "Listen, I know that we promised each other not to talk about Wendi's case."

Eric was intrigued by her comment, especially her referring to Wendi by her first name. It was the first time that he could remember that she referred to Wendi in that way. He wondered how many other times Amanda, or any other prosecutor, referred to the defendants by their first names; he had never heard it done before in all of his dealings with criminal matters. It seemed almost counter to their role as Prosecutor, as referring to the accused by their given names humanized them. It made them more sympathetic than simply referring to them as "the defendant" or a more formal Mr. or Ms., and was exactly the opposite of how a Prosecutor would want the defendant to be viewed by others, especially a jury.

"Anyway, I've tried really hard not to mention it, and I really appreciate how you haven't brought it up either. But I think I need to tell you this one, so you hear about it before she does."

"OK," Eric said, with trepidation, "tell me."

"Well," she said, again blowing her nose, "we finished up a big presentation before the Grand Jury today. There's only one more case before hers, so we are scheduling it for two weeks from today. Notices will go out from the office tomorrow, but I didn't want her to get the mail before you and harangue you with questions." She paused, and reached out to him, gently stroking his arm. "This way, you can prepare yourself."

Eric's heart sank. "Thank you for the heads up," he said in response as he pulled Amanda close to him and hugged her. He immediately felt bile rising in his throat, however, as the reality of the situation struck him like a freight train. The Grand

Jury would be a slam dunk for Amanda and the prosecution. In fact, they probably only needed two witnesses, the kid and one of the EMT people – and maybe even Wendi. Then, there was little doubt the Grand Jury would return an indictment, and it would be on to trial. The chances of getting a favorable plea would erode with each passing day. He had to derail the train before the Grand Jury even got the case. He needed to get more information, more than an alleged affair between Lupe and Sanchez, and more than allegations that either or both of the teenagers involved were in gangs.

"Oh, and Eric," Amanda whispered, her head resting on Eric's shoulder, "I'm worried because I don't want the Grand Jury hearing to come between us." She paused and pulled her head from his shoulder. Eric could see her eyes moistening, and a tear fell down her left cheek. "I really, uh, I really, well you know how I feel. I, uh ..."

"I understand," Eric said, again pulling her close and burying her face against his shoulder, making sure to cut her off before she even thought of telling him that she loved him. He also worried about how the next few weeks might wreak havoc on their relationship. He thought what had happened with Marisol before. He thought about his vow to never love anyone ever again. And yet, he wasn't completely sure if he was in love with Amanda or not. The fact that he was unsure, however, worried him.

Almost as worrisome was that he had less than two weeks. He would really have to press Jim Parker now.

Chapter XXX – The Fax

Sometimes there are events which can make even the most vociferous of doubters believe in the supernatural or other-worldly beings, because there are simply no logical explanations for the perfect timing of these occurrences. Eric did not believe in things like ghosts or fortune-tellers, but he did believe in Guardian Angels. More to the point, he believed that there were those "angels," likely his ancestors, who watched out for him and, on occasion, manifested their presence through a positive sign. Friday was one of those times.

Eric arrived at the office on Friday morning in a despondent mood. The news of the impending Grand Jury hearing for Wendi had soured his planned evening with Amanda, and he had only stayed in her apartment for an hour and a half before begging off under the guise of letting her get her work done. Some of that time was spent clearing the kitchen table of the files that had been strewn across its top, and much of the remainder was spent simply sitting in the kitchen, slowly drinking coffee and eating that evening's purchases, and talking about topics that did not involve Wendi or Jose Gomez.

The urgency of the situation plagued him throughout his time with Amanda, and did not abate after he left her apartment. On his drive home, he called Jim Parker on his cell phone and left a message indicating that he needed the information about the teenager as soon as possible.

Eric hated having to rely on Parker for the information. Unfortunately, however, Eric needed the assistance and Parker was his best, if not only, chance. Obtaining criminal records on adults was not an overly difficult process. Getting such records for juveniles, however, was nearly impossible. That is where being, or knowing, a Prosecutor came in handy. The Prosecutor's office had access to such records, and could therefore gain information that Eric would not be able to find on his own. And he would have to rely on the Prosecution, in this case, Amanda, to even think of looking for the kids' records, because if she did not, then there would be no documents to turn over in discovery, thereby leaving Eric in the dark about any past criminal activity. The Prosecution was likely better off not knowing if their star witness was a delinquent – especially if it was based on information that Eric could not obtain. Otherwise, it could be quite damaging at trial. Not at the unopposed, one-sided process of the Grand Jury, where the defense could not ask questions or raise any such issues, but at the eventual trial, where Eric would have the right to cross-examine any witnesses, if the case even got that far.

He walked over to his desk and sat, looking at his computer in vain for an e-mail from Parker. It was 8:00. Nobody would be at the Prosecutor's office yet, and he did not want to call Parker again on his cell phone, having left a message the night before. He decided to check his other e-mails and, hopefully, wait for some information from Parker later that morning.

Five minutes later, he heard the fax machine ring in the next room. Immediately thereafter, and before he could even consider going into the next room to retrieve the fax, his cell phone began to buzz. Looking down, he realized that it was Jim Parker's cell number. Picking up the phone, he pressed the proper button to answer the call. "Jim," he said calmly, trying to mask his inner turmoil and concerns, "what's going on?"

"Check your fax machine, Eric," Parker replied. "I got the report you asked me for. But I had to fax it from a different place instead of my office so that nobody would track it to me. There's no cover sheet, just the report. Remember, I was not involved."

"Of course, Jim, I know that." Eric paused before asking, "Does it show anything, by the way?"

302

"Take a look for yourself, Eric, and I have little doubt that you will find it both interesting and, likely, quite helpful," Parker answered. "Now let me run so I can get to the office on time. Remember, I had nothing to do with this, but you owe me one, buddy."

"You know I do," Eric said, "thanks so much. I really appreciate it."

"And Eric," Parker added, "Just so you know, I also took a look at the Prosecutor's file. They subpoenaed your ex-wife's cell phone records, which should not come as a surprise to you. You probably don't want to know what those records show."

"No, not really," Eric replied. "Just remember, no matter what those records show, you're talking about a minute here or there difference between them proving guilt or her being found innocent. It's not a matter of whether or not she used a phone, don't forget, the question is when she was using it."

"Suit yourself, Eric. I just thought I'd let you know."

"And I appreciate it," Eric said. "Now let me go and see what you've sent me."

Eric stood and moved briskly to retrieve the fax that Parker had sent. He saw three pages sitting in the tray of the machine, and swept them up in one motion. Looking at the contents of the sheets, he determined that the given address for Ramon Ortiz, also known as Ramon Lopez, was down by the Port, located right in the middle of one of the toughest sections of Elizabeth. Ortiz was 16 years old, and, over the past three years, had been arrested on three different occasions. The first was for drug possession, the second for possession with intent to distribute, and the third for armed robbery. The first one resulted in a guilty plea to a lesser offense, a petty disorderly person's offense which resulted in a small fine and community service, and he was represented at the time by the Public Defender's office.

For the second charge, possession of cocaine with intent to distribute, he was granted a Conditional Discharge, also known as a "CD". This was a diversionary program not normally even offered to juveniles, and meant that he was able to complete a program much like the Pre-Trial Intervention program that Wendi was not offered when they had appeared in court – there is no plea of guilt or finding of innocence, just entry into the program instead of such a plea or finding. Instead, Ortiz essentially had to complete a probationary-type sentence which included, likely, a year of reporting to a probation officer on a monthly basis, peeing in a cup to make sure that he was not using drugs, some community service, entry into some form of drug treatment program, and payment of hundreds of dollars of fines. If he completed the program in a satisfactory manner, then the original possession with intent to distribute charge would be dismissed.

One of the other requirements of any Conditional Discharge, however, was that he could not be arrested while in the middle of serving his probationary term. Any arrest during that time period would void the CD, and the accused would then be facing not only the new charge, but also the resurrection of the original charge for which he was doing the probation-like plan. The shortest time frame for a CD, especially for the crime for which Ortiz was accused, would be one year. It could very possibly have been two or three, but Eric had no doubt that it was at least one.

Yet, the robbery charge was only nine months after the drug arrest, and only seven months after his entry into the CD program was approved. That drug arrest, therefore, should have completely wiped out the CD and exposed Ortiz to proper sentencing on all charges. The record, however, did not show a withdrawal of the CD. To Eric's amazement, the CD remained intact and the armed robbery charge was downgraded to a simple harassment charge. The plea to harassment was entered and fines levied against Ortiz. Shortly thereafter, he completed his CD program and the charge of intent to distribute was dismissed.

Those results completely defied logic and were nothing short of spectacular, in Eric's eyes. They were also completely counter to the applicable statutes. Both emanated from Elizabeth and were dealt with in the Union County court. Maybe the attorney in the last charge did not know about the prior CD and somehow the court failed to pick up on it as well. More than likely, neither the attorney nor court would have even imagined that he was granted a conditional discharge on the prior charge, since such a granting was so unusual, if not unprecedented, for a minor.

But even if that were the case, then how would it have gotten past Trenton when the arrest and plea were logged into the system? It did not make sense to Eric. He scanned the records to locate the identity of Ortiz's attorneys to determine who could have worked such magical results on behalf of young Mr. Ortiz, thinking that the Public Defender's office would not have been able to do so.

To his surprise, the same firm was listed as counsel for both cases – the firm of Samuels, Preston, and Greenbaum, based, like Eric, in Elizabeth.

The firm name sounded familiar, but he could not recall specifically why. Obviously, as the firm was based in Elizabeth and they handled similar types of cases, he had heard the names of the various partners thrown around the courthouse over the years, and had one case where his client was a co-defendant of a kid being represented by senior partner Stuart Samuels. He also seemed to recall that he also knew one of the associates at the firm at some point in the past. At that moment, however, he could not recall which associate.

Regardless of who had represented Ortiz, however, and despite the fact that he had gotten such favorable results in the past, the reality was that Ramon Ortiz was anything but a choirboy. He was a 16-year old drug dealer who had already been arrested three times, for the gamut of charges that are usually incurred by the city's low-level dealers. He certainly could not be the star witness in the case against Wendi, could he? Unless the Prosecution was blissfully unaware of his past criminal history, that is.

Then Eric considered the possibility that Ortiz must have some powerful friends. Even with Clarence Darrow or Johnny Cochrane as his attorney, the chances of obtaining such favorable plea deals would still be minimal. Someone in the court system must have taken a liking to him. Or, worse, could it be that his supplier was the one pulling the strings with his own contacts within the system?

Eric wondered how the existence of such a backer for Ortiz could affect Wendi's case. He had no easy answers, and the case, and its participants, was growing more convoluted by the minute.

As he was pondering these questions and again reading the rap sheet for the now-confirmed juvenile delinquent, Ramon Ortiz, he heard the office door open and Fatima's call of "good morning." She appeared in Eric's doorway shortly thereafter, cup of coffee in hand, and, seemingly in a perky and chatty mood, asked him about whether his prior evening's massage was appropriately relaxing. He lied, deciding not to tell her the events that transpired between him and Marisol, and said, simply, that it was nothing out of the ordinary. He also declined to tell Fatima about the pending Grand Jury notice for Wendi's case, primarily because he had never told her about his relationship with Amanda Johnson and, therefore, would have no way of properly explaining how he had obtained such information. Fatima smiled, remarked that after a long, stressful week she was in need of a massage herself and then placed the cup of coffee on his desk. Turning around, she left the room and returned to her desk to begin her work day.

The notices about Wendi's upcoming Grand Jury hearing, as promised by Amanda, were not going to be mailed until that morning. As such, there was no way that Wendi would receive the notice until the next day, Saturday, or Monday at the earliest. There was no need to obsess about the case that morning, Eric thought to himself. He also was not going to tell Wendi before she received the notice in the mail; much like was the case with Fatima, he would have no proper explanation for his advance knowledge of the notice. Better to allow her to get the notice in the mail. Then she could freak out on her own and then call him, rather than him having to endure her initial, and no doubt overly-emotional, reaction. He put the fax from Parker into the file and tried to focus on getting other work done.

Yet, he kept thinking back to the fax and the young man's attorneys. He knew that firm. He knew someone who used to work there - someone who was not one of the three named partners. He just needed to remember who. Then he could call that person and find out more about Ramon Ortiz, about his other activities, and how he had been able to obtain such amazing results for his cases. He wanted to find out the young man's connections, and, presumably, obtain additional information that he could then pass on to Amanda to make her question the validity of the State's case against Wendi.

But he had to proceed with a great deal of caution. He had to be 100% certain of the facts surrounding Ramon Ortiz before speaking to Amanda, because he did not want to jeopardize their relationship by passing along incomplete or improper information in an attempt to sway her. He did not want her to think that he was using her to achieve a positive result for Wendi. Maybe that was how he began their relationship, but he knew that it had progressed way past that.

He had made his life very complicated by agreeing to be Wendi's lawyer. Now, he realized, he had made it much more complicated by getting romantically involved with Amanda. He did not want to sacrifice his relationship with one for the other. More to the point, he did not want to sacrifice his relationship with Amanda for Wendi. He could not allow that to happen.

Eric spent the next couple of hours essentially pushing paper around his desk. He opened the past couple of days' worth of mail, which had been stacked high and overflowing in his "in" box, and found some court notices for upcoming hearings, as well as a couple of retainer checks from clients which were due over a week ago. He dictated some letters for Fatima to type and mail out to clients about the upcoming hearings, and answered whatever e-mails had arrived since he left the office the evening before for his massage. All the while, however, whether he was opening mail or dictating letters to Fatima, he kept repeating the same names - Samuels, Preston, and Greenbaum - in his mind.

It was almost noon. Eric checked his calendar on the computer, and saw that there were no appointments scheduled for the afternoon. It was Friday, and he was spent, having endured another exhausting week. He knew that if Wendi received her notice for the Grand Jury the next day, then that afternoon would also be a living hell. There was no way he wanted to stay in the office, or even do any more work, for the rest of the afternoon. He needed some time off, and it was time for him to exploit one of the advantages of being self-employed, that of determining one's own hours of work, caseload permitting, of course. "Hey Fatima," he called, "you want to go out for lunch? I need to get out of here."

"Sure," Fatima called from the next room. "Do you want to wait until the mail gets here before we go, though? He should be here any minute. That way we can just make sure that there is nothing we need to deal with right away, assuming we'll be out for a while."

"Good idea," he replied. "Figure out where you want to go and we can leave once the mail arrives."

The phone rang as he was finishing his sentence. Fatima answered, spoke to the caller for a few seconds, and then called out to Eric, "Jonathan Sanchez is on the phone about his divorce case. Do you want to talk to him now or should I tell him you will call him back?"

"It should be quick," Eric replied, "tell him to hang on for a second and then I will pick up. Let me just call up his information on the computer so I can sound intelligent when I talk to him."

"Please hang on for a second, Mr. Sanchez," Fatima said to the caller, and then pushed the "hold" button on the phone. "He's all yours," she called to Eric.

Eric turned to his computer and opened the file for Jonathan Sanchez. Scanning the information on the screen, he muttered the parties' last name, "Sanchez, Sanchez." Suddenly, his eyes opened wide as he remembered something, a recollection that struck him with the force of a hammer between the eyes. It was a recollection that seemed almost incomprehensible to him, even as it was happening.

It was no less than a miracle, or another one of those "Guardian Angel" moments.

"Holy fucking shit!" he yelled, excitedly, forgetting about the fact that his client was still waiting on hold for him, "fucking Jesus Sanchez! I can't believe that I didn't remember right away! That's who used to work at Samuels, Preston and Greenbaum!"

"What?" called Fatima, "what are you yelling about in there?"

"That fucking asshole Sanchez," Eric yelled in response, still sitting in his chair and still ignoring the fact that he had not picked up the phone. "He represented that kid!"

Fatima walked over to Eric's office, and asked, "What kid, Eric?"

Eric spun his chair around so he was facing Fatima, a broad smile running his face from ear to ear. "The fucking kid who says that Wendi was texting when the accident happened, Fatima!" he yelled. "Sanchez represented him twice in criminal court! One time for a drug charge and the other for assault! Holy shit!" he again yelled. "Do you believe this?"

"No, can't say that I do," Fatima replied, somewhat incredulously at the font of information that Eric somehow possessed, none of which she had been privy to up until this moment and information which certainly was not present in the file that she had reviewed previously. She looked at him disapprovingly and her voice took on an accusatory tone. "Should I even ask how you know that?" she asked.

Eric paused to collect his thoughts. He had remembered that Sanchez worked at that firm. In fact, now that he thought about it, he also remembered that Sanchez mentioned Greg Preston when he was being interviewed by Lupe Espinosa. But, he now realized, that did not mean that Sanchez himself had represented the kid, only that the firm had represented him. More importantly, he could not reveal how he had found out about Ortiz's prior arrests. He was sworn to secrecy by Jim Parker.

Suddenly, his elation disappeared. He had potentially explosive knowledge, but he could not use it. He had to think of a way to confirm his suspicions. But first he had to answer Fatima's question.

"No," he answered, his smile completely wiped out by his need to suppress the information about Ramon Ortiz until he could obtain even a shred of properly-obtained, corroborating information. "You shouldn't ask me that question. Let's just say I think I know something, but I need to confirm it." He paused. "In fact, forget that I even said anything."

"Does this mean that we are not going out to lunch?" Fatima asked, sweetly, trying her best to ensure that they would still be leaving the office once the mail arrived.

"No, we can still go out," Eric answered as he began to smile. "I just need a few minutes to make one phone call, and then hopefully the mail will be here and we can go." He paused and leaned back in his chair, his face breaking out into a devious smile. "I need to call a person who I think may be able to help me, even without realizing it."

Fatima looked at him, puzzled, but thought it best not to question him about the call or to whom it would be placed, at least until he carried out his intended plan. Clearly he was not sharing more information with her for a reason. She turned and walked back to her desk, awaiting the arrival of the mailman.

Eric, meanwhile, reached into his desk drawer and produced his wallet. Opening the wallet, he searched in between the ten and twenty-dollar bills for the business card that he had tucked in there after a hallway encounter weeks earlier. He located the card and, reaching for the phone, punched out the numbers. After a few rings, a female voice answered.

"Lupe Espinosa, can I help you?"

Chapter XXXI – Eric Seeks Lupe's Help

Eric had entered the phone number almost instinctively, before even thinking about what he was going to actually say to Lupe Espinosa. When she answered, he had to quickly gather his thoughts. After a prolonged pause, he replied, "hi, Lupe, this is Eric Goldberg." Another silence followed. Eric, remembering that Lupe was not overly intelligent, at least based on what he had seen of her to this time, assumed that she was struggling to remember who he was, or why she should even know the name Eric Goldberg. Having now determined what he would say to her, he decided to help her out when she clearly could not recall for what seemed like a minute or so. "You may remember me, the attorney for Wendi Goldberg." Then he decided to add a joke to both endear him to her and establish a rapport. "You know, the woman accused of hitting that kid with her car. She's my ex-wife, and you said that we are dating again."

Now she clearly knew with whom she was speaking. "Eric! How are you?" she replied, cheerfully. "It's such a surprise to hear from you, a very pleasant surprise." Her news reporter's senses piqued, she paused before adding, "Are you ready to give me an interview?"

"Well, sort of, Lupe. I am ready to talk to you," Eric replied, "but not for the cameras. I would like to sit down with you, but our first discussion has to be off the record. Then we will see, depending on how that goes, if we can do it in front of the cameras. What do you think?"

Lupe sighed and responded in a disappointed voice. "I don't usually do interviews without the camera, Eric. The station does not like when I do that. I especially don't want to interview off the record when it is a case like this. You know what I mean, a big one."

"I understand, and normally I would completely agree with you," Eric replied, "but I think I have some information about the case that you might find interesting. The problem is that I don't know for sure if it is 100% true, and I don't feel comfortable going in front of a camera with this stuff because, you know, if it is wrong I will look stupid and, worse, potentially expose myself to legal troubles. I just can't risk it now." He paused, allowing his last comments to sink in. "If I were you, I would sit down with me, if you know what I mean." He decided to use her ego as bait. "And you, a pretty woman looking to make her name in the news business? You and I both know that this case can do wonders for you. Just talking about me and Wendi won't do it, but the information that I have may do the trick."

There was a brief silence before Lupe responded, as she pondered Eric's comments. He was playing with her, she thought, so she decided to play right back. "You need to tell me more, Eric," she answered, in a voice that could only be described as seductive. Eric always suspected how she got her job. Her "asking voice," which was more akin to a purr, only confirmed his suspicions. "I can't just meet you without any details," she added, but soon realized that she had gone a bit too far for Eric's liking.

"Don't be ridiculous, Lupe," he said, in a scolding manner usually reserved for one's children, but one which attorneys like Eric also often used for their petulant or non-cooperative clients. "You can meet me for whatever reason you want. You may work for the network, but you can still do you own thing when you think it will benefit you, right? Are you going to work there forever? I would say likely not. Sometimes you need to do what's best for yourself, so that you can use it to get the next, and better, job. I assume you want to be an anchor someday, don't you." He again paused, continuing to play with her emotions, and let his last statement sink in before continuing. "Let's do it this way. I think you will find my information interesting. This is your one chance to get it. If you don't meet me now, I'm not going to call you again, and you aren't going to get the interview that you want." He was stunting. He just hoped that she did not realize what he was doing.

Not surprisingly, it turned out that he had played his cards right. He was, after all, the superior intellect between the two of them.

"I'm not saying you're right," Lupe said, sighing, "but I will meet you. How about Monday afternoon at a restaurant? Is there anything local that you would prefer?"

"Honestly," Eric responded, "I would feel much more comfortable meeting you in a non-public place, just because I don't want anyone to even know about it. You may decide that the information that I have is not worth anything to you, and I don't want to be seen with you if that happens. If the two of us are seen together in public, anyone who sees us will think that something is going on, that one of us is giving information to the other. That's something that I cannot risk at this time, either. I would rather do it in my office. It would probably be better for you to do it secretly as well."

Lupe sighed. She knew that he was right. If he did not have any good information, and then refused to give an interview, how would it look to her superiors at the station? She decided to agree to his request, but not without one more comment of a sexually-charged nature to make him think. "Based on what I know about you, Mr. Goldberg," she said in the same purr-like tone, "it might be dangerous for me to be alone in your office with you, but I will take the chance."

Eric did not take the bait on her comment, instead focusing completely on his demands for their meeting. "No cameras, no microphones," he replied so that there was no ambiguity as to his intentions.

Lupe paused before answering, and Eric could hear a deep breath through the phone's earpiece. "OK, no cameras and no microphones."

"1:00 Monday afternoon," Eric said. "And you come alone. If anyone comes with you, or if I see a microphone or camera, then we are not talking. I mean it."

"OK," she said, "I will be at your office at 1:00 Monday. *Solo.* Alone." She paused, and then, more than a little disappointed that he had not responded to her earlier comment, added, "Unless you want to get together over the weekend to discuss this."

Eric thought about that offer for a second, and then thought better of being drawn into such a situation, one that could only lead to difficulties. "No," he answered, "Monday afternoon is better. I wasn't planning on working at all this weekend."

"Well, Mr. Goldberg," Lupe said, her voice taking on a more seductive tone as her comments became less playful and more overt, "I'm sure we could make it where it wasn't all work, but *yo nunca pido.* I never beg. I will see you Monday."

Eric could hear her phone click off. He stood, walked out to Fatima's desk, and told her that it was a good time to leave for lunch – before they were interrupted or delayed by another client phone call or e-mail. If the mailman came while they were out, he would just leave the mail outside of the office door, and there was nothing to be mailed that they couldn't drop in the mailbox in the building's lobby. The call with Lupe was a perfect break for his day. "Just one thing, Fatima," he said as she stood to leave, "please put in the diary that Lupe Espinosa will be here at 1:00 Monday."

Fatima looked at Eric, with a puzzled expression on her face. "You mean the reporter?" she asked, "the woman who keeps saying those horrible things about you on the news? That's the person whom you had to call? You can't be serious. I try really hard not to tell you what to do or not to do, but please tell me that you're not doing an interview with her, especially not here in the office, are you?"

"No," Eric replied. "Not an interview." He saw Fatima's puzzled expression was not waning. "I told you that I have some information on Jesus Sanchez, right? Well, Lupe and I are going to have a discussion. I am going to try to have her do some investigating for me."

Fatima's expression did not change. "I'm confused, Eric. Why would she help you?"

"Well," Eric explained, "she probably wouldn't, if she knew that she was helping me. I am going to try to get her to help without letting her know that she is helping. That's why I need to meet with her, so that I can dangle some information in front of her so that she wants to do the digging."

"I don't know how you do these things, Eric," said Fatima as she bent below her desk to retrieve her pocketbook, "but I hope that it works out for you." She shook her head as she muttered to herself, "always scamming. What the hell?"

"I can hear you, you know," Eric said, sternly. "And for your information, I'm not scamming. I just need to do things a certain way here." He turned to go back into his office to retrieve his cell phone and keys, which he had left on his desk. "You'll see," he added, "Lupe Espinosa will, unknowingly, be the one who helps me get the charges against Wendi dropped. Write it down."

Fatima's look of contempt, both for the conversation and the idea, clearly showed Eric that she did not agree with his plan. Before she could answer, however, he held up his hand as if to signal that he did not want to have an argument with her.

Just then, the mailman walked into the office. He handed the day's mail to Eric, picked up the couple of letters sitting on the shelf waiting to be brought to the post office, and then exited. Eric quickly glanced through the envelopes in his hand and, determining that nothing in those envelopes was critical, again motioned to Fatima that they should go to lunch.

*****

Following a thankfully uneventful weekend, meaning that Wendi did not receive the notice about the Grand Jury and therefore did not harangue Eric with questions about the process, Eric spent Monday morning in Elizabeth Municipal Court. He saw Officer Jack Miller in the courtroom, and the two exchanged quick pleasantries but no mention was made of Wendi's case or the impending Grand Jury proceedings.

The same was not true, however, when Sergeant Woodman entered the courtroom. He approached as Eric was talking to the Prosecutor about downgrading his client's reckless driving ticket. ""Watch what you do with Goldberg, dude," he said to the Prosecutor, "if you don't send his client to the fucking electric chair, you face the possibility of the local news calling you out for not doing your job properly."

"Oh, come on, Adam," Eric pleaded as the Prosecutor broke into laughter, "I'm trying to do a job here. And you know I have no control over the media. It's not like that Lupe Espinosa treated me any better. She's making me seem a lot worse than you guys."

"He's right, Sarge," the Prosecutor chimed in between chuckles. "And don't forget. She may have said that you didn't do your job right, but she did say that Eric here was screwing his ex-wife, which is probably worse in the grand scheme of things." He winked at Sergeant Woodman and the two men began to laugh, as did two attorneys who were seated in chairs directly to the left of the table where the men were gathered.

Eric's face began to redden as his blood pressure started to rise. "Come on, guys," he whispered, "do you think that you can please keep it down? Like I just said, I've got a job to do here, you know. Apparently I am the only one who is looking to work. My fucking client is sitting over there, and I would rather him not see that you guys are picking on me, OK?"

The Prosecutor looked over his shoulder at Eric's client, who was seated in the third row of benches and probably could have heard at least part of the conversation. Feeling empathy for Eric's plight, he turned back around and said, "he's right, guys. Let's keep it professional." He looked down at the paperwork in his hand. "Let's see. What brings your client here today?" He thumbed through the papers. "He got a ticket for reckless driving, huh? And another one for tailgating? What do you want to do with this, Eric?"

"Well," Eric replied, "seeing as you owe me one now that you've embarrassed me, I think you should dismiss the tailgating one and downgrade me to a no-point ticket on the reckless driving."

"You're kidding me, right?" asked the Prosecutor, again laughing. "Reckless is a four-pointer, Eric, it's not like this is for careless. And the other one carries points also. You know that I can't do that. If he's found guilty of these, he's halfway to a license suspension."

Eric knew that he was right and that his request was excessive, but he stood his ground. "Look, man, check out the tickets and your discovery." He pulled the copies from his file folder. "Nobody got hurt, there wasn't an accident, and you know that they are the same frigging ticket so one's going to be dismissed anyway. So the only question is the reckless. On a normal day, you would downgrade it to a careless driving. You know that. So let's give me a little something for the effort, to quote Carl Spangler."

The Prosecutor looked at him with an incredulous look on his face, clearly not understanding the reference to the classic line from "*Caddyshack*." "No points, that's what you want, Eric?"

"Yes, but I don't want the one with the $250 surcharge," Eric said, deciding to see how far he could push the prosecutor. "I want him to plead guilty to obstruction of traffic. No points, he pays his $80 in fines, and I get the fuck out of here so you don't have to see me anymore."

"You know I can't do that," protested the Prosecutor.

"Of course you can, Joe," replied Eric. "You've got Sergeant Woodman here. He can authorize you to take this deal," he added, looking at the Sergeant, "right, Sarge?"

Now it was Sergeant Woodman's turn to look at Eric with a befuddled expression. "Why the fuck are you dragging me into this, Goldberg?"

"Because you started with me and almost made me look bad in front of my client."

Sergeant Woodman shook his head slowly. "Jesus, Eric, you really are crazy. Tell you what," he said to the Prosecutor, in a voice barely above a whisper, "give this ex-wife fucker what he wants." He glared at Eric. "Give it to him this time."

"Thanks, Adam," Eric said, as he turned to his client and gave him the thumbs up sign. He was not pleased about the "ex-wife fucker" comment, of course, but was pleased that he was able to obtain such a favorable result for his client and would be getting out of the court rather quickly. It was worth taking the insult without getting into an altercation with the Sergeant.

Soon thereafter, the Judge came out on the bench. Eric's client was the second case called, and the client dutifully pled guilty to the amended charge of obstructing traffic. The Judge seem quite surprised by the favorable deal that Eric had brokered on behalf of the man, and, after obtaining confirmation from the Prosecutor that he had read the plea arrangement correctly, fined the man $50 plus $33 in court costs before telling him that he had better be extremely grateful for his counsel's efforts in negotiating such an extraordinarily favorable response. The man nodded and indicated his gratitude for Eric, at which time Eric and his client turned and walked out of the courtroom, Eric winking at Sergeant Woodman as he left.

His work in court done, and with the remainder of his fee, a check in the amount of $400, tucked into his shirt pocket, Eric walked back to his office. It was 10:30. He had two and a half hours before his meeting with Lupe Espinosa would begin. He reached his office within minutes, even after stopping to pick up coffee for both Fatima and himself. Handing the coffee to Fatima, he asked what he had missed by not being in the office all morning. She told him that things had been quiet, but that his 4:00 appointment had canceled.

Eric noticed something different about Fatima. He was unable to put his finger on it at first, but as he walked into the next room it struck him, or, more correctly, all of the factors struck him at once: her hair was done, she was wearing more makeup than usual, and she was dressed as if she was going to a party. She was all dolled up, much more so than she ever was before for a typical day at the office.

Then Eric remembered that it was not a typical day at the office. Clearly, he thought, she was doing it for Lupe Espinosa. But why? Was she doing it to assert herself as being an important part of Eric's life? Was she thinking that Lupe would bring her cameraman to the office even though she had agreed not to do so? All things considered, it did not really matter, Eric thought. It was far better, he knew, to allow Fatima to preen a little than to hear her condemn him for meeting with the reporter.

Eric kept himself occupied for the next couple of hours, reading through the day's mail and doing some research for a quirky divorce matter that he had begun working on the prior week. As the clock approached 1:00, he tried his best to clean up his desk so that his office looked at least presentable for his visitor. The appointed hour came and went, however, and there was no sign of Lupe Espinosa. The same was true at 1:10, and also at 1:20. "Don't worry about it," Fatima called from the next room, sensing Eric's concern. "You know that Spanish people are never on time for anything. I wouldn't even expect her before 1:30, or maybe even 2:00. She'll be here."

Fatima was off by five minutes, as Lupe's long legs carried her into Eric's office at precisely 1:25. Not showing any signs of remorse for being so late, she walked over to Fatima's desk, her short skirt making a faint "swishing" noise as she walked, and her tight sweater straining to restrain her chest. She wore what appeared to be at least a half dozen gold bracelets on her left wrist, all of which seemed to strike each other as she moved, creating an incessant clanking noise. Eric heard Fatima call to him that Lupe had arrived. He waited a couple of minutes to make her understand what it was like to wait for someone, even though he knew that she probably would not realize what he was doing, and so he would not seem overly anxious for their discussion. Following a brief period of time, he emerged from the office to greet her. Shaking his hand vigorously, Lupe thanked Eric for the opportunity to talk. He could barely hear her over the sound of her jangling bracelets.

Lupe turned her head toward Fatima, and then toward Eric and asked if they could speak in private. Eric nodded his approval, and extended his right arm in a sweeping motion toward his office. Lupe started to walk into the office, the noise of her skirt drowned out by her bracelet symphony, and Eric followed. He turned back toward Fatima and grimaced. She smiled in response. Realizing that he then turned back to watch Lupe's backside walk into the office, however, Fatima's smile turned to a frown and she shook her head disapprovingly. "No good can come from this," she thought to herself.

Lupe closed the door behind them when Eric entered the room, stating that she wanted to talk without having Fatima being able to hear what they had to say. Eric walked behind his desk and sat in his chair as Lupe sat in the chair across from him, her long legs crossed seductively, with her right foot tucked under her left calf. Her skirt lifted slightly, so that its bottom edge was now slightly above the mid-point of her thighs. "Again, Mr. Goldberg," she said, "I want to thank you for speaking with me. I'm still surprised you didn't want to do an interview, but I am interested in what you want to tell me." She reached into her bag, produced a pen and pad, and then placed the bag back on the floor next to her chair.

Eric shook his head and pointed at the items in her hands. "You should call me Eric, please. But," he said, shaking his head, "we said no pen, no pad, and no notes. We are just talking." He looked at Lupe, and then down at the bag located on the floor to her right. "Now I am concerned. How do I know that you don't have a microphone or tape recorder hidden in that bag?"

"Seriously?" she asked, incredulously, "¿usted no me cree? You don't believe me?" She reached down, picked up the bag, and leaned it forward toward Eric, opening its top widely so that he could see all of its contents. "Do you see a microphone or tape recorder in there? No, I didn't think so." She placed the bag back on the floor. "Are you satisfied?"

"I guess so," Eric replied.

"You guess so?" Lupe asked, angrily. "What do you think, Eric, I am wearing a wire in between my breasts?" Eric started to say no, surprised by the question, but Lupe was already beginning to prove that she was not hiding such a wire. She reached down to the bottom of her sweater with both her hands, and, in one fluid motion brought both of her arms up, pulling the sweater up over her head. She sat, sweater in her right hand, and her bare breasts staring Eric in the face. He hadn't noticed before that she was not wearing a bra underneath the sweater. Now he certainly knew. "Well, Mr. Goldberg," Lupe said as she saw Eric's eyes wander down to her chest, "do you see a wire anywhere?"

"No," Eric responded, "I can't say that I do. I guess we are OK to start talking, if you want." He motioned to the sweater in her right hand. "But you might want to put that sweater back on," he added, "because I'm a little distracted right now."

Lupe looked at him and smiled, like the proverbial cat that had swallowed the canary. "You are?" she asked, clearly pleased that her obviously pre-planned ploy had, at least for the moment, disarmed Eric. Now she wanted to find out why he had called her to the office, hoping that he would reveal more information that he otherwise would have. First, however, she had one more question for him, a question that she would regret asking almost as soon as the words left her mouth because of the ferocity of Eric's reaction. Sweater still in hand, she leaned forward, her naked breasts resting on the edge of Eric's desk. "Eric," she asked, quietly, pointing to the chair where Eric was sitting, "is that the chair where it happened with that Brazilian woman?"

Eric's rage was immediately apparent. He was tired of being asked that question. He disliked it when Wendi asked. He disliked it when Amanda asked. He completely hated it when Lupe asked. "What the fuck difference does it make to you?" he exploded, smashing his right fist to the desk for inflection. "We're not here to talk about what happened last year!" Even Eric was surprised at his own display of fury. It was as if a year's worth of anger and frustration over the situation with Bianca Rodrigues had boiled over at that moment.

He also realized that Lupe Espinosa clearly resembled Bianca, with her tanned Latin skin, long hair and silicone-infused breasts, and this resemblance made his feelings even more acutely painful and strong. Not that the resemblance justified his outburst, he realized, and he was immediately ashamed of his behavior.

His show of raw emotion, however, had a positive effect in that it completely disarmed Lupe. Whereas she clearly thought that she could curry favor with Eric through her attempted seductive maneuver, his reaction to her inquiry swiftly brought into focus to her that he was meaning to conduct business, at least with her, and that her magnificent breasts and the body that had landed her a full-time television news job would not be enough to wrangle information out of Eric Goldberg, at least not on this day. Defeated, and before Eric could apologize, she quickly pulled her sweater back on and sat back in her chair, as far from the desk as she could, in a tacit sign of submission to Eric. The meeting was his to run, and he sensed it. There was no need for him to apologize for yelling; such an apology, now, would only work against him.

Restoring his voice to a calmer, more professional level, Eric looked at Lupe and began to explain why he asked her to come to his office. "Lupe, as you know I am representing my ex-wife in the pending case against her. Contrary to what you have said on the news, however, I am not sleeping with her. I am not involved with her in any way other than as attorney and client."

"Is that why I am here?" Lupe asked, thinking to herself that her suspicions of Eric's newly-rekindled romance with Wendi were correct, despite his denials, and that would be a reason why he had spurned her semi-advances only moments ago. His protestations seemed to strong, she believed, and her mouth curled into a smug grin as she felt vindicated by his comments. Somehow, all of the advantages that Eric had obtained through his outburst were evaporating, and both Lupe and Eric sensed it.

"No, not at all," Eric continued, as he began to get more defensive in his responses and comments. "And stop smiling at me," he added, noticing her expression. "I know what you are thinking, Ms. Espinosa. And let me tell you again, there is nothing going on between Wendi and me. You know that I can't stop you from thinking it or even from saying it, but I swear, as much as I possibly can, that there is nothing between us." He shook his head for emphasis. "She is my ex-wife. She is my client. Period. End of that part of the story."

"OK, Eric, I believe you," Lupe said, even though she was lying. She leaned forward, arms close to her body, perfectly framing and accentuating her cleavage as she continued. "Then why did you want me to come here to speak to you? Certainly the information that you wanted to give to me is not just that you're not romantically involved with your ex-wife."

He leaned forward in his chair. "I do have some potentially important information, Lupe. Some information and I need to find out if it is true. I need you because I want to see if you can confirm for me," Eric said. "I know that you can get in touch with Jesus Sanchez, because you have already done at least one interview with him." Eric did not disclose to Lupe that he was aware that she and Sanchez were having an affair, based on the information provided to him by Marisol. He did not disclose to her that he was aware that Sanchez seemed to simply be using her, but he suspected that she was doing the same to him.

In Eric's mind, giving the basic information to Lupe, so that she could go back to Sanchez, could lead to Sanchez essentially filling in the blanks, providing her with information linking him to the alleged witness, and that she, being a self-absorbed and completely self-motivated reporter, would then bring that information to the public eye, thereby obviating the need for Eric to do additional groundwork. The best part was that she did not even have to tell Eric the information first. He would not then be forced to go to Amanda with the information, possibly harming their relationship. Instead, this plan was perfect - the dirty work would be done by Lupe on the news, before the matter even progressed to the Grand Jury and certainly long before any trial would begin. His defense in the case against Wendi would, to a large extent, be resting on the large, buoyant chest of Lupe Espinosa.

"Here's what I have been told," Eric continued, "that this alleged witness, Ramon Lopez, is also known as Ramon Ortiz. One of the last names is his mother's, and one is his father's. You know how Latinos are with their combined last names, right?" Lupe smiled and nodded in agreement. "Anyway, it appears that Ramon Ortiz has some juvenile arrests and plea deals. He was represented on at least two occasions by the firm of Samuels, Preston, and Greenbaum. Have you ever heard of them?"

Lupe thought for a second before responding. "Not that I can remember," she answered, "Can I write these names down so I don't forget them?" Eric agreed that she could do so, and she again bent down to her right to retrieve her pad and pen. As she did so, her legs spread apart, giving Eric another view, similar to the one from the television interview, of her thong-clad crotch. Pulling herself back upright, Lupe asked, "what are those names again?" Eric repeated the names, spelling each so that she was sure to write them each correctly. "OK, Mr. Goldberg. I have these names. What does it mean to me? What's so special about these three?"

"It's not those three names that are the key ones, Ms. Espinosa," Eric replied. "Of more importance is the name of an associate who used to work for that firm, the person whom I believe was the attorney who actually represented young Ramon Ortiz on these charges. That is what I want for you to confirm, that this other attorney represented him."

Lupe again raised the pen to the pad and prepared to write down the additional name. "And what is the name of this mystery attorney?" she asked.

"Jesus Sanchez," was Eric's curt reply.

Lupe froze as she heard the name of her lover mentioned. She immediately flashed back to their argument and his rage when she first referred to Ramon Ortiz, whom she at that time thought was named Ramon Lopez, as a *delincuente*, a delinquent. Now, assuming that Eric's information was correct, she understood the underlying reason behind Sanchez's strong reaction. Sanchez told her that it was because of what someone had called him when he was young. But that clearly was not the real reason. He knew the kid. He had represented the kid. She had no doubt that Eric's hunch was correct, and that Jesus had represented Ramon Ortiz and knew Ramon Ortiz – and, more importantly, that Jesus knew that Ramon Ortiz was, in fact, a delinquent. But she could not tell Eric. It was her secret. "Jesus Sanchez?" she said, simply, without any discernible show of emotion. "You think that Jesus Sanchez was the attorney for this boy?" She paused. "And you want me to ask him for you?"

"Yes, I do," Eric replied. "You don't have to do it in front of the cameras, of course, but I think that you have the best bet at talking to him about this. I think we can both agree that if I called him, the chances of him talking to me about the witness against my ex-wife would be pretty slim, if any – especially due to the nature of why I would be asking him." He paused and looked out the window to the courthouse. "Plus,

Lupe," he added, again playing directly to her ego, "this could be the sort of thing that really helps your career, you know. Nobody can know that I have this information, and, therefore, nobody needs to know where you got this information, especially that you got it from me. You could always say that you somehow found or stumbled on it, and I could never dispute that. It could work very well for someone who wants to be an investigative reporter, or, even better, an anchorwoman." He looked her directly in the eyes. "I assume that is your ultimate goal, right?"

Lupe pondered Eric's question. She liked Jesus Sanchez. She enjoyed the sex with Jesus Sanchez, and she enjoyed the thrill of being with a rising star like Jesus Sanchez. At the same time, however, she was well-aware of the fact that Jesus Sanchez looked out, first and foremost, for Jesus Sanchez. She had no doubt that if it served his purposes, he would drop her in a second. And this – exposing such an amazing twist to an already emotional story - was exactly the type of news reporting that she could use to catapult her into a better position. "Yes," she said slowly, "this is interesting." She again leaned forward, her breasts resting on the edge of the desk, albeit this time hidden behind the fabric of her sweater. "*Tengo que tener cuidado.* I need to be careful. You know, Mr. Goldberg, of the rumors about Mr. Sanchez, right?"

That was an extremely open-ended question, one which Eric did not feel comfortable answering. "What does she mean?" he thought to himself. Was she talking about the allegations of when he was back in Colombia? That he had killed people there? Maybe she meant the rumors about his dalliance with Lupe? Due to his uncertainty, he simply answered, "what rumors?"

She leaned closer, pressing her chest harder against the side of the desktop, so hard that Eric feared that her saline implants would rupture and cause a flood across his desk. Her voice in a whisper, she said, "I mean the ones about when he was back in Colombia." She looked around to make sure that nobody else was listening, apparently forgetting for the moment that the door was closed and there was nobody else in the room with them. "You know, the rumors about how he killed people. *Dicen que tiene muy mal genio.*" She paused, and saw his confused expression. "Oh, sorry, forgot I was talking in Spanish," she clarified, "they say he has quite a temper." She made no mention of the fact that she had previously been on the receiving end of one of the instances where his temper had flared.

"They say?" Eric replied, smiling. "Who, pray tell, are the 'they' to whom you are referring?" He knew that Lupe must have already witnessed and therefore would possess first-hand knowledge of such a temper, even though she had not yet made any such indication. He thought that maybe she would come clean and tell him, but he underestimated her ability to keep a secret.

"You know, 'they,'" she replied. "*La gente de Colombia.* The local people. People who knew him and his family back in Colombia. From what they say, you don't want to get on his bad side."

Eric again smiled. "Well, then, Lupe, if you are going to talk to him you should stay on his good side. So far, based on the interviews you have done with him, he seems to like you. Perhaps show him your good side. That should work."

Now it was Lupe's turn to smile. "My good side?" she asked, as she sat upright, leaning against the back of the chair. "Which is my good side?"

Eric laughed. "I don't want to get myself in trouble, Ms. Espinosa. All that I have really seen is your front side, and I have to admit, it is pretty impressive."

"You mean these?" she replied, looking down at her chest. "Yes, they have been called impressive in the past." She ran her hands over them. "Tell me this, Mr. Goldberg," she said, her voice again in a whisper, "do you like them? Do you think that they are real?"

Eric again chuckled, choosing to ignore the first question and instead focus on the latter, and only slightly more innocuous, question. "Do I think they are real?" he replied, "Again, I don't want to get myself in trouble by giving the wrong answer."

"Don't be *loco*. There is no wrong answer." She again reached down to the bottom of her sweater and quickly pulled it up so that it was bunched around her neck. "I am going to assume that you like them since you did not give me an answer to that question, and, realistically," she added, confidently, "there is no way that you could say no." Her breasts bounced freely as she stood and started to walk around the desk toward Eric. "Give me your hand," she said, "you can't tell if they are real without touching them, right?"

"Oh, I can tell already," Eric gulped, keeping his hand away from Lupe's grasp. "They're moving as you walk, so they must be real. To be honest, I have always thought they were fake, so I guess that I was wrong. Kudos to you."

Lupe smiled as Eric continued to squirm in his chair, deftly trying to keep his hand away from hers. She looked down at her breasts, noticing that Eric's eyes remained fixed on them as well. "Eric, they say that the mark of a good haircut is that it doesn't look like you had one, right? And good makeup looks like you're not wearing it?" she answered.

Eric eyes wandered upward from her chest to her eyes, and he looked at her with a puzzled expression on his face. "And your point is?" he asked.

"Oh Eric," she laughed, "My point is that good surgery, good plastic surgery, is the same." She cupped her breasts in her hands. "They are nice, right? They're part real and part good surgery, so it doesn't look like I had anything done to them." She smiled and leaned forward, and the sense of déjà vu with respect to when Bianca had been in his office the prior year was not only palpable, it was overwhelming. He was so lost in thought that he almost did not hear her next question - "Thanks for the compliment. So would you say my front side is my good side?" Lupe asked.

Eric pondered the inquiry for a brief second while he tried to properly gather his thoughts. Trying to erase the memory of Bianca Rodrigues from his current psyche, he swallowed hard. "It's hard to say," he replied in an effort to be funny and therefore not have to properly answer the question. "I haven't really seen your back side." Once he said the words 'back side,' however, Eric immediately knew that he had made an error and also knew what was in store for him next.

"Really? Would you like to?" Lupe replied, as if on cue. Eric hesitated. Without waiting for his response, Lupe whirled around and stuck her rear end only a scant few inches from Eric's face, bringing up an entirely new flood of Bianca Rodrigues-related memories. "What do you think?" Lupe asked as she stood next to Eric. "The skirt is pretty tight, so you can tell, right?"

"Uh, yes … yes," Eric stammered as her posterior was inches from his face. He tried to answer her question in as non-incriminating a fashion as possible, "it looks pretty good to me."

"Pretty good?" she barked. "Pretty good? Is that all? We've got to do better than that, Eric." She reached down, undid the zipper on the side of the skirt, and slowly lowered it down her thighs. She then bent over and slid the skirt over the bottoms of her legs and laid the skirt neatly on his desk. As she bent over, her almost fully-exposed ass, cut in half by the string of her thong, invaded Eric's personal space to the point where she could feel his warm breath on it. "Now, Eric," she purred, "still pretty good?"

Eric tried to shift in his seat to move further away from her, but in so doing accidentally forced his head and shoulders in a forward motion. His face struck her posterior, his nose rubbing against the thong strap and gently grazing each side of her ass. Embarrassed, he recoiled as far back in the chair as he could, even though he could hear Lupe laughing and knew that she was enjoying both playing the role of exhibitionist and also Eric's discomfort at the situation. "You know what," Eric said, "I think it's a tie. Both of your sides are pretty damned awesome." He paused. "Now can you do a favor and put on your clothes?"

Lupe turned around to face him. Her sweater was still bunched around her neck like a mink stole, and she was otherwise naked except for her thong. The sight of her standing there, hands on hips, clad only in the thong and the sweater-necklace reminded him, again, of Bianca. He looked up at Lupe and saw her eyes staring at his crotch. Looking downward, he realized the reason for her prolonged gaze. He had not realized how excited and hard he became looking at Lupe and thinking of both her and Bianca. "So you do like what you see, right, Mr. Goldberg?" Lupe purred. "I guess it is true that you do like Latin women." She paused. "Tell me, Mr. Goldberg. What would your ex-wife say?"

Eric stood, the crotch of his pants straining and jutting outward at Lupe. "For the last time, I am not involved with my ex-wife," he said, sternly but quietly so as not to give Fatima cause to come in from the adjacent room and find him in this compromising position. I don't know what I need to do to prove it to you." Looking at Lupe's smile in response to his last comment, he immediately realized he had painted himself into yet another corner from which he had to extricate himself. "I'm not going to prove it that way," he said, adjusting his manhood within his pants so that his erection was less evident, "but you're going to have to take my word for it. Now, Lupe, as much as I have enjoyed this, and as beautiful and spectacular as your body may be, I need to get some work done and you need to go speak to Jesus Sanchez."

"I guess you're right," Lupe said as she walked back to the other side of Eric's desk and pulled her arms through her sweater. She reached for the skirt on Eric's desk and again bent over at the waist, away from Eric, and providing him with one long, lasting look at her ass before pulling the skirt up over her thong. "I will talk to him. How should I let you know what happens?"

"Let me give you my cell phone number," Eric replied. "You have my office number. If I give you the cell number, then you can always reach me." Seeing her take her phone out of her bag, he added, "The number is (908) 555-5873. Call me anytime." This was just another statement that he immediately regretted. "You know what I mean. Use it if you need to. Please don't abuse it. And please do not give it to anyone, especially to Sanchez. I don't need him calling me."

She punched the numbers into the phone. "Of course I won't abuse the number, Eric. I will only use it if absolutely necessary." She reached down and picked up her bag from the floor, and placed her pad and pen into it before slinging the bag over her shoulder. Extending her right hand toward Eric, she said, softly, "It was a pleasure talking to you, Mr. Goldberg." Eric extended his right hand and took hers in his. She leaned closer to him and gently kissed him on the cheek, whispering "maybe we can do it again some time. You know, somewhere other than your office where we have even more privacy."

"The pleasure was entirely mine, Ms. Espinosa," a startled and still evidently aroused Eric replied, "believe me."

"I do, Eric, I do." She again looked down at his midsection before turning and walking toward the door. "I will make arrangements to see Mr. Sanchez soon, and will call you with any information," she said, "and Eric, make sure that you don't go out into the other office for a few minutes unless you want your secretary to see more of you than usual," she added, laughing, turning back and again glancing down at his still-swollen crotch.

Chapter XXXII – Lupe's Dinner With Sanchez

That evening, Lupe Espinosa was unable to sleep. She tossed and turned for hours, her mind whirling. Her head was pounding, her migraine-like headache resulting from the information provided to her earlier that day by Eric Goldberg. She was greatly tormented about how to proceed. Part of her wanted to confront Jesus Sanchez with the information, to report on her first major exposé and be the reporter who saved an innocent woman from going to jail for a crime she did not commit, if it could be shown that Sanchez was somehow using his former client as a pawn to make false allegations against Wendi. If she did so, however, that would not only make the case against Wendi crumble, but it would also have a similar effect, no doubt, on Sanchez's political aspirations. He had promised her that the city would be theirs if he ascended to the Mayor's office. With his political connections, he explained, she would have her pick of television jobs if he were to win the election. And the Mayor's seat was just the first step, he told her. As he continued to rise up the political ladder, he promised, she would go with him.

She was not certain that she wanted to risk losing those opportunities. She was especially wary of risking her future with Sanchez over allegations which could prove to be false.

At the same time, however, she also felt, deep down, that Sanchez was not being completely honest with her. Assuming that Goldberg's information was right, then Sanchez should have told her about his relationship with Ramon Ortiz. The fact that he exploded and almost hurt her in a rage when she referred to the kid as a "delinquent" still haunted her. Now, it bothered her even more. Not just because he refused to come clean and tell her that he knew Ortiz, but also because she was

331

completely right. The young man was a delinquent – three arrests before the age of 17 certainly qualified him for such a label.

She was also worried about how Sanchez would react if confronted with the information. She had heard the rumors of his illegal activities while he was in Colombia. She had seen him flash his legendary temper, most recently at her when she uttered the "delinquent" word. If he caused her such pain just for inadvertently calling his ex-client a delinquent, then how would he react if she basically accused him of orchestrating a fraudulent prosecution? The mere accusation, she knew could completely derail his political aspirations. Even though she thought that Sanchez cared deeply for her, and possibly even loved her, she was well aware of the fact that he loved himself, and his own interests and aspirations, far more. And she had no doubt that his feelings concerning the possibility of political advancement were certainly greater than any amorous feelings that he may have possessed for her.

The last part was the most important. Lupe knew that Sanchez would always put his career advancement before her interests. She was confident in that belief. Her career advancement, therefore, should similarly take priority over any concerns that she had about derailing his aspirations. This was, potentially, her big chance. Was it worth ignoring it, or throwing it away over him?

She rose from bed and walked into the bathroom. Turning on the light, she stared at her reflection in the mirror, as if searching for the image to provide her with the clear answer that she was having difficulty reaching on her own. It was a little before 3:00 in the morning. Lupe was not wearing any makeup, and her restless night of non-sleep left her hair knotted and twisted. There were visible discolorations under her eyes from her lack of sleep. In the absence of foundation, visible blemishes and the faint scars of past acne were visible on her face, blemishes and scars that were never evident under the makeup she donned in front of the television cameras; she hated those flaws and imperfections. She took a step back, and then another. The signs of imperfection gradually faded as she retreated from the mirror.

As the scars and discoloration faded from her field of vision, more and more of her body came into view. When she was standing directly in front of the mirror, a mirror which sat atop the bathroom's countertop and which reached to the ceiling, she could only see her face and the top half of her body. As she moved backward, however, she could now see not only her head and tank-top encased torso, but also the top half of her legs. Her tank top only reached down to a point just above her navel, and she found herself unconsciously rubbing her right hand over the front of her thong, the same thong in which she had attempted to curry favor earlier that day with Eric Goldberg. She began to think of Eric and the prior events which had taken place in his office between he and Bianca Rodrigues, and the thoughts in her head excited her.

She closed her eyes and envisioned herself in place of Bianca, on her knees in front of Eric with her lips wrapped around his erect manhood. There was something exciting about Eric. He was not as physically fit as other men in her life, like Jesus Sanchez. Eric had a paunch of a stomach and had clearly lost most of his hair. The majority of hair that remained on his head was graying. He did not have washboard abs like Sanchez. He was not as facially attractive as Sanchez, and from what she felt through his pants earlier, he was likely not as well-endowed as Sanchez. Still, there was something about him. It was something that was unexplainable, but yet something that enticed her. Perhaps it was simply the fact that another woman found him attractive, or that he was a willing participant in seemingly illegal, or at least improper, activities. She was not sure, not that it mattered. She wanted him.

She opened her eyes and stared at her body. Her nipples were erect, and were clearly evident through the fabric of her tank top. She then realized that her hand was underneath the fabric of her thong, and that her index and middle fingers were thrust inside of her, slowly moving backward and forward in an almost rote, unconsciously rhythmic manner. Chills ran up and down her body as her stimulation increased, resulting in a surprisingly quick and shuddering crescendo.

Struggling to regain her thoughts, she removed her fingers and walked back toward the bathroom vanity, placing both hands on the countertop and leaning forward, staring at her reflection, as if to look completely through her face and into her mind, into her soul. Her decision became clear to her. She must put her interests first. Jesus Sanchez would not make good on his promises to her, even if he were to win the Mayoral election. And she could easily replace him in the bedroom, maybe even with Eric Goldberg if everything worked out properly.

The only question, however, was the means by which she would confront Sanchez. She removed her hands from the countertop and stood, erect, in front of the mirror. Her nipples still made impressions on her shirt. Lupe smiled. She pulled the tank top up over her shoulders and laid it, in a ball, on the counter. She then slipped off her thong and took two steps backward, so that she could see her naked body, from the knees up, in the mirror. She liked what she saw. Thousands of viewers, she knew, liked what she showed them while on the news. And she knew, more importantly, that this was an appealing vision to Jesus Sanchez. That would be the way to get the information, she determined, to ask him the next time that they were in bed together. Once his inhibitions were down, especially as a certain part of his body was going up, he would be more vulnerable to telling her the truth.

She had plans to see him the following (Wednesday) evening. They were having what he had promised would be a romantic dinner at his apartment, which would then, she assumed, inevitably lead to sex. That would be the time to put her plan into action.

*****

The next evening, she arrived at Sanchez's apartment at 7:30 for dinner. She was wearing a slinky, red dress, one which possessed a scoop neck where the neckline lay just above her nipples, and underneath she wore a lacy black bra which left little, if anything, to the imagination. The dress ended about halfway between her crotch and knees, and she took the liberty of going without underwear for the evening so that there would be no chance of panty lines showing through the tight dress, even the faint lines which could be caused by a thong or similar item of clothing. A pair of black stiletto heels completed her ensemble, an outfit which she knew would have Sanchez's heart racing from the time she walked in the door.

334

When she arrived at Sanchez's apartment, Lupe was surprised to find that there were three other people present, not quite what she expected for what was promised to be a romantic dinner. A woman whom she recognized as Sanchez's part-time maid was there, which was not actually all that surprising as, to Lupe's knowledge, Sanchez did not know how to cook even the most basic of dishes. The presence of two large men, however, was certainly not on Lupe's radar and she struggled to determine why they were there, especially because the dinner table was, in fact, only set for two. She suspected that they were bodyguards hired by Sanchez, but they had not been present on her previous trips to his apartment, nor had they accompanied him on their trysts in her apartment.

As Lupe was pondering the presence of the two men, Sanchez emerged from his bedroom, the clicking of his heels echoing off of the apartment's hardwood floors. The tanned, slim soon-to-be Mayoral hopeful was clad in a pale, tan suit, set off by a dark blue shirt and a tie comprised of tan and light blue stripes. His gold cufflinks seemed to illuminate his wrists, and shimmered even more in the light of the apartment when he lifted his arms to greet and embrace her. "*Mi amor*," he said as he swept her up in his arms, "*lucir más bella que nunca* (you look more beautiful than ever)."

"*Y eres muy guapo, papi*," she replied, pulling away from him so that she could see his clothes, "you are very handsome." She then leaned her face toward his ear, and kissed it tenderly before asking, "*¿quienes son esos hombres?* Who are those men, Jesus?" She again kissed his ear. "I thought that this dinner was *solo para nosotros*, you know, just for us."

"Oh, them," he answered, "*no te preculpes por ellos*. Don't worry about them." He motioned to the men to leave, at which time they turned and walked into the room reserved for his office, closing the door behind them. "It's just Paco and Juan. You've met them before, *mi amor, ¿recuerdes?*" He took her right hand in his left. "They're part of my team," he began to explain. "They do things for me. If we need anything, they'll take care of it so that I don't have to leave you, *corazon*. Normally they are not here every night, but I wanted to make sure that tonight was special." He motioned to the table, where the two place settings, located directly across from each other on the long sides of the table, were illuminated by a pair of tall candlesticks. *"Venga, vamos a comer,"* he said, quietly, "come, let's eat. I think you will enjoy it." He paused and lifted his head, his nostrils flaring with an exaggerated smelling motion. "No, I know that you will enjoy. Do you smell that, Lupe?" he asked, *"¿huele a su pais, no?* Right, doesn't it smell like your country?

Lupe also took a deep breath. The aromas of melted cheese and black beans filled her nostrils, and she was immediately transported, in her mind, back to her childhood in her home country, to the special *comidas* that her *abuela* would make for the family. *"Sí, Jesus, que lo huele bien*, it does smell great," she said, adding, "can I ask who cooked it?"

"Mi amor, why would you ask such a question?" he asked, placing his hands on his chest in a show of mock offense. "I did, of course." He could barely finish the word "course" before breaking out into laughter, a seemingly natural, staccato, form of laughter. It differed greatly from the deep, more controlled laughter that Lupe was used to hearing from him, the one that had emanated from his throat at so many public functions and rallies. The show of what she believed to be raw emotion surprised her.

"If you cooked it, Jesus, then why are you laughing?" she asked, the contagiousness of his joy forcing her into her own bout of laughter.

Sanchez wiped the beginning of a tear which had formed in the corner of his right eye, and he tried to bring himself under control. *"¿Por qué estoy riendo?* Why am I laughing? No reason," he croaked out, before again dissolving into laughter. "It's just that …"

"You didn't cook this, *papi*, did you?" Lupe interrupted, in a seductive voice as she placed her hand on his convulsing shoulder.

Sanchez's mood darkened immediately. His face turned stern and the laughter disappeared. Lupe wondered how he was capable of controlling and shifting his emotions so easily, and began to wonder for the first time if his seemingly-natural laughing fit was also just an act. *"¿Cómo puedes pedirme que?"* Lupe looked at him, speechless. "Well? How can you ask me that?" Sanchez thundered, the sound of his voice reverberating throughout the apartment. His face was still flushed red, but this time the coloration resulted from rage rather than joy. Lupe looked at him, her eyes widened in shock at the sudden turn of emotions. Sanchez stared back at her for a brief moment; jaw clenched, but then again started laughing and, as he again grabbed her in a warm embrace, admitted that he had not been the chef for the evening's dinner.

Lupe held him cautiously, unsure of how to process the remarkable span of emotions that Sanchez was somehow able to exhibit in such a short span of time. She would have to proceed with caution, *con cuidado*, she realized, lest she encounter or, worse, cause one of these seemingly manic mood swings or changes. "I didn't think so, *papi*," she said, softly, as he nestled her face carefully into his chest, "but *no importa*. It really doesn't matter. *La comida huele delicioso*. It smells delicious. Let's eat."

The meal was rather uneventful, a situation for which Lupe was extremely thankful. Sanchez's maid, who had already cooked the food, also acted as server. A short, portly woman, she waddled in and out of the room several times, each time bearing a dish with a new delicacy or a new bottle of wine to accompany the food. The two others, Juan and Paco, remained in the office, not even making one appearance during the hour-and-a-half-long meal. By the time Lupe and Sanchez were done with the meal and a delicious flan for dessert, they had consumed almost two full bottles of wine and were both quite tipsy.

Even with her inhibitions compromised by her alcohol intake, however, Lupe remained lucid enough to avoid mentioning Ramon Ortiz during the meal. In fact, the two did not discuss the accident or Wendi Goldberg's prosecution at all while they dined. Instead, the conversation was dominated, as it always was, by Jesus describing his political ascent and trajectory, and how the two could mutually benefit from his becoming Mayor of Elizabeth. It was, as he had told her in the past, just the first political step for the two of them, and that as he continued to advance politically, so would her career. Lupe did very little talking, as was also usual when the two were together, and instead was relegated to a series of nods in approval of Sanchez's comments. When the maid returned to the room and asked if they wanted coffee, Lupe demurred, indicating that she was already way too full to drink or eat anything else. She also did not want Sanchez to drink any coffee, not wanting him to sober up (he had consumed much more wine than her) before she had the chance to ask him about Ramon Ortiz. "Let's skip coffee, Jesus," she purred, "I think I would rather go to the bedroom right now. *¿Quieres acompañarme?*" She stood and started to walk toward the bedroom, and slowly lifted the back of her dress to show Sanchez that she was not wearing any underwear.

"Do ... do I want to come with you?" he stammered, partially due to the liquor and partially due to the sight of Lupe's bare ass, "*creo que sí.*"

"You think so, Jesus, or *¿sabes le que?* Do you know so?" she asked, as she continued to walk down the hallway, reached down and picked up her pocketbook, and strode to the door of his bedroom. When she reached the threshold of the bedroom door, she tossed her pocketbook onto the floor next to the bed and slowly lifted her dress up over her head, so that the only thing that Jesus could see was her bare skin, encased only in a bra strap. The bra was removed seconds later, and a naked Lupe stood in the doorway as Jesus rose from his chair and raced toward the room.

Literally ripping his shirt off of his back, Jesus bounded toward Lupe. One of his cufflinks flew to the side as he neared her, landing on the wood floor with a clatter. He frantically pulled his tie from his neck, almost choking himself in the process, and threw it to the ground, where it lay in a heap alongside a door. It lay alongside the door to the room where Juan and Paco sat, quietly, as if waiting for their cue, their call to action. Sanchez's belt was undone as he reached Lupe, and he grabbed her from behind, one arm wrapped around her waist and the other cupping one of her breasts. "I know, *mi amor,*" he slurred, as he walked her inside the room and turned to his right, forcing them both onto the top of his bed. "I know."

Sanchez then stood and started to remove his pants. As they slid to the floor with his boxer shorts, Lupe gently took his growing penis in her right hand and began to stroke it lightly, making it grow even more under her soft touch. Sanchez's knees began to buckle slightly, as his already alcohol-induced, fuzzy-headed feeling was exacerbated by the blood rushing from his head to the lower half of his body. His breathing became heavier, and he fell to the bed, Lupe's hand still wrapped around his now fully-grown manhood. Lupe bent over and kissed its tip gently, all the while continuing her stroking motion.

Lupe believed that this would be the perfect time to pose her question to Sanchez. She again bent over and rubbed her cheek against his throbbing member, causing him to moan audibly. "Jesus," she said, "can I ask you a question?" Hearing him grunt in the affirmative, Lupe began what would prove to be her last line of journalistic inquiry. "I heard something, *papi*," she said, softly, "and I want to ask you about it."

"What?" he muttered, "Why are we talking now?" He took his hand and placed it on top of Lupe's head, and attempted successfully to guide it to the side, so that her mouth was now hovering directly over and just inches from his erection.

"Not now, *papi*," she whispered. "You'll have to wait a couple of minutes. *Tendrás que esperar un par minutos.* First we need to talk, then I will do that." She pulled her head from his grasp. "I want to talk about the boy who saw that woman kill the kid in Elizabeth, Jesus."

"*¿Qué pasa con él?* What about him?"

"Do you know him?" she asked. "I mean, *¿Lo conocía antes del accidente?* Did you know him before the accident?"

"No, *mi amor*," he answered, his breathing still labored. "*¿Por qué me preguntas eso?*"

Lupe continued to stroke Sanchez, and replied, "Why am I asking you that question? I am asking you *por que* I heard that you did know him before. In fact," she said, "I heard that you represented him in court before. *Que lo representó en la corte antes. ¿Eso es la verdad?*" She moved her head closer to where he had wanted it before, but never reached her quarry. In one quick motion, Sanchez reached up with both arms, grabbed her by her shoulders, and threw her to the side. He rolled to his side and then stood at the edge of the bed, breathing heavily, as he glared down at Lupe.

"*¿Es eso lo que quieres saber?* (Is that what you want to know?) You want to know *la verdad?*" He moved closer to her, and reached out with his right hand. As his fingers found her throat, he leaned down and said, in a whisper, "the truth? I know him; I know Ramon Lopez, or Ramon Ortiz." He raised his voice to a sneer. "Whatever you want to call him, I know him. *Si, lo conozco.*" His grip tightened around the front of her neck, as his left hand pinned Lupe down on the bed. "*¿La verdad? Qué clase de periodista eres tú, Lupe?* You fucking whore. You want the truth? What kind of reporter are you?"

Lupe began to panic as Sanchez's grip around her neck tightened. Instinctively, she reached up with her left arm and swung it outward, her hand finding the only means by which she could free herself from his clutches. She wrapped her hand around his still erect penis and pulled it to the side, causing him to cry out in pain and release her neck. Gasping for breath, she released her grip on him and rolled to the side, but could not gather herself together enough to stand or flee his attack. Sanchez was doubled over in pain, but still was able to grab her leg and keep her within arm's reach. "What do you mean?" she cried, "*¿qué quiere decir?*"

"You *puta*, what do you think?" Sanchez asked, as he held her with one hand and rubbed his sore member with the other. His eyes were blazing red, a combination of wine and his anger. "*¿No recuerdes?* Come on, Ms. Reporter, you really don't remember? We talked about my mother. *¿En la entrevista, que dije el appelido de mi madre era?*" Lupe struggled to remember back to their television interview. He did talk about his mother. He used her last name, but what was it? The pain in her neck continued. Her leg was beginning to ache where he was holding her. She felt herself beginning to cry harder. She couldn't fight him off, especially as his strength appeared to increase when he was enraged. She couldn't think straight, and, in that instant, could not remember his mother's last name. But why did it even matter?

"*No puedo recorder.* I can't remember," she sobbed. "Please let me go. You're really hurting me."

"*No, mi amor,*" he whispered, as he moved closer, putting one hand back on her neck and the other over her heaving left breast as she gasped for air. "*¿No recuerdes?Permítanme recordarles.* (You don't remember? Let me remind you.)" He rubbed her breast gently, and then leaned forward, his again-erect dick resting on her chest. "Think hard, Lupe," he said, and then paused before adding, in a whispered but forceful voice, "my mother's last name, *mi amor,* was Ortiz!"

Lupe gasped. She was already having trouble breathing due to Sanchez's grip around her neck, but the mention of his mother's maiden name was shocking to her and made the situation worse. She had completely forgotten that her last name had been Ortiz. Is it possible that Ramon Ortiz was not just a client of Sanchez? Could it be that Sanchez and Ramon Ortiz were …?

"*¿Sorprendido, Lupe?* Are you surprised? If you haven't figured it out yet, yes, your source, whoever it was, was correct. I did represent Ramon Ortiz. In fact, I represented him twice." He started to move his body upward, so that his groin was hovering above Lupe's neck as he continued to reach down and apply pressure to her windpipe. "In fact, he was not just a client, Lupe." Lupe closed her eyes to try to stifle the pain, but was unsuccessful, "*él era algo mas que un cliente,*" he added as he maneuvered his crotch above Lupe's head. She opened her eyes just as he added, "Yes, he was more than just a client, Lupe. In fact, Ramon Ortiz is my family – he is my nephew! I'll bet your source didn't tell you that." His grip tightened. "In fact, *es una lastima que usted no será capaz decirle a nadie.* It's too bad you won't be able to tell anyone."

Lupe knew that she had to try to escape, and tried to devise a way to escape his chokehold. She could feel his erection pressing against the bottom of her chin. She also knew that his erection was, at that moment, the most vulnerable part of his body. She pulled her head slightly backward, and then thrust her head forward so that she was able to take her mouth and envelop the erection. Slamming her jaw shut as hard as she could, she could feel the warmth of blood spurting into her mouth from Sanchez's shredded manhood. Sanchez yelped in agony, and smashed his right fist against her head, like one would do to an attacking shark, so that she would release the vise-like grip of her jaws. The force of the blow forced Lupe to release her lock, and Sanchez pulled himself out of her mouth as blood trickled onto the bed sheets from several holes which Lupe's teeth had cut along his throbbing and now-shrinking member. He staggered backward against the wall, and then moved slightly to his left to block the door to the bedroom. Lupe stood and, seeing Sanchez blocking the exit, hopped off the bed, grabbed her pocketbook and clothes, and ran for the bathroom, slamming and locking the door behind her.

Lupe feared that she would not make it out of the bathroom unscathed, so she had to tell someone about Sanchez's relationship to Ramon Ortiz. She fumbled through her pocketbook, searching for her cell phone, so she could text Eric, the only other person who knew that she was there and the person who also knew about the possibility of a relationship between Sanchez and Ortiz. As she was fumbling through her purse, she continued to sob. The sounds of her own cries drowned out the noises from the adjoining room, so she could not hear what was happening on the other side of the door. She assumed that Sanchez would be waiting for her to come out, at which time he would do to her what he had done to so many others while he was still in Colombia. What she did not realize, however, was that she would never see Jesus Sanchez again.

The toilet was situated directly in front of the bathroom door. Lupe had placed her pocketbook on top of the toilet, and was standing, naked, in between the toilet and door as she tried to locate her phone. Through her sobs, which echoed through the ceramic tile-filled bathroom, she did not hear Sanchez go out into the hallway and beckon for his goons to come. She did not hear both of the big men enter the bedroom and ask Sanchez if now was the time to undertake their mission, as they thought that they would not be called until after he had, as he put it earlier when laying out his original plan, "fucked her one last time." She did not hear Sanchez go to the other bathroom to tend to his wounds and to distance himself from what was about to occur.

Oblivious to all of those goings-on, Lupe pulled the phone out of her bag and was just about to type in Eric's cell phone number when she was struck from behind by the door. The two men had each kicked the door with such force, and without any warning, that they broke the lock and the door swung open, the knob striking Lupe in the waist so hard that it knocked her onto the toilet. It was the last sensation that she would ever experience.

She did not feel the butt of Paco's gun as it came down on her head with the force that only a 250-pound man could generate, nor did she feel her unconscious, limp body fall onto the toilet and then into the shower door, where the force of her fall caused the door to come off of its tracks and fall onto her. Still unconscious, she did not feel the bullet fired from Paco's gun as it entered the roof of her mouth and passed through the top of her skull, spraying blood and brain matter all over the shower wall.

At least for now, Sanchez's secret was safe. When he returned to his bedroom several minutes later, however, wearing loose-fitting boxer shorts to protect his still-swollen and bleeding appendage, he was confronted with the problem of how to deal with the mess in his bathroom. It was not the first time that he had covered up a murder, but it was the first time that he had been forced to do so in some time. This was common practice when he was with FARC in Colombia and, in fact, evidence of such murders was often left behind as a warning to others that a similar fate could befall them if they were not properly careful. Disposing of bodies and cleaning up crime scenes in the United States, however, was a different story. Luckily, he had experience in cleaning up after others; while he had not personally killed anyone since he came to the United States, he had been involved in the cover-ups of numerous murders as he ran his drug enterprise out of his law office. Looking down at the naked, bloodied body, he could not help but wonder, for a fleeting moment, of what could have been between he and Lupe Espinosa.

He bent down one last time, kissed her on the cheek, and ran his hand down her body, from her breasts to her thighs, one last time. As he stood, he shook his head and spit on her face. "You fucking *puta*," he exclaimed, completely stone-faced and devoid of any discernible emotion, "*mira lo que me hiciste hacer a ti.* Look what you made me do to you." Without showing or, more importantly, feeling any remorse, he instructed Paco and Juan to do just as they were instructed earlier. They were to take the body, clean it up, and bring it back to her apartment, where they were to carefully place it in her bed and hide any evidence which would link them to the crime. She had outlived her usefulness to him, Sanchez had explained to the men when they arrived at his apartment earlier, and it was time to eliminate her before she could do him any damage. He had been thinking about her demise for some time now. She had already provided him with exposure. Now others were picking up on his story, so he no longer needed her to serve as his personal mouthpiece in the media. As people were beginning to whisper about their alleged relationship, he told them, he would not be a suspect in her murder, nor would they, as long as they cleaned up the evidence and covered their tracks properly.

He then walked out of the bedroom, toward the kitchen, and made himself a cup of coffee. He sat at the kitchen counter for the next half hour while the two men cleaned up the bathroom and body, and barely acknowledged their efforts when they carried the limp, now dressed, body of Lupe Espinosa, his former lover, out of the apartment, a body which had enthralled Sanchez for so long but which he would never again see.

All evidence of Lupe's presence in the bathroom had been eliminated in that thirty-minute period. All of her personal belongings were removed, and the bathroom was quickly cleaned and scrubbed so that no remnants of blood or any other part of Lupe's body remained. Paco drove her car back to her apartment, wearing gloves so that he did not leave any fingerprints, with Lupe slumped in the back seat. Juan followed close behind in his own car, and then the two entered Lupe's apartment, laid her in her bed, and again opened the wound on the back of her skull so that blood would leak onto her bed and sheets. They then ransacked the apartment to make it look like a burglary, and even broke the lock on the front door to make it appear as if an intruder had forced his way in prior to killing Lupe.

While they were at her apartment, Sanchez, with the help of his maid, completely sanitized his apartment, removing any evidence, fingerprints or otherwise, which would indicate that Lupe had been his guest that evening.

Lupe had dropped her cell phone when she was struck by the door, and it had fallen to the ground and broken on the tile floor of the bathroom. When the men cleaned the bathroom, they took the phone, smashed it into as many pieces as possible, and then placed the pieces into a garbage bag with all of the dirty rags and towels that they had used to wipe up the blood. They did not want the phone's GPS system to identify Sanchez's apartment as its location. Nobody checked the phone to see if she had tried to call or text anyone after she had locked herself in the bathroom.

Chapter XXXIII – Farewell to A Fellow Reporter

The next evening's newscast began with a somber note, a report unlike any other that the anchors of Channel 14 had ever been forced to deliver. Even for reporters and the stage crew, those whose hearts had been continuously hardened by nightly stories of war, death, and destruction, this story was difficult to write and even more difficult to verbalize. Never before had any of the members of the news crew dealt with the sudden, brutal death of one of their own.

The anchorman who had bantered with Lupe Espinosa only weeks earlier about her stories relating to Wendi Goldberg's case, and the anchorman who, for the past year or so, had sat in a chair a scant few feet from Lupe Espinosa, thereby possessing the best view of her lovely body, was charged with the ultimate task, that of reading the report. It was intended to be a sanitized version, not to reveal the manner of death, so as not to jeopardize what they were told was an ongoing police investigation.

"Tonight, we begin our broadcast with terrible, unimaginable news," the anchor began, "on a nightly basis, we sit in these chairs and report the news to you, our viewers. We do so with as detached a manner as possible, trying to do so without any emotion. Sometimes, however," he said as his voice began to break, "what some call the news becomes more personal, and it becomes a struggle to share without letting part of ourselves be exposed. Tonight is one of those nights." He paused, his eyes moistening, and took a couple of deep breaths before continuing. "As our viewers know, for the last year and a half, we have been blessed to have a wonderful, young, intelligent, insightful, and beautiful newswoman with whom to work. Early last year, Lupe Espinosa joined our staff, and immediately earned a place in all of our hearts. The personal touch that she added to her reports, especially those stories which concerned her fellow Latin Americans, made the stories, well, just that much better."

He again paused. The camera panned back, showing the newswoman sitting next to the anchor clutching his hand for support. "Do you want me to take over?" she whispered to him, but he shook his head and quietly said that he would complete his assigned task, to best honor his friend and co-worker.

Following a prolonged pause, he continued. "Today, we learned that our co-worker, our friend, Lupe Espinosa, has died. Lupe's body was found in her apartment by a relative who had stopped in for a visit. An autopsy is pending, and I have been instructed that it would be improper to report on a possible cause of death." He again paused, and then purposely violated the mandate given to him by the station, adding, "but it appears to be that her death was not due to natural causes. An investigation, we are told, is pending." His eyes moistening anew, he again paused and dabbed at his right eye with a handkerchief. "Lupe leaves behind her parents, a sister, numerous other relatives and co-workers, and legions of fans of her reporting work. Rest in peace, Lupe," he croaked out, "we will all miss you. *Vaya con dios.*" Tears began to stream down the anchorman's face, as they did on all others who were on the studio floor.

The studio went dark, and a photo of a smiling Lupe Espinosa, surrounded by smiling children at a local school, filled the screen. The wording on the bottom said, simply, "Lupe Espinosa, 1988-2014"

Seconds later, Eric Goldberg's cell phone rang. He was in the car, driving home from Amanda's apartment. He had met her for dinner, but left shortly after ten so that she could prepare for her next day's Grand Jury matter, the one that was being held just before Wendi's. Amanda hoped to have the matter resolved by the end of the day, she had told Eric, so that they could proceed to Wendi's the next week. She knew that it would be difficult to see Eric and focus properly on the case at the same time, so the two decided that, pending the outcome of the next day's events, it might be best not to see each other for a while, or at least until the Grand Jury heard the evidence against Wendi and decided her fate. Eric drove home that night, therefore, with a heavy heart.

He did not relish the idea of not being able to see Amanda for the next week, if not longer depending on the progress of the case. The Grand Jury met only once a week. The case could drag on over several weeks, depending on how many witnesses the state would be calling.

He was also anxious about the fact that the case could be heard within the next week, and was nervous about the fact that he had not heard from Lupe Espinosa about whether or not she was able to obtain any incriminating information from Jesus Sanchez. He had even telephoned Lupe earlier that day to check in with her, but the call went right to voice mail and she had not returned his call.

Maybe it was Lupe calling, he thought to himself, wishfully. Without even looking at the number of the caller, Eric pressed the button on his steering wheel to answer the call. "Eric," the caller said, "it's Michael." Eric immediately recognized the voice of Judge Michael Tompkins.

"Judge," Eric replied, "I'm in the car. To what do I owe the pleasure of this call? And calling me on a weeknight, no less?"

"It's really not much of a pleasure, Eric, to be honest with you," Judge Tompkins said. "Is it safe to assume that, since you're in the car, you didn't watch tonight's news broadcast?"

"That's right," Eric explained, "I was just having dinner with a friend and am just driving home." He dared not tell the Judge the identity of his dinner companion, of course.

"Well, then, it looks like I'm going to be the bearer of bad news," he said, and then paused before continuing. "Eric, the lead story on the local news tonight was that Lupe Espinosa is dead. They didn't give any details, but said that it was not from natural causes."

Eric, shocked by the completely unexpected news, gasped and pulled his car into a parking lot off Morris Avenue so that he could better focus on the conversation. "You're kidding me," he said.

"Kidding you?" Judge Tompkins replied. "Would I kid you about that?"

Eric's mind was whirring. "No, I guess not," he replied, as he considered, for the first time, the possibility that he had send Lupe on a mission that had resulted in her death. "They gave no details at all? Did they say anything about where she died or if she was with anyone?"

"No," Tompkins replied. "It was very cryptic. The anchor said that it wasn't from natural causes, and to be honest with you, the way that he said that line made me think that he was ad-libbing, so I don't even think that the station wanted him to say that much." He sighed. "I know that she was helping that piece of shit Sanchez to make our lives difficult, especially yours, but I can't say that she deserved to die."

"Absolutely not," Eric said, consumed with the thought that she had been killed because she confronted Sanchez with evidence against him and that his suspicions turned out to be true. "Do you think that Sanchez had anything to do with it?" he asked, not offering any explanation or reasoning behind why he would even make such a suggestion.

"You're shitting me, right?" the Judge replied, incredulously. "That thought hadn't crossed my mind. If anything, I thought the two of them were in bed together based on the way that she fawned over him and gave him a pulpit to spew his venom from. What motive could he possibly have to kill her? I mean, really, Eric, be serious." He paused. "If anyone had a motive, by the way, it was you. She was fucking with your case and accusing you of sleeping with your client. And you don't see me accusing you."

"Thank God for that," Eric replied. "I can't go through another person accusing me of killing someone. Get accused enough times, and people start to believe shit."

"You've got to start hanging out with better people, my friend. It's not healthy to keep finding yourself mired in this crap, believe me."

"Situations just seem to find me, what can I tell you?" Eric asked, ignoring the Judge's obviously tacit reference to his previous year's dalliance with Blanca Rodrigues. "It's the nature of doing the work I do, I guess. Not like sitting on a bench all day long."

"Alright, smart guy," Judge Tompkins replied. He was not as adept as Eric at hiding his emotions and was clearly not pleased with Eric's comment. "I've done what I wanted to do and let you know about the woman's death so I'm going to hang up now. You drive home carefully and try to stay out of trouble. I think you're appearing before me at some point in the next couple of weeks, and I want to see you in one piece."

"You got it, Judge," Eric said, laughing, "and thanks for calling and letting me know about her death." He realized the irony in laughing as he said such a statement, but he did not know how else to respond to the situation. "It is a shame, and I just wonder how it happened. Hopefully we will find out."

"I think it's safe to rely on Elizabeth law enforcement to figure it out, Eric," Tompkins replied. "Just don't be surprised if they knock on your door asking some questions. Shit, I might even get an inquiry. What a fucking circus you've gotten us into."

"Thanks for the thought, Judge. Hopefully not, for both of us, that is. See you soon," he said, clicking off the phone. Eric sat in the parking lot for another minute, still overwhelmed and shocked by the information relayed to him by Judge Tompkins. He was sure that she died at the hand of Sanchez or one of his "friends." He was equally certain that it was because of what he had told her about Sanchez's presumed prior representation and possible relationship with Ramon Ortiz. He felt guilty for her death, and was now certain that he would need to tell Amanda of his suspicions. She was now his only hope, the only "safe" way that he could prove his case.

Or was she? Suddenly, he began to worry that he would be placing Amanda in some type of jeopardy if he got her involved in trying to investigate Ramon Ortiz. If Sanchez really was behind Lupe's death, and he clearly had no qualms about participating in the murder of a somewhat-public figure, one with whom he was romantically involved, then logic dictated that he would not think twice about taking similar steps against Amanda, even though she was a Prosecutor. He did not know if he was willing to take such a chance with Amanda, even though to give up on his search for corroborating evidence against the young man might spell difficulties for Wendi and their chances at trial. He felt a growing tightness in his chest, similar to his earlier panic attack. He leaned back in his seat in an effort to quell the angina pains, and closed his eyes, breathing deeply, to try to calm his nerves.

At that precise moment, his cell phone began to ring again. This time, he looked down to see the identity of the caller. He was praying that it was not Wendi, and that she had not been watching the news that evening. Wendi had received the notice for the Grand Jury a day earlier, and, as expected, had called Eric in a total panic. A fifteen-minute telephone conversation ensued, with Wendi alternately yelling at Eric for not handling things properly and crying because she was so scared and needed his assistance. Eric understood the range of emotions in light of her surprise at receiving the notice, and barely spoke more than a couple of sentences during the call. He viewed it as more of a catharsis for Wendi than an actual attorney-client telephone conversation, or even a discussion between ex-spouses or friends, and was thankful when he was able to put down his phone and resume the rest of his activities for the afternoon. He certainly did not want to end up in a similar conversation now.

Looking down at the phone, he was pleased to see Amanda's name on the screen. A wave of relief came over him as he was heartened to think that he would not have to deal with Wendi's excitable personality. His relief was tempered, however, by his continued internal debate about the possible need to speak to Amanda about his information and suspicions regarding Sanchez, Ramon Ortiz, and Lupe Espinosa. He did understand, however, that the time to have their conversation with her, should he

352

choose to do so, was not when he was in the car, so he simply answered, "Hello, do you miss me already?"

"Well, yes, I guess," Amanda answered in a somber tone, "but I'm trying really hard not to dwell on the fact that I won't be able to see you for a while. I'm trying really hard." She paused and signed audibly. "So far, it's not working. But to be honest, that's not why I am calling. After you left, I turned on the news."

"Oh," replied Eric, in a matter of fact tone of voice, "is it safe for me to assume that you saw about Lupe Espinosa dying and were calling to tell me?"

"Yes," Amanda replied, in a surprised tone, "how did you know?"

"Well, believe it or not, Judge Tompkins beat you to it," Eric explained, "I just got off of the phone with him."

Amanda gasped at hearing the Judge's name. "Judge ... Judge Tompkins called you? He called you on your cell phone?" she asked, "I knew that you two went to law school together, but I didn't know that you were close enough that he would call you on your cell phone." She paused, and then her voice took on a more panicked inflection. "Please tell me that you didn't tell him where you were tonight, did you?"

"Don't be ridiculous," Eric answered, trying to calm Amanda. "Not that he even asked, but I simply told him I was on the way home from dinner with a friend."

"Good. I don't need that kind of aggravation now," she said, letting out an audible sigh of relief, "and, I think we can both agree, neither do you. The report said that it wasn't natural causes. Do you think someone could have murdered her? I wonder why that would have happened."

Eric realized that this was his best opportunity to broach the topic which was laying so heavily on his mind. "I have an idea why," he began, having reached the decision that he would enlist Amanda's help in trying to find out additional evidence against Ramon Ortiz, "do you mind if I come back to your place for a little while and we can talk about it?"

There was a prolonged pause before Eric received his answer. "I don't like the sound of this and really had no intention of having to think about anything else tonight. My mind is fried from preparing for tomorrow, Eric, and to be honest with you, I really don't know how to react to the fact that the Judge who is presiding over my prosecution of your ex-wife's case feels comfortable enough to call you on your cell phone," Amanda answered, and then sighed audibly. "If you are serious, though, then yes, please come back. But just turn around and let's do it now, because I am exhausted. I was just getting changed for bed."

"I'm still on Morris Avenue so I will be there in five minutes, don't worry."

"OK, drive carefully. See you in a few."

Eric pulled his car to the parking lot exit and, instead of making a right turn onto Morris Avenue, he turned left to head back to Amanda's apartment. As expected, he reached her building within minutes. The door to her apartment was slightly ajar when he reached her floor, as usual, and he entered the apartment to find her sitting in her living room, still watching the news, clad in a t-shirt and underwear as if ready to go to sleep. "OK, Eric," she said without even looking up at him, "Tell me why you had to come back here. I'm really nervous about what you are going to say."

"You should be," he responded, at which time she looked up, puzzled. "It involves Wendi's case."

She stood with her arms outstretched and palms upward in a "what?" motion. Raising her arms caused her red t-shirt to ride up to just below her navel, fully exposing her red-and-white striped thong. Eric's eyes were drawn downward by the display, much to Amanda's chagrin. "Eyes up here, buddy," she said, pointing to her face. "What do you mean it involves Wendi's case? Meaning, that it involves my case? You know, the one with the Judge that you just spoke to without me being involved in the conversation!"

Eric was somewhat surprised by Amanda's obvious annoyance at his conversation with Judge Tompkins. It never occurred to him that she would view it as being improper, and decided that it was a topic best not discussed between them. He sat on the couch and motioned for Amanda to join him, a gesture which she refused with a wave of her hand. "Where do I start?" he asked, mindful of the fact that he could not mention nor even allude to Jim Parker's involvement in any way. He began to explain the chain of events that he believed, correctly, led to Lupe Espinosa's untimely death. "I heard a rumor that Jesus Sanchez may have had a relationship with the kid who is your witness in Wendi's case."

"You mean Ramon Lopez?"

"Well, yes and no," replied Eric. "You are correct that I mean Ramon Lopez, but I am also talking about Ramon Ortiz."

"How did you find out that he was also known by that name?" Amanda asked, coldly, in a tone usually saved for defendants during depositions or cross-examinations.

"Come on, Amanda," he said, conjuring up a lie to explain his improperly-obtained knowledge, "I know people. I've been around this city for a long time, like since you were in elementary school. In this case, ironically enough, I know kids. I've got clients all over the area, and many of them with kids, kids that are in all of these schools, right? One of the kids clued me in to the other name. It wasn't that hard to find out," he added, another clear fabrication. "Plus," he added as he remembered where he really found the name, "it's in the discovery that you delivered to my office."

"Oh," Amanda replied, remembering that there was at least one reference to the boy's hyphenated last name in the police reports. "And?"

"And," Eric continued, "Not only did I hear about the fact that Lopez was also known as Ortiz, but once I had the name I started asking around and I heard that this Ortiz kid was in trouble in the past, and that Sanchez, when he was still practicing law, had represented him. Actually, scratch that. I was told that the firm where Sanchez used to work had represented him twice in juvenile criminal court; but the person who told me was unclear as to whether Sanchez actually represented him or not. Clearly that is something that creates at least an impression of impropriety around the witness, so I had to find out for sure. I wanted to try to find out without you."

The tension in the room abated through Eric's explanation and his stated desire not to involve Amanda in his investigation. Now Amanda sat down next to him. "Well, thanks for not asking me to help you, Eric. You know that I couldn't sabotage my own case."

"Of course, honey," Eric replied, "I know that I couldn't use the resources of the Prosecutor's Office to undermine its own case." That was his second lie. "But I had to figure out if it was true. So I had to find someone who Sanchez trusted to ask him for me."

Amanda ran her right hand through her hair and then crossed her arms in front of her chest. "Don't you have any investigators that you could use?" she asked, still using her Prosecutor's tone of voice. "I would think that a big attorney like you must know some people who can find out information. Instead, you tried to use the newswoman as bait?" She paused, looking skyward as if thinking of her next question – which popped into her head within seconds. "And, by the way, how did you know Sanchez trusted her? Just from that interview that they did together? That wouldn't be enough for me to think so."

Eric grinned, a smile that drew a look of derision and disgust from Amanda as the tension level between them began to rise anew. "First of all," he said, "I do know some private dicks. But Sanchez is a very tough nut to crack. I mean, think about those rumors about Colombia. You know, the drugs, the murders, that kind of stuff. How come nobody's been able to prove anything? You work in the Prosecutor's Office. Certainly you know that they've looked into him in the past and were never able to pin anything on him, even with all of the rumors. Nobody will rat him out."

Amanda nodded her understanding and knowledge of the failed investigations.

"Simply put, I needed someone who could talk to him directly." He paused, and waited for another nod of understanding from Amanda. "And the story gets a little weirder here. You know how I get massages every week or so?" Amanda nodded in agreement. "For the past couple of years, I have been going to the same woman, Marisol. When I was there a couple of weeks ago, she told me that Sanchez and Lupe were there together. She said that Sanchez came onto her …"

"Wait," Amanda interrupted, her face contorted in exacerbated annoyance as she asked, "what does this Marisol look like?"

"Not now, Amanda," Eric scolded. "This is not a time for jealousy. She's a young Latina, OK? But let's focus, please. This is really important. Sanchez came onto her and told her that he and Lupe were just working together, but she didn't believe him and, based on that and the sparks that I saw during the interview, neither did I. So I figured that they were dating and knew that she would have his ear."

Amanda was not listening. She was jealous of the young Latina masseuse, and wanted Eric to know it. "Is she pretty?"

"Is Lupe pretty?" Eric asked. "You know what she looked like from seeing her on the news."

"I don't mean Lupe," Amanda replied, sternly. Her hands returned to her hips, her arms outward, as she leaned toward Eric and pressed her new line of inquiry. "I mean this massage girl. What was her name, again, Marisol? Is she pretty?"

"Please, this is not the time to be jealous, Amanda," Eric implored, "please focus with me and forget about her. Yes, she's pretty. And you're much prettier. But this is not the time to discuss looks. We need to talk about Lupe dying and how Sanchez was involved."

Amanda glared at Eric. She did not want to gloss over the fact that he was so close with his masseuse. She was intrigued, however, about the possible relationship between Lupe Espinosa and Jesus Sanchez. She could not figure out, though, why Lupe would have done anything to help Eric in his investigation, especially if it meant hurting her own boyfriend, her own meal ticket. "OK, I will focus with you, but I am not pleased about this massage thing and we will discuss this later, mark my words. Why would Lupe sell him out for you?" she asked.

He shrugged his shoulders. "To be honest, I wasn't sure at first. But the more I thought about it, the more I figured that she was at least smart enough to see that he was using her to further his political career, and that she was also using him and his exposure to further her television career. So I thought that if she could expose him on this case, and I handed her the information that she had to confirm, that she would do it to make her name as an investigative reporter."

"That's a pretty big gamble, don't you think?"

"Maybe," Eric replied, "but I figured that she was my best hope, if not my only hope. And once I met with her, I knew that I was right. It took me all of two minutes to sell her on the glory that she would gain by blowing the lid off of the story, even if it was about her boyfriend. Our plan was that she would ask Sanchez about the alleged link to the kid and then let me know if he confirmed it or not. We met on Monday, so it was a few days ago. I haven't heard from her since."

"So you think that she went to Sanchez with the information and he killed her right there in her own apartment?" Amanda asked.

"I can't be 100% certain, but what else could I think?" Eric answered as he reached out his right arm, took Amanda's hand in his, and pulled her down next to him so that she was sitting alongside him on the couch. "It's all just too convenient to be anything or anyone else. I mean, it may not have been Sanchez, but there is no doubt that he was involved. It could easily have been one of his goons because he would not want to have actual blood on his hands," he continued. "The timing of this is too incredible for me. We talked about stuff that could incriminate him and could derail his ambitions. And then, days later, the one person whom he knows has that information ends up dead. What would you think?"

"I don't know what to think about her death, Eric," Amanda replied as she moved closer to him on the couch and leaned her head against his chest. "All that I know right now is that I liked it much better when we weren't discussing the case." She paused and lowered her voice to a whisper as she wrapped her arms around his midsection. "And if you're right, dear, I really hope that she didn't tell Sanchez that you had given her the information."

Now Eric had something else to worry about.

Chapter XXXIV – Eric Gets Some New Information

The next morning brought three more instances of Eric being forced to engage in "did you know that Lupe Espinosa was killed?" conversations – the first was with Jon Grant, who arrived for work shortly after Eric and immediately went to his office to discuss the news report. As Grant was leaving the office the clock struck nine. Fatima then walked in, handed Eric a cup of hot coffee, and proceeded to sit down across from his desk and tell Eric various theories of what she believed could have happened to Lupe – one of which involved Sanchez, of course, based on her knowledge of the meeting between Eric and Lupe earlier that week. In response to that scenario, however, he lied to Fatima and told her that Lupe had refused to help him. Then, at 9:30, he received the call that he was dreading the most, the call from Wendi. She, ever the narcissist, was most concerned not with the fact that the woman had apparently been murdered, but rather with the possibility that she or Eric could somehow be fingered for the murder.

"Don't worry about that," Eric replied, attempting to ease her concerns, "while her accusations really bothered us, it's not like they were broadcast all over the world. I sincerely doubt that the police will even suspect that we were involved." He did not tell Wendi, and he had not told either Jon or Fatima, that he suspected Sanchez of committing the crime. He also did not tell any of them of the fact that he knew that she was going to confront Sanchez with the evidence, although Fatima did still think that she was going to do so despite Eric's indication that she had refused to assist him. He also told none of them about Judge Tompkins' seemingly joking comment about the possibility of him being blamed for the murder, so as not to alarm any of them to what seemed like a possibility of such accusations, albeit a remote possibility.

Eric could not dwell on whether or not he would be accused of committing Lupe Espinosa's murder. Of more importance to him, of more urgency, was that he had only one week to get real evidence of the relationship between Sanchez and Ramon Ortiz. If he did not have the information before the Grand Jury convened to hear the case against Wendi, there was little doubt that they would hand down an indictment against her. Once the indictment was done, it would be more difficult to have the process stalled or the case dismissed. Lupe clearly could not be of any assistance to him anymore, and he could not count on Amanda for any information. He would have to find an alternative means.

Also, he was beginning to get more and more worried about his own safety, Amanda's concerns about whether or not Lupe had told Sanchez about him ringing in his ears.

He decided that it was time to go back to his contacts at Elizabeth High School. Maybe one of his classmates would rat Ramon Ortiz out, or at least give Eric enough information to be able to refute his testimony before the Grand Jury. Eric tried to remember which other clients might have a child in the school. When he and Fatima had made their initial round of phone calls trying to locate such classmates, they were met with what amounted to a virtual dead end, with only a couple of kids knowing him and only one providing any information that could be considered as being helpful – information which was later confirmed by the documents provided to Eric by Jim Parker. Who else could there be?

Eric thumbed through the list of clients that he kept in his desk drawer; he scanned down the column on the right side of the pages which listed the home city of the clients, and stopped when he reached one of the middle pages. Sophia Lorenzo was a divorce client from several years earlier – she had three children, one of whom was no doubt in college by now but two of whom were teenagers and were likely in high school. Perhaps one of her children would know Ramon Ortiz. He reached for the phone and slowly punched in the numbers of her cell phone, praying that they were still valid. His prayers were answered, in part, when the voice mail message's voice was that of Sophia, and he left a message asking her to call him back on a personal matter.

He then proceeded to call three other former clients. The response from each was the same - none of them had children in Elizabeth High School and, they presumed, none of their children would know Ramon Ortiz or Ramon Lopez. The rollercoaster ride of emotions that he had been experiencing with respect to his efforts at finding information about Ramon Ortiz, filled more with drops and valleys than positive results, would have to continue, at least until he heard back from Sophia Lorenzo.

The next few hours were consumed with two client meetings, one of which concerned an upcoming appearance before Judge Tompkins. The other was an initial meeting with a new divorce client, the sister of a woman whom he had represented several years earlier on a municipal court matter. That meeting ran almost two hours in length, Eric taking extra time to answer all of her questions to her satisfaction and attempting, as best as possible, to explain to her the entire process of divorce so that there would be no unpleasant surprises as the case progressed. A quick walk down the street to the local pizza place to pick up lunch followed. Eric specifically chose to pick the food up rather than having it delivered just so he could get some air and to remove himself from the office for a few minutes.

That break proved to be fruitful in two respects. First, it allowed Eric to clear his head a little while filling his lungs with air from the outside, rather than the stale air of his office. Second, when he returned with lunch for both he and Fatima, she told him that Sophia Lorenzo had called him back. Ms. Lorenzo told Fatima that she was on a break when she called, and that she would be returning to work shortly and would call Eric after 5:00. Eric lamented that he had missed her and would have to wait another few hours to speak with her, but was heartened that she had at least returned his call.

At 5:15, the office phone rang. Fatima had already left for the day and Eric usually would not answer the phones after 5:00, but this time he did in the hopes that it would be Sophia Lorenzo. Luckily for him, he was correct. "Eric, so nice to hear from you," she said, "but I was a little confused about your message. You said it was personal. Is everything alright?"

"With me, yes," he answered, "but I am really calling more on behalf of a client of mine. Have you seen my name in the news lately?"

"No," she replied, "can't say that I have. Should I?"

"I guess that's a yes and no question, to be honest with you," he began to explain. "There should be no reason for me to be in the news, but I have been. My ex-wife is being accused of striking a pedestrian with her car in Elizabeth. I am representing her, and the story has made the news a few times."

"Is that you?" she asked. "Someone was talking about it a few weeks ago, but I did not realize that it was you. Something about texting and driving and the woman's ex-husband representing her in court. She killed a Spanish kid, right?"

"Well, sort of," Eric answered with a sigh, "you are right that a local Hispanic teenager died after the accident. I try not to use the word 'killed,' though, because it is such a harsh term. She is my client."

"Oh, I'm sorry" Sophia Lorenzo replied, apologetically. "Now that I think of it, Eric, my son mentioned it to me. He knew the kid that died, and apparently he also knew the kid that was with him right before the accident. Is that why you called?"

"Yes, Sophia, it is. I need to find someone who knows these kids. Are you saying that Robert knows them?"

"I think so. I'm pretty sure. Do you want me to check?"

"Absolutely, and I would love to get together with him to talk if possible."

"Well, I'm OK with that," she answered, "but it will have to wait until Monday. You probably won't remember, but this is his father's weekend, and since he moved down to Monmouth County, I don't think we'll be able to convince him to bring Robert back up here, or even let him drive himself, to your office before he is back with me. How about Monday after school? I can leave a little early from work if it makes it easier for you, and be to you a little after 4:00."

Eric was not pleased with the fact that he would be forced to wait until the following Monday to speak with Robert Lorenzo, but he understood that he had no choice. "That sounds great, Sophia," he replied. "I really appreciate it. But do me one favor."

"Sure, what is it?"

"Don't tell him why you are bringing him here. Make up another reason. I don't want him talking to anyone else about this, especially the other kids." He paused. "Also, I want to get a genuine response from him, not something that has time to think about, if you know what I mean."

"I do," she replied. "Sometimes getting the truth from a teenager is one of the hardest things we need to do as parents. Don't worry about it, I will have him there Monday, and he won't know the reason."

"Thanks so much, Sophia, enjoy your weekend," he said, before hanging up the phone and logging onto the computer's calendar program to note Monday's appointment with Sophia and Robert Lorenzo.

*****

That evening, Eric went, as was his custom, for his weekly massage. Contrary to the previous sessions, however, this time Marisol was dressed not in a miniskirt, but rather in a pair of black yoga pants to go with her white polo shirt. She seemed to be acting more "business-like" than usual, Eric thought, no doubt due to the fact that he had rebuffed her advances the last time he had seen her.

"You saw on the news about the woman, right?" Marisol asked as she began to gently rub her hands along Eric's shoulders as he lay, face down, on the table.

"I did," Eric replied. "It is very sad."

365

"People have been talking about it," she added, as she leaned over Eric, her breasts touching the back of his head as she worked her way from his shoulders to his mid-back.

"Really?" he asked, his voice slightly muffled by the donut in which his face rested. "What are they saying?"

Marisol paused, her hands still probing Eric's back while she seemed to think of the words. "*la gente esta diciendo que fue asesinada,*" she eventually said.

Eric thought for a second, trying to understand what she had said. He understood most of it; that people were saying that something had happened to Lupe, but did not recognize the word "*asesinada.*" "What are the people saying?" Eric asked, "I didn't understand that last word."

"Oh, sorry," Marisol said, "I forget sometimes that *usted no habla Español,* that you don't speak Spanish. People are saying that she was killed. *Pero* they don't know who."

"Does anyone have any idea?"

"No. *Dos personas me dijeron que* Jesus Sanchez is, *como se dice,*" she paused, thinking of the proper words, "to give money to the person who finds out who." She grinned, smugly, as if rewarding herself for something. "*Te dije, lo siento,* sorry, I told you … told you that they were dating."

"A reward, you mean?" Eric asked. "Two people told you that Jesus Sanchez is offering a reward for whoever finds her killer?"

"*Sí,*" she answered. The congeniality of their conversation, irrespective of the subject matter, was clearly eroding Marisol's attempt at acting professional. She continued to rub his back, her breasts pressed harder against his upper back, and she was now standing so closely to him that her crotch was pressed up against the top of his head. She moved it slowly from side to side as she rubbed, the fabric of her yoga pants making a faint "swishing" noise against his closely-cropped hair.

"Have you heard anything else?" Eric asked, struggling to ignore the proximity of Marisol's body to his and to maintain focus on the conversation regarding Jesus Sanchez and Lupe Espinosa.

"No," she answered, as she maneuvered herself to his right and began to work on his shoulder, raising his right arm skyward and resting it against her hip. "Oh, *espera. Hay uno cosa más.* There is one more thing. One person said she was killed over drugs. She said cocaine*, pero ellos dicen que cada vez que un latino está involucrado en algo* (but they say that whenever a Latino is involved in something)."

"What?" Eric asked, as he struggled to understand Marisol's Spanish. He lifted his head out of the cradle and turned his head toward her so he could understand her better, and in so doing moved his right shoulder and his arm as well. His hand moved from Marisol's hip across her midsection, and the upward motion of its movement forced it under the bottom of her polo shirt and against her stomach, his index finger coming to rest atop the charm that dangled from her navel. She made no attempt to remove the hand from underneath her shirt, and Eric knew that he was essentially trapped, that he could not move it without also bringing the conversation to an end. "What do people always say?"

Marisol sighed and slowly shook her head disapprovingly as she gently scolded Eric for his lack of understanding what she was trying to say. "*Usted necesita aprender Español, papi,*" she said, as she leaned forward slightly. Eric's hand moved upward as she leaned.

"I know that I have to learn," he said, ignoring the location of his hand as best as he could. "But now is not the time. This is really important, Marisol. It's really important. Please tell me in English."

"OK, I will try," she answered, leaning forward even more and lowering her voice as her mouth neared Eric's ear, "people always say that drugs cause problems with Latinos."

Eric realized that she had moved in so close to him that his hand was now nestled under her right breast. The warmth he felt also made him realize that she was not wearing a bra. He tried to slide his hand back down to her stomach, but she grabbed it through her shirt and slowly lifted it back up, higher, until it was cupped over her breast. "Marisol, please," he implored. "We discussed this last time, remember, that we can't do this, and I really need for us to discuss what you know about Jesus Sanchez and Lupe Espinosa." He again tried to remove the hand from its location.

"I know, Eric," she replied, again placing her hand over his so that he could not pull it from her breast. "I know we did. *Pero* you told me that you were not *con su ex esposa* and the only other woman could be the newswoman, and *ella esta muerta*. She's dead." She moved his hand back and forth over her breast, her nipple stiffening under his touch. "*Así que ahora podemos.* Now we can."

Eric struggled to sit up, trying desperately to remove his oddly-contorted arm and hand from Marisol's clutches and shirt. "No, we can't," he said, as he succeeded in moving to the left and freeing his hand from her grasp. "It's not my ex-wife, and it wasn't Lupe Espinosa," he said, sternly, "but you were right last time. There is someone else. You have to believe me."

"*No entiendo*," she cried, as tears began to form in her eyes, both of her nipples continuing to jut out from the fabric of her polo shirt. "*¿No crees que soy hermosa?*" she asked, as she lifted her shirt to show her flattened stomach.

Eric again found himself in the all-too-familiar but always uncomfortable position of placating a crying woman. "Of course I think you are beautiful, Marisol," he said, "but I have someone else. I can't tell you who." He sat on the table, clad only in his boxer shorts, and put his arms over Lupe's heaving shoulders to console her. "*No eres tú,*" he added, "it's not you. I am extremely flattered. If I didn't have this other person, believe me, I would be all over you."

"All over me? *Supongo que eso as bueno.* I guess that's good," she answered, as she looked downward in an attempt to try and compose herself. She peered down at the crotch of Eric's boxer shorts as she dried her eyes; the fabric in the crotch area had separated slightly, and she could tell that he was not excited at that moment. She took her right hand and gently stroked over the fabric, adding, "*yo no te excito*, Eric. You, I don't excite. *Creo que lo hice.* I thought I did."

"*Lo siento, Marisol, lo siento*," he replied. "I am really sorry, believe me. Can we just finish the massage as if this never happened? I would really like that." He pulled her close in an embrace and then let her go, pulling himself away from her.

She stood and took a step back, continuing to rub the moisture from her eyes and cheeks. "OK, Eric," she replied, "lay down and *nos olvidaremos.* We will forget."

The remainder of the hour was uneventful. Eric was careful to keep his hands out of harm's way, and Marisol did not try to engage him in any further conversation, whether about Lupe Espinosa or any other topic. Eric did leave her a bigger tip than usual, however, and then kissed her lightly on the cheek before leaving.

Eric was in the car for no more than five minutes when his cell phone rang. Dreading the possibility that it could be Wendi again, he looked down at the phone to see who was calling before deciding whether or not he would answer. He was surprised, pleasantly surprised, to see Amanda's name and number on the screen. "Hey there," he said as he clicked the "answer" button on the phone, "I didn't expect to hear from you tonight."

"Your massage is over, right?" Amanda asked, not responding directly to his comment.

"Yes, it is," he answered, "why?"

"Can you come over here now?"

Eric was surprised at the question. "I can, but I thought that you didn't want to see me once the Grand Jury for the case was about to begin. Did you not get through the other case?"

"Almost," she said. "We will definitely be done by next Thursday morning and will begin on Wendi's case that afternoon. But I need to see you," Eric could hear her sigh audibly through the phone, "… I need to talk to you tonight."

"Alright," Eric replied. "I can be there in ten minutes."

"Perfect. Drive carefully."

Eric wondered what it was that Amanda wanted to talk about with him. She had been quite clear about the fact that she did not want to see him around the time of the Grand Jury presentation, and he tried to determine, as he drove to Amanda's apartment, if she had changed her mind or if there had been some important development that she wanted to share with him. He could not think of anything, however, and arrived at her apartment minutes later still completely unaware of the reason for her call.

He arrived at the building and pressed the button next to the intercom. She buzzed him in, and he took the elevator to her floor and expected, as always, that the door to her apartment would be ajar when he arrived there. For the first time, however, it was not and he was forced to knock on the door and wait for her to open it for him. She did so seconds later, still clad in a suit that he presumed she had worn to work that day. Amanda sensed Eric's surprise at seeing her dressed that way, and quickly explained that she had just gotten home fifteen minutes earlier and did not have time to change. She then threw her arms around his shoulders and kissed him passionately before backing away and asking him to come in to the apartment.

"I'm a little confused, Amanda," Eric said as he closed the door behind him and followed her into the kitchen. "I wasn't planning on seeing you this week."

"I know," she replied. "I was dreading it. But I need to talk to you about the case … off the record, of course."

"OK, sure," Eric answered, tentatively, "what's up?"

"Tell me about the information concerning Sanchez and the kid," she began, "where did you get it from?"

"You know I can't tell you that, Amanda," Eric replied. "What does it matter?"

"It matters because I don't want to railroad a case through the Grand Jury just to have it shoved up my ass at a trial, Eric!" she explained, rather loudly. "It will make me look like shit, and could ruin me in the office. So tell me, please, who gave you the information?"

"I promised I wouldn't tell," Eric said. "Listen, I don't want to keep any secrets from you. In fact, the last thing I want to do is keep secrets from you." He paused. "But this one thing, I just can't tell you."

Amanda sat down on the chair next to the kitchen table and began to cry softly. "I really thought we had something," she said, "but if you need to protect your ex-wife so much that you can't tell me something that can totally fuck up my case and my fucking career, then I don't know where we are going together."

Eric walked over to her and put his hands on her shoulders, leaning in and kissing her on the forehead. "You can't look at it that way," he said, "I just can't tell you because I promised the person who gave it to me that I wouldn't say anything. It's about protecting that person. It has nothing to do with you and Wendi." He stood back up. "Besides, I told you what I know. You now have time to confirm it yourself, so you won't be sandbagged with it at trial."

Amanda looked up, her eyes reddened and tears on her cheeks. "I know it was Parker, you asshole!" she yelled. "He told me today. I also know that he told you about the phone records."

"Then why did you ask me?" Eric asked, completely shocked by her revelation and choosing to completely ignore her mention of the possibly-incriminating phone records.

"I didn't tell you because I wanted to see if you would tell me the truth. I wanted to see if you would tell me the truth," she said, again beginning to sob. "And you failed miserably. I can't believe ..." she added, softly, "I can't believe that I fell in love with you. I should have known better."

Eric began to answer, but stopped before any words emanated from his mouth. It was the first time that either Amanda or he had used the "love" word in talking about each other. It was a thought that he had been grappling with for weeks now – but he immediately knew what he should say in response.

"Amanda, please," he said, "you have to understand." He knelt down next to her. "I promised Parker that I wouldn't tell. He did me a huge favor, and I couldn't betray his trust." Amanda slowly shook her head as Eric spoke. "Really, Amanda," he continued, reaching out and stroking her hair with his right hand. "I didn't want to hide anything from you." He paused and took a deep breath, feeling his emotions rising and tears beginning to form in his own eyes. "Listen to me," he implored. "I didn't want to hide anything from you, and I don't want to ever hide anything from you, because ... because I love you too."

Amanda stopped shaking her head when she heard Eric's last four words. In fact, she completely froze when he told her that he loved her. No more tears came from her eyes, and she was so still that it appeared to Eric that she had even stopped breathing. After what seemed like an inordinately long period of time, Eric saw her chest rise sharply as she took a deep breath, and then lower as she exhaled as heavily. Without even looking up, Amanda asked, quietly, "what did you just say?"

"I said that I never want to hide anything ..."

"No, not that," she interrupted, lifting her head, her reddened eyes glistening, "the last part. What did you say to me?"

"I said," Eric replied slowly, as he resumed stroking her hair, "that I love you too."

Amanda stood, a broad smile suddenly erupting on her face. "You're really not making this easy for me, you know, Mr. Goldberg."

"I know, Ms. Johnson," he replied, his eyes glistening with tears. "I'm really sorry about that."

"No, no," she said, wagging her index finger in the air, "no need to be sorry." She leaned over Eric, who was still kneeling on the kitchen floor, and wrapped her arms over his shoulders and lowered her head until it was resting atop his. "Please don't be sorry. You don't know how happy I am right now." She kissed the top of his head, and then lifted her head up and leaned lower to kiss him on the cheek. "I'm so happy."

"Me too," Eric replied, as a tear ran down his cheek. "Me too."

Chapter XXXV – The Prosecutor and the Defense Attorney

"So let me see if I have this straight," Amanda Johnson said, as she lay on her couch, nestled in the arms of Eric Goldberg. "I am a prosecutor, an Assistant Prosecutor in one of the busiest offices in New Jersey. I have been given what is unquestionably the highest-profile case of my career in the Prosecutor's office, a case where a woman driving her car was allegedly texting and struck and killed a pedestrian. It's the first case to be prosecuted in Union County under the texting and driving law. I may never have such a big case again, at least in this office. Meanwhile, my adversary is not only the defendant's counsel, but he is also the defendant's ex-husband, and, to top it all off, I have somehow, inexplicably, fallen in love with that attorney." She paused, and looked up at Eric. "And almost as unbelievably, he has somehow also fallen in love with me. Is that about right?"

"Yes, I guess so," said Eric, laughing, "you know what they say, the truth is often stranger than fiction. I guess that is true, because you couldn't make this up."

"But wait," Amanda said, "there's more. Now you're telling me that the main witness who said that the woman was texting at the time of the accident is, you say, no choirboy. In fact, he's so far from being good that he's a juvenile delinquent with three different arrests, and he was represented for his last two cases by whom?" She chuckled lightly. "Well, of course, the very man who is turning the case into a media circus, presumably for the benefit of the city's Hispanic population but, in reality, to further his own political interests."

"Absolutely correct," replied Eric. "That is all the truth and, like I said, it's stranger than fiction."

Amanda sat up and swung her bare legs over Eric's. Her jacket and skirt lay, folded, over the edge of the chair to the right of the couch. The top two buttons of her blouse were undone, and she had unbuttoned the sleeves so that her cuffs dangled loosely off of her wrists. "I gotta tell you, man," she said, "it's a pretty incredible story, don't you think?"

"Absolutely," Eric again said. "It's crazy," he added, as he stroked her hair with his right hand. "In fact, to tell you the truth, if I weren't right in the middle of it, I know that I wouldn't believe that it could happen." His face turned somber. "But I am in the middle of it, Amanda, and I know the truth. And somehow we need to show everyone the truth so that an innocent woman does not go to jail."

"So tell me, Eric, where do we go from here?" Amanda asked.

"What do you mean?" Eric asked in response, gently kissing her neck. "Go? Go where? We're adversaries, remember?"

"I mean us," she explained, standing. Eric was still lying on the couch as she stood over him, making her legs look even longer than usual and providing him with an excellent view of her crotch as it peeked out from underneath her blouse.

"OK, the question is where we go from here, right? Well, right now, to be honest, I'd like to go to bed with you," Eric said, as he reached out and gently stroked the top of her right thigh. He curled his hand around the outside of her leg and ran it along the outside of her right buttock, which was barely covered by a wisp of fabric. "Is that a good answer?"

"No," she said, giggling as his hand tickled her. "That's not the answer. Let's take this one step at a time," she continued, pushing his hand off of her posterior. "We need to focus on this case first. You have information that can potentially derail my case, and to further muddy the situation it is information that you somehow want me to help you prove. But I can't do that, and you know that, counselor. My allegiance in the case is not to you, or to your client, but it is to the people of this county, so I have to prosecute the case as strongly as possible."

"True," he replied, "but your duty to prosecute really means that you should prosecute a defendant if it is proper. If someone is wrongfully accused, and you know that it is improper, then your duty is to see that proper justice is done. You can't take efforts to convict someone you know is innocent." He paused. "And that is especially true, Amanda, when you are given evidence that could exculpate a defendant." As one of our Supreme Court justices said, your job as a Prosecutor is to do justice – which is served when a guilty man is convicted, and when an innocent person is not.

"But I can't conspire with defense counsel, Eric," she said, "I can't sit here with you and figure out how to sabotage my own case. Aside from being a breach of at least a few ethics rules, it is a breach of my responsibilities to the County and State and can, if you haven't figured it out, threaten my job."

Eric sighed. "Look, I'm not asking you to conspire with me, Amanda," he said, "I just want you to do what's fair. You and I both know that there's something fucked up with Sanchez's involvement in the case. The only question is what, and if this involvement is having the effect of tampering, even if the tampering is not overt, with the prosecution."

"But Eric," she replied, "you know I can't do this. I mean, really, you've been doing this a lot longer than me. In all the time that you have been practicing, have you ever asked a Prosecutor to help you defend your case? And I don't mean just offering you a good plea deal or ignoring some evidence to let a plea go through. I mean actually asking the prosecutor to prove your case." She looked at Eric and waited for a response before asking, "Well, have you?"

Eric sat, silently. He placed his hands on his knees and took a deep breath as if preparing to answer, trying to gather his thoughts so that he could reply in a proper manner. They both, however, already knew the answer. And the answer, of course, was no. Following a prolonged silence, Amanda said it aloud.

"I know you haven't, Eric," she replied to her own inquiry. "So don't even try to fashion some kind of ridiculous answer about how you have. I should also ask you how many times you've been involved, and you know what I mean, with a prosecutor. But somehow I am afraid of that answer."

Eric looked at her, his eyes beginning to mist. "I swear, Amanda," he said, "you are the first Prosecutor whom I have been involved with, or, for that matter, who I have even thought of or wanted to be in any way involved with." He took her hand in his. "I know that you may not believe me, what with the stories that you've heard and the stuff with Bianca, but ..." he continued, as a tear ran down his cheek, "I have never gotten myself involved with a prosecutor, any opposing counsel, heck, with any other attorney. Up until a couple of years ago, I was a happily married man. A monogamous married man." He paused and took a deep breath. "And," he continued, "I don't want to trivialize things by saying only that I'm 'involved' with you. I love you, Amanda, I really love you. You have to believe me."

Now Amanda began to cry again. "I do believe you, Eric," she replied. "That's why you're still here. But," she said, standing and walking toward the kitchen to pull a tissue from the box that sat on the table, "I can't help you on this case. I just can't do it. Please, please do not put me in this position." She took the tissue, blew her nose softly, and then walked back to Eric. "Please, Eric," she said, again sitting next to him, "I'm begging you. This is really hard on me. I love you. I love you more than I ever thought I could love anyone. But I can't do this for you. Don't ask me to."

"I'm not going to, Amanda," Eric said. "But I am going to keep trying on my own, of course. And," he added, "if I find anything, I am going to tell you. I can't let this get past the Grand Jury." He wrapped his arms around her as she sat next to him. "But don't worry about anything, because it won't be because of you. Either way, you're going to come out of this looking great. I promise."

"There's one thing that you keep forgetting," Amanda said as she lowered her head until it rested on his shoulder. "Even if Sanchez is somehow involved in this, and even if he has been coaching this kid since the accident took place, even if, that still does not mean that Wendi wasn't texting when she hit the other kid."

Eric knew that she was right. Her comments were almost identical to Fatima's, and made complete sense. But that was not going to stop him from trying to discredit the witness. If he could do that, he still believed, he could obtain a dismissal of the charges against Wendi. He could have the case dismissed, irrespective of whether or not she was truly guilty. That was his job. Not as her ex-husband, but as her attorney.

Chapter XXXVI – Going "Home" Again

The next few days passed uneventfully. Eric spent much of Friday in court, eventually resolving a divorce matter that had dragged on for months. That night, he met some friends to watch the Yankees' game at a sports bar in neighboring Cranford, and then spent the weekend cleaning his apartment and running errands. He met Amanda for dinner on Saturday night, taking her to an Italian restaurant up in Bergen County where he could be sure than nobody would see them together. After dinner they went back to her apartment, where they watched a movie and fell asleep together on the couch. Eric awakened at 1:30am, carefully kissed Amanda on the cheek and walked, silently, out of the apartment.

No mention was made of Wendi's case during the time that they spent together.

Sunday morning, however, focused entirely on the case as Eric went to Wendi's house, his old house, to have breakfast with his ex-wife and current client. The purpose of the breakfast meeting was to calm Wendi's nerves, as she was again beginning to come unglued at the mere thought of appearing in front of the Grand Jury that Thursday afternoon. Eric thought that he could ease her fears over a cup of coffee and bagel, but he was, as he would find out, sadly mistaken. Just as he had when they dined together on the Sunday morning after the accident, he went out and picked up coffee, bagels, and lox before traveling to his old residence. The similarities between the two dates, however, ended there. The first time, Wendi greeted him in a sexy outfit of t-shirt and tight yoga pants which showed off her newly-toned, taut body. Her hair was perfectly coiffed and she had clearly put effort into her appearance even though it was Sunday morning and her meeting was to be with her ex-husband, not someone whom she had to impress. The house smelled of cooking food, and the conversations between the two were measured, not hysterical, despite the seriousness of the charges that Wendi would be facing.

Now, however, Wendi answered the door dressed in ill-fitting sweatpants and a t-shirt which clung too tightly to her now-thickening mid-section. The threat of indictment was clearly weighing heavily on her, and she was not taking care of herself as she had been only months earlier. Her hair was matted as if it had not been washed in days, and her face was devoid of any make-up. There was only one smell in the house this time, a stale smell that seemed a combination of her dog and Wendi's lack of showering and/or clothes which needed an introduction to a washing machine. No food was being cooked, no coffee was brewing. Eric followed her into the kitchen, carrying the coffee and food. He recalled the last time he was in the house; how impressed he had been with how Wendi looked. She was but a shell of herself now, and he was anything but impressed. He wanted to comment on her appearance in an effort to get her to snap out of her funk, but knew that any such commentary would not be well-received. Instead, he determined, all conversations must focus on the case and on Thursday's court date. He would, however, provide her with some coaching on how to dress.

The conversation was not an easy one. Wendi spent most of the time crying, lamenting her possible fate and questioning why Eric had not been able to get the charges downgraded despite his relationship with many members of the Prosecutor's office. Eric considered the irony of that comment, because the person with whom he now had the closest "relationship" in the Prosecutor's Office was the very one that she knew nothing about; the one that nobody other than the participants knew of, or could know of. He tried again and again to have Wendi focus on how she should dress and act before the Grand Jury, how to answer the questions, and what information she should not offer unless she was directly questioned as to that information. He could sense, however, that none of what he was saying was sinking in as Wendi continued to cry, so he eventually gave up his attempts and resolved that he would have to ensure that he provided Amanda with enough information prior to Thursday that, hopefully, Wendi's testimony would not even be required.

Eric was greatly concerned about what would happen if Wendi, excitable in even simple situations, was forced to take the stand and respond to withering questioning by Amanda or another member of the Prosecutor's Office. This was particularly true in light of the fact that Wendi would be forced to testify that she had received a text from her mother and had returned it just prior to the accident – he wanted to believe, but was not certain, as to whether or she was not distracted by the text just before the impact, and knew that a good attorney could twist the responses just enough to obtain a favorable response from the grand jury members. He also believed that Amanda was a good enough attorney to accomplish that result. Before he left the house, he tried one more time to get inside Wendi's head and provided her with the most basic of instructions: dress appropriately in business attire, answer only the questions asked of her, not to use any profanity, not to guess as to any answers, and to make sure that she understood the questions before providing any answers. He hoped that she at least digested and understood those basic pointers.

During the time that they spent together, he did not make any mention to Wendi of either the information that he had obtained from Jim Parker regarding her accuser or of the meeting that he had scheduled for Monday with Sophia and Robert Lorenzo.

Monday morning, a mentally-exhausted Eric returned to his office at 8:00 to find a voice mail from Sophia Lorenzo confirming that she would be in the office that afternoon with her son. Eric breathed a sigh of relief; he had awakened the night before in a panic, thinking that she would be canceling the appointment. Now he just had to keep himself occupied for the next seven hours until the appointed meeting time.

Surprisingly, the time passed rather quickly, so quickly, in fact, that when Fatima asked him if he wanted to order lunch from the local deli, he was astounded to find that it was already 2:00 in the afternoon. He had been so busy catching up on several files that he had completely lost track of time, and had not even given a second thought to being hungry or wanting any lunch. Now that Fatima mentioned it, of course, he wanted a sandwich. And now he was acutely aware of the time and pulled out what he believed to be his relevant notes on Ramon Ortiz so that he could obtain as much information as possible from Robert Lorenzo.

Lunch arrived twenty minutes later, and Eric ate his sandwich and drank a can of black cherry soda while checking the latest baseball news on the internet. By the time he finished, it was a quarter to three, and the Lorenzos were due in his office in only 15 minutes. Wanting to get the smell of pastrami and mustard from his mouth, he grabbed his toothbrush and walked down the hallway to the bathroom. Returning to the office five minutes later with newly-minty breath, he was surprised to find Robert and Sophia Lorenzo already sitting in the chairs adjacent to Fatima's desk. Robert sat, nervously moving his right leg in a swift, up and down motion. "Robert," Eric said, "Don't be nervous. We're just talking today." He extended his right hand and shook both Robert and Sophia's hands, and then motioned for them to follow him into his office.

Robert, however, was clearly still quite nervous as he settled into one of the chairs across from Eric's desk, as evidenced by his still-jittery leg and the manner in which he fidgeted in the chair. Eric looked at Sophia and smiled before addressing Robert again. "Look, Robert, seriously. Don't be nervous," Eric began. "Did your mom tell you why you're here today?"

"Ye ...ye … yes," Robert stammered, nervously looking between Eric and his mother. "You want to know something about Ramon."

Eric was not overly pleased at his response, as he had asked Sophia not to tell Robert why they were going to see him. At the same time, he understood why she probably had to tell her son why she was taking him to a lawyer's office, so he decided to just deal with the fact that he had time to prepare his answers to Eric's expected questions. "Are you afraid of him?" Eric asked.

Robert looked down at the floor. His leg stopped shaking, and he placed both elbows on his knees as he lowered his head.

"Robert, Mr. Goldberg asked you a question," Sophia said. "Please answer him."

Eric did not wait for a response. "Robert, first of all, you have to call me Eric. Mr. Goldberg is my father's name. And I don't want to stress you out." He paused, and Robert lifted his head and looked Eric in the eye. His eyes were glistening, as if tears were to form any second. "Let me help you out a little. I am going to assume that you are afraid of Ramon. Can I ask you why?"

Robert looked to his left. "Can we talk about this without my mother here?" he asked, clearly to Sophia's surprise.

"I would think that would be OK," Eric said slowly, as he nodded and motioned for Sophia to leave. "I assume that your mother can wait outside with Fatima for a few minutes, right Sophia?"

Sophia looked at Eric and then at Robert, clearly wounded by her son's insistence that she leave the room and worried about what he might say outside of her presence. "I don't know what you will say without me here that you couldn't say with me here, but I will leave." She stood and then bent down to kiss Robert on the forehead. "Just let me know if you need me for anything," she added before she walked out of the room, closing the door behind her as Eric gave her a "thumbs up" sign.

After the door had closed, Eric turned back to Robert. "OK, Robert, she's gone. What's up?"

"Well, Mr. Goldberg, I mean, Eric, here's the deal. I know him a little bit. He's a drug dealer. I stay away from him, but one of my buddies hangs with him."

Eric picked up his pen and placed it atop the papers on his desk, intending to begin taking notes. "What's this friend's name, Robert?"

Robert paused. "I would rather not say, to be honest with you. I can't have this getting back to me. You know what happens to people who talk, even teenagers. Look what happened to that kid that was hit by your wife's car. I don't want that happening to me."

"I'm not going to tell anyone that you told me, Robert," Eric said, more than a little intrigued by Robert's last comment but figuring that he would offer up more information without being specifically asked about Jose Gomez.

Robert looked Eric in the eye. "Come on Mr. Goldberg, let's be serious for a minute," he said, his voice growing stronger as he seemed to gain confidence in his words. "You think I believe that you're not going to take what I say and use it to spring your wife? I'll tell you the basic shit that I know because mom asked me to, but I ain't gonna name anyone." He paused and glanced from side to side, as if to ensure that nobody else could hear what he was saying. "I can't risk it."

Eric laid the pen down and leaned back in his chair, hands on top of his head. "Robert, I understand completely and I don't want you to do anything that is going to cause you any trouble. I'll tell you what," he said, looking out the window to his right, "just tell me some basic shit. No names, no specifics, and I will do what I can. And I will never use your name."

Robert smiled. "Really?" he asked.

"Really," Eric answered. "Trust me." He stood and walked over to the other side of the desk, sitting down in the chair where Sophia had been minutes earlier. "Tell me about this kid."

Robert leaned forward. "OK, but I am not sure of all of this so I can't even say that everything is definitely true. But I think it is. Most of it is shit I've heard from others." Eric nodded in understanding. "Like I told you, he's a dealer." He saw that Eric looked like he wanted to ask a question. Anticipating the inquiry, he continued, "Yes, I have bought weed from him. But never cocaine or the other shit he was selling. He said he got it from his uncle. You know the Colombians, man."

"Yes, I do," Eric said, chuckling lightly.

"So he deals and he's one of the main guys in a local gang. They kind of rule one of the schools over there at the High School. I try to keep away as much as I can, but, of course, I still hear stuff. My buddy told me that he was bragging a while ago about how he was going to whack some kid from the neighborhood, a kid who went to Roselle Catholic, who was moving in on his scene, that his uncle told him to go get the kid and teach him a lesson. That was right before your wife hit the kid."

"She's my ex-wife, Robert, not my wife. You think that was the kid?"

"Don't know, man. But it would be quite a coincidence if he wasn't, don't you think?"

"I guess so," Eric said, again looking out the window. "So you think this Ortiz kid may have had something to do with what happened, huh?"

"Me, nah, I don't know for sure. I don't think about that shit. But if I did think," he said, smirking, "I would think so. I mean, after all, he was there, right?" He paused. "You're not going to tell my mom about this stuff, are you? She doesn't know about the weed or any of that stuff."

"No," Eric replied. "I promised you that I wouldn't get you in trouble, so I won't say anything to your mother. A little advice, though, I would tell her before she hears about it from someone else." He paused. "One more question, Rob, who's the kid's uncle?"

"Don't know, man," Rob answered, shaking his head slowly, "but the uncle is an important dude, to hear him talk about it."

"Sounds like it," Eric said under his breath, "I wonder who it is. Must be someone associated with Sanchez." He stood and walked toward the door to open it and escort Robert out to where his mother sat, pensively. "I wonder who."

Chapter XXXVII – The Grand Jury Convenes

"Listen, I know that you are sick of hearing my commentary on this, but I really think that your witness is going to be problematic for you."

Amanda listened to Eric's comment and then sighed deeply, a breath with such force that Eric could hear it clearly through his cell phone. Following a momentary pause, she replied. "Eric, please. I know what I am doing. I am questioning the coroner first, because he won't be available the next few weeks. Then I am doing the kid. Depending on how he testifies, it will either be your ex-wife next or the cop at the scene." She paused and sniffled. Eric envisioned a tear running down her cheek as she then added, "I'm just trying to do my job, and I am under a great deal of stress, OK? Please don't add to it. We shouldn't even be talking about this."

Eric thought about her statement for a minute. "Stress?" he thought to himself. "She doesn't know what stress is." In his mind, her position was the least stressful of all concerned. The worst that could happen to her was that Wendi was not convicted at trial. The Grand Jury, as was almost always the case, would be a slam dunk for her. And even if she did not gain conviction at trial, it would not be a problem for her. She would not be blamed if her main witness was not cooperating, nor would she be blamed for the Prosecutor's Office expecting such a young and inexperienced Assistant Prosecutor to be able to handle such a high-profile case.

It wouldn't be her fault, he reasoned, so losing would not have any adverse effect on her position in the Prosecutor's office. On the other hand, his position was far more stressful. He had gotten himself into the situation, that was true, but now he was neck-deep, if not worse, in stress. His girlfriend was prosecuting his ex-wife. It was sheer insanity, and extremely stressful. But how could he convey those thoughts to Amanda without totally pissing her off?

He couldn't, of course. He knew that. "I'm not trying to add to your stress, honey," he said, using the term of affection for the first time in an attempt to minimize the stressful effect of what he was going to say. "I just think that you should know all of the information so that the Grand Jury has a complete picture. If you don't know everything they won't know everything, and will not be able to fully understand the case."

"Eric," she answered, "Let's be honest for a second. This whole conversation is highly irregular." He knew that she was right, of course, and was somewhat taken aback by the fact that she replied using his name rather than a similar term of endearment for him. "Prosecutors and defense counsel don't just shoot the shit and discuss the evidence right before the Prosecutor is going in front of the Grand Jury. We just don't do it. Please, let's not have this conversation."

Again, Eric was forced to pause. He understood her position, but at the same time wanted to make sure that her star witness was discredited in her eyes before she even began the process. He had to quickly think of a tactful way of saying something that she did not want to hear, of planting that seed in her mind so that it was not so obvious that she would tune it out and that it would continue to creep in as she questioned the boy when he was in the witness box.

There was no tactful way, so he just blurted something out. "OK, you're right. We won't discuss it all. Just remember to ask him about his uncle."

"Shit, Eric, you've got to be kidding me!" she yelled, clearly upset by his last comment. "We're done with this conversation." Eric heard the phone click, and knew that he would not be speaking to Amanda again before the testimony was to begin. He hoped, however, that his last comment would resonate with her. He was confident that it would. As he thought about it more, actually, his confidence waned. Cautiously optimistic was probably a better way to describe his feelings.

Amanda, meanwhile, was subjecting herself to a wide range of emotions. She was pleased to be finally getting her chance to present the evidence against Wendi to a jury, even though it was the completely one-sided group which constituted the Grand Jury, and excited to be prosecuting what, at the time, was one of the most important, if not the most important, case in the office. A conviction on the texting while driving charge would be, in her mind, a potential springboard for her career, a push to the top of the office or a perfect opportunity to go into private practice with what might be her highest amount of name recognition. At the same time, she was nervous about blatantly messing up the prosecution, because a public failure could haunt, if not completely stunt, her career trajectory, whether in the public or private sector.

She was also conflicted about the prospect of beating Eric at trial, should the case progress that far. More to the point, she was conflicted about having to try the case against Eric. She wondered if she would be able to properly focus during such a trial, if she would be able to put aside her feelings for him and do the job that she was being paid to do. She wondered about Marcia Clark and Clarence Darden, the prosecutors in the OJ Simpson trial who, she had heard, became romantically involved. Were they able to focus on putting that killer behind bars? Possibly not, she reasoned, and maybe, in part, their combined lack of focus was one of the factors that led to the jury acquitting him.

And yet they were on the same side. It would be worse for her, as the object of her affection was not a co-Prosecutor, but rather the defense attorney. The object of her affection was her adversary.

Could she walk around the courtroom, asking hard-hitting questions of a witness, knowing that Eric's stare would be boring a hole in her backside as she passed his table? Could she object to his questions if they were improper, knowing that such an objection, if upheld, could be a source of possible embarrassment for him? Could she even focus on his questioning, or would she find her mind wandering as she watched him practice his craft, using the courtroom techniques that he had likely perfected over his years of practice?

391

All of these questions made her sick to her stomach. Like Eric, she was beginning to wonder if getting romantically involved had been a good idea. It wasn't just that she liked him ... she loved him. And that clearly would cloud her judgment in a trial. She wondered why she hadn't just waited. She wondered why she had gone to his office that first evening rather than waiting until the case played itself out. She had instigated the relationship. Why? And most importantly, she worried that she would be unable to keep her thoughts clear enough to present the case properly to the Grand Jury.

Luckily for Amanda, she had, in conjunction with her superiors, made the decision to put the County Coroner, Dr. Louis Ferrell, on the stand first. The questions for him would be simple, and she was planning on letting him expound in detail to simple questions rather than asking question after question seeking details upon details. She could work her nerves out on him, they agreed, which would then allow her some momentum leading into the next witness, slated to be Ramon Lopez a/k/a Ramon Ortiz.

The prosecution's presentation to the Grand Jury began the next morning. Dr. Ferrell's testimony went fairly predictably. Amanda started with questions about his education and background, his time at the coroner's office, and the number of autopsies – hundreds – that he had performed prior to the autopsy on young Jose Gomez. The line of inquiry then led to the injuries sustained by the teenager, which included cuts and abrasions over multiple parts of his body and blunt trauma to the head, which he concluded was caused either by the impact with the vehicle or striking the street after the initial impact. Dr. Ferrell did note marks across Gomez's midsection which appeared to be initial impact points with the car, which he stated was curious because such marks would not have occurred had the youth been standing when the initial impact took place. Under further questioning from Amanda, Dr. Ferrell surmised that Jose had, in fact, fallen in front of the vehicle, or was in the process of falling in front of the vehicle, when the main impact occurred. It was possible, he further testified, that perhaps the initial impact caused him to fall sideways, thereby explaining the injuries, but that he could not testify as to such events with any medical certainty.

One other item of information provided by Dr. Ferrell was intriguing, and one which Amanda purposely glossed over as being not important for her prosecution. In addition to the multitude of cuts, abrasions, and bruises sustained by Jose Gomez, which were unquestionably caused by the impact with Wendi's vehicle and contact with the street, Dr. Ferrell's examination also revealed a deep puncture wound in Jose's lower back, a deep slicing wound which missed his spinal column by inches but which did lead to internal damage. As there was no indication of a large piece of glass or debris at the scene in any of the police or EMT reports that had been provided to him subsequent to his physical examination of the dead teenager, he testified, he was unable to provide any cognizable reason for the existence of this seemingly incongruous wound. Amanda did not provide any follow-up questions as to possible causes for such a wound, and instead proceeded to questions about Dr. Ferrell's opinions as to the speed of the car when it struck Jose Gomez, questions aimed at showing that the driver of the vehicle clearly was not paying full attention to the road at the moment of impact.

A brief recess was taken before Ramon Lopez was brought to the witness stand. The young man was dressed for the occasion, clad in a tan suit with blue shirt and blue/tan striped tie. The suit jacket was ill-fitting, too large in the shoulders and sleeves, and the pants were bunched at the waist, well secured by a belt to keep them from falling to the floor as Lopez walked to the witness stand from the rear of the room. It was as if the suit belonged to someone much larger than him, and had been given to him for the day without regard for whether or not it would fit on his slender, teenaged body.

As was the case with Dr. Ferrell, Amanda eased into her questions for Ramon Lopez. The first few questions dealt with his age and education, to which he responded that he was 17, and that he attended Elizabeth High School. She asked if he had plans to attend college in the future, to which his answer was in the affirmative, and he then drew laughs from the Grand Jury members when he answered "I don't know, something educational and girls" when Amanda asked what he planned to study while at college. She complimented him on his "sharp suit," which he responded was borrowed from his uncle for the occasion.

Amanda then asked about his relationship with Jose Gomez, at which point he paused, took a few deep breaths as if to compose his thoughts, and then told, hesitatingly, about how they had been friends since grade school, and had remained friends even when Jose went to Roselle Catholic rather than to Elizabeth High School. Jose was a far better student than he was, he testified, and had greater aspirations for a career. His mother, a single mother, was hoping that he would have greater opportunities if he went to private school, and worked two jobs in order to make enough money to pay the tuition at Roselle Catholic. He had received a partial scholarship, Jose had told him, but his mother still would not have been able to afford the remaining tuition without working the second job. Amanda looked over at the Grand Jury members during this testimony. One of the women had a tear in her eye, and several others nodded in acknowledgment as Ramon detailed the monetary struggles of Jose Gomez and his mother. So far, the testimony was steamrolling toward an indictment.

Amanda then proceeded to questioning about the accident itself. Ramon testified, sniffling as if he was about to cry, that he and Jose had been hanging out on the corner of Westfield Avenue and Elmora Avenue for a little while before the accident. They had met there immediately after school had ended; each had gotten a ride there from friends and their intention was to meet up with some other friends and then go to the Dunkin' Donuts on Elmora Avenue for doughnuts and sodas. They were the first two to arrive at the intersection, and were horsing around when Jose ran toward the street, near a car parked on Westfield Avenue. He testified that he then looked toward the intersection because he sensed that something was wrong, and saw a black BMW turning onto Westfield Avenue from Elmora Avenue. The driver of the vehicle was distracted at the time, he said, looking down as if reading her cell phone or typing something onto it.

"Was the driver texting when you saw her?" asked Amanda.

"I can't say for sure, ma'am," he responded, "but if I had to guess I would say that she was. She was definitely doing something with her phone."

Amanda thought that she heard one of the jurors gasp audibly. She heard another gasp when he described watching the car strike his friend, who was walking into the street, and knocking him forward. Ramon then described how Jose fell to the ground and the car continued forward, running over him, so that only his head protruded from the underside of the car, in front of the car, when it finally stopped. Jose's face was covered with blood, he testified, and he was certain that Jose was dead by the time he ran in front of the car to comfort his fallen friend.

Amanda listened carefully to the testimony, and then glanced down at her notes. She reviewed her notes on Dr. Ferrell's testimony, as well as her hand-written notes on the medical records in her trial notebook. Something was wrong. Ramon's testimony did not make sense to her in light of all of the other evidence. She sat back and then leaned forward again, pretending to read over her notes as she asked everyone to bear with her for a moment. Eric's voice was resonating throughout her head as she mindlessly thumbed through the pages. Could he have been right? Was it possible that Ramon's testimony was false and merely a set-up? What simple question could she ask that would tell her, even if not the jury panel, so that she could proceed forward with confidence either proving or disproving her own prosecution? As she looked through the papers, she remembered; something that Eric had said to her.

"Mr. Lopez, this may seem like an odd question," she began, "but you said that you borrowed that suit from your uncle."

"Yes, ma'am, that's correct," he answered, the lilt in his voice making his response sound more like a question as he clearly did not understand the relevance of where he had obtained the suit to a Grand Jury investigation into the death of a pedestrian. Amanda's face brightened, even as she saw the puzzled looks on several members of the jury panel, persons who clearly did not understand this new line of questioning any more than did Ramon Lopez.

"Which uncle was that?" Amanda then asked, rising from her chair and now standing behind the counsel table.

Ramon looked at her, still puzzled, and then answered, simply, "My uncle, you know, my mother's brother." He paused, and then added, stutteringly, "why … why … why does it matter?"

"Please allow me to ask the questions here, Ramon," Amanda answered, her previously genial tone now growing harder. "You didn't answer my question."

"Ma'am?" he replied, still stuttering in apparent fear, "yes … yes … yes I did. My mother's brother, my uncle, lent me the suit. He … he said … he said that I should look nice for the jury."

"Oh he did, did he?" Amanda said, clearly seeing that her witness was avoiding giving her the desired answer, and realizing that she would have to be more direct with her questions. "Now this is going to be a very specific question for which I will require a very specific answer, Ramon."

"OK ma'am."

"Ramon," she asked, "what is your uncle's name?"

Ramon Lopez looked at Amanda as his eyes grew wider. He fidgeted in his chair, clearly uncomfortable. No words emanated from his lips.

"Ramon, what is your uncle's name?"

"It's getting late in the day," a voice boomed from behind her. "Why don't we break and pick this up next week?"

Amanda looked up, exasperated, and glared in the direction of the voice, that of fellow Assistant Prosecutor, but her superior, Ben Kasper. Sighing audibly, she turned back toward the witness and said, "OK, Mr. Lopez. We're done for today. You're back here next Thursday, though, and remember, you can't discuss this testimony or the case with anyone between now and then." Her glare was now focused directly at the young witness, who continued to fidget and squirm.

"Yes, ma'am," he stammered, as he shuffled in his seat. "I won't talk to anyone."

Amanda packed up her paperwork and dejectedly shoved it into her file folders. "I was just breaking through the kid," she muttered to herself as she walked out the door, not even looking in Kasper's direction as she exited. "I could have had something. Who is his uncle?" She was starting to think that maybe Rachel wasn't as guilty as she had originally thought. But was it due to Lopez's testimony, or the fact that she kept hearing Eric's voice in her head?

In desperate need of both air and a cup of coffee, Amanda decided to take a walk to the coffee shop across the street from the courthouse. She could not bear the stifling air or fluorescent lighting any longer, and getting away, even if only across Broad Street, would be refreshing. Head down, she kept watch on her footsteps as she continued to beat herself up over the way that her inquisition had ended. She was oblivious to the traffic going by as she walked, not even noticing as her last witness was whisked away in a dark grey Mercedes.

As she approached the front steps, however, her self-flagellation was interrupted by the roar of a crowd, a groundswell that rose above the sounds of the traffic and the calls of birds inhabiting the eaves of the library across the street from the courthouse. And then a man's voice rose above the crowd. Lifting her head, she was able to make out the man's words: "Do not let my mother die in vain!" The crowd roared again, and multiple voices could be heard urging him to continue. Heeding their call, he added, "my mother died when a driver was texting. We all know someone who has been injured by a distracted driver, or have seen drivers on the road texting, eating, and doing things that should not be done while behind the wheel of a car. This is where it stops!" Again, the crowd roared. Amanda walked closer, and saw a gathering of people, a hundred or so, cheering on the speaker. Most in the crowd were Hispanic, and various cries of *"justicia para Jose Gomez"* and *"te amamos, Jose* (we love you, Jose)" rang out from the assemblage.

Amanda eyed the crowd carefully, and became concerned by its composition. She was not fearful of the large Hispanic contingent, nor did she feel threatened by several teenagers who stood off to the left of the crowd, their garb immediately identifying them as local gang members. To the contrary, she was concerned about the presence of a decent number of Caucasians in the crowd; men and women alike. Not just the man behind the microphone, whose mother had died in a driver-pedestrian texting accident, but the others who had gathered in support of the Hispanic community. This was just added pressure for Amanda – it was one thing to be prosecuting Wendi Goldberg and knowing that the eyes of every Latino were waiting for the results of the Grand Jury hearing, but now, if other ethnic groups were joining the watch, the need to obtain the indictment would increase exponentially. Amanda felt a tightening in her chest as she again lowered her head and hurried past the throng, praying that nobody would notice her. In her haste to cross the street and get herself out of visions' way, she stepped into the roadway just as a van was approaching the corner, its right-hand blinker activated. The passenger's side mirror whizzed by a scant two inches from Amanda's shoulder as it lumbered past, causing her to leap back with a start. Quickly looking behind her, she was relieved to discover that the crowd continued its adulation for the speaker, her misstep seemingly unnoticed.

When the light changed, she quickly hurried across the road's expanse and ducked into the coffee shop, where she ordered a coffee and sat, alone, at a table in the corner. She would periodically glance up and outside to monitor the situation at the courthouse. When she was satisfied that the crowd had properly dispersed, she stood, took the last gulp of the now-tepid coffee, and walked back into the sunlight, intending to return, reluctantly, to the false light and stale air of her office.

Chapter XXXVIII – Amanda and Ramon Have A Tough Week

Amanda was still talking to herself as she walked to her office, the sound of her mumbling drowned out by the loud raps of her heels striking the hallway floors. She strode purposefully, her anger playing out in the form of a spirited gait which culminated in the slamming of her office door before she threw her file to the floor. Collapsing into her chair, she placed her head into her hands and shook it slowly, cursing the fact that she could not complete her line of testimony.

A knock on the door startled her. Before she could ask who was knocking, the door opened and Prosecutor Crawford poked his head inside the office. Seeing Amanda seething in her chair, he asked, cautiously, "tough day at the Grand Jury?"

"Don't fuck with me, Steve," she blurted out, "no doubt someone, like Kasper, has already told you what's going on in there."

"Yes," he said, calmly, "from what I hear it's going very well. That's why I am more than a little surprised to see you in such a snit."

"A snit?" she asked, laughing, "who uses the word 'snit' in conversation? I'm not in a 'snit,' for your information. I'm pissed off."

"OK, Amanda," he replied. "You're pissed off. Sorry for my use of an old-fashioned word." He sat in the chair across from Amanda's desk. "Now, do you want to tell me what's got you upset?"

Amanda started to speak, but then stopped herself. She wanted to say that she was mad at the fact that she had not been able to finish her interrogation of Ramon Lopez, but the reality was that she was angry at herself; she was upset at her own thoughts of self-doubt regarding the guilt or innocence of Wendi Goldberg. She was upset that she was allowing Eric and his statements to cause her doubt. Was it reasonable doubt? Or was she being unreasonable? Her mind raced, but she knew that she had to answer her boss, even if it was not the correct answer. "What's got me upset is that I had that kid. He was, as they say in boxing, 'on the ropes,' and now he has an extra week to talk to an attorney, talk to his family, and change his story."

Crawford stood. "From what I heard, Amanda, you did great today." He turned to leave the office. "Don't beat yourself up so much," he added, "if my sources are right, you may have scared that kid so much that he doesn't talk to anyone about this." Looking back at Amanda, smirking, he said, "go home and get some rest. Or better yet, go out and get a drink. You deserve it. And don't worry about tomorrow. If you don't have any court appearances, just come in whenever you want."

"If you say so, Steve," she answered, surprised that he had so much confidence in her and was willing to allow her to sleep late the next day, and at the same time still tormenting herself over her inability to break down her young witness. She needed comfort. "Maybe I will get a drink," she continued, quietly, reaching for her phone to call Eric. She paused before pressing the "call" button, however, wondering whether or not it was wise to see him with the emotions of the case already so intense.

While Amanda sat at her desk, a tear running down the left side of her face as she debated whether or not to call her boyfriend, the ex-husband of the woman she was prosecuting, the young man who would be her star witness was having a similarly difficult evening. "*Tio,*" he said quietly into his cell phone, "*tenemos una problema.*"

"What do you mean, we have a problem?" Jesus Sanchez replied to his nephew in English. "*Se uno de los oficiales en la sala de audiencias del Gran Jurado, y él me dijo que su testimonio era exactamente como lo planeamos.* (I know one of the officers in the Grand Jury courtroom, and he told me that your testimony was exactly how we planned it.)"

Ramon Lopez sighed. *"Supongo que eso es bueno, pero, ¿te ha dicho acerca de la pregunta de mi tio y el traje que llevaba puesto?"*

Sanchez laughed. *"Si, mijo,* he did tell me about how the Prosecutor asked who your uncle was."

"No te preocupas?"

Still laughing, Sanchez paused to answer the question posed by his obviously overly-concerned nephew. "Why should I worry?" he replied. "Just give her a fake name." His laughter stopped and his voice took on a tone of complete seriousness. "Listen, Ramon, we've worked very hard for this. You are the star witness right now. If this woman, the attorney's ex-wife, *la ex esposa de un abogado,* is convicted of killing your friend, then this city is mine. It is ours. *Esta ciudad es nuestra. El mío, el tuyo, el de la madre.* Ours. All of ours. Think of how much easier it would be for your mother. Think of how she has struggled for you. *¿No quiere hacer su vida más fácil?*

"Of course I want to make her life easier," Ramon replied, as he began to cry. Up until now, his preparing to testify and helping with his uncle's dreams of city-wide, if not greater, domination, were almost surreal to him. It was as if he was playing a role in a play. Suddenly, however, it was all becoming real to him. Sanchez's use of the phrase "killing your friend" hit him in the face with the force of a thousand fists. He felt an aching in the pit of his stomach as if he himself had been run over by Wendi Goldberg's car. His friend was dead. He had killed his friend at his uncle's behest. His friend.

"Then this should be easy for you," Sanchez said, sternly, completely ignoring the sobs that he heard coming from his nephew's side of the conversation. "Make up a name. Say he is still in Colombia and he sent you the suit. And then just say what we have rehearsed. One more day and you are done."

"One more day," Lopez replied, wiping the tears from his face. *"Pero yo quiero que sea mañana. Yo no quiero que esperar una semana más para terminar esto.* (But I want it to be tomorrow. I don't want to wait another week to finish this.)" He looked at the computer screen in front of him. The screen was filled with a picture taken at the previous year's Colombian festival. Five smiling faces were the focal point of the photo. One of the faces was his own, in sharp contrast to his current depressed mood. Standing directly to his right, grinning from ear to ear as his arm was draped over Ramon Lopez's shoulder, was Jose Gomez. As he clicked the phone off, his tears began to fall anew.

Amanda Johnson was also crying as she held her cell phone in her right hand, still debating, minutes later, about whether or not to call Eric Goldberg. She desperately wanted to see him, but did not know if she could see him without having him ask her about his ex-wife's case. She wanted to tell him about what had happened that day, but knew that she could not say anything to him, Seeing him, she knew, would be a terrible idea.

As she sat, her phone began to vibrate. Looking down at the screen, she saw Eric's number. Composing herself, she slowly lifted the phone to her face and pressed "answer."

"Hi, Eric," she said, calmly, "I was just thinking about you."

"Something good, I hope," Eric replied. "I know that you probably don't want to talk to me tonight, but I really just wanted to check in and, without asking for any details, just make sure that everything went alright for you today and that you are doing OK. I know that it must have been a rough one for you."

"No, it wasn't so bad," she lied. "So far it is going well, but we did not finish up with the kid yet so we're going to pick up with him again next week before moving onto the next witness." She did not identify the next witness by name, even though both knew that it would be Eric's ex-wife.

"Well," Eric said, sighing, "I guess that means another week without seeing each other. I don't want to sound overly dramatic or needy, but I have to be honest with you, I'm not enjoying this time apart."

Amanda began to cry again. "I miss you too, Eric. I really wish that I could see you." She paused and looked at the large file lying on her floor, the name "Wendi Goldberg" emblazoned in large black marker across its front side. "Meet me in a half hour at my apartment," she said, quietly, "I need a drink and hate drinking alone."

"If you insist," Eric replied in surprise, "I had a client coming in but will cancel her. I will be there in a half hour. But we're not discussing this case at all. I can't deal with it today, and I am sure that you feel the same way."

Amanda knew that Eric was saying that for her benefit. "Thank you," she said quietly before clicking off the phone, and then silently mouthing to herself, "that's why I love you so much."

Eric placed his phone down on his desk and leaned back, smiling. "Fatima," he called, "please cancel my appointment for later. I'm leaving in a few minutes. I'm going to go home and relax."

Chapter XXXIX – Sanchez Conducts Another Vigil

Eric and Amanda saw each other not only that night, but also on two other occasions in the intervening week leading up to the second day of Ramon Lopez' testimony. Showing respect and tremendous restraint, Eric never asked Amanda about the substance of his first day's testimony or her plans for the second day. He never asked her about whether or not his testimony was truly incriminating to his ex-wife, nor did he ask about any possible testimony as to his possible relationship with Jesus Sanchez.

The following Sunday, Sanchez led yet another vigil outside of the courthouse, this time leading the crowd in a march from the courthouse steps to the Elizabeth police station. As the crowd of dozens made its way up Broad Street, enough of the people left the sidewalk and walked in the Eastbound lanes of the roadway, blocking both lanes of travel and bringing traffic to a standstill. Some shopkeepers along the pathway pulled the metal gates down over the windows of their establishments, fearful that the crowd might turn destructive. Luckily for those proprietors, however, the crowd remained essentially under control, with the exception of a couple of altercations with irate drivers. Three people were brought to the Police Station ahead of the other protestors, and all were charged with disturbing the peace and released later that day. Two of the arrested men were Hispanic, and they walked out of the police station that evening after being released, each of them flanking Jesus Sanchez as the three walked arm-in-arm out of the building, onto the sidewalk, and strode back to Broad Street. A small contingent remained at the corner of East Jersey Street and Broad Street, anxiously awaiting their friends' release. They remained there for the better part of the evening, continuing to call for the indictment of Wendi Goldberg and justice for Jesus Gomez. All the while,

Sanchez basked in the glow of adulation from the crowd, alternately preening for photographs with those present and engaging the crowd with fiery rhetoric.

Meanwhile, Ramon Lopez did not speak with his uncle for the duration of the week, until the night before he was to take the witness stand for the second time. During that week, however, he continued to torment himself over his participation in the murder of his own friend, and the fact that he had done so solely to further his uncle's political aspirations. He was beginning to feel tremendously guilty over the murder, a feeling that he somehow had not felt until the last telephone conversation with Sanchez. As he was watching television the next Wednesday night, trying in vain to calm his nerves in anticipation of the next day, his cell phone rang. It was his uncle calling him to reiterate that he was to "*acuerdas de lo que habíamos discutido* (remember what we had discussed)" regarding his testimony about the death of Jose Lopez.

"*No te preocupes, tío,*" Ramon replied, "Don't you worry, Uncle." He paused. "I know exactly what I am supposed to do. "*Sé exactamente lo que debo hacer.*" He paused again. "In fact, I know exactly what I have to do. *De hecho, sé exactamente lo que tengo que hacer.*"

That night, Ramon Lopez had his first restful sleep in weeks. He awoke the next morning, dressed himself in the other suit provided to him by his uncle, this one also too large in the shoulders, and ate a bowl of oatmeal before waiting to be picked up for his second day of testimony.

At the same time, Amanda Johnson was feeling exactly the opposite. Where she had been somewhat confident only a week earlier, she was overcome with a fear of dread of the coming day's events, the pressure of the populous weighing even more heavily on her. She was haunted by the pictures of Jose Gomez, and she was disturbed by her memory of the racially-mixed assembly outside of the court following the last day's testimony. Following a night of sleep, often interrupted, she woke, took a long, hot shower in a futile attempt to clear her mind and prepare mentally for the day's events, and then slowly sipped a cup of coffee and ate breakfast while thumbing through the newspaper. She then dressed in a conservative navy blue skirt and jacket over a cream-colored blouse. Checking herself in the mirror as she pulled her hair into a ponytail, for the first time, she allowed herself some peace. Gazing at her outfit, she smiled. This was the exact clothing, she recalled, that she was wearing when she first seduced Eric Goldberg in his office. Little did she know that she would be back in his office that evening.

Chapter XL – A Grand Jury Surprise

"Honestly, it was all very surreal," Amanda said, "the kid's testimony was very easy-going at first. Last week started off with basically cream puff questions and answers about his age, education, stuff like that. He then testified about his friendship with the dead kid, and gave some details about how the accident happened. But his details didn't jive with the other evidence. He testified that Jose's head was essentially sticking out in front of the car when the rest of his body was underneath it, but that made no sense because everything else said that Jose was sideways when the impact occurred, so his head could not possibly have been in that position. So before I went any further, I had to figure out for myself whether or not he was actually telling the truth."

"I would think that any Prosecutor would do the same thing."

"Don't patronize me," she said, disapprovingly. "Anyway, he was wearing this big suit that clearly did not fit him, just like last week. He testified pretty early on last week that it was his uncle's suit, and I guessed that the same was true this time. And sure enough, he testified that he had gotten this suit, like the other one, from his uncle. Meanwhile, a little bird had whispered into my ear that his uncle may be someone fairly important, so I figured I would ask who his uncle was and that would, or could, tell me if he was on the level or not. He was evasive until we were told to break for the day, which gave me exactly what I needed to know that he was a bullshitter, and it all just went from there."

"Really? I think that it must have been the great questioning of the Assistant Prosecutor, even if you had some information from a little birdie."

Amanda smiled. "Thanks for saying that, but I don't think so. I got really lucky on that one. I don't know how I would have been able to explore his possible family relationships, to be honest with you. I also don't know how I could have asked him about his criminal stuff, because, you know, he's still a juvenile. Anyway, I asked him who the uncle was, and he was very evasive. Last week, that is. Today, he was a completely different witness. It was almost as if he was aching to tell me."

"Tell me," Eric replied. "I want to know. I'm actually dying to know. Who is this uncle and what is the guy's relationship to Sanchez?"

"It was crazy," Amanda said. "You know how on television and in the movies the attorney asks the 'smoking gun' question and the witness folds like a house of cards? It was just like that. It's funny, in law school we used to talk about that with each other, you know, getting that 'gotcha moment' out of a witness. To put it into terms that you would understand, Mr. Baseball Fan, it's like hitting a game-winning home run."

Eric was pleased with her analogy, but could not stand the suspense any longer. He had to know the uncle's name. He had to know how the uncle knew Sanchez. "I get it, believe me," he answered, "but you have to tell me, who is this guy?"

"You're not going to believe this," Amanda replied, further prolonging Eric's anticipation at the answer. "You know that the kid's mother's last name is Ortiz, right?"

"Yes, we've already discussed that, remember. Why?"

"Well," Amanda answered, "it's an important part to the answer." She leaned in as if to whisper something to Eric, but then backed away and smiled.

Eric waited out the long pause, but after a minute could not contain himself any longer. "Damnit, Amanda, tell me," he barked, "you're killing me here."

Amanda's smile broadened. "I am going to ignore the fact that you just yelled at me," she said, kissing him on the cheek before whispering, "guess who else has relatives named Ortiz? Or, more to the point, guess who's mother's last name is Ortiz?"

"How the fuck should I know?" Eric cried, "Just tell me already."

"Begging does not become you, dear," she replied. "And clearly you have difficulty paying attention, or a lousy memory, because you should know this answer." She paused and chuckled to herself. "But because you are so pathetic, I will end the suspense. The uncle that you speak of has no relation to Jesus Sanchez, Eric," she said, forcefully, "the uncle has no relation to him." She paused again for dramatic effect. "The uncle has no relation," she explained, "because the uncle is none other than Jesus Sanchez."

"Holy shit!" Eric exclaimed. "You're kidding me."

"But there's more," Amanda continued. "Those arrests? Not only did Sanchez represent Ramon for them, but he was actually the ringleader behind the kid's gang. Once I got the information about his relationship with Sanchez, the kid started blabbing about how he was in a gang that dealt cocaine and marijuana, and he actually started to cry and talk about his prior arrests. I didn't even have to ask him about them. From what he said, Sanchez was getting weed from all over and importing cocaine from Colombia, just like the rumors said, and was using kids like Ramon to run the stuff for him. That's how he avoided getting fingered for everything; by having these kids do all of his work and then representing them in court when they got pinched.

It wasn't even just Ramon – there were a couple of other kids who also got arrested and got representation from Sanchez. And just like what happened with him in court, all of the kids got what amounted to little more than slaps on the wrist. Also of curiosity is that all of the charges stayed at the municipal court level, no matter how much they were caught with. We're going to be looking into that, and try to find out if some of the cops and one of the local prosecutors were also in Sanchez's back pocket."

"Unbelievable. But how did this relate to Jose Lopez?"

"Well, Jose Lopez, the honor student at Roselle Catholic, was also apparently beginning to get involved with a gang and was looking to deal some weed to earn the money needed to cover his tuition. The Lopez kid was trying to move in on Sanchez's territory and Sanchez told his nephew to take care of him, to send a message to his gang and any other local dealers that he would not tolerate their presence in his neighborhoods."

"Seriously?" Eric asked, his eyes growing wider. "Wait, let me get this straight. Are you saying that Sanchez put a hit on the Lopez kid?" He paused. "Shit, Robert was right."

Amanda nodded. "It looks like your ex-wife was really just in the wrong place at the wrong time. Acting on his uncle's instructions, Ramon stabbed Lopez in the back, which explains that deep wound in his back that we all noticed, and then threw his knife into the bushes next to the building. Lopez, bleeding from the wound just next to his spine, stumbled into the street and fell just as your ex was turning onto Westfield Avenue. He fell in front of the car, and that's why the impact of the car was across his whole body and he was dragged underneath the car. Then Dr. Ferrell's testimony actually made some sense."

"So the stabbing is what killed Lopez, not Wendi," Eric said, excitedly.

"Yes and no, to be honest with you," Amanda said, shaking her head. "I did speak to Dr. Ferrell about what Ramon said after the jury was released for the day. From what he told me, the stabbing was his initial injury and started the process of his death. That was the wound on his back that you pointed out to me, and the one noted by Dr. Ferrell when he was on the stand. It looks like the knife also caused some nerve damage due to the location of the cut, which may have actually caused partial paralysis. That could also explain why he lurched into the street and fell in front of the car."

"Makes sense to me," Eric said, "so that's what killed him."

"Not so fast. Dr. Ferrell still could not say for sure, however, if he would have bled out and died or if the impact from the accident is what killed him. Each was likely a contributing factor, though. It does seem clear that without the stabbing, he would not have been in the street and there would have been no impact with Wendi's car. Would he have died just from the stabbing? Maybe. It would have depended on how fast they were able to get him to the hospital. And you know that flash of light that she told you about and included in her statement? That was the knife. Freakin' Ortiz threw the knife into the bushes next to the stores on the corner after he stabbed his friend. Wendi saw the sunlight reflecting off of the knife."

Eric gasped. "But at least because the actual cause of death is uncertain, so you can't keep going against Wendi, right?" he asked.

"Well," Amanda replied. "To be honest with you, it seems like we won't be able to. There is no real evidence that she could have avoided the accident if the kid fell in front of the car. It doesn't mean that she wasn't texting, though."

Eric shrugged his shoulders. "Maybe so, Amanda, but here's the thing," he said. "It doesn't really matter whether she was texting or not. If you can't prove that she killed the kid, then you can't prosecute her under that statute."

Amanda's eyes narrowed. "Please don't tell me how to do my job, Eric. Here's what is happening from here, because I've already spoken with Crawford. They're going to pick Sanchez up for drug running and for conspiring with his nephew to kill Jose Gomez. That will be all over the news tomorrow, so make sure to watch Sanchez being led into the police station in handcuffs because no doubt it will be a wild scene." She smiled. "Now, whether he and his nephew are also charged with actual murder is up to the Prosecutor. At the same time, we are a little unclear now because your ex's running into the kid was a possible intervening cause that may actually prevent prosecuting them for the actual murder. But that doesn't mean we can't get them for conspiracy or attempted murder. More than likely, they'll give some type of immunity to the kid for his testimony against his uncle."

"That's unbelievable," Eric said. "Un-fucking-believable."

"Everything in this case is unbelievable, Eric, you know that. To be honest with you, I wouldn't be surprised if they also try to pin the Espinosa murder on him." Amanda responded. "As for Wendi, she will be charged with some motor vehicle summonses, like Reckless Driving and failure to yield, but yes," she said, smiling, "because of the uncertainty surrounding the time of death and actual cause of death, the state won't want to waste resources prosecuting Wendi under that statute. The main charge will be dismissed, and replaced with the others. They will be sent down to the city for disposition instead of in my office, so my job prosecuting her is over and we are no longer adversaries. Good work, counselor."

"Reckless? Failure to yield?" Eric replied as a smile creased his face. "That's fine. We'll plead them down, she will pay some fines, and then she can try to put this whole episode behind her."

"And how about you, Eric?" Amanda asked. "What about you? Do you want to put this whole episode behind you?" She looked at him, her eyes moistening. A tear formed in the corner of her left eye.

"The whole episode?" Eric asked, as he reached up with his right hand and wiped the tear from Amanda's left eye as it started to roll down her cheek. "No. I would sure like to forget about some parts of it, of course, but, I did learn a lot about this type of case and how to handle, or not handle, the media when I am involved in a big case. So I guess I would still like to have lived part of it."

"Is that it?" Amanda asked.

"No, silly," he answered, "if not for this case, I wouldn't have met you." He stroked her hair. "You know, getting that kid to confess and bringing down Sanchez can be just the type of case that can catapult you to the top of the Prosecutor's office."

"I don't know," Amanda said, "they've already told me that they will be assigning the Sanchez prosecution to another person in the office, you know, someone with more experience because they really want to nail his ass, so it's not like I am making a name on that one. In fact, I actually liked tearing down the case, looking for the holes in it, rather than building it up. I enjoyed the chance to pick apart Ramon's testimony once I realized he was lying." She paused. "I think it is time to leave the office and go into private practice, you know, as a defense attorney. It seems like much more fun, not to mention the fact that I hear that the really good ones make much more money than civil servants."

Eric looked at her, puzzled. "You want to go into private practice now? So soon?"

"Well," Amanda said, "I know a place where I think I can learn from someone who is really good at it. Someone who I know I can work with. Maybe someone who can be like a mentor to me, but who also will treat me as an equal because, well, because he's that kind of a nice guy."

"Who is this guy?" Eric asked, again smiling. "I know you're not talking about me."

"Of course I am, silly," she laughed, "think about it. The two of us together? It would be great. Not partners yet, but I can come work with you and learn more. If I can start to bring in the revenue, we will talk about partnership."

"Don't you think it's a little close to the end of the case to be seen working together? Won't people talk?" Eric asked.

Amanda snorted in derision and sat up, placing her hands on her hips. "Look at me," she commanded. "What do you see?"

Eric looked at Amanda. "I'm not sure how to answer that question, Amanda," he replied. "My initial answer would be your bare chest."

"Good answer," Amanda said, "my bare tits. Here's the deal, Eric, I am lying here naked with you in your office, telling you about how your ex-wife is going to escape prosecution for a crime that, between you and I, she almost certainly committed. Do you really think I am going to worry about who is talking about who I go into private practice with after what will unquestionably be my biggest case in that office?"

"I'm going to assume not," Eric answered, still lying next to her, "but think about this instead. Now things are great between us. What happens, though, if we break up? What if I do something stupid? Then how are we going to remain partners? I mean, how are we going to be able to continue working together?"

Amanda leaped to her right, on top of Eric, and straddled his midsection, leaning forward so that her face was next to his head and her breasts brushed against his chest. "Break up, you asked? Not going to happen, my friend." She kissed his ear. "Listen carefully to me, Mr. Eric Goldberg. You're not going anywhere. You're going to be stuck with me for a long, long time." She pulled herself up so that she was sitting upright. "There isn't going to be any breakup, Eric. I love you." She leaned back down and kissed him passionately.

After Amanda removed her lips from his, Eric smiled. "Well, that's a good thing, because I love you too. Welcome to the firm." He kissed her again. "But just so we are clear on this issue," he added, "my client was not guilty."

"Yes she was, you ass," Amanda replied. "She was definitely texting when she hit the kid. I don't care about the bullshit with Sanchez and his nephew. You know it and I know it. She was texting, and she was certainly guilty of something."

"It doesn't matter, Amanda." Eric said. "It doesn't matter. If you're going to work this side of the case, you're going to have to start thinking that way."

"Honestly, none of that shit matters. All that matters is right here," Amanda said. "Johnson and Goldberg. No, Goldberg and Johnson. I like the way that sounds."

"At least I get top billing," Eric replied. "That's very fair of you."

"Age before beauty, my friend." Amanda said, laughing, "Age before beauty." She leaned over to kiss him again. "Just remember, Eric, just like whether or not your client, or our client, is actually guilty does not matter when we're representing him or her, a little difference in age between us, well, that just doesn't matter either."

Eric smiled again. She was totally right. None of that stuff mattered. Not now, at least.

Chapter XLI – The Final Press Conference

The next morning, Jesus Sanchez was accompanied into the Elizabeth Police Station by two of the department's officers and two of his most trusted advisors. He was booked, fingerprinted, and walked to a jail cell, where he remained until the local Municipal Court judge would be able to decide what bail, if any, would be appropriate based on the charges that he was facing. Moments later, Ben Kasper, followed by several other members of the Prosecutor's Office, strode out of the front door of the Courthouse, walked to the top step, and stood in front of the microphones which had been placed at the top of the staircase.

"My name is Ben Kasper," he began, clearing his throat, "and I am the first Assistant Prosecutor here in Union County." He glanced down at the papers in his hand. This time, he was intent not to stray from the script. "I am going to read a statement from the Prosecutor's Office now. I will not entertain any questions afterward, and information will continue to be provided as this case moves forward."

He continued to speak as the crowd groaned. The heat of the sun beat down on him, and the sweat that was beginning to emanate from his pores distracted him momentarily. Again clearing his throat, he adjusted his reading glasses on the tip of his nose, breathed deeply, and continued. "Some time ago, I stood on these very steps and gave a statement in the wake of the death of Jose Lopez, a young man from this very city, who died following a motor vehicle-pedestrian accident. At that time, the Prosecutor's Office requested everyone's cooperation in allowing us to do our investigation into the events leading up to that fatal accident, and charges were brought against the driver of the car that struck Mr. Lopez.

"Thankfully, most people heeded our requests to allow our office to conduct its investigations. There were some, however, who sought to exploit the fact that the accident involved a Caucasian woman and a Hispanic boy. There were some who sought to advance an improper political agenda, to further their own selfish goals. Luckily for all of us, the protests and demonstrations that followed were peaceful in nature, and this great city of ours did not dissolve into anarchy and acts of retribution for a perceived wrong.

"Much has happened over the past couple of days. To clarify, as best as we can, the most serious charges against the driver of the vehicle have been officially dropped by the Prosecutor's Office. This was done after an exemplary job by one of the junior members of our office, Amanda Johnson, revealed that the precipitating factor in young Jose Lopez's death was not the automobile accident itself, but rather a planned murder which was done at the behest of Jesus Sanchez, the man who has led the overwhelming majority of the public outcry over the young man's death."

He paused, turned, and motioned behind him. "Assistant Prosecutor Amanda Johnson is here with me today," he said, pointing to Amanda, who stood behind him and to his right. "I think we should recognize her efforts at this time." The crowd broke into applause. Amanda sheepishly stepped forward and waved to the media crowd, smiling faintly as she peered beyond the assemblage and spotted Eric standing in the shadows of the building located across the street, away from and out of the glare of the assembled media. He smiled in response, and then stepped back as far as he could so as to blend in with the building's exterior. Amanda then stepped back as the clapping subsided, allowing Kasper to continue.

"As I said, the most serious charges against the driver have been abandoned. I can also report that, this morning, Jesus Sanchez voluntarily turned himself in at Elizabeth Police Headquarters where he is awaiting arraignment on a variety of charges relating both to the murder of Jose Gomez as well as certain other activities that have allegedly been perpetrated within our city over the past few years, including the recent murder of television reporter Lupe Espinosa. More details on those charges will be forthcoming.

"The Prosecutor's Office and the Elizabeth Police Department would like to thank the people of Elizabeth for their restraint and understanding during this difficult time, especially our Hispanic population. All too often, a perceived wrong against a member of an ethnic community results in acts of retribution, whether through violence or property damage and looting. Thankfully, none of that took place here; as a result, no violence resulted. No property damage was done, and there was no looting. Those appearing at the various rallies in support of Jose Gomez and the Gomez family acted in an exemplary manner, and it is the hope of the Prosecutor's Office and Police Department that this positive conduct continue through the prosecution of Jesus Sanchez. This is your city. This is our city. Let's continue to work together to protect it. That will be how we achieve our mutual goal of respect for people of all nations, people of all cultures, and people of all races."

He paused, and a smattering of applause emanated from the crowd. He carefully folded the pages in his hands and placed them into the inside pocket of his suit jacket, turned, and walked toward the now-opened front door of the courthouse, entering the vestibule and disappearing from view. The other members of the Prosecutor's Office followed suit, including Amanda Johnson. Before she turned to walk into the building she again peered across the street to catch Eric's attention. He was already gone, however, and was making his way down Broad Street to his office as Amanda sighed, turned, and then walked into the building with her fellow members of the Prosecutor's Office. The media members began to disassemble their camera stands and began to walk back to their respective vehicles, the Press Conference having ended and the first chapter of the saga, which had clearly taken a completely unexpected turn, having concluded.

All the while, Jesus Sanchez sat alone in a cell in the Elizabeth city jail, about a mile away. Nobody was chanting his name, and nobody was praising him now.

THE END

ALSO BY ANDREW WOLFENSON

"*People may hate lawyers but they love to read about them and this book proves why. **In His Own_Defense** is a realistic look at the human drama that surrounds a high-stakes criminal case. The pitch-perfect prose and provocative plot compel you to read on, late into the night. New Jersey's own Andy Wolfenson is a north-of-the-Mason-Dixon line answer to John Grisham.*" – Henry Klingeman, Esq., Criminal Defense attorney and former Assistant U.S. Attorney for the State of New Jersey.

What happens when an attorney is wrongfully accused of murdering a client's husband? Are conversations and interactions between the client and attorney protected by the Attorney-Client privilege, or is the attorney capable of defending himself against the false accusation, even if his actions prove damaging to the client?

Eric Goldberg is a New Jersey attorney who is first seduced, and then falsely accused of murder, by one of his clients. While testing the boundaries of the attorney-client privilege in conversations with the local police, he travels to Brazil to locate the one person who can clear his name. There, while the police from two countries search for him, he gains the assistance of a transplanted American architect and his free-spirited girlfriend, who lead him through the streets and clubs of Sao Paulo searching for his accuser.

***In His Own Defense** is available on Amazon.com and for Kindle*

ALSO BY ANDREW WOLFENSON

The perfect gift for fantasy baseball players and/or fiction lovers

"Who would ever think a game amongst friends would turn to deception and murder? ... Andrew Wolfenson takes loyalty and the American Pastime where they've never been before by playing Fantasy League Baseball with a life and death scoreboard, unquestionably making this book a home run." – Jon D'Amore, Author of the true mob story, "The Boss *Always* Sits In the Back"

Over 33 million people in the United States participate in fantasy baseball and/or football leagues, and these leagues generate over two billion dollars per year in revenue. Some take their participation in such fantasy leagues more serious than others, suspending reality as they try to fulfill their dreams of serving as a major league owner or General Manager. For Jeff Goldstein, fantasy baseball is not just a game; participation in the league takes over his life. His obsession with winning his fantasy league, and its $150,000 prize, consumes his every thought and threatens his relationship with his girlfriend, his friends, and his job. How far will Jeff go in his desire to win the league? What actions will he take, or ask others to take, as he struggles to separate fantasy from reality?

Deadly Fantasy: A Baseball Story *is available on Amazon.com and for Kindle.*

www.ingramcontent.com/pod-product-compliance
Lightning Source LLC
Chambersburg PA
CBHW071640260626
47170CB00001B/179